THE KEY of RAIN

DAVE MASON
with MIKE FEUER

Dave Mason

As I'm writing this, I'm realizing how strange it is to reserve rights in a Biblical Fiction book, for Torah law has no conception of rights. Thus, let us add:

All Obligations Also Reserved

Some may call this a distinction without a difference, but it was the fascination with such distinctions between the modern and the Biblical world that drew me to write Biblical Fiction in the first place. You see, modern law would say that the author has a right to not be stolen from, whereas Torah law would say that the reader has an obligation not to steal. Practically, they are the same. No portion of this book can be copied or distributed without permission of the author.

The difference is where the onus lays. Rights by their nature are the domain of the government, which both grants and enforces rights. Obligations reside in the individual.

Interestingly, both systems allow me as the author leeway in defining the parameters of what constitutes stealing, for to the degree that I give permission, there can be no theft.

So let me clearly state that I am OK with small segments of the book being used for quotation or teaching purposes. Indeed, I want the book to spark discussions and learning. I just don't want anyone other than myself selling the book, distributing it for free, or making so much of it public that it undermines book sales.

For more specific queries regarding usage, or to place massive book orders, contact me directly at Dave@TheAgeofProphecy.com

Yes, I know this is more than you're looking for in a copyright page, at least those of you who bother to read a copyright page at all, but since so many of you commented on my rambling copyright page from Book 1, I felt pressured to do it again.

Cover Design by the amazing Juan Hernaz. Check him out at JuanHernaz.com

To the members and educators of the Sulam Yaakov Beit Midrash.

This series owes its very existence to the life-changing work we did together over the past decade.

Two quick notes before you begin:

1) The Key of Rain is the sequel to The Lamp of Darkness. While one can read The Key of Rain alone, we highly recommend starting with The Lamp of Darkness to really understand the characters and the world. You can download a free digital copy of The Lamp of Darkness on our website TheAgeofProphecy.com.

2) We are continually looking to improve our books and love getting reader feedback. If there's an idea you find confusing, or something you'd like more elaboration on, or (Heaven forbid) a typo, please let us know using our feedback form at: TheAgeofProphecy.com/feedback

And now, please enjoy The Key of Rain...

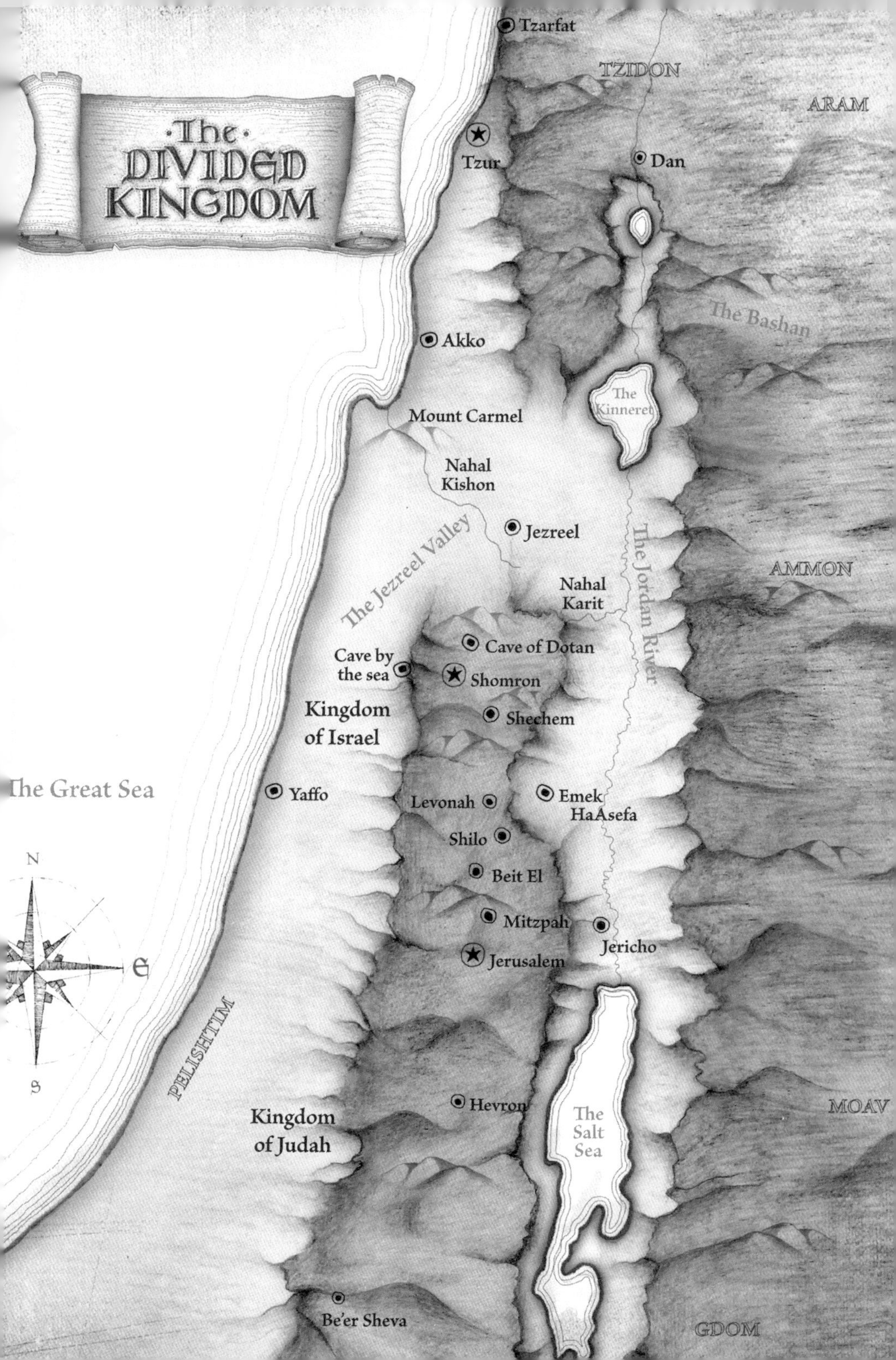

The DIVIDED KINGDOM
Tzarfat
TZIDON
ARAM
Tzur
Dan
The Bashan
Akko
The Kinneret
Mount Carmel
Nahal Kishon
Jezreel
The Jezreel Valley
The Jordan River
AMMON
Nahal Karit
Cave of Dotan
Cave by the sea
Shomron
Shechem
Kingdom of Israel
The Great Sea
Yaffo
Levonah
Emek HaAsefa
Shilo
Beit El
Mitzpah
Jericho
Jerusalem
N
E
S
PELISHTIM
Hevron
Kingdom of Judah
The Salt Sea
MOAV
Be'er Sheva
EDOM

Prologue

The Priest's Mistake

"Rise, Yambalya, and report," Izevel commanded the giant of a man bowed before her.

The priest rose to his full height. Though he stood a few steps below the two thrones, he towered over the young queen. "The men of Shomron journeyed to honor their god, yet they bent their knees to Baal upon their return."

Izevel leaned toward her priest. "How did you do it?"

"It was simple, my Queen. The men made the annual pilgrimage to bow before their beloved Golden Calf in Beit El. When they returned home, they found their way blocked by Baal."

Izevel gave him a sideways glance. "What of the King?"

Yambalya's eyes flashed over King Ahav's empty throne. "The King's escort was long past when we brought Baal onto the road."

Izevel's long fingers gripped the arms of her throne. The great oaken chair with the cedar emblem had been made for the visit of her father, King Ethbaal of Tzidon. Months later, the throne remained, now the seat of his sixteen-year-old daughter, Izevel, the Queen of Israel. "Did any resist bowing?"

"Indeed, for those already loyal to Baal did not journey to the Calf at all."

"How did you handle the stubborn?"

Yambalya laughed. "The people of Israel are sheep. If the men in front of them bow, they bow as well."

The Queen relaxed her grip and leaned back in the overlarge throne. "Did none cause any trouble?"

"The tale grows even better, my Queen." A grin played at the corner of Yambalya's mouth. "Come," he called.

Two men stepped from the shadows. Like Yambalya, the younger one wore the deep violet robes of the priests of Baal. The other wore a soldiers' tunic embroidered with the cedar tree of Tzidon. The soldier bowed before the Queen, holding out a sword for her inspection. "We took this from one of the men at the roadblock, my Queen." He spoke without lifting his face.

Izevel reached out and took the weapon. She fingered the cedar tree emblem carved into the hilt. "This belonged to one of my soldiers?"

"It did, my Queen. To one of the four who never returned from…" his eyes flickered to her face and returned to the floor, "…from dealing with the prophets."

Her eyes narrowed as she stared at the sword. "Was the man who carried it a prophet?"

"He looked like no prophet I've ever seen. He had the face of a soldier, covered in scars."

Her hand closed on the sword's hilt. "You killed him?"

"The ground has already swallowed his blood, my Queen." The soldier bent his head to the side, pointing to a tattooed pattern of dots stretching down his neck and extending below his tunic. He touched an inflamed area on his neck, a newly printed black splotch at its core. "This one is for him." The soldier met her eyes. "And so may all of her majesty's enemies perish."

"Excellent." Izevel gave him a cold smile. "One man did not kill four of my soldiers on his own. Had he no companions?"

The soldier shot a glance at the young priest standing at Yambalya's side, then returned his gaze to Izevel. "On this point, we disagree, my Queen."

"What is this?" Izevel eyed the young priest. "Explain."

The young priest bowed low as he stepped from behind Yambalya's protective shadow. "An old man passed soon after your soldiers killed the one with the scars."

"An old man?" Yambalya's eyes shot to his priest. "What old man?"

"He was too old to bow," the priest said to his master, "but he caused no other trouble."

The soldier scoffed. "If he was strong enough to walk from Beit El, he was strong enough to bow."

"He was old and confused," the priest said. "His grandson made that clear."

"What grandson?" Izevel's eyes darted back and forth between the speakers.

"There was a boy who passed before the one with the scars," the young priest said.

"If the grandfather was merely confused," the soldier said, "why did his grandson not pass through with him? Why separate himself?"

"You forced the people to pass through one at a time." The priest's voice rose to meet the soldier's. "They separated in the crowd."

The soldier shook his head. "He did not look confused to me. He exposed his neck to the sword. He wanted us to strike him down."

"Why would a man do that?" Izevel's eyes narrowed.

The soldier only shrugged, but Yambalya offered an answer. "Israel venerates mercy, the virtue of the weak. The prophets think showing the people we do not share their love of weakness will rouse them against us."

"So he was a prophet?" The Queen turned her full gaze on the young priest.

He shrank back. "I cannot be certain, my Queen."

Yambalya placed his hand on his disciple's shoulder. "Trust your instincts. Was this old man a prophet or no?"

The priest lowered his head. "I expect he was, Master."

Yambalya's hands closed on his neck and lifted him clear off the ground. "You let him pass through alive?"

"We couldn't kill all who refused to bow," the young priest said. "Sixty men waited to get through."

"Those men would have done nothing had it not been for the boy." The soldier grimaced. "He was the one who roused them to resist."

Yambalya released the priest, who fell to the floor.

"Agreed." The priest nodded at the soldier, the unlikely ally who had come to his defense. "Once provoked, we could not have handled them all. Even if our soldiers had won the battle, we could have sparked a rebellion."

"Did you not think to follow them?" Yambalya asked the soldier. "Kill the old man and the boy where no one would see?"

"There were too many men on the road," the soldier replied. Not all the mistakes belonged to the priest. "Someone would have seen."

"Fool! You let a prophet escape?" The Queen turned her wrath on the soldier. "Now he's perhaps in Shomron itself. He could be rallying others around him even as we speak."

"There is nothing to fear, my Queen." The soldier straightened. "These prophets are far easier to kill than we feared. Many are old, most unarmed. Some even came out to greet us when we arrived."

"So much for their prophecy," Yambalya said. "Their powers are as false as their god."

"Are they?" The Queen's eyes burned at the high priest. "What of Eliyahu? Even you acknowledge he holds back the rains."

"Indeed." Yambalya's face grew dark. "But once the storm god asserts dominion over the land, we will have nothing to fear from Eliyahu's drought."

"There is still no news from the hunt?" the Queen asked.

"None, my Queen," Yambalya replied. "He has not been seen since issuing his curse."

"Now we have another prophet to track." The Queen turned on the soldier. "Do not underestimate them. I will not have a prophet in Shomron."

"I will hunt him myself," the soldier said. "Shall I seek the boy as well?"

"There are too many prophets running free to worry about a child. If you find him with the old man, kill them both. Otherwise, leave him. There's nothing a boy can do to harm us."

As water reflects a face back to a face, so one's heart is reflected back by another.
Proverbs 27:19

1

The Grinding Stones

As warm light touched my face, I opened my eyes expecting to see the dawn of a new day. But the sun was nowhere to be seen. A thick fog surrounded me, a grey cloud dry to the touch. I squinted in the shimmering light as a figure approached through the haze. I had never seen the man who approached, yet everything about him was familiar. My gaze flitted from his curly grey hair to his lanky frame, coming to rest on his eyes.

"You look as I did at your age," he said.

My ache at hearing his voice. "Father?"

"I am here, Lev."

Tears clouded my vision. My whole life had unfolded without his guidance. Why had he come now? The question had hardly arisen before the words I could not share with anyone else came tumbling out. "Father, I failed. I killed Shimon."

His smile disappeared as he shook his head. "Shimon was murdered by a soldier of Tzidon, Lev. You are not to blame."

I wanted to believe him, but I knew better. "He died because he listened to me. It was my idea to pass the roadblock without fighting."

He seemed to float closer through the fog. "There were nine soldiers at the roadblock, all trained killers. Had a battle begun, there is no telling how many would have died. You and Uriel might now lie among them."

"He saved us the last time. The spirit of the Holy One filled him, and none could stand before him." My heart pounded. I tried to lift my hand and reach out to him, but I was frozen in place.

"The Holy One gives the gift of prophecy with an open hand, Lev, yet few are blessed to receive it even once in a lifetime. You cannot know if he would have saved you again. You did the best you could for him. As I tried to do for you."

Hot tears stung my eyes. "Why did you have to leave me so soon?"

I heard my own voice in his sigh. "I wanted better for you, Lev. I did not want my battles to become yours. Certainly not when you were so young. Now you find yourself at the center of a war larger than any I ever fought."

"I don't want it." My voice dropped to a whisper. "I want to go home."

His eyes lifted to a spot above my head. "You may return to your uncle if you wish. None will begrudge you leaving after all you've been through. You may still be safe there."

"I'm no use to anyone here anyway. Not in any meaningful way."

His eyes caught mine and it was like staring at my reflection. "You have more power than you imagine."

"The power to get my friends killed?"

"Forget how Shimon died. Think instead about how he lived."

His words sank in. "He gave everything for the prophets."

"Indeed." The fog swirled, and suddenly I could only hear his voice. "If you choose, so can you."

"But who am I?"

"Who was Joseph? He was the lowest of us all, a prisoner and a slave. From those depths, he rose to save the entire nation."

I looked down at my travel-stained tunic. "He was a son of Jacob."

"You are a descendant of Aaron the Kohen." His voice was next to me now. "It's not humility to make yourself smaller than you are."

"I'm a boy, not even of age."

"Even King David was twelve once. There is greatness inside you, Lev. You only need to awaken your will. Your *ratzon*."

"Awaken my *ratzon*? How do I do that?"

"Lev!" a voice broke through the fog, but it was no longer my father's. The last of the light disappeared, and I awoke in total darkness. "Lev!" I heard again. It was Batya, Ovadia's wife.

"Coming," I called back, but I closed my eyes again and burrowed deeper into my straw bed, hoping to hear my father one last time.

"Lev!" she called a third time.

I rolled myself out of bed, my back groaning. I had never been so sore. Not even when I stranded my flock on the far side of the *nahal* below Levonah as the rain fell in torrents and the dry gully became a rushing stream. I carried each sheep back across in my arms, as stones and branches driven by the water pounded me. My uncle called me a fool for trying to get back, saying I should have taken cover and waited for the rains to subside. I still remember the agony of getting out of bed the next day, but this was worse. At least then I'd gotten a good night's sleep and had risen to Aunt Leah's hot porridge. But how could I complain about rest to Batya, who worked later than the moon and rose to wake the dawn?

I climbed down the ladder to the kitchen. One touch to the oven told me it was still warm from the baking the night before.

"Fire the oven and get grinding." Batya didn't look up from the dough. "I've almost finished kneading the flour you milled yesterday."

"How could you finish it?" I asked. "I must have ground for twelve hours."

She snorted. "Each of them like a man. I'll need you to grind for another twelve today, and this time do it proper, like a woman."

"You said I'd get faster."

"You have been getting faster, but five more prophets arrived yesterday. There's more to do than ever before."

"We can't send it out to a miller?"

"We've been through this, Lev. We can send a little bit out, but any more and he'd wonder why we need so much. We can't have any questions about what we're doing."

Ovadia had sent away his slaves and maidservants for the same reason, which was why all the work fell to me. Batya caught my gaze. "I can do some of the grinding today if you want to try your hand at the baking again."

I scanned the burns on my fingertips from pulling bread off the red-hot oven walls. "No, no. I'll grind."

"Light the oven first, it needs time to warm."

I stirred the coals back to life, laying splinters of wood on top. Once I saw the flames rise, I threw a handful of barley onto the lower millstone and dragged the smaller upper stone back and forth over the grain with as much energy as I could muster. My muscles protested, but I wanted to make as much flour as I could before the entire house became unbearably hot. There was a reason the rest of Israel baked outside.

"We can't use the outdoor oven today?" I wiped the sweat from my face.

"We can do two hours. Any more and the neighbors might wonder why we're baking so much."

"And grinding outside?"

"Perhaps for another hour. Any more…"

"And the neighbors will wonder why we're grinding so much," I finished. I cursed under my breath as I lifted the grindstone. It was heavy, but only about as long as my foot and made from a hard, charcoal-colored rock that Batya said was common in the northern part of the kingdom. I held it in both hands and pulled it back and forth over the barley kernels, grinding them to dust.

Outside, the sun finally rose. It would be a cool, dry day, as all the winter days had been since Eliyahu brought the drought. Inside the house, the oven grew hot. Sweat dripped from my forehead and pooled under my arms.

In my family, Dahlia ground the flour each day before making the next day's bread. The wealthier families in Levonah had their flour ground by their maidservants, or else would send the grain out to a miller, who let donkeys do his work. Only in Emek HaAsefa had I ever seen men grinding flour and baking bread, and they were slaves.

Ovadia sent his slaves away because he couldn't trust them. Now I'd become the trustworthy slave. Still, if it kept my master and the other prophets alive, I should do it with joy. So I told myself, but the joy refused to come.

Late in the afternoon, we finally finished, and I loaded the bread into saddlebags. A knock came against the gate, four hard raps followed by one soft one. I recognized the signal, but nonetheless lifted the flap and peered through the peephole.

I unlatched the gate, and Ovadia stepped in, holding three vine cuttings. "Where did you get those?" I asked as I secured the gate behind him.

"From Shmuel the Carmeli, a local farmer who makes excellent wine. He was gracious enough to let me choose the vines myself."

"What do you want them for?"

"For my orchard."

"You're planting an orchard during a drought?"

Ovadia's eyes flashed a warning. I had spoken of the drought loud enough to be overheard. He opened the gate, glanced up and down the street, then shut it again with a sigh. When he replied, his voice was a whisper. "No, Lev. You're going to plant an orchard during a drought."

"Me?" Didn't I have enough to do? "Isn't that like pouring out water on bare rock? Nothing will grow."

"Nothing need grow." I felt the intensity of his eyes as he watched me.

"Why else plant an orchard?"

Impatience crawled up Ovadia's brow. "Never forget how great a responsibility rests in your hands, Lev. You and I are like men on the edge of a cliff, one slip and all is lost. It is not enough to hope to evade discovery. You must anticipate discovery and prepare for it."

Ovadia stared at me, waiting for me to understand. I put aside my annoyance long enough to think on his words. "The orchard is my excuse should anyone see me near the cave."

"Exactly. Soldiers may question you, but as long as you have plausible answers, they will let you be." Ovadia grabbed a shovel and a pick from the corner of the courtyard and strapped them onto the donkey. As he did this, he sniffed the saddlebags. "I don't smell the bread. You waited until it cooled?"

"Yes."

"Good. The smell could attract attention. If anyone examines your bags and sees the bread, what will you say?"

I shrugged. I hadn't given it any thought.

"Never get caught without a story." He rubbed his brow. "There's a widow named Zilpah in Shomron who bakes and sells bread to support herself. Should anyone ask, say you live near Dotan, your mother is dead, and your father sends you once a week to Shomron to buy bread. That story should suffice."

Ovadia led the donkey toward the gate. "You'll need to reenter the city before the sun sets. Remember," he caught my eye with a hard look, "entering and leaving this house is the most dangerous part of your journey. Your greatest value is that no one takes notice of you. Once it's known you associate with me, you'll draw attention, and we'll be in danger of discovery."

I nodded and led the donkey out into the deserted alleyway. Ovadia silently shut the gate behind me. I saw no one until I reached the main road, though even this was mostly empty on a non-market day.

Two guards stood in the open space of the triple city gate as travelers passed around them. One wore the royal ox of the House of Omri, the other was Tzidonian. My heart pounded as I eyed the cedar tree emblem embroidered on his tunic. His eyes were turned outwards, inspecting those entering the city. He had no attention to spare for the boy with the donkey taking his leave.

I hurried on the King's Road, hoping to arrive at the cave quickly enough to snatch a brief visit with my master. Before long, I spied a mangled fig tree, with one of its lower branches broken off near the trunk. Beneath it passed the head of the trail which would take me to the Cave of Dotan. I followed it to the base of a hill I knew by sight and climbed the waist-high stone walls that formed terraces in the hillside, like the staircase of a giant.

The terraces bore no signs of being planted in recent memory. Whole sections had fallen away from the walls, and little soil remained on each shelf. Only once I reached halfway up, to an olive tree so gnarled that it may have been from the time of King David himself, was there any sign of planting. Here a few saplings stood in freshly turned soil, and before I left, I would need to add my vine cuttings beside them. But my first duty was to the prophets.

I unloaded the pick and shovel and propped them against the terrace wall where they could be seen from the path below. I tethered the donkey's lead rope to the great olive tree and untied the saddlebags. A quick glance at the trail revealed that it was empty, so I slipped behind the tree into the hidden entrance to the cave.

I had not gone far when a cold blade rose to my chest. A voice demanded, "Who is there?"

"I am Lev," I stammered, "a disciple of Master Uriel."

The sword came down and the wielder sighed. "That's a relief."

"Afraid the Queen's soldiers had discovered you already?" I asked.

My question was met with laughter. "No, I knew from your footsteps you were a boy, but I don't know what I would have done if you were a stranger who stumbled upon us. Could I spill the blood of the innocent to preserve our secret?"

My eyes adjusted to the dim light of the passageway revealing two disciples before me, both a few years older than myself. The one who had been silent laid a hand on his friend's shoulder. "He's never held a sword before."

"How did I do?" The sword bearer ran his fingers through his scraggly beard. "Did I sound frightening?"

"You scared me," I said truthfully.

"Really?" His chest expanded. "You're not just saying that?"

"Oh no, I was definitely scared."

"Ha!" He raised the sword again toward the empty entranceway. "Let all who enter tremble before Peleh, guardian of the gate." He lowered the blade. "I will guard this entranceway valiantly as long as no true enemies attempt to enter." His shoulders drooped as he looked at his companion. "Not sure what I would do then."

"If you've never held a sword," I asked, "why are you the guardian of the gate?"

"It's the only place where there's enough light for Sadya and myself to learn the ancient scrolls. You're the first person who's entered today, so guarding has been light duty."

I cringed at the mention of learning. Master Uriel had told me I could begin my studies in the cave and that as a Kohen it was not my place to serve others. Yet, here I was, baking and delivering bread to others so they could learn. "You're lucky," I muttered.

Sadya shot me a quizzical look. He was broader shouldered and darker skinned than Peleh and stood like one who knew how to hold either plow or sword. His strong hands held a scroll, browned at the edges from age. "You bring bread?" He pointed to the saddlebags. Without waiting for an answer, he rolled his scroll and grabbed the saddlebag with one hand, easily carrying it into the cave.

I stepped in after him. The prophets in the main room gathered around Sadya to receive their portions. Uriel stood to one side, his eyes on me. "Come with me, Lev."

I followed my master away from the broad cavern into the dark passageways. He took a lit lamp from a niche in the wall and led me into the recesses of the cave. He ducked his head to enter his low quarters and sat on his sleeping mat. I lowered myself to the ground before him, and he held the lamp aloft between us.

"So," he began, "you believe those of us hiding in the cave to be lucky?"

I dropped my eyes to the ground. "No, Master."

"Do not hide from your feelings, Lev. Speak only the truth."

"No, Master, I do not consider you lucky."

"Why not?" he asked.

I lifted my eyes to meet his. "You are a prophet of Israel. You traveled the Kingdom, giving guidance to the people. Now you must live like an animal in a cage."

"Ah, so for me you feel sympathy and even anger at those who've put me in such a place. But for Sadya and Peleh?"

I dropped my eyes again. "I only want to learn as well."

His wrinkles were deep in the lamplight. "Then rejoice, for you are learning right now."

"Rejoice?" I gave a dry laugh. "Rejoice in a few moments between baking and delivering the bread?"

"Of course. If learning is what you desire, rejoice when you have it, rather than lamenting that you don't have more."

His words stung, but I would not show it. "It is so little, Master. You told me when we arrived at the cave that you would begin my instruction."

"I'm teaching you now, Lev. The question is—do you want to learn?" He held my eyes until I looked away. "You think I have much to tell. In truth, my most important teachings are few."

"Then why must the disciples study for so many years? Why do so many fail?"

"Because it is not enough to learn the teachings, you must live them. Most lack the *ratzon*, the deep will." His words echoed in my dream and held me fast. "Even those who find the will to learn may discover along the way that it is not their deepest desire. They will run out of years before they succeed in embodying the words of the prophets. I will give you what words I can when you come to me, but only you know whether you have the *ratzon*, the will, to live them."

Uriel paused, and I felt an invitation in his silence. "Master, you told me Kohanim were not meant to serve."

"I spoke the truth. The Kohen serves only the Holy One. Tell me, Lev, can you think of any greater service to the Holy One right now than keeping the prophets alive?"

My ears grew hot with shame. I could not hold back the words on my heart. "Ovadia tricked me."

My master's eyes grew wide. "Tricked you? How?"

"He told me I must persuade you to come to the cave, even against your will."

"Which you did."

"Yes, but he let me believe I'd be able to hide with you."

"Did he ever say this to you?"

I paused. It had only been a week since Ovadia told me to bring Uriel to the cave, but it already felt like another lifetime. "No, but he never told me I would be his servant either."

"Had he told you this, would you have brought me here?"

I frowned. "No, Master."

"Then he was wise to remain silent. The fool sees only what is in front of him, the wise anticipate what will come to be."

"So I am a fool?"

Uriel placed his hand on my knee. "You have not learned to see as far ahead as Ovadia. Indeed, for him to remain in the palace and keep all of us alive, he would soon perish were it not for his wisdom."

"I still don't like being tricked."

"You are too quick to cast blame, Lev." He tapped my knee so I would look up. "Was it a trick that he allowed you to hear what you wanted to? Ovadia does not need any more mouths to feed—he needs more hands to help."

I balled my fists but kept my face calm. Ovadia had outsmarted me, and now I was his slave.

"You cannot change the past, Lev. All you can do is choose how to approach the future. I feel your anger toward Ovadia. You even directed it toward Peleh and Sadya, who have done nothing but help the prophets and learn our ways."

"Didn't you say I shouldn't hide my feelings, Master?"

"You must not hide from your feelings. Only by acknowledging them can you hope to change them."

"Isn't changing my anger simply another way to hide from it?"

The old prophet sighed. "Be not so clever that you cannot hear simple truths, Lev. Your anger will not serve you. As long as you hold it dear, it will compromise your ability to help anyone, even yourself."

Uriel stretched his arms above his head. "Do you recall the first lesson I ever taught you on our journeys together?"

Several moons had passed, but I could easily picture myself walking away from Levonah with my master. "You spoke to me about how Jacob could not reach prophecy because he was mourning the loss of his son, Joseph."

"Never forget this, Lev. Prophecy only descends in a state of joy. Just as joy may open the gates of prophecy, your anger makes you easy prey for the Baal and other dark forces that Izevel is mustering against us."

My heart went cold. "How do I protect myself?"

"You must strengthen your will."

It was as if my master had heard my dream. "I'm trying, Master. I've ground flour from dawn till dusk each day since we parted."

"It is not enough to exert your will outside of yourself. You must direct it inwards." He paused to let his words sink in. "You wish to learn the ways of the prophets? Strengthen your heart until your life flows outward from it. That is the way of the prophets. If your heart follows that which lies outside of you, you will fail yourself and us in the difficult days ahead."

"How do I strengthen my heart, Master?"

"The first step on the path of wisdom is always to listen. Never ignore your heart's message, but beware, not every feeling is an expression of higher will." The old prophet paused, then added, "The sun will soon set. As you grind tomorrow, think on what we spoke of today. Strengthen your heart, Lev, and your arms will never fail you."

Bread of falsehood tastes sweet, but afterward one's mouth will be filled with gravel.
Proverbs 20:17

2

An Old Friend

All the next day I struggled to apply my master's words, to keep a grasp on my emotions as I dragged the grindstone back and forth. Perhaps the prophets found it easy to master their hearts, but the disciples worked for years under the watchful eye of a master prophet. Uriel was crazy if he thought a few choice words would teach me a skill it took others years to develop.

I piled another batch of flour on top of the powdery mountain rising beside me. The bin of barley kernels waiting to be ground was even larger, but I couldn't bring myself to reach in and take another handful. I wiped my forehead and lay the upper grindstone on the lower one. I needed a break.

Cool winter air dried my sweat as I stepped out into the courtyard. My breath still came short from the grinding, though standing in this cramped courtyard brought little relief. I eyed the gate. Didn't Ovadia keep saying I was valuable because no one ever took notice of me? I was already allowed to leave the house to deliver bread, so why shouldn't I step out to get some air?

I unlocked the gate and pushed it open. No doubt Batya signaled some objection behind me, but I kept my eyes forward knowing she wouldn't dare scream out or pursue me.

The alleyway was empty, as it almost always was. Once away from the house, I no longer had to worry about being associated with Ovadia. There was no reason I shouldn't walk around without fear.

When I hit the main road, I turned up the street toward the palace rather than taking my usual route down to the city gates. My footsteps were light with freedom, brief though it might be. The last time I walked this stretch of road was three months before, during the King's wedding, when I was just a shepherd boy, and Uriel was still free to roam the land as a prophet. Now everything had changed.

In the upper marketplace, a grain seller called out, "Barley, a *seah* per shekel, a *seah* per shekel. Wheat, two shekels a *seah*, two shekels a *seah*." The barley price was higher than in previous years, but it was not because of the drought, just a reflection of last season's poor barley crop. I knew this because the wheat prices were lower than the prior year because of the strong harvest. Once the merchants sensed drought, the costs would soar. Was this why Ovadia purchased so much grain, despite the lack of adequate storage? Was he trying to build a stockpile before the prices rose?

I continued up the road, drawn to the cloud of dust and noise I heard at the top of the hill. Where an orchard had once stood, fifty slaves labored away at an enormous building, second in size only to the palace itself. The floor of cut stone was already complete, covering an area three times the size of Ovadia's house. The violet robed priests overseeing the work meant this was the new Temple of the Baal. I ought to seethe seeing such a giant structure rising to a foreign god in the heart of the capital, but instead I found myself admiring the work. At least Yambalya was doing something useful, unlike the prophets who just waited in the cave for me to feed them.

Only Eliyahu took a true stand against the Baal. All of our hopes rested with him. But what impact could one man alone have against all of this?

Without warning, two arms wrapped around me from behind. The arms tightened across my chest, cutting off my air and lifting me off my feet. My thoughts spun. Had the tattooed soldier who killed Shimon tracked me down? I heard a familiar laugh and went cold. It wasn't the soldier—it was worse.

An Old Friend

"Lev! You came back!"

Zim put me down facing him, his hands on my shoulders. "Did you come to see the Temple? No one's ever heard of such a massive structure going up so fast, but then, Yambalya himself comes at least twice a day to measure the progress. Come, I'll show you."

My heart pounded as I struggled to keep the smile on my face. At least the soldier would have killed me quickly. How could I be so stupid? Ovadia warned me to anticipate discovery and prepare for it. I knew Zim had returned to Shomron, he was bound to spot me eventually. Why hadn't I concocted a story to give him? Zim knew my connection to the prophets. Worse, he played for the priests of the Baal, who wanted my master dead. In a single moment, all my secrecy had disappeared.

My thoughts raced, trying to conjure the excuses I should have worked out days ago. Nothing came to mind, but one thing was clear: trying to break away now would only make matters worse. Whatever I did, I couldn't make him suspicious.

I followed Zim to the partially constructed Temple. "The altar will be over there, facing north toward Tzidon. There will be an attic covering half of the building, and Yambalya is putting a small room there for me. Until then, I'm back in the old musicians' quarters. How about you? Where are you staying?"

In Shiloh, when I had last seen Zim, I avoided his questions by distracting him with food. Now I had nothing to offer. "I'm not sure yet. I just arrived."

"So where's your kinnor?"

My mouth went dry as I stammered, "at…at Ovadia's," unable to come up with a convincing lie. "I stayed with him during the wedding, so it was the first place I thought to go. His wife let me leave my things there while I looked around."

Zim grimaced and lowered his voice. "You'll want to be careful. Yambalya doesn't trust Ovadia. Says he's fallen out of favor with the Queen."

I lowered my voice to match his. "Thanks for the tip. What do you suggest?"

"Why not stay in the musicians' quarters with me? There are only three of us there, not like during the wedding."

"That might be a fit." I needed to find more intelligent responses to Zim's questions. Ovadia would know what to say, but I wouldn't see him until the evening.

"So, where did you go after we parted at Shiloh?" he asked.

Again, I could think of nothing better to say than the truth, or at least part of it. "I tried to return to Uriel. He stayed behind in Emek HaAsefa with a few disciples. I thought they could use a musician, but it didn't work out." That at least was true. "So I went home to Levonah, and my aunt took me back in."

I could see Zim getting ready to ask another question. I needed to break his momentum and get away until I could consult with Ovadia. Having no food to offer, I turned to his other great love. "Are you still playing every night?"

Zim shook his head and held up a hand in mock protest. "Every night, plus during the day more often than not."

"Mostly for Yambalya?"

"Whenever there's not some bigger festival or banquet that needs me."

"Still playing for Uriel's son?" I had been shocked in Shiloh to learn that Uriel's son Gershon was the High Priest of Israel, serving the Golden Calf his father despised.

"No, not for some time." Zim paused. "Truth is, Gershon hasn't hosted a single banquet or celebration in the past month that I can recall." He shrugged and moved on. "Say, if you just arrived you can't have begun to look for work. There's a banquet tonight—I'm sure we could use your kinnor. Shall I ask?"

I was needed at Ovadia's. The number of prophets had already grown to over forty, and they needed every moment I could spare to grind flour. Yet, if Zim thought I was in Shomron to feed myself as a musician, I couldn't say no. I couldn't even say I would live off my copper until I settled in, for Zim knew music was much more than food to me. My fingers ached for my kinnor, which I had not played in weeks. "I'd love to play," I said, and it was the truest thing I'd said yet.

"Great. Bring your things to the musicians' quarters an hour before sunset, and we'll go together." He gave me a last hug. "Yambalya calls, but stay and watch as they build the future of Shomron."

I sank onto a stone at the roadside and looked at the horizon. An hour before sunset. At least I had enough time to deliver bread to the cave. How many more deliveries could I make now that I had been discovered? I needed to figure out what to do next.

An Old Friend

Ovadia was not home, and I didn't dare seek him out at the palace. Batya worked on in cold silence. If she was this mad because I went for a walk, how would she react when she learned I'd been discovered?

There was no time to let the loaves cool. I shoved them into the saddlebags and shut them tight, but the smell of warm bread wafted through. It was one thing to be in a hurry, but another to be stupid. If the guards found the bread, I might never arrive at the cave. I rubbed dried manure from the courtyard over the saddlebags and sniffed again. No more bread smell.

Without a word to Batya, I led the donkey out into the alleyway. I managed to control my steps as I exited the city, only breaking into a run once I was out of sight of the gates.

"Is this Naftali ben Jacob reborn?" Peleh said as I arrived at the cave out of breath. "Why the rush?"

I had no desire to tell Peleh all that happened. Fortunately, I knew few prophets or disciples could resist a chance to teach. "Who was Naftali?" I asked, feigning interest.

Peleh took the bait. "You know Naftali." He received the first stack of bread from me and passed it to Sadya behind him. "When our father Jacob died, his twelve sons brought his body back from Egypt to lay him with his fathers in the Cave of Machpelah. When they arrived at the mouth of the cave, they found Jacob's brother Esau blocking the way. He claimed that there was only one grave left, and as the firstborn, it belonged to him."

My uncle had taught me the stories of our fathers. "Didn't Esau sell his birthright to his brother?"

"Precisely." For a moment, we were teacher and student, not fellow fugitives. "Naftali was the fastest of the brothers, so he ran back to Egypt to retrieve the deed showing the grave belonged to Jacob."

"They left Jacob unburied long enough for Naftali to go all the way to Egypt and back?"

"No!" Peleh's enthusiasm took the bite out of his instant response. "Hushim ben Dan was deaf and could not understand Esau's words, but he saw his grandfather's body lying dishonored while the brothers argued. He took a club and with one mighty blow sent Esau's head flying into the cave behind him."

I handed Peleh the very last of the bread. "No man can hit another hard enough to knock off his head."

Peleh placed his hands on the last stack of bread but didn't take it from my grasp. "You must learn to understand the stories of the prophets. Esau's wisdom merited an eternal place amongst our forefathers, and so his head was allowed to be buried in the cave. But he never learned to control his cravings. Whatever his body desired, he gave it, be it for good or ill. His wisdom failed to purify his body, and thus it was left to rot by the roadside."

Peleh raised an eyebrow and turned back into the cave. Did he guess that my craving for freedom had led me astray? I grabbed the donkey's lead rope and hurried back to the city. I had no time to spare for stories.

Back at Ovadia's, I slipped past Batya's silence and up the ladder into my room. I threw my few belongings onto the straw bed and rolled them into my sleeping mat. The sun descended over the palace outside in an orange haze. I would miss this room.

I hid my father's knife under the straw of the bed. A Kohen's knife was sure to raise uncomfortable questions if anyone saw it in the musicians' quarters. I grasped my bedroll under my arm, took my kinnor, and slipped down the ladder.

"Where are you going?" Batya demanded, breaking her silence.

I hung my head. "I was seen."

"By whom?"

"Another musician." I decided to leave out the part of him playing for Yambalya. "He invited me to stay in the musicians' quarters, and I had no excuse to give him."

"And the bread?"

"I'll come every day. Whenever I can."

Batya groaned, followed me to the gate, and locked it behind me.

The houses near Ovadia's were all built from cut stone, but further down the hillside they shifted to uncut stone, and then to mud brick. The alleyways grew narrower and the stench stronger as I descended into the poorer part of the city. These streets were already in shadow, and I stepped carefully to avoid the puddles of rank water which dotted the road.

I could not remember precisely how to get to the musicians' quarters, but I wasn't too worried. Finding Zim was only difficult when he slept. The pounding of his drum drew me like a beacon. Hearing Zim's rhythms made my fingers tingle in anticipation.

The door to the musicians' quarters was open to capture the last light of the day. All three musicians were there, though only Zim was playing. One sat whittling a halil, and the other lay with his tunic over his face.

Zim rounded off his playing with three loud blows. At this sign, even the one lying down sat up and uncovered his eyes. "This is Lev. He just arrived in Shomron, and he's going to be staying with us. Lev, this is Betzalel and Avihud."

Neither seemed bothered, or even terribly interested, that another musician was joining their ranks. I found an empty corner and lay out my sleeping mat, feeling the bumps of the floor through the thin sheepskin.

"Come, we're late as it is," Zim said. We cut over to the main road, crowded now with those rushing to get in or out before the closing of the gates. As we climbed back up the hill, my nose caught the scent of roasting meat. Wherever the smell was coming from, I certainly hoped that's where we were headed.

Zim turned off the road right where we'd met earlier in the day, and I saw the source of the smell: an entire bull hung over a giant fire pit. My appetite was suddenly gone, and I paused at the edge of the Temple grounds. "Zim, you said we were playing a banquet tonight?"

"We are. In honor of Mot, sent by King Ethbaal himself to see the progress of the Temple."

"Who is he? An aid to the King?"

"He was Yambalya's teacher in the ways of Baal."

Zim waved me on, but I didn't budge. The Tzidonian soldiers hunted the prophets in the name of the Baal. "I shouldn't play tonight," I blurted out.

"Why not?"

Had I known earlier that Zim wanted me to play for the Baal, I could have thought of some excuse. Again, I found myself unprepared. "Yambalya didn't like my playing at the wedding."

"He prefers drums for a festival to Baal, but this is a banquet. He's expecting you."

I tried again, adding a shred more truth as I lowered my voice. "Yambalya scared me at the wedding."

Zim laughed. "He scared a lot of people. He wanted to make an impression. But only priests will be attending tonight. They won't be cutting any flesh but the bull's."

If I really wanted to get out of playing I could plead my loyalty to the Holy One. There were still enough people left in the Kingdom who rejected the Baal that such a response on its own might not raise any suspicions. But Zim knew my connection to the prophets. I told him I'd returned to Uriel after Shiloh, and that I'd sought out Ovadia when arriving in Shomron. If I revealed myself as a believer, would he guess I was still involved with the prophets? If he told Yambalya his suspicions, could the priest and his spies follow my trail back to Ovadia? I couldn't take that chance.

"Play tonight," Zim said, "and if you don't like it, I promise I'll never bring you to play for Yambalya again."

I nodded and followed him to the hillside above the roasting pit. Zim went for a piece of meat. I took advantage of the moment alone to tighten the strings on my kinnor. If Zim heard it now, he'd wonder why I hadn't been playing. Certainly, he would never go this many weeks, or even a day, without his drum.

Zim returned with a piece of bread wrapped around a hunk of meat. "It's still a little raw," he said, "but you'll want to eat before we play as it's just the two of us tonight. Not sure we'll get a break."

It had been over a month since I'd tasted meat, and my mouth watered at the smell. Yet, Yambalya cared nothing for our laws of the clean and unclean. My stomach growled as I shook my head.

"You don't want meat?" Zim's eyebrows went up as a bit of juice ran down his chin.

"I don't like it so raw," I lied.

"Alright, but there's no promise any will be left by the time we get a break."

I got myself a piece of dry bread, the only thing I felt safe eating. I soon went back for a second piece and was halfway through it when Yambalya nodded in our direction. Zim shoved his third helping into his mouth, filling it to capacity to leave his hands free to drum. I did the same with my bread and picked up my kinnor.

My fingers, raw from grinding flour, felt awkward on the strings. My initial playing drew a puzzled look from Zim. He had played with me enough to know something was wrong.

Once I found the rhythm, I relaxed into the flow of the music. I broke off to retune my kinnor. The sound was good, but not quite perfect. The strings had too much give, falling out of tune too quickly after weeks of not being played. Once the sound rang out clearly, I fell back into rhythm with Zim.

The two of us had played together so many times that there was no need to watch him. I played with eyes closed, hearing from the subtle shifts in his drumming when a transition was coming. We moved from melody to melody as if we'd rehearsed.

Zim's drumming always grew louder as the night wore on, so when I heard him soften his strokes, I opened my eyes. Over sixty violet robed priests stood in two lines, with Yambalya towering over them all. Four torchbearers approached, surrounding a short man whose bald head reflected the torchlight. His robes were frayed at the collar and sleeves, as if worn for many years, their dye so dark that they appeared black.

Yambalya fell to his knees, bowing before his master. Mot smiled down at his disciple, displaying several missing teeth and deep wrinkles at the eyes. He touched Yambalya on the head, and the giant of a man rose, standing so tall above his teacher that Mot's head barely reached Yambalya's chest. Though Mot was the elder and perhaps the wiser, it was easy to see how Yambalya ascended to the rank of High Priest. He commanded fear and respect his elderly master could not.

Yambalya led Mot through the foundations of the new temple. The priest's small eyes darted around, taking in each detail, his face glowing with pleasure.

After the inspection, Yambalya brought his master to the fire pit. He pried open the mouth of the roasted bull, drew his knife, and cut out the tongue to present to his honored guest.

This was the signal for the feast to begin. The smell of roasting meat filled the air as the junior priests pressed forward to receive choice portions. Zim increased the intensity of his beat, and I followed his lead. I was a horrible baker, an adequate hand in my uncle's orchard, and a good shepherd. But in my heart, I was a musician.

The way of fools is right in their own eyes, but the wise accept advice.

Proverbs 12:15

3

The Prophet Finder

The following morning, my back hurt from sleeping on the floor. I missed Ovadia's straw bed. My eyes were heavy from playing until the moon set, but I dragged myself upright. The prophets would go hungry if I didn't.

By the time I arrived at Ovadia's, sunlight brightened the tops of the city walls. Batya must have woken long ago to light the ovens. That was my job. I gave four hard raps at the gate and one soft one. The peephole opened first, then the heavy, wooden door swung on its leather hinges. Batya filled the entrance, one hand holding the gate half open, the other planted on her hip. "You're here to help?"

I swallowed. "If you'll have me."

"You know we need to make enough for two days?"

Obviously, I knew there would be no baking on Shabbat, but I bit back my reply. "I should have come earlier."

She stepped aside, giving me room enough to pass. She secured the gate and followed me into the house.

I scanned the kitchen with faint hope. "Ovadia isn't here, is he?"

"No." The word hung in the air. "He left you a message."

My eyes jumped to Batya's.

"You must remain where you are."

If Ovadia saw no way out of the musicians' quarters, I was stuck.

"Go back to grinding." Batya crouched to stoke the coals in the indoor oven. "Do it outside today."

Why was I suddenly allowed to labor outside? Was it safer on the eve of Shabbat when everyone baked additional bread? Or did Batya no longer want me present?

I quickly hauled the grindstones to the courtyard. I needed to make up for lost time.

"All hail Lev, bearer of the staff of life," Peleh called out in mock salute as I arrived outside the cave. It was less than an hour to sunset.

"We'll take the bread and bring water for the donkey," Sadya said. "You can go to your master."

They went to work unloading the saddlebags, and I slipped past them into the cave. Peleh's voice carried as I stepped into the darkness. "So little, Sadya? This is a Shabbat feast for neither man nor beast."

Sadya slapped him on the arm. "Hush."

Even if I'd ground by the light of the moon, we would have struggled to make bread for the prophets for two days. With me spending the night playing before the Baal, the amount fell far short.

I felt my way through the cave to my master's sleeping quarters. He was not there, though an oil lamp flickered in its niche. I was arranging my sleeping mat when Uriel appeared, his hair glistening wet in the lamplight. "Ah, Lev," he greeted me. "If you hurry, there is still time to wash for Shabbat."

"Wash, Master? Where?" The prophets would not risk leaving the cave to clean themselves for Shabbat, would they?

"Remember, our ancestors dug out this cave long ago, back in the time of Gidon. When they hid from the Midianites water was as precious to them as it is to us now. A spring runs through the lower reaches of the caverns. Our hands are idle here, and lest they learn to eat the bread of laziness, we have set the disciples to work deepening its channel into a cistern. Soon it will be fit for proper immersion, but even now its waters flow sweet and cool. Go to them."

Flour, dirt, and sweat clung to my body. I must have smelled little better than the donkey, but I did not rush to take Uriel's offer. "No thank you, Master."

His eyebrows rose at my refusal, and he examined my face in the flickering light. "There is a shadow in your eyes, Lev. What has happened?"

I looked away. "Zim saw me on the streets of Shomron." Once I forced out the first words, the rest came easier. "I had to move into the musicians' quarters so he wouldn't be suspicious. Then last night, to keep up the disguise, I had to play for the…," the next word wouldn't come—I couldn't tell Uriel the truth, "…for a banquet in honor of one of King Ethbaal's ministers. Now there is not enough bread for Shabbat." Peleh's words still echoed in my head.

Uriel took my shoulders and turned me toward him. "The prophets eat from the hand of the Holy One, no matter who labors to bake their bread. Do not let this trouble your heart. We will eat, be satisfied, and bless the Holy One for all we have. Is there anything else?"

There was so much more to say. I hadn't mentioned my anger, which led me to wander and get caught, nor that I had played before the Baal, but not all things could be said, even to Uriel. "No, Master."

The prophet's eyes seemed to narrow as he held mine, but it may have been a trick of the light. "It is well," was all he said.

"Have you nothing more to say, Master?"

"Go wash for Shabbat," he replied. "Hurry now, there's not much time."

Uriel spoke to me no more over Shabbat, though in truth, I gave him little chance. My stomach churned as I watched the prophets ration the bread that night, breaking the loaves between them. My neck burned as I received two whole pieces, for mine was the Kohen's portion which no one else would eat. I retreated to Uriel's cavern and chewed my bread in the dark so I would not have to eat in front of all those hungry eyes, then collapsed onto my sleeping mat.

I woke in the darkness, and my groggy state told me it was already late in the day. I heard the prophets' voices as soon as I stepped into the passage, and they drew me like a light to the main cavern. I recalled Emek HaAsefa, where our voices had filled the valley, echoing from the cliffs when the melodies reached their heights. Now the prophets pitched their voices to remain in the cave, but I felt the power of their motion as they swayed together, moved by the soft *nigun* on their lips.

The disciples sat in a ring around the prophets in the center, and two of them opened the circle to let me join. The rhythm captured me first. I rocked back and forth in unison with the disciples, my breath deepened, and a calm descended. The faces of the prophets swaying before me were lit by patches of orange sunlight which penetrated the cracks in the cavern wall. The *nigun* spiraled, rising and falling on itself. The prophets' voices may be hushed underground, but their wordless song still held its power. As the *nigun* drew me deeper, the union of our voices squeezed a tear from my eye. I glimpsed the unbound horizon of the prophets in the fading light.

Our unity did not last. As our chant rose to its peak, it shattered when one voice fell away. Yissachar, an elder even among the prophets, sat with his mouth hanging open, as if the *nigun* still held him. The circle tightened as the prophets leaned toward him, the air thick, as before a storm. Then, like a crack of lightning, the old prophet fell trembling to the ground.

A breath of clean air flowed through the cave. The prophets watched silently in the fading light—the only sound came from Yissachar's shaking, which came to an end as darkness fell. The old master pushed himself upright, but no one pressed him for an accounting. I could no longer see Yissachar's worn face in the growing darkness, but I heard him weeping as he spoke. "Oy! May the Holy One wipe the tears from our faces and bring an end to the reproach of our people." The prophets sighed together. "Our brother Pinchas has survived an attack in the Galil. Many of his disciples were not so fortunate. He fled south with two others. They are hiding in a hollow not far from Mount Gilboa. Blessed be the Righteous Judge."

"Do they know where we are?" a voice asked in the darkness. "Are they coming to us?"

"I have never seen Pinchas more disturbed in spirit. Prophecy is beyond him. He will not be able to find us."

"Then the Holy One is calling you to him," Uriel's voice cut through the murmur of discussion which filled the cave. "Can you find his hiding place?"

"I saw it clearly."

"Master Yissachar is no less hunted than they, and well known in this part of the Kingdom," a disciple called out. "Wouldn't it be wiser to send another?"

"The Holy One sent the vision to me," Yissachar replied. "I will fulfill it."

"That may be so," Uriel said, "but it does not mean you must go alone. Take Lev with you, if he will consent to go."

I started at his words. "Me? You need me for your bread."

Uriel turned toward me. "As I said when you arrived, the prophets eat not from your hands, but from the hand of the Holy One." He let the rebuke sink in for a moment, and I felt, more than heard, grumbling from some of the disciples. "Only you among us can pass the Queen's soldiers every day. So too you can serve as a scout or decoy if the master must flee. Will you go?"

Coming from my master's mouth, this was a command, not a question. "If that is your wish, Master."

"It is. Come with me now, and I will instruct you on what you must do."

I saw no need for instruction, as I would be traveling with Yissachar. Nonetheless, I followed my master out of the cave. The sun was long set now, and the moon would not rise until midway through the night, so the only light came from the stars. This was the one time the prophets ever ventured out of hiding, when there was little chance of being caught by stray eyes.

Uriel walked around the olive tree, out onto the terrace and past the budding grape vines. The orchard took less effort than I feared, as the prophets had taken to watering it at night. Once we were away from the entrance, Uriel faced me.

"You would prefer not to go?" he asked.

"There was already not enough bread for Shabbat, Master. If I don't return tonight, the prophets must go another day without full portions."

"I am not concerned for the prophets. Sometimes an empty stomach makes room for the heart to grow. Hunger is not yet our greatest threat." Even in the starlight, I saw my master's eyes soften as they held mine. "Right now I am more concerned for you."

"Me?" Had Uriel seen through my half-truths?

"Do you not see the gift I offer by sending you on this journey?"

"Gift, Master?"

"Yes, the gift of forgiveness."

The darkness hid the flush which rose to my face. "You are saying…that if I go, you will forgive me for my foolishness?"

Uriel's laughter was the last sound I expected to hear. "I? I have nothing to forgive. Do I not owe you my very life?" The prophet placed his hand on my shoulder. "I am offering you the chance to forgive yourself."

"For allowing Zim to see me?"

"For that. For Shimon's murder. Perhaps even for that of your parents. And more which I cannot see." Uriel leaned close to me, and his voice dropped to a whisper. "You take too much upon your young heart, Lev. Are you the Holy One that you can cup the waters of the seas in your hands? We are all called upon to do what we may, and to trust the Holy One will do the rest."

"I didn't do all I could. Being seen by Zim was my fault."

"You were doing your best—you must never doubt that."

I shook my head. "My anger drove me out of Ovadia's house. I brought it on myself."

"Do you know why you were angry?"

I shrugged, it seemed so obvious. "Because I am doing the work of a servant rather than learning from you."

"If learning is truly your desire, let me teach you this. To rid yourself of anger, you must first recognize its true cause." Uriel squeezed my shoulder. "Ask your heart why you are angry."

We stood in silence for a few moments, but I knew no more than before.

The old prophet sighed. "I see your guilt plainly."

"I don't understand, Master."

"You blame yourself for Shimon's death, despite doing your best to keep all three of us alive. Your guilt fueled your anger—at yourself. That is what drove you to Zim."

His words sunk in. Had Shimon safely reached the Cave of Dotan, would I have been so angry at baking bread for the prophets? Had I not been so angry, would I have walked out of Ovadia's right into the hands of Zim?

"Know this. Guilt over an action can be more destructive than the act itself. I say again, you did your best last week in Shomron."

"No, Master. I could have done more."

"So long as you blame yourself, your power is limited. Learn to forgive, and you will be capable of more than you know."

"It's too late. Zim's seen me. I had to move out. I must play festivals and banquets to keep the appearance of a musician in Shomron. I can no longer help care for the prophets as I once did."

"Do you hear the poison in your words? Your guilt over Shimon drove you to Zim. What will your guilt over Zim drive you to? If you are not careful, the Baal lies at the end of that path." Uriel's words stung more than he could know. "What then will become of the prophets you hope to sustain?"

"But why must I journey with Yissachar?"

"I can see your heart is not yet strong enough to forgive yourself. Let this trip be your atonement. You blame yourself for your role in Shimon's death, so go now and save the lives of three hunted prophets. When you return, I bless you to see your debt as paid. Only then can you free your strength to help the prophets."

Uriel turned back toward the cave. "Come, you have a long journey ahead, and it will be safest to return before the rising of the sun."

Yissachar tilted his head back, took in the open sky, and descended the terraces. Whether it was his hunger, the lack of light, or weeks underground, the old prophet moved slower than even his age merited. I gave him my hand, but it did little to speed our descent.

Uriel's words echoed in my ears as we crept down the hillside, but they rang false. Walking out on the baking had nothing to do with Shimon, and I certainly hadn't done all I could in Ovadia's house. I am a musician, not a baker. There should be callouses on my fingers, not burns. Sacks of barley packed Ovadia's courtyard—there is only so much grain one boy can grind. Yissachar stumbled and almost pulled me over in my distraction. As I regained my balance, a question rose in my heart. When I walked out of Ovadia's house, was I hoping to be discovered? Is that why I walked right to Zim, to avoid being a house-slave?

As we crawled along, my master's words echoed louder. Every night since Shimon died, I had seen his face in my dreams. Did Uriel believe accompanying Yissachar as he saved three prophets could atone for Shimon's death?

We reached the bottom of the hillside, and the frail prophet released my hand with a squeeze. We turned north on the trail, away from Shomron. "How long is our journey, Master Yissachar?"

"Oh, quite far." He didn't look at me as he replied.

I fought the urge to tell him that his shuffling steps would bring the dawn far before we found the prophets. I didn't belong here. I belonged back in Shomron, trying to make up for the time I had already squandered. I buried these thoughts. I was here because my master ordered it, and if this was what he wanted, this is what I would do.

I tried to distract myself by listening for night birds, but the old prophet had other ideas. "Your Master holds you in high esteem."

True or not, I was in no mood to talk about Uriel. I grunted in reply.

We walked on in silence, but I had barely sunk back into my thoughts when Yissachar stopped. His breath came heavy, and he leaned against a tree at the side of the trail. "I must rest."

I looked at the dark sky, wondering long it would be until moonrise. We would never rescue anyone at this rate. The prophet took a step and waved us forward. He no longer leaned on my hand, but perhaps talking would help his feet along the trail. "Master Yissachar, have many of the prophets arrived this way?"

Yissachar shook his head. "Each has come in their own manner. These are the first I have gone to retrieve. Indeed, they are the first we have discovered via a vision."

His words made no sense. "With a cave full of prophets?"

Yissachar nodded. "The cave is full of prophets, yet all but empty of prophecy. Vision has been exceedingly rare since we sought refuge underground."

"Then how have so many masters arrived?" In Emek HaAsefa, Uriel taught me that being together made the spirit of the Holy One stronger among the prophets. Why should the cave be any different?

He weighed his response. "We were drawn."

"Drawn to the cave?"

"Drawn to Shomron. Have you not felt it, Lev?"

I said nothing.

"The capital has become a giant lodestone, drawing prophets as that stone draws iron. We gathered from across the Kingdom. Some already knew of the cave at Dotan, others made contact with Ovadia. He is known to us as one who fears the Holy One."

"Why would the Holy One draw them to Shomron? Surely there are safer places in the Kingdom."

"Safer? Indeed." The old prophet paused again and leaned on my arm. When we continued, he did not release it. "I do not believe the prophets are being drawn for our safety."

Our trail wound its way north until it intersected with the King's road. When we reached the junction, Yissachar was once again out of breath. "Lev, bend down for me and pick up a pebble."

I did as he asked and dropped the stone into his hand. He reached over and placed it in the largest knot of an olive tree which stood at the head of our trail. "When you come back, the pebble will tell you this is the correct trail."

"When I come back?"

"Yes, Lev. From here you walk alone." The prophet may have been frail, but there was no weakness in his voice. "Such is the way of visions granted by the Holy One. Their intent is not always clear before we seek to fulfill them. When the prophecy came to me, I thought it my journey to take. Yet, I lack the strength to continue."

"I cannot leave you here, Master Yissachar."

"You must leave me here, Lev." Yissachar lowered himself onto a rock by the side of the trail. "Your master is wise; he has eyes to see. He did not send you to hold my hand along the way. I too sense there is something which awaits you at the end of this journey."

How could I leave the old prophet alone in the dark? "At least allow me to escort you back to the cave."

"There is no time. Do not worry about me, we have not come so far from the cave. I will rest until the moon rises then make my way back." Yissachar drew raspy breaths. "The designs of a man's heart are many, but the Holy One's will is done. I cannot hope to rescue any besides myself. You will go on alone."

My head sank as Yissachar described his vision. His words gave me only a vague picture of where to look. Years of chasing stray sheep had taught me how hard it is to find something lost, and my sheep wanted to be found. Without Yissachar's guidance, what hope did I have of finding hidden prophets on my own?

"The Holy One blesses those who strive to succeed. Uriel believes in you. You will find the way. Go now. As it is, I have caused you much delay."

I turned away from the old prophet and took to the road. The silence was absolute; even the night birds slept. I had barely noticed the stars when we set out, but now that I was alone, they felt close enough to touch. Their light would be my only guide until the half-moon rose over the hills.

The road grew wide and smooth as I approached Dotan. The city was shut for the night, though the low wall and single gateway seemed a feeble defense compared with the massive gates of Shomron. It was much more like Levonah, and the sight of it stirred thoughts of home. Only a single guard stood on the wall above the gate, his shadow dark against the stars. I would be invisible to him in the weak light. As I passed beneath the walls, I flirted with the urge to keep walking, not to look for hidden prophets, not to go back to the cave, never to bake another loaf of bread or sleep another night on the dirty floor of the musicians' quarters, but just to keep walking and disappear.

I swallowed a bitter laugh—it was a child's dream. I knew of only one man who could disappear. No one had seen or heard anything of Eliyahu since he declared his curse, though Ovadia said the King was overturning the world searching for him. His soldiers had spread throughout the Kingdom, and Ovadia himself had dispatched messengers to all the surrounding lands. Even Ethbaal's merchant fleet had been recruited, with a King's reward promised to the ship that discovered him. Ovadia laughed at this, saying only a fool sought what the Holy One hid.

Now who was the fool? I had laughed with Ovadia at King Ahav, but now I sought three prophets hiding in the dark, with nothing but the words of an old master to guide me. Since I couldn't run away and disappear like Eliyahu, I had to find them and bring them back before sunrise, which drew nearer at every step. Yissachar told me to look for a craggy mountain, but all I saw were jagged shadows blocking out the stars. How was I supposed to know which one was my destination?

As I walked on, my eyes returned to the innumerable stars above. While fleeing the Queen's soldiers, Uriel had told me about our father Abraham, how he trusted in the Holy One and his fortunes were lifted above the stars. "Holy One…" The words surprised me as they left my lips, for it was the first plea I had voiced since leaving home months ago. "I know I've erred and am not deserving of your help, but these are prophets I seek, your servants. For their sake, please give me a sign of where to go."

The stars seemed to dip down from the sky, and I closed my eyes with hope. But I felt nothing. Sighing, I opened my eyes to move forward again when my foot caught on a stone and sent me sprawling into the dirt. This was useless. I couldn't even see rocks on the road, how was I supposed to find hidden prophets? Better to admit defeat and turn around. It was not too late to get back to Shomron for the morning baking. I pushed myself up and turned to go. As I did, my eye caught the glint of flame high on a mountain in the distance. I hadn't noticed it with my eyes focused on the trail at my feet. According to Yissachar's description, the mountain ought to be closer, but my heart told me this was my destination.

The fire drew me like a beacon, and I pressed on as the stars moved across the sky. Soon the sound of a drum reached me, and I as drew nearer I could make out chanting as well. My trail passed below the ridge where the bonfire burned, but I knew I would be invisible to those in the circle of its light. Shadows danced in the firelight above, and I caught a flash of violet robes. A sacrifice to the Baal.

At that moment, the moon broke over the horizon, bathing me in silver light. I dashed toward the cover of the hillside. I was in no danger for I was not yet in the company of prophets, but my chest still pounded in rhythm with the drum. At least the moonlight illuminated my path. Ahead, a trail left the road and followed the foot of the mountain around to the west, exactly as Yissachar had promised. The prophets were close. Now I had a different problem: I didn't know precisely where they were hidden, and I couldn't call out to Master Pinchas. The moon had risen, and the sacrifice to the Baal would be ending. How could I call out to a prophet without risking being overheard by hostile ears?

The answer came to my lips as a *nigun* which started as a low rumble, a hum in the quiet of the night. Many of the prophets and disciples who chanted this melody deep in the cave in Emek HaAsefa now lay dead. Its first sounds filled me with the sense that the melody was many generations older than any of us. I had never once heard the *nigun* anywhere else, not even among the prophets, but I would never forget it. To unfriendly ears, I was a boy humming in the dark, but to a prophet, I was one of his own. Or so I hoped.

The hum grew into a song whose energy sent my voice echoing from the surrounding hillsides. It grew loud enough that I would no longer hear friend or foe, but I kept singing. I ran through the melody once, three times, five times. As I came around to the beginning again, two powerful hands pinned my arms behind my back. I tried to drop to my knees and push my arms free, but the grip was firm. I went slack the instant cold metal rose to my throat.

Like a cooling snow on a harvest day, so is a faithful emissary to the sender, refreshing the master's soul.

Proverbs 25:13

The Blood of Dotan

"Not another breath or I will spill your life blood." I held still, and the blade lifted from my throat. "Where did you learn that song, boy?"

Too late it occurred to me that Zim had also spied on the prophets in the chanting cave. Later, he'd boasted about learning their melodies so he could free them from the narrow circle of the prophets. Could he have taught the *nigun* to the servants of the Baal? My hesitation brought the flat of the knife back against the soft skin beneath my chin.

My captor stepped around from behind me, keeping the knife pressed in place. His face was hooded, and he looked like a shadow in the weak moonlight. I was still held tight, and I dared not turn my head to see how many there were. He spoke Hebrew with a smooth tongue, so I knew he was Israelite, but he could still be loyal to the Baal. Who in Shomron feared the prophets any longer?

If the men behind me were priests, saying I was a friend of Zim and had played before Yambalya and Mot might save me. But if they were prophets, it could mean my life. "I am a shepherd boy, unarmed and alone. I'm no threat to anyone. Why do you grab me like bandits? Who are you?"

My words were met with a laugh. "That's no shepherd's song you were singing, boy. If you're so innocent, tell me where you learned it!"

"Emek HaAsefa." I gave him the truth, for if he was loyal to the Baal, I could tell him I learned it along with Zim.

The blade eased off my throat, though strong hands still held my arms. "Very well, shepherd. I am Pinchas ben Asaya, and the one holding your arms is Ariel ben Shema." He paused, and I felt his eyes even from within the darkness of his hood. "Now, who are you?"

"Lev ben Yochanan HaKohen."

At the mention of my father, the grip on my arms relaxed. "Yochanan's son lives?"

"I have been sent by my master Uriel to retrieve you."

"Uriel sent you?" Ariel had to stop me from pitching forward as he nearly dropped me in surprise. "My apologies for the rough treatment, son of Yochanan." He steadied me on my feet and stepped around to join Pinchas. "We had to be sure. The servants of the Baal are everywhere."

"Of course." I rubbed my arms—there would be bruises in the morning. "Are you prepared to leave immediately? We must arrive by daylight." Even as I said it, I knew our hopes were few. Was it wiser to lay in hiding and travel by night? Perhaps, but that would mean another day of the prophets getting less than a full ration of bread.

"First tell me where you lead us?" The moonlight still shone on Pinchas' drawn knife.

"There was a sacrifice to the Baal tonight on this mountain. I will not speak of our destination until I can be certain none can overhear."

"That is well." Pinchas sheathed his knife. "We will retrieve our belongings and one more companion."

The two men disappeared into the darkness as silently as they had come. The half-moon edged over the treetops. When it reached overhead, the horizon would grow light with the dawn.

Fortunately, the prophets were not long in returning. Their brother stood only a hair taller than me, with narrow shoulders. I peered at his face in the dark, wondering how young one could be to attach himself to a prophet, but his hood was pulled low. I set off at once, moving quickly down the trail, but my pace was still too slow for Pinchas. As soon as the path widened, he elbowed past me to take the lead, and the four of us moved on in swift silence. At least, the three of them did.

The young one whispered from behind me, "Silence your steps, Lev." The soft voice was unmistakably a woman's. "Heel to toe," she said, "and keep your knees bent." My footsteps grew quieter, though my heart pounded from the effort of keeping pace this way.

The warbling of a nightjar broke the quiet of the night, and I bumped into Ariel as he stopped short in front of me. His hands grabbed my shoulders as he turned, holding me still. Pinchas stood in the middle of the trail, his right hand held at shoulder height. The nightjar's call had come from him.

In the silence, I heard voices approaching. Ariel's hands nudged me to the side of the trail, and I stepped into the brush, placing my heel down first. As I rolled my foot forward to my toe, a dry branch cracked. Ariel reached for my ankle, directed my foot to a secure spot, then tugged at my tunic, coaxing me to lower myself to the ground. Pinchas and Ariel drew their knives.

The group moving toward us felt no need for silence. "I don't blame you for not cutting yourself," a voice thick with wine said. "I wouldn't do it either. Leave that to those tattooed foreigners. What I want to know is, why did you pull out your knife?" Many voices laughed. "There those two priests were, cutting themselves up, and you're just standing there, knife drawn, doing nothing." The laughter rang louder as they drew near.

The group passed directly in front of us, six men in all. A year ago these drunkards would have paid homage to the prophets, be they faithful to the Holy One or not. Now they staggered fearlessly through the night while we crouched beside the trail, weapons held ready against any threat.

Pinchas watched until the darkness reabsorbed them. "May the Holy One straighten the path of Israel and keep our feet from stumbling," he muttered.

We reached the King's Road without any other encounters, but when we turned south, torchlight appeared ahead of us. Once again we eased off into the brush and this time I was as noiseless as Ariel. The torch illuminated the violet robes of the two men approaching.

Pinchas went tense. "Kohen, you wait here," he hissed into my ear. He drew his knife and nodded to Ariel to follow. I grabbed his arm and pointed at the moon. Time was passing. His words were silent as a breath. "There are greater priorities than safety."

The two prophets slipped across the road while the prophetess remained beside me, knife drawn. I had lied to Pinchas earlier when I told him I was unarmed. My heart thumped as I pulled my father's knife from under my tunic. My companion's eyes grew wide at the sight of the stone blade. She spoke against my ear. "Put it away, Lev. We will have no Kohen desecrated on our account."

My hand closed tight around the hilt. Kohen or no, it was my duty to deliver them safely to the cave.

The torches lit the path before the approaching priests but blinded them to Pinchas and Ariel crossing the road beyond their ring of light. The torches blinded us as well. More revelers or even a troop of soldiers could walk behind the two men—there was no way to know until they passed.

I held my breath when the priests reached the road across from our hiding place. We remained silent as the circle of light moved past. Were Pinchas' preparations purely defensive? I could now see empty road behind them—the priests walked alone.

The nightjar warbled again in the darkness. The prophetess rose without a sound and crept into the road. I waited for a dozen pounding heartbeats and followed her.

The priest with the torch held the greater threat, as his companion couldn't draw his weapon without dropping the wooden cask which held his god. Nevertheless, Ariel grabbed the one with the idol, threw a hand over his mouth, and wrenched back his head. The torchlight flashed in his eyes, which went wide before the descending blade. He gave a gurgling cry as Ariel cut his throat.

The torchbearer turned to respond, but it was too late. Pinchas seized his torch hand with an iron grip, clamping the other arm around the priest's neck and throwing him backward over his half-turned hip. There was only a moment to cry out before the prophetess sank her knife deep into his chest.

"Keep that fire burning," Pinchas said. "We'll need it to destroy this abomination."

Ariel grabbed the torch before Pinchas dropped the dead priest to the ground. "Where?"

"Back up there." Pinchas pointed toward the mountain. "We'll burn the Baal and his servants on their own altar."

I saw his face for the first time in the torchlight, and my protest about the approaching daylight died on my lips. Pinchas' hard eyes would hear no opposition. "Lev, watch the road to the south. Tamar, to the north."

Tamar moved toward me on the roadside as the two prophets swung the dead priests onto their shoulders and disappeared up the mountain trail. "Slow your breathing," she said with her eyes on my face, "it will calm the trembling."

Her words made me aware I was shaking. The bright spots left by the torches danced before me in the darkness.

"Bend your legs." She spoke directly into my ear. "Put your hands on your knees." My heart raced as I struggled to catch my breath. "What is it?"

I could not answer. My shoulders shook as images rose in my head. The priest's eyes in the torchlight, Shimon's body, a head coming to rest at Uriel's feet. Tamar's voice sounded far away.

"Hold fast. This was all sudden. It will pass."

Violet robes. Firelight. Dancing circles at the wedding. My insides turned, and I doubled over.

"Easy, let it come. It's better this way."

Tamar stepped slightly back as my vomit splashed to the ground. "Have you never seen a man die?"

Her question brought another wave of retching. "Just like Shimon. Didn't see it coming…" My eyes and nose ran, tears mingled with the mess in the dirt. A deep flicker appeared in Tamar's eyes as I choked out Shimon's name. "Ariel slit his throat like a sheep."

"Better they than we. Shed no tears for their blood, Lev."

I gagged out the last of my Shabbat bread, then drew an unsteady breath. "It didn't have to be. They didn't see us. Had we let them pass, they would never be the wiser."

"Perhaps, but what blow would they strike tomorrow? In war, you strike when the enemy is at hand, or else you bring blood upon your own head. Did your father not teach you this?"

I went cold at her question. Still shaking, I straightened to face her. "My father was dead before I knew him."

"He may yet live on in you if you will it. Your father taught many whom he never knew. I come from the north, but I knew his name. If you cannot take his counsel, then hear mine—war is not a time for mercy."

My trembling calmed as she spoke. "These men weren't soldiers, they were priests."

"So much the worse. Soldiers may kill their thousands, but priests of the Baal will take tens of thousands if not uprooted."

I knew the truth of what she said, but the hard reality of her actions still turned my stomach. It didn't fit with the soft look in her eye as she watched my face. My thoughts turned to the drunk men who passed us, laughing in the night. Had the priests done anything to them which merited murder?

Her eyes never left mine as she answered. "Know this, Lev—those who are merciful to the cruel bring cruelty upon the merciful." Tamar handed me a waterskin, and I rinsed the filth from my mouth. My breath came steady now, and my heart beat softly in my chest. As we stood in silence, my worries returned—the attack had cost us precious time. By the time Pinchas and Ariel rejoined us, the moon's silver disc was almost directly above our heads. There was no longer any hope of reaching the cave before daybreak.

Without exchanging a word, we followed Pinchas south on the road. The walls of Dotan appeared as a shadow in the distance, lit by the grey dawn. "If we hurry," I said, "we can pass the city and be on the trail to the prophets' cave before they open the gates."

Pinchas frowned at me. "Is there no guard watching the road?"

"There was one last night, but I expect he was an Israelite."

The prophet raised an eyebrow. "You believe we have nothing to fear from an Israelite guard?"

"The King has not allowed them to enter the fighting. On either side."

Pinchas gave a mirthless laugh. "Loyalty to his King is not a man's only motivation."

"You fear he may be loyal to the Baal as well?"

"To the Baal?" He shrugged. "None can say. Certainly, he is loyal to his pocket."

"Meaning what?"

Now it was Ariel's turn to laugh. "The Queen spends more treasure than blood in her search for the prophets."

"You think a man of Israel would sell us to the Queen?"

"He well may," Pinchas said. "This is Dotan, after all."

Pinchas' tone allowed for no argument, but I didn't grasp his point. "What's wrong with Dotan?"

He stopped and faced me. "Do you not know what happened in Dotan?"

I shook my head. There were so many massacres, so much secrecy. Had the Queen attacked another group of prophets right here?

"This...," his outstretched hand quivered as he pointed at the city, "was where Joseph's brothers sold him into slavery."

"Joseph's brothers?" I had heard the story many times from Uncle Menachem. "That was hundreds of years ago."

Pinchas nodded. "Almost a thousand."

"What does that have to do with the Queen?"

"Boy," now he turned his finger on me, "know that every handbreadth of this land cries out with the blood and memories of our people. If you believe the events of a thousand years ago are irrelevant to us now, you might as well join forces with Izevel. Those who feel as you do believe she will prevail. As for us, we will go around Dotan."

I bit my lip. It was already too late to get the prophets hidden before daylight. At least if we raced past Dotan, we could reach the trail to the cave before the gates opened, and we might have a chance of making it back without being seen.

What should I do? To hide them before it became light and come back when darkness fell again would mean another sleepless night. Plus, more hours away from helping with the bread. Still, it might have been the best option if not for the dead priests. Once their charred bodies were discovered, the search for their killers would begin.

That left only one choice—to reach the cave in daylight. That meant we had to get off the King's Road. I waved the prophets after me as I stepped into the furrowed field which lay on the opposite side of the road from Dotan. Green stalks of ankle high barley covered the ground, and I winced as we trampled our way forward. My uncle had raised me to never cross a planted field, but the lives of three prophets were in my hands. Besides, I saw no stream or spring nearby. Unless Eliyahu relented soon, these stalks would never see the harvest.

When the sun poked above the horizon, we were well out of view, but my path through the fields wandered as I lost sight of the road. Pinchas sensed my confusion. "Is that the path to the cave?" he asked, pointing ahead.

It was a hard-packed trail, but I had not managed to get a good look at our path in the blackness of the night. "I'm not certain."

"You do not know your way?"

It was more of an accusation than a question, and I swallowed my first reply. If they had followed as I asked, we would have been safe in the cave by now. "I marked the trailhead, not the middle of the path. Stay here, and I'll investigate."

I walked toward the King's Road. A young shepherd watched his flock graze along the roadside, as I had done so many times. I ignored the feeding animals and headed for the olive tree at the junction. I reached into the knot and retrieved Yissachar's pebble.

Satisfied, I settled myself at the foot of the tree with my back against its trunk. I would wait until the flock passed. The shepherd was just a boy, but I didn't want him to see me double back the way I had come. It would strike him as curious that I would walk to the road merely to turn around again, and was sure to stick in his mind. No one knew better than I that shepherd boys were not as harmless as they appeared.

Tamar lagged behind on the trail to the cave. I knew she must be exhausted, so I slowed for her to catch up, but to no avail. As we dropped our pace, she slowed hers to match.

Peleh stood aside as we entered, and I paused for his greeting. All we received was a silent bow, though there was a twinkle in his eye as he stood upright. The prophets gathered in the main cavern to greet the newcomers. Yissachar stepped forward first, followed by Uriel and the other masters. Pinchas embraced each one in turn and introduced Ariel as his disciple.

Only one person did not join the reunion. Tamar stood just inside the entrance, her hood pulled forward over her face. After releasing Pinchas, Yissachar approached her. "Welcome, Tamar *haneviah*." He bowed, his palms held upward.

She bowed her head in response, but did not speak. Nor did she move any deeper into the cave.

Yissachar turned back to Pinchas. "You must be weary from your journey."

"Indeed," Pinchas replied. "We have not slept in three days."

"Our home here lacks many things," Yissachar said, "but for resting it is unparalleled. Come, let us find you a place."

Pinchas and Ariel followed Yissachar into the cave, but Tamar did not move.

My eyelids hung heavy from one night without sleep. How could Tamar stand arrow straight if she had gone without for three? "The caverns are vast," I said to her, "there is room for you to rest as well."

She shook her head once. "This is the realm of the prophets."

"You are a prophet."

"I am a prophetess."

The yearning for sleep weighed upon my whole body, and my mat called to me from my master's cave. Still, the prophets ignored her needs. "Yes, you are a prophetess. There is room for all. There is nowhere else to sleep."

"The world is wide and offers many places to lay one's head. This is the realm of the prophets. I will seek my rest elsewhere."

"You are hunted," I protested. "Shomron is close at hand here, not like it was in the north."

"I am a prophetess." It seemed this was her only answer.

"You think you are safe from the Queen and her soldiers, that they will have mercy because you are a woman?"

Tamar threw back her hood, and I flinched at the fire in her eyes. "Foolish boy. If I were not so sure you speak in ignorance, I would strike you. I should do so anyway, for the sake of the lesson."

My face flushed, and I was glad the cavern was dimly lit. "I…I apologize, prophetess."

"I expect no mercy from Izevel nor any man, hers or otherwise. I've never seen savagery like that of the Tzidonian soldiers. At least the prophets died quickly."

"Then why do you refuse a place to rest? No one here would deny you sanctuary."

"Deny me?" Her face was hard, but I saw the sadness in her eyes. "No, no one will deny me. Neither do they wish for my presence." She drew her hood back over her face. "You are young, Lev, but you are almost a man. Have your thoughts never turned to a woman?"

Now I was doubly grateful for the dim light. I turned away from her gaze as Dahlia's face rose in my mind.

"There is no need to be embarrassed. It is the way of life. But a man cannot encompass two desires at once. Moses separated from his wife to always stand ready for prophecy. These prophets too have wives, but when they gather, they gather alone."

The first time I ever saw a man bake bread was at the gathering in Emek HaAsefa. I thought it strange at the time, but only now did I realize that not a single woman had entered the valley during the time I was there. Now I was the one helping to bake the bread. The thought of the oven brought my eyes to my hands.

The glance was not lost upon Tamar. "Where did you get those burns?"

"Baking bread for the prophets," I replied.

Tamar pulled a small vial from beneath her robe. "Hold out your hand." She poured a single drop of oil onto my fingertips. "Now rub that in." I rubbed my fingers together, and a coolness passed over my hands. "I bless you to find your true calling Lev, for baking bread is surely not it."

"No, but I'm getting better."

Her eyes held a warmth I had not yet seen. "I am sure you are. Why has a woman's job fallen to you?"

"Batya, Ovadia's wife, bakes the bread. I mostly help with the grinding now. They had to send away all of their servants—no one can know what we're doing."

"Indeed, the tongues of maidservants are notoriously loose, but the man has not been born who can bring my tongue under his control."

Was she saying what I thought?

"I cannot remain here, Lev. A prophet's heart must serve one master if he is to remain a prophet, and a woman born to service will not be locked up and fed. If Batya sent away her maidservants then their quarters sit empty, yes?"

"Yes."

"Take me to her home."

This had to end. Whatever Tamar's objections to staying in the cave, walking into the capital was insane. "You are hunted! Don't forget the dead priests as well. Do you think we can walk you past the guards of Shomron?"

"The men you fear have heard of a prophetess on the run, but they have never seen me."

I held back a laugh. If any woman looked like a prophetess, it was Tamar. She was younger than Aunt Leah, with sharp cheeks and a flat chin. It was her eyes that gave her away. Their depth was not that of a simple woman. She stood straight, as if labor had never bowed her back. Even if she changed the brown, fine-wool cloak fastened tight about her neck for poorer garments, she would never pass for one of the people of the land. If I were charged with spying out a prophetess, there is no way I would allow her through the gates.

The lamplight reflected in her eyes. "Judge not by what you now see. I am a woman who knows my power as well as my place. I restrain myself in the presence of my brothers to avoid clouding their minds, but weak-minded guards will be clay in my hands. I can shape their vision of me into whatever form I desire."

Tamar might be confident, but I was not. The risk was too great. If she were caught, we would all be lost.

"Fear not," she said, "I will do nothing to endanger you, or anyone else. We will enter the city separately. Should I fail, the consequences will fall upon my head alone."

"And if Batya should refuse your service?"

"Then I will turn elsewhere, for I will not remain here. But why should she refuse?"

I was out of objections. "Very well. When would you like to go?"

"At once."

I knew the answer before she said it, and my knees sagged at the thought of the walk to Shomron. I needed to sleep, and here with the prophets was the perfect place to do so. But Tamar's needs were greater than my own, and she would have no rest as long as we remained.

Ovadia's donkey waited for us outside the cave, already packed by Sadya. He had even strapped my sleeping mat on top. As we stepped out under the open sky, Tamar paused behind the olive tree. She loosened the cloak at her neck to expose her throat and pulled back her hood, setting free a few strands of hair. When she stepped out from the shadow of the tree, there was a subtle sway to her step that had not been there before.

She gave me a full-lipped smile which softened the sharp lines of her cheeks. With her hood down, her hazel eyes shone in the sunlight. Then her smile disappeared, and her eyes went dark. "All this I've done for any stray eyes that should happen to catch us on our journey. You keep your gaze forward. Whatever thoughts I may invoke in others, to you I remain a prophetess."

I whipped around and led the donkey down the terraces. Only once I hit the trail did Tamar descend and follow from a distance. When I reached the gates of Shomron, I passed through as easily as always. The attention of the guards was already fixed behind me.

Though Tamar had warned me to keep my eyes forward, I could not help but stop twenty paces from the gate and turn to watch. The guards' eyes followed her as she approached, and I reached for my father's knife under my tunic. Tamar must have felt their suspicions, for she hurried through the gate, her hand drawing her cloak tight about her neck.

Why was I so stupid? I never should have listened to her. I watched as her composure fell apart under the gaze of the guards. I unfastened the knife from my thigh. I would not let another prophet die as I watched.

The Tzidonian stared at Tamar as she passed through the gate, but did not reach for his sword. A grin spread across his face as he watched her, then his eyes drifted back to the next person approaching the gate.

"Eyes forward, Lev," the prophetess said as she passed me, her voice perfectly calm.

I hurried up the hill of Shomron, passing her on the road. At the corner of Ovadia's street, I stopped to tighten the straps on the saddlebag. Heads turned to watch Tamar, and with all attention on her, none saw my subtle sign. I remained at the corner after she passed to make sure no one followed, but once Tamar stepped out of sight, those on the main road returned to what they were doing as if she had never passed.

I caught up to Tamar and led her to Ovadia's door. I raised the hammer to bang on the gate, but she held up her hand.

"Not yet," she said. "I am about to enter another woman's domain." She refastened her cloak at the neck and tucked the loose hairs back under her hood.

She looked at me with piercing eyes. "I have left your mind untouched, but I wanted you to get a glimpse. I have the power to enter a man's dreams, or his nightmares. Lest you ever come to consider your thoughts to be your own, remember that moment back at the gate. Each of those guards considered himself strong and me weak. Yet, I chose what they saw. I wished to draw their attention and hold it for only a moment. I could as easily make them fear me or fall sick with desire, but neither would have served our purposes.

"There is nothing unique about these gifts. If you were only battling in the world of men, it might do to strengthen your body, but Izevel will use all her powers to achieve her ends. To survive in her realm, you must strengthen your will.

"Now, knock upon the gate."

One's gifts make room for them, and bring them before the great.

Proverbs 18:16

5

The Spy

The gate opened a crack. Batya's eyes fell on me and her dark brows drew down. Only when she opened it a bit wider did she see Tamar. I stood braced for questions, but Batya merely stepped back to let us both in the courtyard.

"You are a prophetess," Batya said after bolting bolted the door. There was no question in her voice.

"I am Tamar bat Yoram. I have come to help with the bread—if you will have me."

"She has hardly slept in three days," I said, afraid Batya might put her right to work. "Nor I since Shabbat," I added.

"Come in and eat, then you may both rest. I can manage the baking today. You are welcome in my home, Tamar bat Yoram."

Hot bread was less tempting than sleep. Bypassing the kitchen, I went straight up the ladder and dropped like a stone onto the straw bed.

The Spy

Ovadia shook me awake early in the afternoon. "I hear you've had a busy few days?"

I pushed myself into a sitting position. "I'm so sorry I've messed everything up."

He waved away my apology. "The main problem was we needed your help with the baking, but I expect Tamar will prove equally capable."

I allowed myself a laugh. "What will you have me do now? Remain with the musicians?"

"Now that Zim knows you're here, we have no choice. We can't risk having anyone so close to Yambalya grow suspicious."

"I could still come help in the mornings. Zim rarely wakes before midday."

Ovadia shook his head. "Sooner or later they'll wonder where you're going."

I had failed. Much as I hated baking, at least it helped keep the prophets alive. "I understand. I'll go live with the musicians and find work where I can. I'll bring whatever copper I earn for you to buy grain."

Ovadia's grin grew wider as my voice sank. "Oh, I believe you can still contribute more than that. In truth, I've had another role in mind for you from the beginning."

"What? Why have you said nothing about it?"

"Batya thought it too dangerous, and she needed your help with the baking."

"And now?"

"Now you've already brought danger upon yourself, and produced a substitute to help with the bread."

All this time I felt Batya's resentment, and she had been trying to protect me. "This role is no worse than baking, is it?"

"Oh, I daresay you'll appreciate it more."

"What is it?"

"I'll say no more until I am sure it will work. For now, do the following—take today's bread to the cave, and when you return, go directly to the musicians' quarters. Let them think you've just returned from Levonah. If any of them invite you to play tonight, say you're exhausted from the journey. Once they're all gone, come here."

Ovadia stepped over to the ladder. "I must return to the palace before the King misses me. We will speak after sunset."

"You want me to spy on Izevel?" I stared at Ovadia, my jaw wide open.

"It's crucial that I know what happens in the Throne Room." Ovadia paced before me. "Izevel makes her most important decisions in private, but you might still learn enough in the Throne Room to ward off disaster."

"You're the palace steward. Can't you go into the Throne Room whenever you want?"

"Yes, but whenever I'm there these days, it's not for long. Izevel usually finds some trivial mission to send me on. It's clear she doesn't want me around." Ovadia stopped pacing. "That's why I need you."

"What will I do?"

"You will be my eyes and ears, invisible before Izevel, seeing all she does without drawing any notice."

"How can I see without being seen? You intend to hide me?"

"I said invisible, not unseen. She will see you every day, just as she sees the carvings on the wall. Do your job well, and she will pay you no more notice than she pays them, less even—the carvings were made by a master craftsman. You were made by a peasant woman of Israel."

None of this made sense. "She'll kill me if she catches me spying on her."

"Not right away. First, she'll torture you until you tell her everything you know about me and the prophets." Ovadia patted me on the cheek. "So make sure you don't get caught."

"I can't just stand in the Throne Room watching."

"Of course not. That's what makes you perfect for this job. You will be doing what comes most natural to you."

Why must he speak in riddles? "Which is what?"

"Playing your kinnor."

My ears perked up at the word. "I've only been in the Throne Room once, but there were no musicians."

Ovadia fingered the signet he wore around his neck. "Many things have changed since the wedding, Lev. King Ahav models his Throne Room on those of his fathers in Israel and Judah—the heart of the Kingdom, where the people can seek the justice of the King. Izevel prefers the ways of Tzidon. Ethbaal's Throne Room is the seat of the powerful, where he makes decisions of importance. His people come there only to bring tribute or provide entertainment."

"So there are musicians there now?"

He nodded. "Soon after their marriage, Izevel told Ahav that she could not bear to be apart from him the entire day. Then she pleaded boredom, saying she could not focus on the important affairs of the Kingdom for so long, and music would help pass the time." Ovadia sighed. "I saw her face as she said it. The truth is that she fears to be absent from the seat of power, even for a moment. The needs of the poor of Israel are no concern of hers."

"The poor are no longer welcome in the Throne Room?" My uncle taught me that the King's ear was open to all of Israel.

"They still gain entrance—her will does not rule Ahav yet. Izevel is wise enough to make her changes slowly, except when provoked. Remember that. For now, she shares the Throne Room with the people of Israel, but she has succeeded in making it her personal salon, complete with musicians playing and servants bringing her delicacies. But let her have her entertainments if they enable me to have my spy."

My mind jumped. "Is Dov still the master musician?"

"Yes, and it's a good thing you made such an impression on him at the wedding. All I had to do was mention that you had arrived in Shomron, and he had the idea of bringing you into the Throne Room. It was the Holy One's grace. Had I pushed you upon him, it might have planted seeds of suspicion."

"You could have forced him?"

"Of course. He may play at the will of the Queen, but he collects his silver from me."

"What is your business in the palace?" The guard at the gates stood a full head taller than I, and I had to crane my neck to meet his eyes.

"I have come to speak with Master Dov, the head musician of the Court." My voice shook. I had asked Ovadia to accompany me, but he insisted we could never be seen together.

The guard grinned at the quiver in my voice. "Dov is playing before the King and Queen. You can wait."

"I'm a musician." I swung my kinnor around from my shoulder. "Master Dov told me to meet him at this hour." It was a lie, but it worked. The guard frowned once at my instrument and waved me past into the courtyard.

The sentry at the door to the Throne Room was less suspicious and immediately sent a page in to retrieve Dov.

The heavy cedar door pushed open enough for Dov to slip out. "Lev, I'm so glad you returned." A warmth spread in my chest at his words. "The Queen has us playing twice as often as the King ever did, and we need the help." He scanned me from head to toe, and his expression tightened. "I can't have you looking like one of the peasants coming to petition the King. Come."

Dov led me out through the courtyard, and I hurried to keep pace with his long strides. "When do we rehearse?" I hoped he would slow down to answer.

"There's no time now." We passed through the gates onto the stone streets of the upper city. "While the Queen is on her throne, we have at least two musicians playing at all times, ideally three. She often requires us again at night. The only time we could rehearse is while the Queen sleeps, but we need rest ourselves."

The prospect of laboring over my kinnor for long hours did not bother me. Better callouses from its strings than from grinding grain. But no rehearsal posed a bigger problem. "When will I learn the music?"

"You'll pick it up as we go."

I stopped walking, and it took Dov a moment to realize I was no longer racing along beside him. He took a half step back toward me with a fatherly smile. "Don't look so worried. No one else picked up the melodies for the wedding as quickly as you did."

His words brought me little comfort. Those other musicians had arrived at the first rehearsal hung-over from the King's wine. My mission depended on my invisibility, and nothing drew attention like a misplaced note.

We arrived at the marketplace below the palace. Batya had sent me once to the capital's other market, in the square just inside the city gate, where farmers sold fruits and vegetables from their donkey carts. Now I found myself walking a street lined with stalls of cut stone, where vendors sold oil, wine, meat, and other luxuries. Only grain was sold in both marketplaces.

Dov entered a stall with walls draped in wool and linen cloth.

"Dov, back so soon?" A bald man with a sharp nose rose from a stool. "How can one who sits all day wear out his garments so fast? Or perhaps the Queen feeds the musicians too well?"

"I'm not here for myself today, Asher." Dov pushed me gently forward. "Meet Lev, the newest Court musician. He needs a full set of garments, the same make as the rest."

The cloth cutter's keen eyes took me in with one quick glance, coming to rest on the worn collar of my woolen tunic. His smile faded. "Who will pay?"

"Ovadia has commissioned his first set. After that, Lev will pay for his own. How long will they take?"

His smile returned at Ovadia's name, and he rubbed his hands together. "Two days. If it's pressing, I can squeeze it into one."

"Make it one," Dov said. "Lev, come to me at the palace once you have your garments. I leave you in good hands." He slapped my shoulder and hurried out of the stall.

The cloth cutter picked up his measuring rope. "I've been cutting the musicians' clothing since King Omri first moved the capital to Shomron. I've never fit anyone of your age before."

I bit my lower lip. Would my age draw the Queen's notice as well? "I played during the King's wedding," I said. "Master Dov invited me to return."

"Ah, you must be talented indeed." His words were truer than he knew—more than my success as a musician depended on my talent. "Stand over here." He stretched his rope across my shoulders. "I'm going to make them extra big. They'll still look right if you keep the sash tight, but they're too precious to replace at the rate you'll be growing."

As he looped his rope around my waist, his hand brushed the bulge under my tunic. "What is this?"

My heart raced at the question. Out of laziness, I'd taken to keeping my knife with me rather than hiding it after each journey. "It is my knife," I said, unable to think of a good excuse why I wore it under my tunic instead of around my waist as normal.

"Hmm," he said, still staring at the bulge. "There is more to you than there seems. It will stick out even more under the new linen garments. Leave it behind if you don't want anyone to notice it."

I nodded eagerly. "I'll do that tomorrow."

He knelt and measured from my foot to my waist. "That's a beautiful kinnor you have. Where did a boy dressed like you come by such a fine instrument?"

Once again I was caught without a story. "It was my uncle's. He gave it to me."

The cloth cutter's eyes went back and forth from the instrument to me. "A generous gift," he said at last. "That is all I need." He folded the rope between his hands. "You may return at this time tomorrow."

I stepped out of his stall, my face pale. I needed to make some changes. From this point on, I would leave my knife behind at Ovadia's. The clothing would help me blend in with the other musicians, but there was nothing I could do about my age. The only way to make up for looking too young was to play my kinnor perfectly, so anyone hearing me would know I belonged. Without a chance to learn the melodies in advance, that would be impossible.

"Fear not, my servant Jacob," Peleh called to me when I arrived with the bread.

"Why are you calling me Jacob?" I asked.

"Why do you look so afraid?"

There was nothing Peleh could do to help me, and I was in no mood for his talk, so I ignored his goading. Sadya removed the saddlebags from the donkey and replaced them with a second set of saddlebags filled with grain from the stores we kept at the cave.

Peleh caught my eye as I turned the donkey for the return trip. "Don't let worry too deep into your heart, Lev. Never forget that a power greater than any of us is in control."

I held my silence. If the power was so great, why was Peleh hiding in a cave? I returned the donkey to Ovadia's and dragged my feet each step of the short walk to the musicians' quarters. At least if I were well rested, I might make less of a fool of myself the next day in the Throne Room, but with musicians coming in at all hours of the night, there was little chance of that.

I stepped into our one-room house and found Betzalel hurrying to leave. "I'm playing a banquet tonight," he said. "There's room if you want to join."

Other than the first night with Zim, I hadn't played my kinnor in weeks. Nothing would feel better than playing, but it wouldn't help me be ready for the Throne Room, nor make me better rested. "I'd better not."

"As you like." Betzalel shrugged and disappeared out the door.

Zim sat up on his sleeping mat. "You'd better not? You're a musician. There's nothing better you can do. How do you expect to eat?"

"Eating is my last concern. Master Dov took me on as a Court musician today."

"The Throne Room?" Zim whistled. "I didn't take you for one to chase the glory of Kings."

I couldn't help grinning at his reaction. "You dreamed of this once yourself."

"True, but that was before I'd arrived in Shomron. I'd rather play my music before Baal than Dov's melodies before the King."

"His melodies weren't so bad at the wedding."

"There won't be wedding music in the Throne Room."

"I wish there was." At least I already knew the wedding music.

Zim squinted at me. "What's wrong, Lev? You say you're not worried about eating, but you look sick to your stomach."

I couldn't tell him about my real concern, but the flood of words I'd held back from Peleh came tumbling out. "I'm going to make a fool of myself. I'm the youngest musician ever to play in the King's Court, and I'm being thrown in without a single rehearsal. I haven't even heard the melodies. At the first missed note, the Queen will ask Dov why he brought some talentless boy before her. I'll be lucky to make it through my first day."

Zim's head dropped back on his sleeping mat as he laughed. "Nervous, are you?"

I regretted my words, but at least they'd let something out. I already breathed deeper. "I am."

Zim jumped up and grabbed his drum. "Bring your kinnor," was all he said as he headed out the door.

"I don't want to play for Yambalya tonight," I said as I hurried behind.

"Don't worry so much."

He led me further down the hill, where small, mud-brick houses lined the alleys. At this hour before evening, the air was heavy with the smell of burning dung. Zim stopped in front of a house that looked much like all the others, where a baby cried within. "Peretz!" he called out.

A man with a closely cropped beard pushed aside the reed mat covering the entrance. "Yambalya looking for another musician tonight?" he asked. "It's a little early for him, isn't it?"

"I'm the one looking tonight, Peretz. I've come to collect a favor. Allow me to introduce Lev, who joins the King's Court tomorrow. He's…" Zim caught my eye, "he's eager to make a good first impression."

Peretz's gaze was kind and knowing. "Shalom, Lev, I remember you from the wedding. You played well enough then. You'll find the music in the Throne Room far easier."

The blood rushed to my cheeks. "It's only the first day that worries me. I've never even heard the music of the Throne Room, and Master Dov said I'm expected to perform right away before the Queen."

"The King as well," Peretz said, "not to mention nobility, army generals, foreign dignitaries, and a load of commoners. But you're right, the Queen is the only one you must please. Here, come in and sit, both of you."

The single room barely held us all. We took seats against the back wall. Peretz picked up his daughter and stilled her cry with a gentle bounce. He returned her to the floor and pulled his halil from a niche in the wall. He blew a soft melody, which had none of the complexity of the songs we played at the wedding. I listened through one round, then swung my kinnor around for the second. The instrument sounded awful, and I broke off playing to tune it, stretching and tightening the sheep-gut strings until its voice rang true.

Zim tried to join us but soon gave up. "Yambalya will be expecting me," he said.

Peretz removed his halil from his lips. "You can go. I'll sit with Lev a while longer." When Zim left, Peretz said, "It's still early. The priests of the Baal never begin until after dark."

"He's not running toward the Baal; he's running from this music."

"It's just as well. Master Dov does not allow drums in the Throne Room." Peretz lay his halil in his lap. "You speak as one who knows Zim well. Where did you meet?"

I regretted having spoken. "At a gathering for the prophets."

Peretz lifted his eyes to mine. "The prophets? I've heard much about them these past few months but mostly whispers. Do you know where they are now?"

I shook my head. "I've only heard whispers as well. Some have been killed, the rest have fled."

"May the Holy One keep them safe. I have seen a number of prophets in my two years playing in Shomron."

Prophets in the Court? "On what business?"

Peretz shrugged. "Advising the King, I suppose. I am only a musician. I know sometimes they came at the King's request and other times without being called. I haven't seen them since the engagement."

"The lentils are ready," Peretz's wife said as she walked in with a steaming, clay pot. "Lev, will you join us?"

I gladly accepted. As we ate, Peretz told me of his life as a Court musician. The copper was less than I had imagined, but the work sounded easier than I feared.

When we finished, Peretz and I played through all the melodies Dov preferred for the Throne Room. I picked up each one by the second or third time through, yet we played each until I had their feel in my fingers.

I left Peretz's house after midnight, my hands sore but my heart calmer. As Ovadia said, music was what came most natural to me. If the Queen were to close her eyes and listen, I was confident that she would hear a musician fit for the palace. Unfortunately, her eyes would be open.

The sleeves of my tunic hung down over my hands. I tripped over the skirts that dragged below my feet.

"I made them a little big, so you'll have room to grow," the cloth cutter said. "Just tighten the sash, and you'll look like all the others."

I pulled on the cloth belt until my waist hurt, but the linen still fell in heaps around me.

"You told me you wouldn't bring your knife," he pointed to the giant bulge on my thigh. "I told you it would show through your garments. Do you want the Queen to know you're a spy?"

"I'm not a spy!" I rolled the sleeves over and over again so my hands could peek out the ends.

"Do you know what the Queen does to spies?" His eyes glistened as he leaned close to my face.

"She wouldn't kill—."

"Kill? You're afraid she'll kill you?" The cloth cutter laughed. "Before she's done, you'll beg for death. She'll grant your request, eventually. First, you'll tell her everything you've ever known. You'll betray your own mother to stop the pain."

"My mother's dead."

"So much the better for her! When the Queen sees a child playing in her Court, it won't take long to guess he's a spy."

"But when she hears my music...," I held up my kinnor, but the strings were all rotten.

"You'll be lucky to play a single note. She'll know you by your kinnor. The Queen won't fall for that pathetic lie that your peasant uncle gave you a master's tool. I knew at a glance it was prophet made. If you're holding one of their instruments, you know where to find them."

"I don't. I—."

"Don't be a fool!" His voice dropped as he moved in close. I could smell the stink of his breath. "Tell the Queen where they are before she sees through your feeble disguise. Then she'll fill your hands with gold rather than cutting them off at the wrists. With gold like that, you can buy the biggest farm in Levonah, and your uncle would never deny you Dahlia. You could live the life you dream of."

"How do you know about—?"

He drew me toward him. "I know all about you, Lev. You're a child playing a man's game. You have no secret I cannot pierce. Perhaps I'll tell the Queen and keep the reward myself."

The door of the musicians' quarters creaked open, and I bolted upright on my sleeping mat. My heart pounded in the darkness as Zim pulled the door shut and set his drum on the ground. His snores soon filled the room, even as I lay awake, dreading the dawn.

The cloth cutter held my folded garments in his hands but didn't pass them to me. He sniffed the air and turned his sharp nose at the smell. "Perhaps you should bathe before putting them on?"

His expression made plain that he didn't approve of a peasant boy wearing his precious handiwork. He was well paid for making the garments—it was no business of the cutter who wore the cloth. I nearly told him so but mastered my tongue. In my dream, his clever eyes had seen through my disguise. Why not use them to make it stronger?

"How should I smell when wearing your garments, master?"

His look softened at the title. "Clean, for one." He paused. "Scented oils would also be appropriate."

"Where do I find these oils?"

"Right over there." The smugness left his face as he led me to a stall three down from his own.

"Yossi," the cloth cutter said to the shopkeeper, "this boy will play in the King's Court. What can you do for him, so he doesn't offend his majesty's senses?"

"I don't cut hair," he said. It was meant as an insult, but I felt a rush of gratitude. I hadn't thought of my hair.

The cloth cutter stepped back toward his stall. "Just sell him something for his smell."

I left Yossi's stall with a small vial of oil that cost enough to feed ten prophets for a week. I didn't regret giving him most of the copper I earned from the King's wedding—if I failed there would be no more prophets left to feed.

The barber drew the thinnest knife I'd ever seen across a sharpening stone and frowned as I entered. Boys who dressed like me got their hair cut at home by their mothers, not by barbers in stalls of cut stone. "What do you want?" he asked, wiping his blade on his tunic.

"I will be a musician in the King's Court," I said, no longer shy. "Make me look like I belong."

His eyes widened, and I could tell at a glance that this was a man who enjoyed a challenge. "Sit." He jerked his chin toward a stool, put down his stone, and tested his blade across the tip of his thumbnail.

I hated haircuts—Aunt Leah's blade always pulled at my hair—but now I felt barely a tug as clumps of hair fell at my feet.

When he finished, I headed to the pool of Shomron, outside the gates of the city. The spring which fed the city was as old as the hill itself, but Ovadia told me the pool that received its waters and the stone plaza surrounding it were among the first things King Omri built. At this hour of the morning, a few maidservants filled their water jugs, so I went to an empty spot at the far side of the pool. I scooped double handfuls of water over my head. Once I had scrubbed myself clean, I waited in the sunshine until I was dry.

I barely recognized my reflection in the still water of the pool. My hair, so thick and curly when I woke that morning, was cropped short. My new linen garments hung loosely on my shoulders, with none of the heaviness of my woolen tunic. The garments were white, with a fringe of blue at the neck and cuffs. There was a bit of bagginess to the fit, but they looked natural when I tightened the sash, as the cloth cutter promised. I could easily pass as the son of a nobleman.

I looked deeper into the pool, staring into my eyes. The last time I looked at my reflection, a few months earlier, I was struck by how old my eyes looked. Now I saw a scared boy pretending to be a man.

I strode back through the city gates with my woolen tunic balled under my arm. The guards in the gates halted their conversation as I passed by, the Israelite one standing a touch straighter. When I put my woolen tunic back on, would I be able to pass the gates as invisibly as I once had?

I dumped my shepherd's clothes on my sleeping mat and retrieved my kinnor. It was time.

Not an eye turned my way as I entered the Throne Room. The King listened to a petitioner, and the Queen sat back in her throne, examining a scroll. Dov, Peretz, and a third musician sat off to the Queen's right against the wall, where they could be heard, but not easily seen. When Dov caught sight of me, his hand nearly stumbled on his harp. Peretz gave my shoulder a welcoming squeeze. The third musician nodded to me, and I recognized him from the wedding, a halil player named Tuval.

I waited until their melody came back to the beginning and joined in on the first note of the round. The Queen glanced up at the change in the music. I fought the temptation to look back, forcing myself to stare at the far wall.

My hands grew sweaty, and the grip on my kinnor loosened as her eyes passed over me. Then she dropped her focus back to the scroll in her hand. That was it. The Queen had seen enough to find me unworthy of attention.

I exhaled, and only when my shoulders dropped did I feel how tense I had been. Now I was positioned to be Ovadia's unseen eyes.

I glanced around the Throne Room as we played. A guard stood by the door, and two scribes sat at the King's left hand, recording his instructions. In addition to the petitioner who stood before the King, four other commoners awaited their turn against the back wall. A magistrate stood before the line of petitioners, keeping order and signaling each one when he could approach the throne. Two pages stood behind the thrones, ready for any command.

Even with four of us playing, the music had no more energy than when Peretz and I played alone. The sun shifted in the windows as petitioners moved forward one by one. I had pictured myself entering a lion's den, but after a short while, I found it quite tame.

Once the King dismissed the last petitioner, the magistrate rapped the floor twice with his staff. All present stood straight, and the King and Queen rose to make their exit. Once the great wooden doors clanged shut behind the royal couple, their servants slouched as one. Dov brought our music to an end, the scribes put down their quills, and many voices broke out at once.

"A fine effort for your first day." Dov said. "I knew you picked up melodies quickly, but you hardly listened at all before joining in."

"All thanks to Peretz," I said. "He took me through the music last night."

Dov raised an eyebrow at Peretz. "Very good. The essence of surviving as a Court musician is supporting one another."

"It certainly isn't playing invigorating music," Tuval said. "When you spend an entire day playing at the tempo of a lullaby, it's hard enough to stay awake."

"It's not always like this," Peretz told me. "Since the Queen's arrival, we play in the Throne Room, but also for festivals, banquets, ceremonies, wherever we're needed."

"True," Dov said. "We have slow days, and others when we're wanted in three places at once. You play at the will of the King now, and his demands are unpredictable, so we need to back each other up. Be there for the rest of us, Lev, and we'll be there for you."

Walking out of the Throne Room with the other three musicians, I felt a lightness in my step. For the first time since I played with Daniel, Zim, and Yonaton in Emek HaAsefa, I belonged.

As we neared the palace entrance, Tuval asked me, "You hungry, Lev?"

"Famished. But I have some bread at home."

"No need to eat cold bread. As servants of the palace, we eat from the King's table."

"Are you all going?"

"They go home to their wives at night, but I see no need to cook my own food. Come."

Dov and Peretz headed out through the courtyard, and Tuval directed me down an arched hallway of cut stone. I walked on toward the dining room at the end, but Tuval grabbed my arm halfway down the hall, turning me through a narrow doorway in the side. "You don't think we're eating with the King and Queen, do you? Eventually, you'll be welcome in the royal dining room, but only as a musician. The servants eat in here."

He pulled me into a cavern of uncut stone. A hearth as large as the musicians' quarters stood against one wall, with six sweaty cooks working before it. A giant pot of stew and a stack of bread stood on a counter between the hearth and a small eating area where seven men sat. We stood as far away from the hearth as possible, but sweat beaded on my forehead nonetheless.

Tuval pulled off his linen tunic and swapped it for a woolen one hanging on the wall by the entrance. "If you eat in your linen, you're either neater than I or freer with your silver. We may not be nobility, but we're expected to look like them when playing before the King and Queen. Stain your tunic, and Master Dov won't let you back in the Throne Room until you've washed or replaced it."

"So what should I do tonight? I don't have another tunic here."

"Take it off and eat without, no one who eats here will care." He laughed at the shame on my face. "Suit yourself. If you don't want to eat in your undergarment, be extra careful or go home to your cold bread."

Tuval filled us two bowls of hot lentils, and I ate standing, bent forward over my meal so I wouldn't spill. Men ate quickly in the kitchen, and there was a constant stream of them coming in and out. Some entered in finer clothes like Tuval and myself, either changing them or throwing something over them before eating. Others came in wearing workmen's tunics and ate as they were.

Three maidservants helped themselves to bowls of stew, and I was grateful I hadn't taken Tuval's advice about eating in my underclothes. Yet, when one of the scribes came in and slipped off his linen tunic, neither he nor the maidservants showed the slightest embarrassment.

The cooks flew around the kitchen, stopping only to drink, which they did constantly due to the heat of the hearth. Every now and again fresh bread was thrown on top of the stack for the servants. Each time I looked up at the slap of the bread being thrown down, the cook had already turned to work on something else.

"New boy among the musicians?" the scribe asked, taking a stool next to Tuval. Had I not seen him change out of his fine garments, I wouldn't have recognized him.

"This is Lev," Tuval said with a nod. "He's one of us now. Lev, this is Amram."

"Aren't four musicians a bit much for the Throne Room?" Amram asked.

"We won't be four for long," Tuval said, "just until Lev finds his place. But if you ask me, even one is too much for the Throne Room."

"I won't argue with that. It was hard enough catching the King's words when I didn't have to hear him over music. Twice he had to repeat himself today with the four of you playing at once."

"I bet the King hates repeating himself," one of the workmen said.

"No one likes it," Amram said, "but the King never objects—he wants the record right. The Queen on the other hand…"

There was so much I wanted to know. "So what do you do if you don't hear her right?"

Amram leaned in close and lowered his voice, like one sharing a secret. The others halted their conversations, so all still heard. "If it's not important, or you're sure the mistake won't be noticed, let it go. No reason to draw her anger for nothing. But if you've missed something important, if you value your head, you'd better ask her to repeat it, even at the cost of drawing her ire. Two scribes have already been flogged for missing a command."

Amram shoved a last bite of bread into his mouth and got up to go. He still wore his woolen tunic, and carried his linen one carefully folded over his arm.

❦ ❦ ❦

I left the palace soon after dark and headed straight back to the musicians' quarters. Had anyone been there, I would have been stuck, but it was empty. I stowed my kinnor in a corner, changed back into my woolen tunic, and ran off.

I slowed my pace when I reached Ovadia's street, walking calmly so I wouldn't attract attention. Seeing the alleyway empty, I knocked on the gate, four hard raps followed by one soft one.

The gate swung open, and I found myself facing Ovadia himself. His eyes flashed wide, and he gestured me inside. He looked into the alleyway before locking the gate behind us.

Batya and Tamar kneaded dough in the kitchen. Tamar scrutinized my newly cut hair and sniffed at the air. She turned away without a word.

"Are you hungry?" Batya asked.

"I ate at the palace," I replied, wondering if that had been a mistake.

"Excellent," Ovadia said. "I want you eating there whenever possible, both the morning and evening meals if you can."

"I understand." I pitched my voice so Tamar would hear. "Better that my portion of bread should go to a prophet if I have another source."

Ovadia waved this away. "I don't want you in the kitchen for the sake of your stomach. You eat the Kohen's portion in any case. I want you there for your ears. You'll often learn more from a meal in the kitchen than from a day in the Throne Room. The servants will speak of matters in your presence they would never mention in mine."

"Is the kitchen to be trusted?" Tamar didn't look up from the dough. "Is the information he learns worth him eating impure food?"

"Idolaters may eat from the Queen's table, but that does not make the kitchen impure," Ovadia replied. "One of the only times I have seen Ahav stand up to his wife was when her soldiers caught a wild boar, and she wanted to serve it at the royal table."

"He bows to her gods, why should he not eat their beasts?" Tamar asked.

"King Ahav insists all should be welcome at his table. He's uncompromising on the sanctity of the kitchen. I would feed the prophets themselves from there."

Ovadia drew a stool opposite me. "Now Lev, tell me what happened today in the Throne Room."

"I arrived late as I had to wait for my garments."

"Did the Queen notice you?"

"She looked up when I started playing, just for a moment, then went back to reading her scroll."

"And the rest of the day?"

"She never turned my way again."

"Excellent. That means nothing about you caught her attention. It was wise of you to get your hair cut. You're young for a musician, but otherwise, you don't appear out of the ordinary. If she paid you no mind today, she's unlikely to notice you again. Did you hear anything notable?"

"No. Six petitioners spoke before the King, all commoners, but I was only able to hear two of them over the music."

"The commoners concern me little. They only petition the King once the chief matters of the day have been heard. Tomorrow you'll start the day at the beginning and hear more."

"What do I do if I hear something important? Come find you?"

"Oh no." Ovadia held up a finger in caution. "Remember, we must never be seen together."

"I thought I'm to be your eyes and ears?"

"You are. But if a connection between us is even suspected, you'll no longer be invisible. Even coming here tonight was foolish." He waved away my protest. "It was my mistake, not yours. I should have realized you'd want to come."

"So what do I do if I hear anything important?"

Ovadia thought for a moment. "Come tell Batya. As long as I'm not home, I don't think anyone will be watching the house. Batya can come find me without attracting attention."

The next morning, I found the servants' area of the kitchen deserted. A bit of cold bread and the remnants of a chickpea mash were all that remained.

I hung my linen garment on a hook and sat to eat. I chewed my bread as slowly as I could and watched the chefs working at the hearth. Once I finished eating, I would have no excuse to remain. Finally, Tuval came in. "Morning, Lev," he said, grabbing a piece of bread and sitting beside me. "You just arrive?"

I nodded, not wanting to admit I was already on my third piece. "No one else eats at this hour?"

"Most palace servants rise before the sun. Only after all-night festivals am I ever at the morning meal when it's crowded. A cold meal is a small price to pay for a warm bed."

"But they're still baking now," I said, pointing to the cooks carrying stacks of bread in from the courtyard.

"Oh, yes. There's hot bread, cakes fried in date honey, cheese, and many other things we'll never taste. All that is for the King's table. Though the cooks call it the Queen's table now, as her priests take up most of the seats."

A young man with a fair complexion and scribes' robes entered. "Ah, little Otniel," Tuval called out to him.

A faint blush appeared on Otniel's pale cheeks. "Good morning, Tuval." The scribe gave me a quiet nod as he sat at one of the empty stools. He helped himself to bread without bothering to change his linen tunic.

"Otniel, you'll be glad to know you're no longer the youngest member of the Court. Meet Lev, the most recent addition to the musicians."

Otniel made eye contact again. "Pleased to meet you."

"Lev, I used to carry this boy on my back when he was no larger than that piece of bread you're eating. His father Merari is among the nobility of Tirza, but for some reason, he eats with us commoners."

"Only on mornings when I serve the Court," he said. "I can never extricate myself from the King's table fast enough to be at my position on time."

"Where is Tirza?" I asked.

"Be careful what you ask this one," Tuval said. "You're likely to get more information than you want. His family has been among the Royal Chroniclers since Yeravaum declared the Kingdom."

"Not so," Otniel said. "Yeravaum first made his capital in Shechem. My family only became the chroniclers once he moved the capital to Tirza, next to our inheritance. King Omri asked my father to accompany him when he moved his throne here to Shomron, but he refused."

"Your father refused the King?" I asked.

Otniel nodded. "My father always says, 'it's a foolish man who abandons his land to follow a King, especially a King of Israel.'"

"What's wrong with the Kings of Israel?"

Tuval drew his finger across his throat. "They have a nasty habit of losing their heads at the neck."

"Actually, King Zimri died by fire," Otniel said, "though admittedly he hardly counts, having ruled for only seven days." Otniel turned to me. "Once he saw his revolt was going to fail, he burned the palace down on himself rather than fall into the hands of Omri, who laid siege to the city."

"Omri?" I asked, pointing to the royal banner above the hearth.

"Yes, King Ahav's father. He became King when he won the civil war."

"So he moved the palace to Shomron because the old one was destroyed?"

Otniel shook his head. "It's far easier to rebuild a palace than to build a new capital city. But as Tuval said, it is rare that a King of Israel dies in his sleep. Omri moved the capital from the tribal lands of Ephraim to that of his own tribe of Menashe, hoping his brethren could protect him."

"It worked?"

"So far. King Omri went peacefully to the grave of his fathers, and his son Ahav still sits on his throne."

Three trumpet blasts shook the palace. "What are those?" I asked Tuval.

"The signal Court is about to begin," he said, shoving the rest of his bread in his mouth. He stripped off his woolen tunic. "Move quickly when you hear them. We must be ready to play when the King and Queen arrive."

Otniel wiped his hands neatly and stood to leave. "You didn't bring a second tunic?" I asked him as I pulled mine off.

Tuval snorted. "It will be a mighty cold day indeed before any son of Merari wears wool."

A hint of color came to Otniel's sallow cheeks. Though he had eaten hardily, not a crumb marred his garments. He stepped out of the kitchen as I hung my woolen tunic on a hook. "Can I leave it here during the day?"

"Yes, but don't leave your linen ones here at night. They're far too valuable."

I threw my musicians' tunic over my head and was about to tighten the sash when Tuval said, "There's no time now. We're not even allowed in the hallway when the King and Queen walk to the Throne Room."

We hurried out of the kitchen and down the hall. My baggy garments puffed out behind me, and I held them with one hand so I wouldn't trip over the skirts. Another scribe ran ahead of us, clutching a roll of parchment, his quill, and a jar of ink. The guard at the Throne Room door waved us in, then pulled the wooden doors closed behind us.

A line of petitioners stood along one wall, and four others of high birth stood before the empty thrones. Dov sat tuning his nevel, which was three times the size of my kinnor, with longer, thicker strings. "Morning," he said. "We are only three today. I have Peretz and Uzzah playing for Zarisha this afternoon."

I neither knew nor cared who Zarisha was. I needed to look presentable before the King and Queen arrived or I'd risk standing out. I folded over my garments and tightened the sash, but still looked like a boy dressed in his father's clothes.

Tuval put his hand on my back with a weight that told me to relax. "You can take your time now. The King and Queen come at their own pace, which isn't very fast. That's how it is around here: run, run, run, then wait."

I undid my sash, gathered the excess material in my garments, and folded it back on itself around my waist to make the front taut. When I retied the sash this time, I looked presentable. I plucked all the strings on my kinnor, listening to each one in turn.

The door shook with two heavy knocks. "That's our signal," Dov said, resting his fingers on his nevel. "Did Peretz show you this melody?"

He launched into a tune faster than anything we'd yet played. Apparently, not all the music in the Throne Room would be as dull as yesterday's. "No," I replied, already plucking at my strings.

"When they open the doors," Dov said to me, "play quietly this time."

I finally got to play music with life to it, and Dov wanted me to silence my kinnor? But he was the head musician. I bit my lower lip and nodded back.

"King Ahav and Queen Izevel," the guard at the door announced. The King and Queen stepped in, holding hands. As they walked down the center aisle, I fumbled two notes. It was a good thing Dov had me playing quietly. The Queen climbed the three stairs to the dais and seated herself alongside King Ahav without so much as a glance in our direction.

Dov brought the fast-paced song to an end and began one of the slow tunes we'd played the day before, soft enough that it wouldn't overshadow the discussions in the Court. The King turned to the magistrate standing before the throne. "Who is first today?"

More than all that you guard, guard your heart, for it is the source of life.

Proverbs 4:23

Ashera

"You look miserable," Zim said.

"Just bored." Unable to visit Ovadia, or even return to the cave lest my absence be noted, I had spent the entire Shabbat alone. Zim returned late in the night and was only stirring now that the sun was going down.

"How's the music in the Throne Room?" he asked.

If there was one thing I could never lie convincingly to Zim about, it was music. "Awful," I admitted. For the last three weeks, I'd played the same slow melodies over and over, never allowing my kinnor's true voice to ring out.

"When things are quiet in the Temple, I can hear the music from the palace. I think it would put me to sleep."

"I'm sure it would, especially as Master Dov expects us to play while the sun is up. But try giving ear to petitioners over the music you play for the Baal."

"If I were King, there would be no petitioners in the Throne Room. The people should listen to the King, not the other way around. Yambalya says

King Ethbaal never opens his palace to the peasants of Tzidon. If they're not there to work or bring tribute, what use are they to the King?"

I knew the people mattered to Ahav. It was written across his face when he listened to even the poorest of the land. How could I explain that to Zim?

"I suppose there are worse fates than being a Court musician. At least you get to play your kinnor, and receive copper for your efforts." Zim rolled over as if going back to sleep. "If it were me," he said over his shoulder, "the moment I finished in the Throne Room, I'd play my music. You're not, are you?"

If there was ever a time to lie to Zim about music, this was it. He was never here the first half of the night. I could tell him I played for hours after the Throne Room. But his instincts were strong. He'd hit on my frustration—he knew it, and I knew it. "I miss the music we used to play."

Zim turned back to me. "Yambalya is always happy to have another musician. You won't find him so scary once you get to know him." I shook my head. "Well, how about this. I'm playing a festival elsewhere tomorrow night. Come with me. The music's better before Baal, but it will be far more exciting than the Throne Room—I can promise you that."

"Anyone cutting themselves up?"

"No man's blood will be spilled," Zim replied with an odd grin.

I told myself it was dangerous to refuse, that I couldn't have Zim grow suspicious. "I'll come."

"Excellent. Be ready an hour before sunset."

The next night I skipped the evening meal and ran back to the musicians' quarters. Zim sat tapping his drum. "Good," he jumped up, "I thought you weren't coming."

"Court ran late today." I yanked off my linen garments, dumped them on my sleeping mat, and pulled my old tunic over my head. Zim was already out the door, and I rushed after him back to the main road. We climbed up in the direction of the palace, not turning off until we reached the site of the half-completed temple. The fresh cut stone walls already rose taller than Ovadia's house. "I thought we weren't playing for the Baal?" I asked.

"Don't be frightened." He shot a smirk at me over his shoulder. "We're not." We skirted the temple and entered a clearing lit by tall torches thrust into the ground. A small crowd already gathered around a newly planted tree which stood in the center of the open field. "Would you believe Izevel had this tree brought all the way from Tzidon? Yambalya says it's a sapling; the mature ones are impossible to dig up and could never be transported."

A sapling? It was already larger than an olive tree, and its wide branches and fat leaves seemed out of place in the mountains of Israel. "What kind of tree is it?"

"Ashera."

My heart sank. I had been so worried about the Baal that I had given no thought to Ashera, the other god Izevel brought from Tzidon.

Zim laughed. "Don't look so downtrodden. True, the music before Baal is better, but Ashera offers other benefits." His eyes flashed.

A woman in crimson robes drew toward us as we entered the torchlight. Her hair was wound in a high crown, but it was her eyes that drew me. They locked on mine, daring me to break contact. Tamar's words of warning echoed in my ears, and I knew I ought to look away. Yet, my eyes remained fixed on hers even as I felt the blood rising to my cheeks.

Flowers weaved through her chestnut hair, each the same shade as her crimson gown. She stood a full head taller than me and wore a silver pendant of a bare-chested woman with wide hips and pregnant belly.

"High Priestess Zarisha," Zim bent at the waist before her.

"This is your friend?" she asked, and I caught my breath at her voice.

"Yes, High Priestess." Zim kept his head bent.

"He's a child." Her eyes held me as my faced burnt. I felt naked before her.

"He plays the music of a man." Zim grinned at me sideways, but I couldn't look away from Zarisha.

Her eyes released me and turned to him. "Perhaps I would do well to hire more children. The last time, I lost four musicians to the festivities. You were one of them."

Zim raised his eyes a notch but didn't look up. "It is the price you pay for my drum, High Priestess. If Ashera does not desire it, I will not play."

"I do not blame you for sharing the weakness of men." Her lips curled in a disdainful smile. "Just recall I've hired you for music. There will be no fewer than three musicians playing at once."

She turned back to me. This time, I dropped my eyes before she could catch my gaze. "I expect you will not disappoint me?"

I swallowed as I looked down. "I will not disappoint, High Priestess."

"Good. Take your places."

Master Dov might not have a drummer in the palace, but tonight there were three, with Zim in the lead. There was one string player other than me. His nevel was smaller than Master Dov's, though he still sat to play it. Betzalel added his halil, which I could barely hear over the pounding rhythm.

Fifteen priestesses ran toward the tree, the oldest no more than twenty, the youngest just entering womanhood. All wore crimson dresses like Zarisha's. They lit incense and poured water on the roots. They wound the trunk with swaths of crimson cloth and hung polished metal on the low hanging branches. Two women brought carved wooden breasts and fixed them on the trunk. The tree transformed into the likeness of a woman, the goddess Ashera. Firelight sparkled from the offerings adorning the goddess. The upper boughs, lit from below, reached up into the darkness like a cloud of hair.

Zim rapped twice upon his drum, and we all fell silent. With a sharp blow, he hit a third beat, and all of the priestesses bowed toward the goddess. Zarisha bowed last of all, falling to her knees with her arms outstretched and lowering her forehead to the ground.

Zim led us into a wild rhythm as Zarisha rose to her feet. A young girl, no more than five, ran in to kiss the trunk of the goddess. Others followed, caressing, kissing, and even trying to bow, though the press of the crowd made that difficult.

Three young priestesses approached the musicians, and placed goblets of wine on the ground before us. One smiled at me as she stood, and my nose tingled with the sweet smell of honeysuckle. The other musicians drained their goblets, but I left mine untouched at my feet.

The crowd danced to our rhythms. A weaving mass of people ringed the goddess. Priestesses pulled bystanders into the dancing, while others circulated through the crowd with wineskins. Zim's rhythms built in intensity as the crowd swelled. A man with gray streaks in his beard scooped up a crimson-robed priestess. She put her arms around his neck and planted a kiss on his cheek as he carried her away into the darkness of an orchard at the edge of the clearing.

Betzalel tucked his halil into his belt and ran in toward the goddess. He soon weaved his way out of the crowd, dancing hand in hand with one of the older priestesses. I forced my eyes away from the tree but found myself looking at the full goblet of wine at my feet. I forced my eyes to focus on the one place I could safely look, my hands.

Despite shunning the wine, my blood raced as my fingers flew across the strings of my kinnor. Zim's rhythms filled the clearing and lifted me with the energy I longed for while strumming Dov's melodies. I danced in place, with notes pouring from my hands.

The better the music felt, the more the great tree pulled at me. My eyes kept returning to the mass of people surrounding it, and the priestesses winding their way through the dance. My uncle taught me from a young age that only a fool thinks he can serve two masters. What was I doing here? My heart belonged to the prophets. No one would even notice if I disappeared now. They would assume I had followed Betzalel into the darkness. Whatever she said, that was certainly no more than Zarisha expected of any man.

Still the music…and Zim would grow suspicious. He was the only one in Shomron who could guess my true loyalties. If I left now, I would not be paid, and no honest musician would do that. Even Betzalel would surely be back to finish the night. And that extra copper would help feed the prophets. I grasped to whatever excuse I could to play on, but the truth was that I lacked the strength to leave.

The clearing filled with an intoxicating mixture of frankincense, rose, and lavender. The great tree blossomed in the smoky haze. As the crowd swelled into the shadows, I felt the goddess calling to me. Kinnor still in hand, I took a step toward the tree.

A small voice rose within me. I recognized it from my dreams. *"Strengthen yourself, Lev. Do not be drawn after your eyes' desire."*

Eyes? Music pounded in my ears and flowed through my body. Incense wafted around me, and my parched mouth longed for the wine at my feet. Why my eyes?

I closed my eyes, and my father's voice rose in my ears. *"These are the false gods killing the prophets. You must resist."*

With my eyes closed, my concentration returned. My fingers leapt across my kinnor, and I finally felt free. This is how I wanted to play since returning to Shomron. The music replaced my longing for the wine, the dancing, and the goddess. The power of the notes grew as the melody ran through me.

Zim bumped up next to me, and my eyes flew open. The great goddess Ashera filled my sight. Zim nudged me with his shoulder toward the crowd and the priestesses. I planted my feet and pushed back against his pressure. He laughed at my innocence, then saw the full goblet at my feet. He snatched it with one hand without losing the rhythm and held it out before me. I shook my head. He shook his own in disbelief and drained it himself. With a last two-handed flourish, he set down his drum and went off to join the dance

Two priestesses reached out from the crowd as Zim approached. He took the hand of the smaller of the two, and she drew him into the circle. The other turned away with a pout. As her eyes came up, she saw me watching her from the musicians' area. Her lips curled into a mischievous grin as her eyes locked on mine. It was the same priestess who laid the wine at my feet, the one whose hair smelled of honeysuckle. She took a slow step toward me.

Be strong, Lev, I told myself. Where was my father's voice now? As she drew nearer, I searched for words to strengthen my heart.

"As the Holy One, the Lord of Israel, before whom I stand, lives..." My fingers slipped on the strings as Eliyahu's voice rang in my ears. I saw his eyes blaze as he declared to the King *"...there will be no dew nor rain during these years except by my word!"*

These were the idols that provoked his curse, and we might all die from famine because of them. How could I claim to be for the prophets if I walked off with a priestess?

Torchlight illuminated the flowers woven into her brown hair. The priestess swayed her hips as she stepped slowly, the tassel of her dress bouncing on her thigh. Blood pulsed in my temples as she raised her hands toward me. Still, music poured from my kinnor.

There was a game I used to play with Ruth and Shimi before I left home. I'd slip toward them slowly, hands bent like claws, a deep bear growl in my throat. Their eyes would lock on mine, unable to look away, giggling wildly. As I crept closer, they inched back, caught between watching and running. Eventually, I'd get close enough to swoop down on them. Then they'd run, but it was too late. I'd grab one in each arm and tickle them into hysterics. Dahlia would cheer me on while their laughter filled the courtyard.

The fun of the game came from being caught in the end. But the memory of Dahlia hit me like a slap across my face. My playing didn't falter, but I felt the wild edge of the energy draw back from the strings. The crimson-robed priestess still advanced, but now it was the blood of shame pounding in my face. My anticipation dissipated, leaving a sick feeling behind. Dahlia's faced shone as I gobbled up her laughing siblings—how would she look if she saw me now?

In an instant, it was no longer a struggle to look away from the priestess or the tree. Betzalel came stumbling out of the woods, fell to his knees, and heaved twice before the evening's wine splashed to the ground before him. His priestess rejoined the dancing without a glance in his direction.

I sighed deeply as my stomach settled. Only a single drummer and I played on. I nodded to him to take the music, and he flashed back a knowing smile. I placed my kinnor on the ground and untied the sash from my waist. My priestess had already faltered in her steps, and now her smile turned to confusion. I would never know what she looked like next because I wrapped the thin cloth several times around my eyes and tightened it behind my head. I grabbed my instrument and slipped into the drummer's rhythm, receiving a roll of beats when he saw I was not abandoning my post.

I could no longer see the priestess, nor hear her footsteps over the din of the music. I only knew she arrived by my side from the faint scent of honeysuckle, now overpowered by the odors of sweat and wine. "You play beautiful," she said, in the unpracticed Hebrew of the Tzidonians.

"Thank you." I kept my voice even.

"Why cover eye?"

"To focus on my music," I said, which was the truth.

"Not dance?" She placed a warm hand on my upper arm.

I almost laughed aloud. Only moments ago I was her slave from afar, but even at her touch, I now felt free. "No," I shrugged my arm away from her grip. "I want to play my music."

I was tempted to lift my blindfold and watch her sulk away in defeat, but I resisted. The wise man has his eyes in his head, and that's where I'd keep mine for the rest of the night.

As we played on, Betzalel's halil blended back in with the music, though it lacked the energy with which he'd begun the night. My music kept growing stronger. When the festivities began, the voice of my kinnor was barely audible. As it drew to an end, all the musicians followed my lead.

Like a bird that wanders from her nest, so is a man who wanders from his place.

Proverbs 27:8

Ravens

"Zim right; your music strong." Zarisha's eyes didn't meet mine as she handed me two pieces of copper for the night's work.

Had I acted foolishly? Had covering my eyes allowed an enemy of the prophets to guess my true loyalties? As if hearing my thoughts, Zim asked, "Why did you cover your eyes?"

I gave my most innocent grin. "I was having the hardest time concentrating on the music."

Zim rustled my hair. "I completely understand." His smile was knowing, but was it too knowing?

My stomach growled, reminding me I had skipped the evening meal to meet Zim. There had been roasted lamb during the night, but I refused to eat the meat of idolaters. The light of dawn showed in the eastern sky, and I recalled something Tuval told me on my second day at the palace. Zim, Betzalel and I walked back to the main road, but when they turned down the road toward the musicians' quarters, I turned up. "Where are you going?" Zim asked.

"I'm hungry. I'm going to take my morning meal in the palace."

"That's the best reason I've heard for playing in the Court," Zim said.

Servants crowded the kitchen. A cook dropped a stack of hot bread on the counter as I entered, but it disappeared before I reached it. I helped myself to a bowl of wheat porridge from a steaming pot and ate it standing against the back wall. The sky brightened outside, though the sun had not yet risen. A cook brought more bread from the kitchen's small courtyard, and this time I managed to grab a piece.

I tore into the hot bread and finished it without a pause. With my belly now full and the energy of the festival gone, my head sagged, and I squinted out at the growing light in the courtyard. If I lay down now, would I wake in time to play in the Throne Room?

The cook brought in another stack of bread for the ever-changing crowd of servants. A raven, pure black in the red light of the hearth, glided in behind him. The bird landed on the top piece of bread, grabbed it in its claws, and took flight again.

The cook screamed, but he could do nothing without dropping the bread in his hands. Not so his companions, who snatched knives and whatever kitchen tools came to hand. One jumped into the doorway to block the bird's escape, but he was facing the wrong way. A second raven sailed between his legs and landed on a tray of freshly roasted meat. It seized a dripping piece in its claws and rose into the air with a beat of its wings.

The cooks chased the birds around the kitchen. They thrust at their prey, aiming less to recover their food than kill the thieves. The air filled with their shouts. The head chef lunged at one raven, plunging his knife deep into a wood cutting board as the bird soared beyond his reach.

The servants eating in the kitchen depended upon the cooks for our food, so we dared not laugh aloud, but I saw the glee in everyone's eyes as the chase ensued. Amid the chaos, a door flew open as one of the guards entered for his meal. The ravens seized their chance and shot out into the hallway. The head chef yanked his knife from the wood with a final curse.

I whispered to the house servant next to me. "Why are they so upset? Surely the King won't miss a piece of meat or bread."

He raised his eyebrows at me. "You're new here?"

"I'm a musician in the Court. I normally eat later."

"You've never seen the birds before?"

"No."

He smoothed the front of his woolen tunic. "Well, I'm a page in the King's service, and I eat here every morning before the sun rises to be ready for my Lord's command." He gave me a superior smile. "Every day at dawn the ravens come back to steal."

"For how long?" I wasn't sure why this was important, but an itching in my gut told me it was.

He rubbed his chin for a moment. "Over a month now, I'd say."

"The cooks have never caught them?"

He shook his head and lowered his voice. "Not for lack of trying."

A maidservant next to him tipped her head in my direction. "In the evening too."

"What's that?" I asked.

"They come back in the evening too." Her eyes were wide with wonder. "Steal twice a day, they do."

I frowned. "I'm here in the evening, but I've never seen them."

"When are you here?" she asked.

"Right after Court."

"That's too early. They come just before sunset." She pushed her hair back and leaned in closer. "I clear the King's dining hall and sweep the floors, and I'll tell you something few others can say—sometimes they steal from the King's table itself!" She giggled. "Bird's got to eat, I guess."

And musicians need to sleep. The sun streamed through the eastern windows, and the crowd in the kitchen dispersed to their duties. I would soon be due in the Throne Room, but the festival left exhaustion in its wake. Whatever the mystery of the birds may hold, I needed to sleep.

I struggled to keep my eyes open as I left the palace gates. I needed to lay down for more than a nervous hour or two. Four musicians in the Throne Room were more than enough. I went first to Peretz's house and asked him to beg forgiveness and tell Master Dov I had played for the Queen's goddess through the night. He agreed with a laugh. I trudged back to the musicians' quarters and collapsed on my mat.

When I finally rose from sleep, the sun had passed its peak. Despite the odd hour, I woke refreshed. Perhaps Zim was right that the night was for song and the day for sleep. Certainly, our music last night was better than any I had played during the day. I looked closer at the shadows out the door. If I went now, I could get to Ovadia's in time to take the bread.

Tamar answered my knock at the gate. The donkey stood in the corner of the courtyard, its saddlebags nearly full with the day's work. Its soft bray was my only greeting.

"I'll take it today," I whispered, nodding toward the donkey.

Tamar stared at me in silence. Since I began playing in the palace, she had barely spared me a glance. With my new duties, I was rarely present in the house for longer than it took to load the donkey, so I had not thought much of it. Now I wondered. She turned and waved for me to follow her into the house. When I pulled the door shut, she turned to face me.

"You are uncomfortable with me looking at you."

It was not a question, so I gave no reply.

She examined my face. "Something happened last night."

How could she know? "Master Dov keeps us busy. Many things happened yesterday."

"I said last night, not yesterday." Her eyes narrowed. "You are proud of something."

I looked away with a modest smile. "Not proud so much as—."

"Silence!"

I flinched at her voice. I tried to reply, but the words died on my lips.

She drew close, walking a slow circle around me.

"It is late in the day, and yet I see from your face that you have just risen. Where were you last night?"

I had risked my life to rescue Tamar and find her a safe haven in Ovadia's house. For weeks, she'd ignored me, and now she spoke to me like a disobedient child. "I was playing my kinnor." I dropped my eyes. "As I have been commanded."

"For whom?"

I opened my mouth and shut it. I did not want to answer, but could not hold back. "Zarisha."

"Who...," the blood pulsed in my neck as she paused, "is Zarisha?"

I swallowed. "The High Priestess of Ashera."

My answer hung in the air until she continued in a quiet voice. "Did this...priestess reward you well?"

"Two pieces of copper." I patted the pouch on my belt. "I brought them now to give to Ovadia."

"You would have prophets eat the wages of abomination?" She spat the last word out.

I met her eyes. "If it keeps them alive, what does it matter where the copper comes from?"

"You might sustain a prophet's body with bread, but if the price is honoring an alien god, how long do you expect he will remain a prophet?"

"I..." I closed my mouth, having no idea what to say.

Tamar sniffed, then grimaced. "I smell her on you stronger than ever."

"Zarisha?"

She shook her head. "Izevel."

"The Queen wasn't even there last night."

Tamar circled me again. "You played before her god, who she brought from Tzidon to kidnap our daughters and poison the souls of our sons."

"I didn't know." My voice sounded hollow. "Zim told me we wouldn't be playing before the Baal. I forgot about Ashera."

Her voice was harsh from behind me. "You enter her den every day. Last night only brought you deeper into her grips."

This was too much. "I'm there to help the prophets."

"Are you?" The question hung in the air as she stopped before me.

"You know I am."

"I know that's what you tell yourself. Now tell me, had the war not broken out, where would you be?"

The question caught me by surprise. "With...with my master."

"Doing what?"

"Serving him. Learning the ways of the Kohanim."

Our eyes locked. "And if tomorrow Ahav opposes his Queen and brings this bloodshed to an end, where will you go?"

I swallowed again. I wanted to say I'd return to my master, but the words wouldn't come. I had barely spoken to Uriel since coming to Shomron. If the prophets were no longer hunted, if I no longer had to be a spy, if all the copper I earned would be my own to keep, would I return to him? Or would I remain in the palace and show Uncle Menachem I was worthy of his daughter's hand?

Tamar watched me struggle for a moment, then turned to her kneading. I packed the last of the day's bread in silence and led the donkey off to the cave.

"Has the sun stood still, as once it did for Joshua ben Nun?" Peleh said when he saw me. "How else could Lev appear so early in the day?

"I wasn't needed in the Throne Room," I replied, in no mood for his banter. "Can you two distribute the bread? I want to speak with my master."

Sadya took the donkey's rope. When my eyes adjusted to the dim light, I saw Uriel was not among the prophets assembled in the main chamber. Several clay lamps sat next to the entrance, clustered beneath the only flame. I lit one from the burning wick and used its halo to guide me into the depths of the cave.

I found the old prophet asleep on the floor of his cavern. The dust in the cave made me sniffle, then sneeze. The sound echoed against the stone walls, loud in the silent space. Uriel stirred. "Elon, is that you?"

I felt a pang at hearing my master name another. It had been too long since I came to him. "No, Master. It is me, Lev."

"Lev," his face brightening. "I think of you often." He sat, crossing his legs before him. "Peleh tells me you now play before the King."

"Yes, Master." The praise in his voice warmed me. "Master Dov had enough musicians without me today, so I came to sit with you."

"The generosity of a young heart. Please light the lamp. I wish to see you."

Did he not see the flame between us? I held the lamp up. The prophet's eyes were milky-white and did not shrink from the light. My heart fell. Could Uriel not smell the burning oil, nor hear the sizzling of the wick? Apparently, even prophets could depend too much upon their eyes.

If Uriel did not know he had become blind, I would not be the one to tell him. Better he should learn after I left, when the other prophets would know how to comfort him. Fortunately, I had become adept at lying. "I'm sorry, Master. There is no more oil for the lamps."

Uriel sighed. "I knew the day would come when oil would become too precious for Ovadia to provide, but I had not expected it to come so soon."

I pulled the lamp as far back as I could reach, placing it gently on the ground behind me. I didn't dare blow out the flame—the smell of an extinguished wick was far too strong. The lamp's odor was still strong enough that Uriel would soon notice it unless I could distract his attention.

I wanted to tell him about playing before Ashera. I badly needed his counsel, to hear his words about my struggle and how I could avoid such challenges in the future. But I could not bear it if he also thought I was falling into Izevel's grip. Instead, I said the first thing that came to mind. "Something funny happened in the palace kitchen this morning."

Uriel's head tilted to the side. "If you were not needed in the Throne Room, what brought you to the palace?"

I bit my lip. How stupid—I should have considered that. "As a servant in the palace, I'm entitled to eat in the kitchen."

"But you can eat *challah*. Of all the mouths Ovadia must feed, yours is the easiest. Unless..." Uriel's brow furrowed. "Has Ovadia stopped separating *challah* to provide more bread for us?"

I may have lied about the olive oil, but I didn't want Uriel believing Ovadia had stopped taking *challah*. Besides, a partial truth was always more effective than a total lie. "Ovadia commanded me to eat in the kitchen to hear the gossip among the servants."

Uriel nodded. "A wise thought. You will hear words from servants that will never be spoken aloud in the Throne Room. What amused you there?"

I breathed deeper. "Two ravens flew into the kitchen and stole food."

"What did they steal?"

"One stole bread, the other meat."

Uriel sat straighter. "Cooked meat or raw?"

"Cooked, Master."

I had expected Uriel to laugh, but his face grew grave. "Did they take the food in their beaks or their claws?"

Why should that matter? "Their claws, Master."

Uriel's milky-white eyes popped wide open. "There were people around?"

"Oh yes. We all had to hold back from laughing as the cooks chased them around the kitchen in a rage. Apparently, the birds have been coming to steal twice a day."

"The same birds?"

"What?"

"Is it the same birds which come to steal every day?"

"I couldn't say if they are the same. I've only seen them once."

Uriel had not cracked so much as a grin during the entire story. "How long has this gone on?"

"Over a month."

"In all that time, the cooks have never caught even one of them?"

Why had my distraction worked so well? "Perhaps they have caught some. I don't know."

Uriel leaned close to me. "Ask your heart, Lev. Have the cooks ever caught these ravens?"

My heart? His question brought me back to our first day traveling together, on the road from Levonah, when the old prophet had first told me about the power of listening to my heart. It had been only two months since coming to Shomron, but already his question felt foreign.

I took a deep breath and closed my eyes. That morning there had been chaos in the kitchen, but not from the ravens. They eluded the cooks easily and did not caw once. I opened my eyes. "No, Master. The cooks have never caught the ravens."

"Very good, Lev. You must practice listening. You now know, as I knew the moment you spoke, that these are no ordinary birds."

I knew ravens stole, but only when no one was looking. "No, Master, they are not."

"Knowing this does not solve our mystery, it only deepens it. We must discover their mission."

"What mission could birds have other than to fill their bellies, Master?"

"Your thought is sharp, Lev, but narrow. To be a prophet, you must expand your imagination. The more you can conceive, the more you can comprehend creation, and realize your potential within it."

It was the first time my master had ever spoken to me about becoming a prophet. That had been my goal when I first arrived at Emek HaAsefa, but it felt like the distant past.

"There is a will behind these ravens," Uriel said. "We must discover why they steal and where they take their spoils."

"How can we do that?"

"Ask yourself, Lev. Can you think of nothing we can do?"

How could I learn why birds stole? "No, Master."

"Ask your heart, Lev."

Once again, I closed my eyes and breathed into my heart. What did I know about these ravens? Just that they came twice a day to steal.

"You need not grasp it all at once. Is there no way to learn more?"

"Well, I know when they come each day. I could watch for them and see if they go in the same direction each day."

"Very good. If they do, we will follow them."

"Follow them? How can we follow birds?"

"Far more is possible in the Holy One's world than you imagine, Lev. You need not worry how, for I will follow them myself. I do not fear the risks which lay beyond these walls. I know in my heart if I remain here, I will wither. Still, it would be foolish for me to enter Shomron. You must only watch to see if they fly beyond the city walls, and what direction they fly. I will track them from there. It is time I took another journey, even if it should be my last."

I said nothing. No doubt Uriel expected some protest from me. He tilted his head at my silence. He sniffed, and the smell of burning olive oil told him what I would not. Uriel's cheeks fell, his back bent, and his head dropped into his hands.

I sat mute while his tears flowed. My master wept for more than the loss of his eyes. His dreams of ever again traveling among the people, of being their prophet, disappeared into the darkness.

"I do not begrudge your lie," he eventually said, forcing himself to sit up and stare at me through unseeing eyes. "I knew I had withered, but did not realize how far. Travel is beyond me now. This is indeed my last sanctuary. If I am not to leave, I will not send another prophet in my stead. Prophecy has been driven underground, and here it will remain."

"So you will not track the ravens, Master?"

"No. You will."

My body tensed. "Me?"

"Of course. I should have grasped this from the first. The wise know the message is intended for the one who receives the scroll. You saw the sign from the Holy One."

"What sign?"

"You saw the ravens. This is your mission to undertake."

I shook my head. "The ravens have been coming for a month. Many have seen them."

"Others have seen only birds stealing food. You saw that they are messengers."

"I too only saw birds stealing food, Master."

"The ravens stuck in your mind, and you sought an answer to their puzzle. Curiosity is the beginning of seeing."

Should I admit to Uriel that I only mentioned the ravens to distract him from the lamp and to avoid talking about Ashera? Taking my silence for agreement, he continued. "When I was no older than you, a master taught me the burning bush flamed for hundreds of years before our master Moses heard the voice of the Holy One speaking from its heart. Many passed by, but few took notice. Only Moses turned aside and wondered at the source of this miracle, so it was only a sign for him."

"How will I follow them? Shall I sprout wings?"

"Did you think I would fly after the ravens? That flight is among the powers of the prophets?" Uriel laughed. "Your imagination is broader than I thought." His laughter petered out into a cough. "Perhaps you are right, perhaps one day a prophet will fly. But I am a simple servant of the Holy One. I intended to follow them on foot, and so may you."

"Can one chase birds on foot?"

Uriel's response brought me no comfort. "Yes, if one is strong of heart and unwavering in will."

I swallowed. Had I been unwavering in will, I never would have been discovered by Zim. Had I been strong of heart, I never would have played before Ashera. My master sat straight again as we spoke of this impossible mission. If going on this journey bolstered his strength, how could I refuse?

"Master, you said these were not ordinary birds. What are they?"

"The ravens are still birds, Lev, just as a prophet is still a man. Being a man does not make one ordinary."

Once I had dreamed of remaining in the cave with my master, but now I longed for the simplicity of the Throne Room. Dull as it was, at least there I knew what was expected of me. Uriel had finally begun sharing secrets of the prophets, and all I felt was my ignorance. "I don't understand."

"Just as the Holy One may send a prophet on a mission, so too the Holy One may send an animal."

"Birds have prophets?"

"No, messengers."

"What's the difference?"

"When a prophet receives a vision, he remains a man and so maintains his will. Woe to the prophet who turns away from the word of the Holy One, but the choice is in his hands nonetheless."

"What happens if a prophet refuses to heed the voice of the Holy One?"

"When Yeravaum built the altar to the Golden Calf, the Holy One sent a prophet to reprimand him. He carried out his mission almost perfectly but violated a seemingly insignificant part of his instructions. As he left Beit El, a lion struck him down."

"How do you know the Holy One sent the lion? There was a boy in Levonah killed by a lion last year."

"The lion attacked the man rather than his pack animal, killed but did not eat, and stood guard over the body until others came to bury him. Such is not the way of lions, but a lion sent by the Holy One will fulfill his mission. Unlike the prophet, it has no will to disobey."

I thought of the festival the night before. "And me?"

"You are a man, not an animal, and so have freedom of will. With that comes the power to refuse. I present you with a mission, but the choice rests with you. Will you go?"

The next morning, I woke before the sun, slipped into my musicians' clothing, and headed to the palace. My garments and instrument allowed me to sit unnoticed in the twilit courtyard and tune my kinnor as I waited for the birds. Outside of Uriel's presence, it was hard to consider the ravens as anything but hungry birds. I devised a test.

The sky grew steadily lighter until a shout from within the palace alerted me the ravens had arrived. A moment later, two birds shot out of the palace doors, one clutching meat in its claws, the other a piece of bread. Here was the moment of my test. Everyone knew ravens were greedy. If these were normal ravens, they would land as soon as they were out of danger and eat their spoils. The two birds beat their wings and soared over the outer wall of the courtyard. They gained height steadily as they passed over an old carob tree to the north of the palace.

Though the ravens had flown beyond the courtyard wall, I could not yet consider my test complete. Could they not have landed beyond the carob tree to enjoy their spoils? I rose early again the next morning but did not bother with my musicians' clothing or kinnor. Instead of entering the courtyard, I followed a dirt path which skirted the palace walls, following it in the dim light until I reached the old carob tree. The houses of the nobility descended like steps down the north side of the city. I settled myself on a rock outcropping between two houses and waited.

My eyelids drooped, and I pinched my arm to stay awake. Better a bit of pain than an entire day lost. I fought sleep, but pried my eyes open just in time to see the first raven, meat dripping in its claws, pass over the carob tree. The second followed, bread in its grasp. The two birds flew over the north side of Shomron, crossed over the city walls, and faded into the grey dawn. I lost sight of them right as they passed over a ridge not far from the Cave of Dotan, with three olive trees on its summit.

I could no longer deny what I had seen. Uriel was right; my imagination was too narrow.

I flew over mountain after mountain, the ravens mere specks in the distance. As we moved north, the yellow earth grew greener and the crags steeper, until jagged peaks jutted out above thick cedar forests. After an eternity of flight, the birds descended, gliding between cliffs of naked rock toward a fortress of grey stone.

The ravens flew in through the lone window in the tower, and I came behind, landing silently on the sill. The ravens came to rest on a cedar table, where an elderly man sat alone, studying a scroll by the light of a single flame.

He greeted the birds with a wide grin and a nod, and I went cold as I recognized the frayed robes of Mot, the master priest of the Baal. The birds placed their treasures on two empty plates before their master. The old man stroked their head feathers while they cooed at his touch.

One of the ravens croaked, and Mot cocked his head. He turned toward the window where I peeked in. His eyes widened in recognition. "You are that musician from Shomron." Wrinkles gathered around his eyes as a smile full of missing teeth showed that nothing could make him happier than discovering I'd followed his minions home.

"Sit." He pointed to a chair across the table. "This is more meat than one old man can eat." He cut the flesh in two, putting the larger portion onto a second plate and placing it before my chair. "I do not often receive company. I have my scrolls, but a man nonetheless grows lonely. Sit, sit."

I eyed the meat. At least I knew it came from the King's kitchen. Mot's lamp lit the table, but the corners of the room were shrouded in darkness. For all I knew, soldiers stood ready to pounce as soon as I sat, but my heart told me I was safe for now. I stepped in through the window and joined him at the table. I took a bite, savoring the first meat I had tasted in over a month.

"I have many questions for you," Mot said, "but you are the guest. You ask first."

I met the old man's eyes, seeing a calmness there which told me he would wait as long as my questions took. "Why must you bring meat all the way from Shomron?"

Mot sat back in his chair. "Yes, that is a puzzle, isn't it? I have all I need here in Tzidon, so why bring meat from Shomron? I do not even like the meat from your King's table. It always arrives cold."

"Then why do it?" I asked again.

He leaned forward, planting his hands on the table before him. I stared into his small, unblinking eyes. "Because it is a puzzle."

I swallowed the meat in my mouth. "I don't understand."

"Yambalya claims to have rid your land of prophets. He killed those he could find and drove the rest into hiding. My pupil is terribly devoted, but too easily satisfied. The wise are patient. They may hide, but they are never idle. Just when you think they are gone, they reappear, stronger than ever, and snatch victory from your jaws."

"I don't understand."

"Do you not? Do you not know that the prophets of Israel are hidden, waiting for their opportunity to return?"

"But the birds?" I said, avoiding his question.

"Yes, the birds. Why would birds steal from the King's table? Quite a puzzle, is it not?"

I did not like the direction this conversation was taking.

"I have long observed, Lev, that most men have little interest in puzzles."

I sat up at the mention of my name. He learned more in Shomron than I realized.

"Yet, puzzles are of great concern to the wise." He pointed across the table at me. "Do you understand now?"

"You wanted one of the prophets to come investigate?"

"Actually," he sat back again, showing off his remaining teeth as his grin grew wider, "I was worried one of the prophets might come himself."

"Why would that worry you?"

"As long as any prophets remain alive, they remain a threat. The stronger ones would sooner let me cut out their tongues than reveal the location of their friends. I am ever so glad to see you."

"Me?"

"You. Do not tell me a mere musician sought to answer this puzzle on his own. You were sent, and sent by the prophets, I expect."

"I don't know any prophets."

"No? You've never met a prophet?"

How much could Mot know? He had seen me playing with Zim. Yambalya knew Zim played before the prophets. Did Mot know from Zim that I played there as well? Should I admit to playing before them in Emek HaAsefa?

"You think too long on such a simple question," he said before I could answer. "The truth is written on your face. You know the prophets, and you will lead me to them."

"I—."

"There is no need to protest. We both know you will not reveal all you know so easily. We will discuss it no more tonight. As I said, the wise are patient."

The wise might be patient, but I was not. I'd heard enough. I got to my feet and turned back to the window, but found only a stone wall.

"Sit. Sit. There is no need to hurry. We will have plenty of time to discuss the location of the prophets in the coming weeks. Before long, I'm sure you'll be eager to tell me all you know. For now, enjoy your meat. Savor each bite. It might be your last."

I woke with Mot's laughter ringing in my ears. I took a few deep breaths as I trembled on my mat, grateful to be safe in the musicians' quarters. As if following the birds were not enough, I now had another worry to add to my burden. What fate awaited me at their destination?

"Remember, you are traveling only to observe." Uriel's voice held a warning note. "Once we know the ravens' destination, the prophets will hold a council and determine the proper course of action."

Shabbat had just ended, and the silver light of a near-full moon streamed in through cracks in the cave. My pack was full on my back as I took my last instructions.

"What if I'm seen?" I asked. There was no knowing if the ravens went to friend or foe. Though a full Shabbat had passed, my nightmare of Mot was still fresh in my mind.

"No one will be there to advise you." Uriel placed one hand on my shoulder. "You must trust your judgment."

My judgment? Didn't my judgment get Shimon killed? Hadn't it led me to play before Ashera? It was pointless to argue with my master—mine was a fool's journey anyway. Who had ever tracked birds through the sky? Perhaps one of the prophets could have done it, but Uriel refused the idea when I raised it again, reiterating that the sign came to me.

At least I knew where to begin. I had watched the ravens for nearly a week. At first, I'd hoped they would land close to the three olive trees I spotted on the second day, but it was not to be. From there, I'd seen them continue to the northeast, finally disappearing over a crag in the distance. That was where I was headed now. Hopefully, their destination was not far beyond it.

Master Dov frowned when I begged for time away from the Throne Room, but he did not refuse. Fortunately, I had a ready excuse. Two days after the full moon, Dahlia would come of age. Uncle Menachem was sure to slaughter a ram from the flock and throw a feast for his eldest child. Of course, I couldn't attend. My family believed I'd fled the Kingdom, and it was best to keep it that way. But Master Dov didn't know that.

The night was mild, yet a shiver passed through me as I left the cave. It was the same at the beginning of all my journeys—the first steps were always the hardest.

My path again took me past Dotan, and I walked unafraid beneath the city gates rather than avoiding them as Pinchas had done. The prophets might walk in the shadow of ancient events, but I would not. Eager to reach my destination, I walked through the moonlit night and continued after the arrival of the new day. Soon I had passed farther north than I had ever ventured.

I didn't see the ravens that morning, but it mattered little. The naked crag rose in the distance, and I knew they would be there by sunset. The almond trees along the road were beginning to flower—they were always the first sign of spring. I pictured my flock in Levonah, ready to grow fat. Wheat and barley fields lined the road, their bright green stalks a testament to the strong early rains. Would any of them make it to harvest?

By late morning I had to leave the King's Road, taking an overgrown path east. Just before heading up to the rocky heights, I spied a patch of green among the dried grasses above the trail. I followed the strip of life to its source and refilled my water at a trickle which flowed out between two rocks. Full skins meant it was safe to climb on in the heat of the day. I reached the summit as the ravens flew toward me over the green mountains to the south. I stood on the bare rock, and watched them approach. The birds passed so close I could hear the beat of their wings, yet neither one even turned its head in my direction.

If only they would land, I could end my journey a mere day and a half from Shomron, but once beyond the crag, the ravens floated along the brown hillsides which descended toward the Jordan River below. Men didn't settle out here, for the land was too poor to farm. Only a few nomadic shepherds grazed their flocks on the meager grasses which grew on the edge of the wilderness. Their pastures would not last long without rain—soon they would have to guide their flocks back toward the high mountain valleys. Who was out here to receive the ravens' burden? Or were the birds passing over the wilderness to the river, or even flying beyond the Jordan River to the red mountains on the eastern horizon?

I watched their descent as far as I could, but the hills already lay in shadow, and I lost sight of them well before the river. As darkness fell, exhaustion took hold. It was not worth climbing down in the fading light, so I found an overhang sheltered from the wind and laid out my sleeping mat.

I woke in the pre-dawn light and scrambled down the rocky height into the Jordan River Valley without waiting for the ravens. When the sun rose over the peaks on the far side of the river, I stopped for long enough to chew a hard piece of bread. I carried enough food for a week, but only water for a day, two if I was careful. The river still flowed, if I had to go that far, but I had no idea how I'd cross it or if I'd find water on the far side.

I watched the pale sky as I ate. The ravens passed over the crag and down the slopes toward the Jordan. I lost sight of them soon after they passed a rounded hill just above the final drop into the river valley. That hill was my goal for the day.

The heat rose as I descended, but I didn't mind. There was a quietness to these hills that I had not experienced since Emek HaAsefa. I had twice dreamed of living in these barren hills, once when I thought it my fate to be a shepherd in the wilderness, and again when I joined the prophets. Since fleeing with my master to the cave, I had not dreamed of the future. Each day I returned undetected from the Throne Room was a success.

I walked alone in the desert sun, sweat soaking the tunic under my pack. My shadow shrank as the sun moved directly overhead, then it stretched on the path before me. I saw no sign of water among the brown rocks and sharp grasses, so I took only cautious sips from my skin. Nevertheless, I soon found myself squeezing the last drops into my parched mouth.

The eastern sky was growing dark as I reached the base of my hilltop destination. I turned back to the west and saw two dark spots against the orange sky—the ravens were coming. Though it was the end of a long, hot day, I broke into a run. I needed to reach the top of the hill before they arrived if I was to see the next leg of their journey. The birds gained speed as they coasted from the heights, and by the time I reached mid-slope, they were already overhead.

The ravens dropped out of sight beyond the summit, but I pushed myself upward nonetheless. Reaching the top, I scanned the fading skies, looking toward the river and over the mountains beyond. They were nowhere to be seen.

I had no choice now but to descend all the way to the river, refill my water, and climb back up to await their return in the morning. My legs burned with the wasted effort of my rush to the top, and my head dropped in defeat. That's when I saw them, in a gully just beyond the hilltop.

I needed water. The climb down to the Jordan would be easier while light remained in the sky. I could climb back at night and be perfectly situated to watch the birds deliver their bundles in the morning. No doubt that would be the smartest thing. But my curiosity proved stronger than my thirst.

The ravens no longer held their meat and bread. Had they already delivered it to someone? My mission was to observe without being seen. I saw no one, but the gully was full of crevices. Someone could be anywhere. I crept down the hill toward their resting spot. The birds leapt into flight at my approach, cawing as they swerved to avoid me.

With my eyes following the birds, I failed to adequately muffle my footsteps. Pebbles shifted beneath my feet. I held still, but it was too late. The stones gave off an audible crunch.

"Lev ben Yochanan."

I froze at the deep voice, then shivered with recognition. The speaker stood off to the right of the trail, as if awaiting my arrival. His hair and beard, so neatly trimmed months ago, were disheveled, his garments dirty and worn. Only his eyes remained unchanged. They burned with the same fire, undimmed by the months of drought he had brought upon the land.

All one's ways are clean in their own eyes, but the Holy One weighs the spirit.
Proverbs 16:2

8

Will and Free Will

I stared at Eliyahu, but he said nothing more. My throat itched, and I held up my empty skin. "Do you have water?"

"You will find what you need below in Nahal Karit."

The gully dropped steeply behind him, becoming a deep cleft cut at the edge of my trail. Without a word, I headed for the bottom. I picked my way down a staircase of natural rock, grey and mottled, until I reached the stream bed. The tinkling sound of falling water greeted me, and, ignoring the meager flow at my feet, I pushed my way through lush reeds that rattled in the wind. A trickle of water fell over a short cliff into a narrow pool, too deep for me to see the bottom. I dropped to my knees at the edge and cupped my hands together in the cool water. I drank until my belly hurt, knowing I was a fool for running out of water in the wilderness. It was a mistake most people only made once.

The sun had set as I climbed back to Eliyahu, and the nearly full moon was rising over the mountains. The prophet ate his bread and meat, making no offer to share, so I pulled a piece of hard bread from my pack.

Uriel told me not to interfere, but he also said to rely on my judgment. Could I sit with Eliyahu and not ask his intentions or tell him the news of the land? "Master Eliyahu…?" I began, unsure what to say.

He looked up from his meat. "Yes?"

"How long will… it go on?" I meant to say the drought, but the word stuck in my throat.

Eliyahu raised an eyebrow. "How much longer will Israel serve foreign gods?"

"Israel? We're not struggling with the people, we're fighting against Izevel and her servants."

"We?"

The word stung like a nettle. "I apologize, Master Eliyahu. You fight for all of us, and you fight alone."

Eliyahu shook his head. "Perhaps you battle the Queen. I do not waste my effort with one such as she. My struggle lies elsewhere."

"Elsewhere? What other battle can there be when the Queen kills prophets of the Holy One?"

"How is it that the Queen strikes down the prophets?"

Could Eliyahu not know? I witnessed his declaration of the drought to King Ahav, but the hunt for the prophets had not begun right away. Only once the King returned from Jericho to Shomron and told Izevel what occurred did she unleash her soldiers. If Eliyahu had gone into hiding immediately after his curse, perhaps he was unaware of the massacres. No passing travelers would bring him news in this deep wilderness.

"Master Eliyahu, since the drought began, Queen Izevel has ordered her soldiers to hunt and kill all of the prophets of the Holy One."

Eliyahu's tone did not shift. "I know of the killings. My question is: how is it that she strikes them down?"

"How? By the sword, of course."

"I ask not about the instrument of death, but about its cause. Tell me how she is able to do it."

His words made little sense to me. "She…she has her own soldiers. From Tzidon. They attacked the places where the prophets gather. They watch the roads and the gates of the cities."

"Foolish boy." Eliyahu was a shadow in the moonlight. "Do you not know the Holy One created the heavens and the earth?"

"Every child in Israel knows this."

"So if the Holy One is master of the heavens and the earth, how can this child Queen kill the prophets?"

He did not wait for my answer. "Izevel may wield the sword, but the Holy One wills that it be so."

Were it not Eliyahu speaking I would have taken the words for madness. "Why would the Holy One wish the prophets dead?"

"When the flock wanders, who does the master punish—the sheep or the shepherd?"

"But Izevel—"

"Izevel is nothing. The Queen has no power over the prophets."

"No power! I spend my days spying upon her, under Master Ovadia's command. All day long she receives messages from Kings and ministers of foreign lands. Priests and soldiers alike bow before her, ready to carry out her every will. She kills the prophets without mercy or restraint, and only through Ovadia's position have we kept a few safe from her hunt. You call this no power?"

"The One who grants her power today can withhold it tomorrow. Only the will of the Holy One matters."

He had not seen the gaunt faces of the prophets hiding in the dark, eating their meager bread. "The Holy One's will? This drought is your will. I heard your curse myself."

For all the fire I had seen in his eyes before darkness fell, Eliyahu's voice remained calm. "Can man bring a drought if the Holy One does not will it?"

My words were like the fists of a child, pounding against the gates of Shomron. The prophet would not be moved. Still, I could not give up. Who else in Israel would have a chance to change his mind? "What of those who refuse to bow to the Baal? Will you let the faithful die along with the idolaters?"

"You are not Abraham, nor I the Holy One that you should plead before me. The wicked of Sodom perished and so may all the enemies of Israel."

"Your word brought this drought."

"Justice brought this drought." His voice held neither softness nor regret. "Our Master Moses taught that if Israel worships strange gods, they will receive no rain. Let them rectify their ways, and the rains will return."

Even if justice would destroy all? "The Baal and Ashera get stronger every day. If your goal is to make the people turn back, the drought is not working."

"Do the people yet speak of a drought?"

Grain prices in the marketplace had gone up a bit, as they did during any year when there was a significant break in the rains, but nothing like they would if the merchants suspected a true drought. "No, not yet," I answered.

"Then we cannot yet know its effects."

"Ovadia is already feeding fifty prophets, and more keep coming. He cannot continue to sustain them forever."

"The righteous will receive their reward."

It was pointless to go on. How could I argue about the rewards of the righteous with a man eating meat delivered by ravens? I chewed my hard loaf in silence. When Eliyahu finished his meal, he retreated from the moonlight into a nearby cave. He neither invited me to stay nor told me to go.

I laid out my mat on the rocky ground as the full moon rose over the Jordan. I was exhausted from my journey, but sleep would not come. Since the prophets retreated underground, Eliyahu had been my one hope in the struggle against Izevel. Only he had taken up the battle against the Baal, but now I knew he did not even see himself as part of our war. Without him, what champion could rise to redeem us from this darkness?

I woke to the grey light of the approaching day and went directly to the spring. Climbing down, I could just make out the bends in the trail ahead. The wind shook the reeds around me as I drank deeply and filled my water skin.

The sun lit the sky above the mountains to the east by the time I returned, and I could see all of Eliyahu's camp, except into the darkness of his cave. Whether he still slept or had already risen and walked off, I didn't know or care. I had fulfilled my mission—the flight of the ravens was no longer a mystery. There was no more to be done here. The battle raged on in Shomron, and that's where I was needed most.

Still, I lingered. After all, there was no rush to return. Without Eliyahu, what hope did the prophets have? Should I speak to him once again? As I turned toward his cave, the ravens dropped silently out of the sky. Watching their appearance, I grasped what I should have understood the night before: there would be no change in Eliyahu. He would not question the justice of his path nor give ear to pleas for mercy.

I shouldered my pack and turned up the trail. I needed to gain as much ground as I could in the coolness of the morning and rest in some shady spot through the heat of the day. To preserve my water, the glow of the moon must guide me, not the brightness of the sun. As I trudged upwards, the image of last night's moon hovered before my eyes. It had lacked only a sliver, which meant tonight it would be full. That meant Dahlia came of age in two days' time. No doubt she and Aunt Leah were already hard at work preparing the feast. They believed I'd gone south to the Kingdom of Judah, never to return. It was safest for all of us if they continued to do so.

With a squawk, the ravens flew past me above the trail. Moments ago, they were messengers of the Holy One, unconcerned with predators, prey, or even water. Now, their task complete, they were free, just like every other animal in this wilderness. In Uriel's story of the lion eating the prophet, both man and beast were messengers. The lion lacked choice, only the prophet had the free will to disobey. What of me? Was I like the prophet, with a path of my choosing? Or perhaps I was more akin to the ravens after delivering their burdens. Their mission was complete, and so was mine. I had tracked the birds, discovered their destination. Was I not now free to choose my path?

The sun rose higher in the sky, beating on my back as I climbed the next hillside. How many more peaks lay ahead until I reached the mountain plateau? Too many to count. My feet dragged—there was no need to hurry back to a war which could not be won.

I pictured Dahlia coming of age, her curly red hair pulled back from her eyes, a new dress in place of the old. Family and neighbors would gather to wish her a long life filled with the blessings of family and prosperity. Shelah would be among them. Now that Dahlia was entering womanhood, would he ask Uncle Menachem for her hand?

My duty was clear. My master must know where the ravens flew. I must return to Shomron to report on my journey. Yet, was there any hope that even Uriel and the prophets could shift Eliyahu?

Master Dov believed I had gone to Levonah for Dahlia's coming of age. Hadn't Ovadia told me to avoid lying whenever possible? I laughed aloud at the weakness of the excuse. Going to Levonah was more than foolish, it was dangerous. But my heart leapt at the thought of home, and my feet felt light on the trail.

No longer bound to follow the ravens, I took a more southerly route up the mountains. My present path would still arrive back at Shomron, but it could also be the beginning of a journey to Levonah if I wished. I crossed one ridge, then a second as the day grew warmer. At the base of a third rise, I came across a spring trickling out of the rock.

Uriel told me the wise see signs which others miss. My path from Shomron had been dry and barren, but the route to Levonah flowed with life. A full waterskin meant I could walk through the heat of the day. I could think of no greater sign. If I hurried and used the cut-through to Shiloh, I could arrive home in time for the celebration. I kneeled to drink my fill from the spring, then refilled my skins. I practically ran up the next hillside.

Just before sunset two days later, I climbed up from the King's Road toward my uncle's farm. I heard the celebration before I saw it. At least thirty people gathered, talking, drinking, and waiting for the lamb that Eliav roasted over the fire. Staying out of sight, I cut behind the house, going directly to the spring to wash off the dirt and sweat of the past week's journey. Despite the months of drought, the spring flowed near its normal winter strength, still blessed by the early rains.

By the time I was clean, darkness had fallen, and the party had swelled to over forty guests. The moon had not yet risen, and the firelight left the edges of the celebration hidden in shadow. I slipped in unnoticed, grabbed a piece of bread, filled it with meat, and sat on the ground among the other guests. After days of stale bread, the hot food tasted better than anything at the King's wedding feast. I took bite after rapid bite, and juice ran freely down my chin. Several of the guests waved at me, probably unaware I'd ever left.

Dahlia stood near the roasting pit, her face lit by the fire. Her thick curls were woven into a long braid, revealing the curve of her neck. Her old dress had barely covered her knees, but the one she now wore stretched to her ankles in the way of women. Dahlia's true beauty was in her smile. Her face glowed as I had rarely seen, as she accepted the blessings of a neighboring family.

My cousin Shimi jumped into my lap and threw his arms around my neck. "Lev! You're home!" I hugged him back and heard my name echoing from all corners of the celebration. Ruth and Naama ran over and piled on as well.

Uncle Menachem grabbed my hand and pulled me to my feet. "It's good to have you back." The warmth in his eyes showed he meant it. Aunt Leah stood behind him, but the thin smile drawn across her face failed to mask her disappointment.

Dahlia stood by the fire, her arms frozen in some forgotten gesture, mouth hanging open. The moon peeked over the hills to the east, bathing the courtyard in silvery light. Naama and Ruth clutched my hands, and I drew them with me as I stepped toward her.

"You came?"

"Would I miss your coming of age?"

She finally managed to drop her arms, though she held them stiffly by her side. Now that she was of age, she could no longer embrace me as she once did—certainly not before all of these people.

"Did you return from...," Dahlia caught herself, and I saw that she knew of Aunt Leah's plan to send me to Judah. None of the younger children seemed surprised at my return. What explanation had Aunt Leah given them?

Fortunately, I could readily share part of the truth. "I've returned from Shomron. From my position as a musician in the King's Court."

Eliav let out a low whistle, and Aunt Leah's head fell. Dahlia's eyebrows rose. "The King's Court?"

"I assured Master Dov, the head musician, that the King and Queen could do without me for a few days."

Part of me cringed at the emptiness of my words. Dahlia, who had always seen through me better than anyone else, failed to notice my deceit. "You left the King for me?"

"For you," I told Dahlia, then bent down and wrapped my arms around my younger cousins, who still clung to my legs. "For all of you. It's good to be home."

Will and Free Will

I did not speak to Dahlia again during the celebration. Too many guests waited to congratulate her, and my younger cousins were too persistent in demanding my attention. Yet, we never lost track of one another in the crowd. Unlike her daughter, Aunt Leah never made eye contact with me, though I felt her gaze when I was looking away.

Uncle Menachem brought me a third helping of meat, giving me more attention than any but the most honored guests. Eliav dropped beside me. "Have you seen the priestesses of Ashera yet?" He asked about the palace, the King, the Queen, Yambalya, the soldiers of Tzidon with their strange tattoos, the merchants, petitioners, and generals of the army. Never once did he mention the hunted prophets. Had their plight failed to reach his ears, or did he not care?

Aunt Leah stepped over. "Eliav, please take a turn with the meat and give your father a rest." When he got up to go, she strode away, saying only, "Follow me."

I didn't dare disobey. She led me behind the house, speaking quietly enough that only I could hear. "You defied my wishes."

Of all my responsibilities in Shomron, one stood above the rest. More critical than spying on Izevel, retrieving lost prophets, chasing ravens, or delivering bread, was the obligation of secrecy. Seeing the disgust in my aunt's eyes, I made my choice. "I did not defy you."

She planted her hands on her hips. "I told you to flee to your family in Judah."

"Judah was your second choice. I followed your first."

"My first? You returned to Uriel?" The anger disappeared from Aunt Leah's face, replaced by a hungry searching. "That was a bold lie you told, saying you play at the palace."

"I do play in the palace. Under Uriel's guidance." I saw no reason to mention Ovadia.

"Where is he?"

"Hidden in a cave outside of Shomron, where the Queen's soldiers can't find him. I bring him bread and news from the Throne Room." A lump formed in my throat. "You won't tell Uncle Menachem?"

Aunt Leah stepped forward and took me in her arms. My head dropped to her shoulder. "Your secret is safe with me, Lev. I'm sorry I scolded. I'm proud of what you've done. Of who you've become. You've learned of your past?"

"Yes, Aunt."

She released her embrace, holding me out at arm's length. "You remind me more and more of your mother."

I stared into her eyes. "My mother?" I was used to comparisons with my father.

"Oh yes. It took a brave woman to attach herself to a man like your father, a man hunted, yet unwavering in his devotion. That is what you are for Uriel, is it not?"

I nodded, not finding the words to speak.

The next morning, I was the only one with no responsibilities. Eliav left early with the flock while Uncle Menachem led a donkey loaded with produce into Levonah for market day. Dahlia baked, and Aunt Leah cooked, while the younger children helped as best as they could.

Squatting before the oven, Dahlia once again looked like herself, with her red curls hanging before her dark eyes. "I can't believe you came back for my coming of age. You left the King and Queen for me?"

"Yeah," I said lazily. I couldn't abandon my lie from the night before, but it felt worse in the light of day.

"Do you see them every day?"

"Most days."

"Is the Queen as beautiful as they say?"

I wanted to tell Dahlia that the Queen was nothing compared to her, but couldn't bear any more empty words. "The Queen is very beautiful."

"Does the King always wear his crown?"

"Only when he enters the Throne Room each morning. It doesn't look very comfortable." I felt my irritation rising with her questions. She had no idea what was happening in Shomron.

"And the Queen?"

"The Queen always wears her crown." I focused on the coals glowing beneath the clay oven rather than meeting Dahlia's eyes.

"You remember Chava, who lives just inside the gates? She went to Shomron last month with her father and saw the Queen from a distance. She said Queen Izevel has beautiful black hair that flows—"

My restraint broke. "Yes, her hair is black. As black as her heart."

"Lev!"

It was a stupid thing to say, but I could not take back the words.

"How could you say that about our Queen? Ow!" In her distraction, Dahlia's hand had brushed against the inner wall of the oven. She sucked her burnt fingers, tears welling in her eyes.

I ought to say no more. What was the harm in letting her picture the Queen as beautiful? Or life in Shomron as exciting? It was just that my life was a tangle of lies already. Must I include Dahlia in that web?

I reached into the oven and pulled out the two remaining pieces of bread stuck against the oven walls. Then I took a handful of fresh dough and patted it into a flat disk. Dahlia's eyes widened—she had never seen me handle dough before.

I slapped the dough against the inner oven wall, and heard a satisfying smack as it stuck. Somehow baking, which I'd despised at Ovadia's, calmed my inner fire.

"The Queen is evil," I said, keeping my voice low, "and the King is weak."

Overheard by the wrong person, these words could cost me my head. Worse, the truth about Ovadia and the prophets would be beaten out of me first. All our secrets could be exposed, but there was no stopping it now. Only as the words poured out did I feel how great a burden I'd been carrying.

"You think it's glorious playing before the King and Queen? It's vile."

Dahlia still held her burnt hand in her mouth, but she didn't look away.

"I don't do it to entertain them, or even for the copper. I play in the Throne Room to listen to their conversations."

Dahlia pulled her hand out of her mouth long enough to ask, "Why?"

I took another fistful of dough and patted it flat. "Do you know the Queen is hunting the prophets?"

She shook her head.

"There's a war going on, Dahlia, and I'm fighting on the side of the prophets."

"Isn't that dangerous?" she asked.

"Extremely. If I'm found out, I'll be killed."

"Is this why you went to Shomron? This is what you want?"

"What I want?" I smacked another piece of dough into the oven. "You think I want this?"

"My mother told me you fled to Judah. If you don't want this, why did you come back?"

"I never left. Had I known what was coming, I may have gone. But it's too late now. I've made my choice." I reached into the oven and pulled out my first piece of bread. It was neither as round nor as pretty as Dahlia's, but was a vast improvement from when I first arrived at Ovadia's.

"When did you learn to bake?"

"In Shomron."

"You bake your own bread?"

I shook my head. "As a member of the Royal Court, I eat from the King's table."

"So why are you baking?"

I knew I should say no more, but couldn't stop myself now. "We are feeding hidden prophets."

Dahlia gasped and put her head in her hands. It was too much. I had grown into my new reality for months, but I had burdened her with it all at once. "I don't know you anymore," she said from between her hands. "You were a sweet shepherd, and now you're fighting the King and Queen? What happened?"

"War happened."

Dahlia shook her head. "Not in Levonah."

"Even here. Your father brought a Baal into the house. We saw him bow, remember?"

"He doesn't anymore, it was only that first night."

"What about Eliav?"

Dahlia's silence was all the answer I needed.

"People are choosing sides, Dahlia. It will be worse once they feel the drought."

"Drought?" Dahlia stared at me, her eyes raw. Few words evoked as much terror.

"The rains are not late, they are over. A great drought is coming, and it may last for years." I pictured Eliyahu's face, and I knew I was not just trying to scare her. All my hopes for a quick end to the drought had vanished.

"How can you know this? Did you hear it in the Throne Room?"

I gave a humorless laugh. "They do not speak of it there, though the King knows it's true. I learned of it from the prophets."

"Have you told my father?"

Her question brought home to me how foolish I'd been to share my secrets. "I can tell no one." I looked over her head, out toward the city. "Neither can you."

"You must tell my father! He could buy grain. We could dig a cistern before the spring dries."

I shook my head. "If your father prepares, others will ask how he knew." I looked her straight in the eye. "From there it's a short step to me and the prophets."

"Why did you tell me?"

I shrugged. "I shouldn't have, but..." my words had poured out without thought, but now I struggled to answer "...I wanted you to know what I am."

"You expect me to do nothing?" Now it was Dahlia's turn for anger. "To starve instead of prepare? You're risking your life for the prophets, won't you do the same for your family?"

I pleaded with my eyes. "People will find out. If the prophets are lost, there is no hope for any of us."

"You think you can keep a secret but your own family cannot?"

"They'd see you digging and buying grain."

"We could dig at night and buy grain little by little. My father trades for grain all the time."

I shook my head—it wasn't that simple. "Eliav will know."

"Eliav? You think Eliav would betray you? He sees you as his older brother."

"No, he doesn't." I knew it was never far from Eliav's mind that he was the true heir of the family. "I see where his loyalties lie. He already bows to the Baal."

"Eliav would never do anything to harm you."

"Perhaps not intentionally. But one misplaced word could bring ruin." Like the words I had spoken to her. Now it was too late to take them back.

That afternoon, I wandered through the vineyards and came upon Uncle Menachem pruning his vines. He put down his curved knife when he saw me.

"Playing in the King's Court is a good position," he said.

"Yes, it is," I agreed. "The work is easy, and the King is generous."

"I wondered if it was demanding. You look stretched thin—like you've been working too hard."

This was not my aunt or Dahlia, this was my uncle, who bowed to the Baal. I couldn't confide in him the reason I looked so tired. "There are many feasts in Shomron at night," I said. "They pay even better, but they mean I don't get much sleep."

Uncle Menachem nodded. "Music is a good path for you, Lev. Better than shepherding. You'll be able to stay in one place and build an inheritance."

"At this rate, I'll be able to purchase land before too many more years." It was a lie, as the prophets ate all the copper I earned. But my uncle didn't need to know that.

"Land." He rubbed his hands together and nodded. "Indeed, if you choose, you could buy a piece of land." Uncle Menachem's voice trembled as he spoke. "Is that your path, Lev? Do you hope…to buy land?"

There was a message embedded in Uncle Menachem's question. A chill settled on my heart as I deciphered the hidden meaning of his words. If I told him what he wanted to hear, a new horizon would open in my life that had nothing to do with owning land. But I couldn't bring myself to say the words. I had lied about why I looked so tired, but I couldn't lie now. I had chosen my path.

"No, Uncle," I had to admit. As I spoke the words, my vision for my future came crashing down. "It is not my path to buy land."

He nodded back. "You're growing to look more like your father."

"That's what I hear."

Uncle Menachem bent to pick up his knife, and I turned back toward the house. I had intended to remain through Shabbat and return to Shomron early on the morning of the first day. But this was no longer my place. My obligations were to Ovadia and the prophets, and they needed me. I would begin the journey back to Shomron immediately. And I would say nothing about the drought.

Before ruin, one's heart is proud; Humility goes before honor.

Proverbs 18:12

9

Empty

My footsteps dragged on the way back to Shomron. When I'd announced my plan to leave so late in the day, I'd expected a protest from Aunt Leah, but only understanding lit her eyes. All she said was, "Are you sure you wouldn't rather begin the journey in the morning?" When I said no, she didn't argue, just filled my satchel with fresh bread and stood in the doorway to watch me go.

The sun set before I reached halfway to the capital. There would be no entering Shomron that night—the gates would be locked long before I arrived—and I still had to complete my mission by delivering my report to my master.

"Is it Lev returned from outshining the wisest of all men?" Peleh grabbed my shoulders as I entered the dim cave. "Three things are beyond me, said Solomon, and four I cannot fathom—the way of a bird in the sky, the way of a snake over a rock, the way of a ship in the high seas, and the way of a man with a maiden."

I shook free of Peleh's grasp.

"Did you trace them back to their nest?"

"Master Uriel sent me after the ravens," I said. "It is only proper that I report to him first."

"True," Sadya said as he stepped between us, "Wait here in the main cavern, and I will summon your master."

"Is it not proper that I go to him?" I said, but Sadya was already lost in the darkness. I had hoped to speak to Uriel alone, but knew that little from the outside world penetrated the cave. My mission hadn't been a secret, and all would be eager to hear what lay behind the mystery of the birds.

Once all were seated, Uriel opened without introduction. "To whom did the ravens fly?"

"To Master Eliyahu." The prophets gave a collective gasp.

"I wondered if it were he," Uriel said.

I didn't know whether to be surprised or hurt. Had my master sent me on such a mission when he already knew the destination?

"The raven is the most miserly and craven of birds, one which will place its young in the nest of another to be fed. In the wake of the flood, Noah first sent out a raven to see if the waters had receded. But it refused to go. To force such a one into an act of boldness and generosity, the Holy One had to overturn its very nature. Who else, then, should be fed by ravens but the one who overturned the natural order of the world?"

Other prophets grumbled in assent. Uriel said, "You must recount all you saw, but do not reveal Eliyahu's location. This was a secret revealed to you alone."

"Do you trust us so little, Uriel?" Pinchas's voice pierced the quiet.

"Why speak of trust, Pinchas? You have earned my trust many times, and to you I would bare the secrets of my soul. I also know you to be a man of action, and it is not your way to seek permission before you act. After we have heard Lev's words, the prophets will hold a council. Should we decide to pursue Eliyahu, I will instruct Lev to reveal his location."

"He is your disciple," Pinchas said. "Do with him as you wish."

The prophets listened as I recounted my story, holding silence until I mentioned Eliyahu's greeting to me. Uriel broke in, "When you first met Eliyahu in Jericho, did you address him in your father's name?"

"No, Master."

"Then he must have known about your coming."

The cavern filled with the sounds of agreement. "Why is that a surprise, Master? Is Eliyahu not among the prophets?"

"Yes, he is among the prophets." Uriel sighed. "The springs of vision have dried up among us since entering the cave."

"Why is that, Master?"

Pinchas interrupted. "Because prophets are not meant to hide underground while enemies overrun our land."

"We have spoken of this many times, Pinchas. I for one do not fault our taking refuge in this cave. Lev, do you remember the first words we ever spoke about prophecy?"

"Yes, Master. The word of the Holy One can only descend on a prophet in a time of joy."

"Or rather, in a state of joy, for even in dark times, one with strength of mind can be joyous."

Why was my master teaching me something which we all knew? I shook my head. "Eliyahu did not seem joyous to me."

"I expect the sources of his joy lie deeper than your own." Uriel's voice made it clear he was addressing the entire cave. "He derives joy from aligning his will to the Holy One's."

"So you believe the drought to be the will of the Holy One?"

"My belief is of no matter. Eliyahu believes it, and the arrival of the ravens each day surely encourages him. He may even derive joy through his very suffering."

"The prophets are suffering as well," I said, "but you said vision has dried up."

"Suffering without meaning will never bring joy, and we fail to see the purpose of our hardship," Uriel said. "Did you tell him about the cave?"

"Yes, Master, but he sees only the nation's sin. He did not listen to my words."

"Do not be so sure, Lev. The seeds we plant may lie dormant a long while before they sprout."

"Or wither and die." Pinchas spoke through gritted teeth. "Especially during a drought."

"Is there something you wish to say, Master Pinchas?" Uriel asked.

"There are fifty-five of us hidden in this one cave and more coming. How long can one man continue to feed us all? If I have to choose between fighting for my life or starving to death, the choice is clear."

Uriel held his silence, merely nodding for me to finish my tale. Only months ago, he also preferred to die in struggle rather than retreat from the world, but I persuaded him to hide. Now he lacked the strength to leave even if he wished.

Ovadia himself opened at my knock, and I cringed, knowing we weren't supposed to be at his house together. He peeked into the alley, then let me in without a word. As soon as he shut the door of the house behind us, I said, "I'm sorry, I did not think you would still be here."

Ovadia waved away my apology. "I haven't much time. Did you succeed?"

"I did. The ravens fly to Eliyahu."

"Eliyahu?" Ovadia sat at the table and motioned for me to take the seat opposite him. "Where is he?"

"Master Uriel instructed me not to tell."

"That is wise. It is better if I do not know. Did the two of you speak?"

I recounted our discussion, relieved that Ovadia had no questions about my journey. "You did well, Lev," he said when I finished. "Far better than most would have fared, I'd say." He stood to go. "Now I need you back at your post."

"What's happened?"

"A merchant named Elifaz arrived on the third day of the week. He is a member of the dyer's guild and owns twenty ships out of Tzidon. He takes his meals at the Queen's table, always sitting at her right."

"What's his business here?"

"That's what I want to know. He claims he's exploring trade, and I'm sure he is, but I suspect there's more. There's a feast celebrating Izevel's seventeenth birthday tomorrow night after Shabbat ends, and Elifaz will be there. Make sure you let Dov know you're back; he's sure to want you playing there. Now I must go before I'm wanted."

He left without another word, and I was left alone with Tamar. My stomach tightened—the memory of our last conversation was still fresh.

"Will you not share the rest of your story?" she asked.

The kindness in her voice surprised me, and I looked up as I answered. "The rest?"

"As Ovadia said, it is no simple task to follow a raven to roost. Yet, your face shows no joy."

She sat across from me, and I turned away. "Eliyahu will not end the drought—"

"You believe you were sent to bring an end to the drought?"

"No." I felt her eyes on my face, but I would not meet them. "My task was to track the ravens, but once I found whom they were feeding—"

"You discovered that your notions of justice and mercy do not move Eliyahu." She gave a quiet laugh. "We will speak of that another time."

I watched the clouds drift across the square of sky visible through the window.

"Lev." I brought my eyes to hers. "What happened after you left Eliyahu?"

A pit opened in my stomach. It had been easy to hide the truth of my return trip from both my master and Ovadia—they were only interested in Eliyahu. What told Tamar there was more to my story?

"Tell me, Lev." Her look was kind but insistent. Only Aunt Leah spoke to me like this, asking and offering at the same time. But if Tamar questioned my loyalty for accidentally playing before Ashera, what would she say about my intentional betrayal?

"I went home to visit my family." The words left my mouth before I knew what was happening.

"Why?" The question was a simple one, and I heard no judgment in her voice.

"My cousin Dahlia came of age." I steeled myself for her reproach. Even the danger of going home was plain to see.

"What happened while you were home?"

"I told Dahlia and my aunt about the prophets." I had risked everything—my life, her life, all the prophets. I watched her face, almost wanting her anger.

Aside from a flicker deep in her eyes, Tamar seemed unmoved by my confession. "I see. What else happened?"

What else? I played with my cousins and told Eliav about Ashera and the Baal. I told Aunt Leah about Uriel and Dahlia about the drought and the Queen. I admitted to feeding the prophets! But my heart knew Tamar was interested in something else. "My uncle asked me about my prospects as a musician."

Tamar rose silently, went to the hearth, and filled a drinking bowl from the kettle over the fire. I inhaled as she placed the steaming drink on the table in front of me and the smell of sage filled my nostrils. Closing my eyes, I pictured the pastures above Levonah. When I opened them, Tamar was waiting.

"What did you say?"

"That if I wish, someday my earnings will allow me to buy a piece of land." I pictured my Uncle's face, feeling the same reluctance to lie. "But this was not my path."

"What does owning land mean to him?"

I held the hot clay bowl with both hands, and breathed deeply. "My uncle would never give Dahlia to a man without land."

"Ah." It was a sound of total understanding, and we sat in silence for a long moment. "I can see the love in your heart. Why was this your answer?"

I looked at the steaming herbs. "I have chosen my path."

Tamar's smile held no mockery, but her words stung nonetheless. "I am glad, for the time has long passed for choosing sides."

"Choosing sides? Whose side was I on when risking my life time and again these past few months?"

"Your own."

My mouth snapped shut, and I felt hot blood rise to my ears. "You think I've done all this for myself?"

"Yes, I do." A kind smile still lit her face, and my anger dissolved into confusion. "There is no question you have been brave and capable in defense of the prophets, Lev. The only question is, why?"

It seemed obvious, but my heart wasn't with me as I answered. "For... my master, for the prophets...for the Holy One!"

"I watched your face when you first came in here with your linen clothing, your scented oils, your trimmed hair."

Her words felt like a goad. "They are a disguise. Would you rather I be caught as a spy? It would mean your neck as well."

"No doubt it is a wise strategy. The risks are indeed great." She paused before adding, "You were less concerned with our safety in Levonah."

All the anger I'd been suppressing surged up. "You turned away from me the moment I came in with my new garments! Why? Because I would no longer help with the bread?"

Tamar's laugh was still kind, but it made me feel like a child. "I assure you, Lev, your skills at the oven have not been missed."

"Then what was it?"

"Pride." The sudden truth of the word deflated me, and I sagged on my stool. "It was there before your first day in the palace, tucked beneath your fear. I have watched it since, growing as the fear diminished."

"I was never too proud to serve."

"You need not be ashamed of pride, Lev. Indeed, men would do little without it. But beware when it lies at the root of your actions, lest as they grow it does too, and together they bear fruit of gall and wormwood. The tree fed on pride grows swiftly and rots just as fast. It did not take you long to follow your kinnor from the Throne Room to Ashera."

"I told you, that was a mistake. I didn't know we were playing for Ashera, and once there I could hardly refuse."

Her smile faded as she studied my face. "Perhaps not. But can you say in your heart that you felt no desire?"

"I was tempted." I blushed. "But I overcame my desire." I met her stare. "By the end of the night, I was the strongest musician there."

"And your pride grew."

I didn't understand Tamar. I divulged our deepest secrets, putting us all at risk, and she didn't care one bit. But an accidental performance before Ashera was a betrayal. And overcoming temptation only pride. "Yes, it made me proud. Should I not be proud of such a thing?"

"Pride has its place—as a strong medicine, taken in small doses. Woe to the heart filled with pride, which quickly becomes deaf and blind. There is no greater danger."

I frowned. "If I am so filled with pride, why do you speak to me now?"

"Because you are no longer full. What you gave up in Levonah has left you empty."

"Empty?" A tremor passed through my hands. "I'm not empty."

"Some will deep in your heart has been broken, leaving a great hole behind, yet your pride does not rush in to fill it. I see the way you hold your head, as if it were too heavy to lift. The pain of your heart is plain in your eyes."

"You don't—"

"There is no shame in this, Lev. Indeed, it brings me hope."

"Hope?" Even saying the word made the room feel lighter.

"The arrogant man learns no more than the fool. You are no fool, Lev." She smiled warmly. "Now that you are empty of arrogance, you can fill yourself with wisdom. If you have the will to learn, I will share what I know."

No doubt every prophet had wisdom to share, but since arriving, Tamar had berated me twice and ignored me the rest of the time. "I already have a master."

"Thank the Holy One for that. You must draw closer to him, even in hiding. You lack a teacher, not a master."

I wasn't quite ready to forgive. "What would you teach me?"

Tamar leaned across the table. "That depends on your will to learn. The way of the prophets is different for everyone who treads it." She studied me with a frown. "My wisdom might keep you alive and help save the prophets." Her eyes lingered on my face. "Master what I offer, and it could even bring an end to the drought."

"End the drought? The Key of Rain is in Eliyahu's hand."

"Grass will grow from the sockets of your eyes before Eliyahu concedes defeat."

"Then why speak of hope? We're all doomed to die."

"No doubt." She sat back. "There is one end for all flesh. Life and death do not lie in your hands, but victory may."

I snorted. "To Eliyahu, only the destruction of the wicked will bring victory, even if the innocent die with them."

"You presume to know the mind of Eliyahu?"

I hesitated. "He told me rain would be unjust as long as the sin persists."

"So you believe that as long as one person in Israel bends a knee to the Baal that Eliyahu's justice requires the complete destruction of the land?"

Even for Eliyahu, that seemed extreme. "No, I expect if only one idolater remained that Eliyahu would bring the rains." Then I remembered Eliyahu asked about the devotions of one person. "Unless that one person is the King."

"Very good, Lev. If you are blessed to hear a prophet speak, pay careful attention to his words. You despaired of victory because you believed Eliyahu cared little for the suffering of the people. Eliyahu is the greatest prophet of the age. I believe the suffering from his drought pains him more than you can imagine. He does not wish to destroy the land, only to bring the people to repent. Anything you can do to speed that repentance can bring victory and the rains a step closer."

"What can I do? I'm only one person."

"Noah was only one person, yet the entire world was saved for his sake."

"Only after everyone and everything in it was destroyed."

Tamar sighed. "You know some of our stories, that is good, but make certain they are sources of wisdom and not merely words. The flood did not have to come to pass. Noah bowed to the will of the Holy One without protest, unlike our father Abraham who interceded on behalf of the wicked. Had Noah done the same, he might have saved the entire world."

I drained my cup. "What does it matter? I'm neither Noah nor Abraham."

"Nor will you ever be, but if you learn from me, you may become something far more important."

"What is that?"

"Lev."

"That's what I already am."

"It is your name, but until you embody your deepest *ratzon*, you will not know the fullness of who you can be."

I heard my father's wisdom in Tamar's words. I had little to lose by learning what she had to teach. "What should I do now?"

"Do your duty. Take the bread to the prophets, report to Dov, and return to the musicians' quarters. You must spend Shabbat there, so they will know you've returned. On the first day of the week, resume your place at the palace."

"No other instructions?"

"Listen and see."

"I was doing that before. What will change now?"

"If we do our work properly, *you* will."

When you sit down to dine with a ruler, consider well who is before you.

Proverbs 23:1

10

Beggars at the Gates

I recognized Elifaz right away. He entered the dining hall conversing with one nobleman and trailed by two others who hung on his words. His blue embroidered robe spoke of wealth that exceeded even the King's. His hair was pure black, except where turning to grey along his temples, and shone with oil. A page led him to a seat of honor at the right of the Queen's empty chair, though I suspected he would have taken that place on his own had it not been offered.

At a signal from a footman, Tuval and I struck the opening notes of our song. It was the same melody we played whenever the King and Queen entered a room; Otniel claimed it was an ancient melody from the King's tribe of Menashe. The guests, all noblemen, rose as Ahav and Izevel entered hand in hand, and remained standing until the royal couple took their seats. The scent of afarsimon oil wafted from the Queen, and I pictured my friend Seguv with a sad tug at my heart.

The King commanded the head of the table, and his Queen sat opposite him at the far end. Once they sat, only Elifaz remained standing beside his chair. "Your majesty! Seventeen years ago, I was present at the great celebration King Ethbaal threw in honor of the birth of his first daughter." He addressed the King, but the whole room watched as he spoke. "I have been blessed to watch that daughter grow from a baby, to a maiden, to a woman of beauty, wisdom, and strength. To a Queen who brings acclaim to King and Kingdom."

Izevel glowed. "The people here have a custom," she said. She held Elifaz's eyes and raised her goblet. "To life!"

The noblemen of Israel raised their goblets and replied, "To life!"

Elifaz picked up his goblet and raised it to Izevel. "To life, my Queen. May your rule be long and prosperous." He took his seat by her side, and servants came forward with the first course.

Tuval and I played a steady flow of quiet but intricate melodies as food crowded the table and wine stewards refilled empty goblets. Ovadia instructed me to watch Izevel closely and catch any conversation I could, but for the first half of the meal, all talk happened in small groups clustered around the King, the Queen, and Elifaz.

Midway through the meal, the Queen gave the slightest nod to a nobleman sitting across from Elifaz. He spoke in a voice which drew the attention of the whole table, "You are a merchant to the world, Master Elifaz. Tell us what you think of our humble capital."

Elifaz waited a moment too long before replying, "In most respects, Master Micha, I have found it admirable."

The table fell silent, and the notes from my kinnor sounded loud in the large banquet room. Elifaz looked directly at Micha, but everyone else's eyes turned to the King.

Ahav looked up from his plate. "Most respects, Elifaz?"

"Pardon me, my King. I did not realize you were listening." There was no need to be a prophet to see that Elifaz only feigned embarrassment. He signaled a servant to fill his cup as people shifted in their seats around him.

"Indeed I was," Ahav said. "Do tell us how my father's capital fails to satisfy."

Elifaz dropped his eyes. "My apologies, my King, I do not wish to offend."

The Queen put a reassuring hand on his arm. "There is no offense in a word truly spoken. No one here, not even my royal husband," Izevel gave

Ahav a dazzling smile, "has seen the great capitals of the world as you have. Is that not so Elifaz?"

"If you say it is so, my lady, then so it must be." Though his head was still bowed, a grin rose on Elifaz's face.

"Do you know, my Lord," Izevel shook her hair forward over her shoulders as she spoke and another wave of afarsimon wafted across the room, "in my father's court Elifaz is legendary not only for his wealth, but for his wisdom as well."

The King spoke to Elifaz, but he looked at the Queen. "Fear no offense Elifaz, you are an honored guest here. Where does our fair city fall short?"

"Shomron is a young city, my King, and from what I see she may someday rival Tzidon herself." A pleased murmur passed down the table. "The new Temple to Baal will be a magnificent building, a fitting jewel to crown your capital. But…" he paused, looking around as if uncertain how to continue.

It was Micha, the nobleman who had started the conversation, who prompted him. "Please, Master Elifaz, do not be afraid. Surely our King desires to hear your wisdom on how to bring glory to our city."

Elifaz looked back toward the King, and when Ahav nodded, he continued. "It is the beggars, my King. No other capital would allow the poor to beseech a visitor of rank for bread or coin."

I watched the conversation closely now, grateful the musicians were nothing more than wall decorations to the noblemen gathered around the table. Not everyone greeted Elifaz's wisdom with sounds of approval, and one of the guests, who sat not far from the King's right hand, scowled. I recognized him as Yishai ben Avraham, one of the largest landholders in the kingdom.

"Come," Ahav said, "every city is home to those in need."

"You misunderstand me, my King. No doubt need abounds everywhere, or so I am told. In a great city, the poor know their place. In Tzidon, a beggar would lose his hand for accosting a visiting merchant at the gates of the palace itself."

"This makes Tzidon great? Cutting off the hands of those who stretch them out in need?" Yishai's voice was louder than it needed to be, even speaking from the far end of the table.

Izevel eyes were like daggers. "It is not your place to interrupt a conversation between your King and his guest."

A shocked silence followed her words, but Yishai laughed.

"You and your guest may be new to this table, my lady, but I sit where my father sat before me. I need no man," he paused with a scornful look, "or woman, to tell me my place."

Izevel did not respond, but her eyes burned. The King sat straight in his chair.

"It is true our customs are different than those of Tzidon, ben Avraham." Ahav frowned across the table. "The custom in Israel is also to hold the honor of our guests, and our wives, above all else."

The command was clear. "I apologize, my Queen," Yishai said with a slight bow of his head. When he looked up, their eyes locked, and the men around him studied the food on their plates.

"The nobleman of Israel raises a valid point," Elifaz said, "though in a clumsy manner. I do not deny a great city may aid the hungry. But those who live by the grace of the powerful should never harass those who feed them."

Yishai flushed in anger. "It is the hand of the Holy One which feeds us all, and it is the pride of Israel to raise up the weak. What you call harassment we call *tzedakah*, the demands of righteousness. The people of Israel will not let the poor starve to spare your feelings." Several men at the table nodded in agreement.

This time Izevel ignored him. "How is the problem of the poor managed in the great cities you have seen, Elifaz?"

"The beggars may not approach the gates, rather they are given a designated place to sit outside the city walls. That way, anyone who wishes to help them will know where to find them."

"Ban beggars from our city?" Ahav's hand went to his mouth, and a deep crease appeared on his forehead.

"Such would be my counsel, my lord." He looked around the table before adding, "but I have heard the Kings of Israel are merciful even to a fault. Say then that beggars may enter, and only begging is banned. There are other great cities where it is so."

Before Ahav could respond, Izevel said, "Come Elifaz, what difference could such a fine distinction truly make to a capital?"

"All the difference in the world, my Queen." He shook out his sleeves and brushed a fleck of dust from the brocade on his chest. "A merchant trades on his reputation. Nothing is more valuable to me than my dignity. In a city where I am honored, I return. When I am degraded…"

"Say no more," Izevel said. "My husband desires nothing more than to bring prosperity to his land. Such a thing seems a small price to pay for it. Don't you agree, my King?"

Ahav's eyes flitted between the Queen and the merchant at her side. All around the table were silent. All but Yishai. He rose to his feet. "It is not the beggars whose hands have grown too bold in our capital. I beg your forgiveness, my King, but the honor of my house cannot abide this talk. Our master, King Solomon, saw his kingdom divided by his foreign wives, and if your bride rules over you, no better will come to you house."

Yishai turned his back without bowing and strode toward the door. At a signal from the Queen, the guard stepped into his path. The King gave a single shake of his head, and the soldier retreated, but not before the angry nobleman noted it.

Ahav stood, and all rose with him. "Stay and enjoy," he said to his wife and guests, "this meal has given me much to think on." The guard opened the door, and the King walked out.

"What else have you heard?" Tamar bent over the dough as she asked me the question. More than a week had passed since the banquet. Each morning I came to report to Tamar before going to play in the Throne Room.

"Only rumors in the kitchen."

"Of what?"

"Yishai, the nobleman who defied the Queen at her birthday feast. The scribes and the pages say he has retreated to his estate, but they could not agree why. Some said he refuses to enter the Throne Room so long as Izevel sits by the King's side."

"What do the others say?"

"That he is no longer welcome there."

Tamar lifted the dough and smacked it on the counter, folding it in upon itself with surprising strength. "It will not end well for this nobleman. Only a fool provokes the serpent in its den."

I shivered from the cold in her voice. "What do you think the Queen will do?"

"There is no way to know, but she will not leave his challenge unanswered." She gave the dough several more sharp thrusts and turned to face me. "Her power is growing, and we must be ready. It is time to begin a new stage in your training."

"Now? I must be in the Throne Room before too long."

"I said begin, nothing more." Tamar pulled a stool forward from the table and sat facing me where I stood in the middle of the kitchen. "Tell me exactly what you heard in the Throne Room yesterday."

"Nothing of importance," I replied. "Two of the King's messengers came in with reports, but neither mattered to us."

"What did the Queen do?"

I shrugged. "Nothing unusual."

"Nothing made her angry?" Tamar asked. "Nothing excited her?"

"No."

"Excellent. Tell me about it."

"There's nothing to tell."

"I understand. Now I want to hear every detail."

I frowned. "Every detail of what exactly? I said nothing happened."

"Izevel is growing into the role of Queen. To fight the prophets, she used her own soldiers, and she brought priests and priestesses from Tzidon to honor her gods. Her move against the beggars shows she seeks to rule the King as well. Her power is growing with her experience. Using Elifaz was clever. What King would fail to defend the honor of his capital?"

"What does that mean for me?" I asked.

"It means that if you're waiting for her to scream when she's angry or sing when excited you'll grow old before hearing anything of value. You must learn to *see*."

What did she think I'd been doing? "I can see."

"Can you? Did Izevel receive any scrolls yesterday?"

Did Tamar think me so blind? "Yes, one."

"What did it contain?"

I laughed. "She doesn't read them aloud." I raised a hand to hold back her response. "Don't tell me I have to see better, because the musicians stand so far back from the thrones that no one could hope to read them."

"True, if you aspire to read the words. Even if the scrolls were dropped into your lap, it would not help, as the most important ones are not written in our tongue."

"So what can I do?"

"I don't want you to read the scroll, Lev. I want you to read Izevel. You must learn to see when she is angry, when she is eager, when she is frightened, and when she is bored. Now, describe to me how she looked while reading the scroll."

"How she looked? She sat on her throne." I tried to picture more detail. "She held it in her left hand."

"Did she sit like this?" Tamar moved the stool into the corner, reclining with her back against the wall. "Or more like this?" Now she leaned forward, both feet pulled in toward the base of the stool, her eyes intent.

"More like the first. She looked bored."

"What was she doing with her hands?"

"She held the scroll with her left," I said again. "I don't remember what she did with her right."

"Next time you must. I want to know what her messages contain, and her reactions are our greatest clue." Tamar drew close to me. "You must see everything, and remember everything you see. Especially we must learn who she favors, who she ignores, who she hates, and who she fears." Tamar put a handful of barley on the grindstones. I knew I was dismissed for it was impossible to talk over the sound of the grinding. As I moved toward the door, she called out, "Lev."

I turned to meet her eyes. "We will repeat this each morning until you can describe her every move."

"You are tired," was all Tamar said to me at the end of another week of watching the Queen.

I nodded. "It's exhausting trying to see everything, especially when I can't be noticed noticing. And I still have to play my kinnor."

Tamar's smile was the only reward I would get, so I tried to enjoy it. "Watching becomes easier with practice. Once you know what you are looking for, it will call out louder than a crow. Now," Tamar said, "who went first yesterday?"

"A royal messenger from Ashur."

"Did he come with an offer or a request?"

"Neither. He brought greeting from his King and made promises of friendship."

"This was a great day for our young Queen." Seeing my confusion, Tamar explained. "Ashur is a far greater power than Israel—they care little for our kingdom. Now that Izevel sits on the throne, the path to Tzidon, and Ethbaal, lies through Israel. Praise for the daughter is a way of currying favor from the father."

"Where is Ashur?" I asked.

"To the north and east, past the river, the mountains, and the wilderness which lies beyond them. They are a powerful but cruel people."

"Are they less powerful than Tzidon?"

"Far more powerful than even Tzidon."

"Then why try to win favor with King Ethbaal?"

"Not everything can be taken by force, Lev. The strength of Tzidon lies in their command of the seas and their ties to ports throughout the Great Sea. Even Ashur must pay them homage if they wish Tzidonian merchants to carry their goods. Did Izevel speak to the messenger?"

"No, but her eyes were on him the entire time he spoke."

"How was she sitting?"

I was ready for her question. I placed a stool in the corner and sat. "She leaned forward, across the arm of her throne, her head turning back and forth between the King and the messenger."

"What was she doing with her feet?" Tamar asked.

"They were flat on the ground."

"Good, you noticed. Place your feet that way as well. What of her hands?"

"They were on the arms of her throne."

"Loosely placed or gripping it tightly?"

Tamar had warned me to watch for this. "Her left hand, the one facing the messenger, was loose. Her right hand was gripped tight."

"What does this tell you?"

"She was pleased, like you said."

"I do not need you to repeat my words, I need you to see it in her body." Tamar's eyes bored into mine. "How do you know she was pleased?"

I lowered my eyes and bit my lip. "She was smiling and watched the messenger as he spoke. With the commoners, she stares off at the walls."

Tamar shook her head. "Not enough. If Izevel wishes to appear happy, she will smile. If we are to succeed, we must know what is in her heart."

"How can I know that?"

"Before we finish, you will feel her emotions even with your eyes closed. For now, you must learn to see the signs which her body cannot avoid. What lesson can you learn from what you observed in her hands and feet?"

I shrugged.

"Only masters can fully rule their bodies and thus hide their feelings. Izevel is growing day by day, but a master she is not. Her hands and feet told you everything you need to know. She must preserve her dignity before such an important messenger, so she kept her feet on the ground and the hand facing the messenger loose. The other clenched the arm of the throne, for her excitement must express itself somewhere."

"Izevel's pregnant?" I asked.

"*You* are pregnant." Tamar pointed to my belly. "But I cannot yet say if she is."

I sat once more upon the stool, mimicking Izevel's posture. "See the way you're holding your hand on your belly?" Tamar said. "Are you sure her hand was there, or was it lower?"

"I'm not sure."

"The first is the posture of a pregnant woman. Any lower and it may be nothing more than a belly ache."

"If she is pregnant, is that good or bad?"

Tamar still studied my position on the stool. "Pregnancies are as different as women themselves. At best, she may lose interest in running the Kingdom and focus on her child."

"And at worst?"

Tamar turned back toward the oven. "I have heard that at her wedding, men challenged a bear for treasure."

"Yes, I saw it. Some even managed to get a few jewels off of it."

She spun back to face me. "Was anyone killed?"

I hesitated. "I don't think so. Why?"

"Had they changed the contest a little, had they taken a mother bear and placed her cub behind the challengers, not one of those men would have left the cage alive." Tamar pressed her hands together and closed her eyes. "We must be certain. I will come to the Throne Room myself."

The Priest's Suspicion

Late in the night, the drumming finally broke off, and the priests stepped out of the Temple. Laughing with one another as they dispersed, their freshly dyed robes shimmering in the torchlight, they took no notice of the old man among the shadows. He waited until most had departed, then slipped through the door, pausing to breathe in its cedar smell. Though the roof was only half complete, the Temple already rivaled all but the greatest in Tzidon for size.

Twenty or more priests remained within, yet Yambalya was the first to spot his master. He ran forward and fell at the old man's feet, and seeing him, the other priests broke off their conversations to bow as well. "Master, why did you not inform me you had returned?" he asked as he rose. "I would have prepared a celebration—"

"A celebration?" The wizened priest frowned at his onetime disciple. "What is there to celebrate?"

There was a time when Yambalya would have cowered at Mot's question, but those days had passed. Now Yambalya only smiled. He was master in Shomron and were it not for the honor he paid his former teacher the old man would be forgotten, left to study his scrolls alone in his barren fortress, deep in the mountains of Tzidon.

The words of his master could no longer sting him, but it would not do for any of his disciples to hear the old priest criticize him. He turned to the twenty remaining in the Temple, who delayed to observe the two masters. "Leave us."

There was a shuffling of feet as the young priests hurried through the door. The last out did not wear the violet robes, and he pulled the heavy doors shut with one hand, grasping his drum with the other.

The door shut with a bang that echoed as Yambalya burst into laughter. "As you can see," he stretched out his arms to the walls of the Temple around him, "there is much to celebrate. We have taken great steps since your last visit."

Mot did not follow Yambalya's sweeping gestures. "Your Temple adds nothing to the greatness of Baal."

"True." Yambalya swallowed the rage he felt whenever his master corrected him. "But it adds much to the people's fear. They cower before me now as they see how Baal grows. By summer, we will have over two hundred priests. Meanwhile, their prophets are dead or driven into hiding."

The old priest raised an eyebrow. "So you believe victory is close at hand?"

Seeing Mot impressed made Yambalya sorry he had sent away his disciples. "Indeed. Victory for Baal is certain."

"Fool!" The elderly priest poked Yambalya in the chest, showing no fear of the powerful giant. "If you would stop declaring victory, you might notice we are losing this war."

"Losing? I arrived here with twelve priests, and now our sacrifices grow week by week as the people of the land flock to me."

Mot's voice was cold. "To you or Baal?"

Yambalya drew himself to his full height. "All I do is for Baal. The victory is his, not mine."

"Is that so?" Mot held his eye, and a tremor passed through the big priest. "Baal rules the storm wind, does he not? If Baal is so victorious, where are the rains?"

Yambalya tried to break eye contact, but his old master held him. "Baal must be angry—"

"Angry? Angry at what? At your victory?"

"We are on the verge of wiping the memory of their god from this land."

"You speak of memory? I am speaking of the present. One of their prophets declared a drought, and all of your efforts to break it have yielded nothing. If the rains do not come, who will appear more powerful, the storm god or the god in whose name Eliyahu holds back the rains?"

Yambalya struggled to look away. "We have killed over three hundred prophets of Israel. Whoever remains has been driven into hiding. Their power over the people has ended."

"You ordered them all put to the sword?"

Yambalya nodded. "Every one."

"And their sacred scrolls?"

"Burnt."

"You were a precious student, Yambalya—few disciples showed such devotion. If only your wisdom matched your loyalty."

Yambalya's eyes narrowed. "My wisdom has built all you see."

Mot shook his head. "Your strength built all of this, and it will destroy it as well. Had you acquired wisdom, you would not have killed all their prophets."

"You would let them live and preach against us?"

"Preach? Certainly not. But what good are their corpses? Could you not capture even one alive? Could you not have kept their scrolls?"

"I do not share your love of scrolls. I see no value in preserving their creed."

"No value? How do you propose to understand the source of their power?"

"Baal is the greatest power." Yambalya raised his hand toward the statue of the storm god. "You taught me that."

"Yet, all of our devotions, all of our sacrifices, have failed to bring back the rains."

"You think Baal is angry that so many still worship the god of the land?"

"You will repeat this to no one." Mot released Yambalya from his gaze and turned away. "I think Baal is fighting to bring the rain and is losing to a stronger hand."

"Their god still has power in this land," Yambalya said. "Once all who fear him are dead, Baal will reign supreme."

"Their prophet's power is not just in this land. Why do you think I have returned so soon?

Yambalya had no answer.

"The merchants of the dyer's guild have consulted their oracle—the drought will strike Tzidon as well. Our King sent me to see what has gone wrong. And you speak of victory?"

Yambalya would accept no question of Baal's power from his disciples, but this was his teacher who stood before him. "What do you want me to do?"

"I must understand the source of their god's power. Then I will know the path to victory. Are there no prophets left in all of the land? Are there no more sacred scrolls?"

"There is one place where they still dwell in safety."

"Why have you stayed your hand?"

"It is the Queen's will that the killing of the prophets remains a secret. We have slain those who have witnessed their deaths, but many eyes surround their last refuge. We could not silence them all."

"I will speak to the Queen in her father's name. This final stronghold must fall."

A ruler who listens to lies, all his ministers will be wicked.

Proverbs 9:12

11

A Gift Fit for a King

We snuck Tamar into the Throne Room on the next market day, taking advantage of the extra-large crowd. She slipped in just before the doors closed, at the height of the chaos, and made her way to the back of the line of petitioners. She wore a coarse wool cloak and stood with her arms across her chest like one of the commoners. She kept her eyes down, which was unremarkable in a peasant woman but critical for a prophetess. I doubted even she could hide their power.

Two of the King's messengers presented first. One brought word on the royal garrison stationed in Jericho, on the eastern border. Another came from the Bashan, bearing word that a city in Aram, just across our border, was fortifying its outer walls. The Queen listened to the reports with half an ear, but as the first of the noblemen approached the King, a page brought her a scroll. She did not even look as he placed it in her waiting hand. She laid back on the embroidered cushions behind her, her free hand caressing her belly as she read.

Tamar had a story prepared, a dispute regarding a well that bordered her property, but she never spoke it aloud. When she had observed enough, she slipped out of the Throne Room and did not return.

The next morning at Ovadia's house, Tamar put down the bread and drew a stool as I entered. Her posture mimicked Izevel's perfectly now. She leaned back against the corner of the wall as if it was her throne and pretended to read a scroll with her hand upon her belly.

"Is she pregnant?" I asked.

"Without doubt." Tamar shifted her position, leaning forward now. She shifted it again, leaning back against the other wall. "There is something more."

"What's that?"

Tamar shifted again, playing with the end of an imaginary strand of hair. Her movements so matched Izevel's that I had no trouble picturing the Queen's black hair between her fingers. Tamar dropped her imaginary hair and reached out as if taking a cup from a page, sipping from it, then placing it beside her. All her movements were perfect, but they told me nothing.

"I don't understand."

Tamar sat straight, and the Queen disappeared. "Izevel cannot sit still. She couldn't focus on anything for more than a few moments, even the message she received."

"Could it be the baby?"

"No. The only times she appeared relaxed were when her hand rested on her belly. The baby is a source of comfort to her, and well it should be. Nothing will win her the hearts of the people more than bearing an heir."

My brow furrowed. "Then what is it?"

"I do not know. but she does not take waiting well."

"Do you think something troubles her?"

Tamar shook her head. "Her body was not troubled, it was expectant."

I watched Izevel closely for the next two weeks, and soon even my eyes caught her growing restlessness.

On the morning of the fifth day, I came to report to Tamar before my shift in the palace. Ovadia sat at the kitchen table while Tamar and Batya worked the dough. I stopped at the threshold. "I didn't realize you'd be home," I said to Ovadia.

"I've been waiting for you. Sit."

"What is it?" I asked as I slid across from him.

"Elifaz has returned. He arrived yesterday, and he didn't come alone."

"Who was with him?"

"A woman. She entered the palace hooded and cloaked."

"Could she have been his maidservant?"

"No. Her garments were fine linen, and she received her own quarters in the palace. I've been instructed to deliver meals to her chamber twice a day. I even brought her food myself this morning in hopes of learning more, but she answered my knock with an order to place it outside her door."

"Who could she be?" I asked.

"I don't know. It could be she has nothing to do with Shomron. Elifaz's ship landed from Tarshish, and this is a stop on his return to Tzidon. Or so he says. It could be he is escorting a noblewoman with reasons of her own for secrecy." He leaned back and shook his head. "But I don't think so."

"Why not?"

"There is no reason for Elifaz to be in Shomron, especially if he is serving as an escort. Only a fool would pass through Israel on a journey from Tarshish to Tzidon. He says he came on matters of trade, and I have seen him speak with various noblemen since his arrival, but he has purchased nothing."

"If not for trade, then why?"

"Oh, he wants to trade here. With the Queen as his patron, there is much profit to be made. But a man like Elifaz trades in far more than wheat and wine. Information is a valuable commodity to those who know how to use it. Perhaps he knows of the drought and came to see the situation with his own eyes. But why the woman?" Ovadia drummed his fingers on the table.

"How do we find out?"

"That is why I came to you. The servants have the freest reign of the palace, and you have the best access to their talk. I want you to listen closely in the kitchen. You might even risk an innocent question or two if they mention her. Or even if they don't." He stood and put his hands behind his back. "Keep your eyes open even wider in the Throne Room. By the time she arrives there, it may be too late to thwart their plans. But it may not."

Tamar silently kneaded the dough as we spoke. At Ovadia's last words, she stepped out of the kitchen to her quarters, then returned with a clay vial. "How certain are you that this woman will bring us harm?"

Ovadia turned to her. "What do you have in mind?"

"Place three drops of this in her food, and the Queen's plot will never come to be."

"Poison? She may be nothing more than an innocent noblewoman." Ovadia said.

Tamar shrugged. "I have no hesitation killing the priests of the Baal, nor the Queen's soldiers. Is she among them? Is she a threat? If so, dispose of her now. Have the food delivered by some servant who has turned toward the Baal, and make sure that your hands are clean."

Ovadia glowered at her. "Even if she is a threat, I will not sentence an innocent servant to death. Even if he bows to the Baal."

Tamar did not flinch under his gaze. "Tell me where her quarters are, and I will deliver the food myself."

Ovadia shook his head. "I am not Izevel. I will not kill a woman who may or may not mean us harm."

Tamar turned back to her kneading. "In that case, all we can do is wait."

Otniel sat alone in the palace kitchen. "Ah, Lev," he said as I came in, "it has been some time since you joined us for the morning meal."

"I need all the sleep I can get." I patted the wood of my kinnor. "This keeps me up later than your quills." In truth, my early mornings with Tamar kept me from the palace kitchen. Only Tuval and Otniel ate this late, and I had long since given up hope of overhearing important gossip from either of them—Tuval because he didn't know anything, and Otniel because he only spoke when spoken to.

"Scribes need as much sleep as musicians," Otniel said, "we just get it at night, when respectable people sleep. I don't see why musicians are incapable of doing the same."

"It's not our fault," I said with a grin, "the non-respectable pay more for their music."

Otniel laughed. "What then brings you here this morning?"

"My belly. The music was in such demand that I didn't get a chance to eat last night. It's hard to sleep on an empty stomach."

I helped myself to a piece of bread, and Otniel went back to eating in silence. But I had come to talk. "Where is Tarshish?" I asked without introduction.

Otniel put down his bread. "Tarshish is the farthest port on the great sea. It takes more than a month's journey toward the setting sun to reach it, if one arrives at all."

"More than a month! How do you know?"

"My father deals with many great merchants that come to the Kingdom. I have heard their tales around our table many times."

"Really?" My interest was not entirely feigned. "I have only seen one foreign merchant. Not long ago, at the Queen's table. Eliraz was his name."

"Elifaz," he corrected me.

"Elifaz? Are you sure? I thought it was Eliraz."

"No, no, Elifaz. Elifaz of Tzidon is one of the great traders of the world."

"You know him well?"

Otniel's face lit up at the question. Maybe he did not eat in silence by choice. "He has called upon my father more than once, always bearing exotic gifts."

"So he spends his days traveling the world?"

"A great trader like Elifaz has agents in each port. He only travels himself for the most important missions."

"I keep hearing whispers about him," I said.

"I'm not surprised. We in Israel are poor at trade. King Ahav means to change that, but it can be a tough transition for a nation used to dwelling alone."

Could Otniel tell me what I wanted to know? "They say this time he returned with a woman, and she's staying in her own quarters here in the palace."

Otniel gave a silent laugh. "You should know, Lev, the Tzidonians do not share Israel's views on chastity. Elifaz rarely travels alone, and his companions can be extraordinarily good company."

Otniel's smile made the blood rise to my cheeks, and he laughed to see me blush. Could it be that simple? Were Ovadia's fears unfounded?

Before I could ask another question, Tuval rushed into the kitchen.

"Have you heard?" he asked as he grabbed a piece of bread from the stack on the counter.

"Heard what?" Otniel replied.

"Yishai ben Avraham is dead. You knew him well, didn't you Otniel?"

Otniel's face went pale, and his only answer was "Blessed be the Righteous Judge."

A wave of dizziness washed over me. I pretended to listen to their talk, but all I could hear were Tamar's words echoing in my ears, 'only a fool provokes the serpent in its den.'

"How did he die?" I asked.

"I don't know." Tuval shrugged. "I guess the same way as everyone else does. They found him in his bed."

"You don't think it was murder?" I blurted out.

Tuval looked at me in horror, and Otniel jumped up from his stool. "How could you even suggest such a thing?" he said.

Before I could even think of an answer to cover for my stupidity, the trumpets sounded throughout the palace.

Tuval shook his head and shoved the last of his bread in his mouth. "Come on Lev, we'll be late."

I threw on my linen clothes and hurried after him. Otniel's shocked stare followed me out the door.

The next day, Zim announced he was leaving the musicians' quarters. The Temple of Baal neared completion, and Yambalya wanted Zim in the loft he had built for him above the main chamber. Zim had no reason to hide his excitement and therefore did not notice mine. Of all the musicians in our quarters, only Zim took notice of my coming and going. He was also the only one who knew or cared about the ongoing battle between Izevel and the prophets. The next day, I was again able to spend Shabbat with my master in the prophet's cave.

Even though Court was dismissed early on the eve of Shabbat, I only reached the entrance of the cave when the sun was hanging above the sea to the west. Even Peleh and Sadya had left their post to prepare for the coming holy day, and my master was not in his niche. I dropped my sleeping mat and headed into the heart of the caverns, hoping to clean myself before sunset.

The disciples had succeeded in carving out a pool to receive the waters of the spring, which was fortunate as I could hear in the dark that the flow had already slowed. I stood knee deep on one of the broad steps until the man ahead of me ascended, and only when I slipped into the water did I realize it was too deep for me to touch the bottom. I dunked my head under a few times to let the dust of the road float away.

After the prophets shared their Shabbat bread together and sang a few *nigunim*, I finally had a chance to speak with Uriel. We retreated to the darkness of his cave and sat together. "Master?"

"I am here, Lev."

"Tamar desires to be my teacher."

"Praise be the Holy One." I heard his smile. "Acquire for yourself a teacher, and doubt will never overcome you."

"I want to learn from you, Master." I felt like a little child.

"There is no conflict between the two, Lev. On the contrary, I see a great blessing. Tamar sees your life as you live it now, whereas I know only what you tell me. It is her words which must guide you along the dangerous path you tread. Let our time together be for a different type of question."

"Master, Tamar says I must awaken my *ratzon*. How do I do that? How can I even know what my deepest will is?" I thought of the priestess with the honeysuckle in her hair, and a flash of heat passed through my body.

Uriel did not answer me right away. Time was the hardest thing to measure in the darkness of the caves, and when he answered me, I had no idea how long we'd sat in silence.

"Tamar is right about awakening your *ratzon*. The power which comes from embodying your deepest will is astounding. This entire war hinges on the will of two people: Izevel and Eliyahu."

"Only two? What about Yambalya and Zarisha?"

"At one word from Izevel they would retreat to Tzidon."

"And the King?" Even Eliyahu had asked about Ahav's devotion.

Uriel sighed. "True, King Ahav could end the war. But his will is too weak."

"What of the prophets?"

"We are irrelevant." I heard the sadness in his voice. "So long as we remain hidden, only Eliyahu's *ratzon* is left to guide the people toward the Holy One. Just as Izevel's will is to guide them away."

"How do I discover my deepest will?"

"You will know your deepest will by expressing your deepest will."

I stifled a frustrated reply, but Uriel must have heard something.

"I speak to you in the language of the heart, Lev, which you must learn to understand. By expressing the deepest will you have, you come to connect to deeper and deeper levels."

"Until when, Master? Until I discover my deepest *ratzon*?"

"There is no until, Lev. There is no limit to how deep your *ratzon* can be, so too there is no limit to the power your *ratzon* can have. The depths of Eliyahu's *ratzon* allowed him to demand and receive the Key of Rain, an act as powerful as Moses splitting the sea."

"How can I better learn to hear the language of my heart, Master?"

"By listening to it. Accept Tamar's guidance, and you will unlock its secrets."

A crowd of beggars huddled outside the city gates when I returned to Shomron in the early morning of the first day of the week. At the end of the previous week, the Queen's soldiers caught a cripple begging alms from a grain merchant in the lower city. They stripped him to the waist and lashed him right in the middle of the market. The throng of beggars outside the gates showed the Queen had made her point.

I kept my eyes distant as I passed; it was too hard to meet their searching eyes when I could do nothing to help. A Tzidonian soldier watched the beggars from the shadow of the gate, whip in hand. If a traveler wished to give a coin or piece of bread, so be it. But woe to the beggar who accosted anyone that passed the gates of Shomron. None ever approached me, for there was little reason to risk the whip to beg from a peasant boy.

Yet, as I neared the gate, one of the feeble-looking men broke away from the crowd and approached me. I ignored him and rushed toward the gate, but he called out, "Lev."

My back tensed. I turned toward the voice. My life depended on not being known, as did those of more than sixty prophets. Now someone had called my name within earshot of the city gates, and many eyes bent in my direction. I wanted to run, but that would only attract more attention.

The beggar who called out had a bent nose and crooked teeth, and his black beard covered half his face in thick growth. He blended in perfectly with the indigent, but he had the eyes of a prophet. Raphael.

Poor, trusting Raphael. Any other prophet would know not to call out my name, but he stepped forward, his arms spread before him, and I could see tears of relief in his eyes.

"I have no copper to spare for you, friend." I pitched my voice to carry and kept my tone cold. Raphael stepped back as if slapped. The soldier in the gate shook loose the coils of his whip. "If you come with me," I added, keeping the soldier at bay, "I know where to find you a morsel of bread."

Confusion clouded Raphael's face, but he was wise enough to follow in silence. I dared not lead him through the city gates, nor could I turn back toward the prophets' cave without drawing attention from the other beggars. Izevel paid good copper for information on the 'troublers of the Kingdom,' as she called the prophets. The prophets were beloved by the poor, but it was too much to risk—the demands of a man's stomach could be louder than those of his heart.

I led Raphael past the city gates, and we followed the line of the wall until we struck a path that wove around a nearby hillside. Only out of sight of the city walls did I dare turn and embrace him. "Praise be the Holy One that you are alive," I said.

His arms tightened behind my back. "I feared you had forgotten me. Or worse."

"These are no days to publicly embrace a prophet."

He dropped his arms. "Some prophet I am. Everyone knew what was coming but I."

"They attacked Yosef's school?" Most prophets lived in the hills and when they gathered it was in wilderness areas like Emek HaAsefa. Only Yosef built a home for his disciples inside a city. Beit El was home to the Golden Calf and contained no lack of witnesses. So long as the Queen waged her war in secret, Ovadia assumed they would be safe. "Master Yosef?" I asked.

"Dead."

"His disciples?"

"Only I remained. The others are also dead, or runaway, or..." His face crumpled. Whatever the last option was, it was too much for Raphael to say.

"You fled here, to Shomron?" I asked.

Raphael gave a weak nod. "Clever, wasn't it? Who would seek a prophet in the heart of the Kingdom?"

The sun lit the high hilltops surrounding the city. "I am required soon in the Throne Room, and I cannot be absent. Can you remain hidden among the beggars for the rest of the day? I will come to you before sundown and lead you to safety."

"You can hide me?" he asked. "How will I eat?"

"I can feed you as well. I'll explain later. Unfortunately, I have nothing to give you now."

Raphael gave a grim smile. "I can last another day."

I took a step toward Shomron, then recalled Raphael's lack of caution. "Do not try to enter the city gates, and do not call out my name," I said. "Wait until I pass, then follow from a distance."

"It will be as you say, Lev."

If Raphael could reach Shomron on foot, a King's messenger could certainly make the journey on horseback. Whatever rumors circulated about massacres in the hills, an attack upon a prophet school in the middle of the most sacred city in Israel was entirely different. Even the King could not ignore that. Could he?

The doors of the Throne Room opened early in deep winter to take advantage of the daylight hours. I left the prophets' cave while it was still dark to have enough time to eat in the palace kitchen, but meeting with Raphael had made me late. Now I hurried to arrive before the King and Queen. "You walk in late, everyone takes notice," Ovadia had told me when first instructing me to play in the Throne Room. "Your job is to stand invisible before the Queen, which means no one else should notice you either. Make sure you are always on time."

I ran to the musicians' quarters and threw on my linen garments. I grabbed my kinnor without trying out the strings and was back on the road to the palace in a matter of moments. My stomach rumbled, but there was no time to eat. I heard the ram's horn warning of the imminent arrival of the King and Queen before I made it through the palace gates, and it took all my speed to slip into the Throne Room before the closing of the double doors.

Dov gave me a quizzical look as I settled into place, breathing heavily. "Oversleep, Lev?"

I nodded as I checked the strings of my kinnor, tightening each in turn. I used to place it on my lap while tuning it, but Tamar instructed me to hold it in front of my face instead. That way I could look through the strings, inspecting the assembled crowd without them noticing.

I spotted the messenger from Beit El right away. His black tunic adorned with the royal ox set him apart from peasants and noblemen alike. He stood at attention before the empty thrones clenching a tightly-rolled scroll in his hand. Eight commoners stood in a line against the far wall, where they would wait until the King finished the priority matters of the day. Three members of the nobility lingered by the scribes' table, not far from the throne. The King heard the commoners in the order they arrived, but he called the nobility at will. The nobles hovered near the throne, hoping to be honored by an early nod from the King.

My eye fell upon a man and woman in the far corner of the Throne Room. There was no mistaking Elifaz, in his blue embroidered robes and trim beard that failed to hide his contemptuous smile. The woman by his side was wrapped in pale red from her neck to her feet. Her dress wound around her body rather than being slipped over her head in the local manner. A matching hood hid her face.

One of the door guards banged his staff three times against the stone floor, and the room went silent. All stood as the double doors opened, and we struck up the first song of the day as the King and Queen entered with clasped hands. As soon as the King sat in his throne, his eyes fell upon the messenger, who took a half step forward. The Queen turned her eyes toward him as well, and he hesitated.

The messenger cleared his throat and bowed before the throne. "My King, a message from Ephraim ben Ulah, captain of the guard in Beit El. On the morning of the sixth day of the week—"

"Ah, Elifaz," the Queen said, as if she had just noticed him. Her voice was calm, but higher pitched than normal. "I wondered how long it would take you to appear in Court. Why do you hide in the back?" She motioned him forward. "Come. A man like you belongs amongst the nobility of Israel."

"You are too gracious, my Queen." Elifaz stepped forward, drawing his companion with him.

The Queen turned back to the messenger. "You may continue your report."

"Thank you, my Queen." The messenger again cleared his throat, but the King struggled to draw his attention back from the merchant and his escort. "My King, on the morning of the sixth day, in the Holy City of Beit El—"

"She is lovely." The Queen's whisper carried, and all eyes went to the red-clad stranger. None but the King ever interrupted his messengers, and Otniel looked at his fellow scribe in confusion.

Elifaz reacted as if they were alone in the room. "You only see the wrappings, my Queen."

Izevel looked up at the silence in the room, her face that of an embarrassed child. Only my hours with Tamar enabled me to see the falsehood in her overwide eyes and perfectly rounded mouth. She placed a finger to her lips and with the other hand motioned to the messenger. "Continue."

The young man was no fool—the King's eyes never returned to him, so he held silent. The messenger did not continue his report as the King still looked upon Elifaz's companion. "Who is this woman?" Ahav asked his wife.

The Queen licked her lips, and her right hand trembled with suppressed excitement. "She is a gift. One which I asked Elifaz to arrange. That is his true purpose in Shomron. When they arrived, she was weary from the journey, so Elifaz advised that we wait a few days for her to recover." Izevel glanced back at the messenger. "Perhaps they should wait outside; their presence appears to be a distraction."

The King ignored her last comment. "A gift?"

The Queen blushed and brought a hand to her mouth. "I spoke too soon, and now I've spoiled the surprise. Ignore my words. There will be plenty of time once you have settled the affairs of the Kingdom."

"Ah, a gift for me, is it?"

Izevel dropped her eyes. "Yes, my lord and King."

"Now you have aroused my curiosity." Ahav's eyes remained on his gift.

I was the only one not staring at the slave girl. My fingers worked effortlessly across the strings as I watched the Queen's face. I felt a cold shudder at the smile that brushed her lips. "Would you prefer to receive her now?"

"Yes, yes," Ahav replied. "Better that the messenger should wait than receive less than my full attention."

The messenger bowed his head and backed away.

Elifaz drew the hooded woman forward by her elbow. "My King, I have journeyed to the lands beyond the River Euphrates, lands which few have seen and from which even fewer return." Even the noblemen craned their necks to keep their eyes on Elifaz. "The lands beyond the river are known for the richness of their soil, the fierceness of their warriors...," he looked up with a grin, "and for the beauty of their women. At the behest of my lady, your Queen," he bowed in Izevel's direction, "and at great risk and expense to myself, I brought back one of that land's fairest jewels. Allow me to present, Ahba."

Elifaz pulled back her hood and stepped aside with a flourish. The entire room drew its breath. Her skin was a polished bronze, and dark chestnut hair fell thick and straight past her shoulders.

Without turning, the King asked, "What is the meaning of this?"

Izevel's hand went to her belly, and she gave a feline smile. "When I first arrived in Shomron, I was distraught to find that there were no royal concubines. I was raised amongst kings, my lord. I know great rulers have great passions. King Ethbaal, my father, warned me before our marriage that passion unquenched clouds the heart of a King. It robs him of...judgment." She lowered her voice. "With the help of your loyal servant Elifaz, I sought to correct this. Does my gift find favor in your eyes?"

The King's eyes remained on Ahba. "It finds great favor."

"Then take her. She is an expression of my love, and my care for your Kingdom—our Kingdom. Elifaz brought back many such treasures for my father, and developed a reputation in Tzidon for unsurpassed judgment in taste."

The King pulled away his gaze to nod at the merchant. "I thank you, Elifaz."

"She is indeed a gift fit for a King," Elifaz replied with a low bow.

The King turned to one of his pages. "Show Ahba back to her quarters. I will attend to her at the close of Court."

Elifaz bowed once more, and as he straightened, I saw him squeeze Ahba's elbow. She knelt and stretched her hands flat on the floor toward the throne. "Whatever pleases the King."

Izevel turned to her husband. "Have mercy on the poor girl, my Lord. The affairs of the Kingdom wait while you take your morning meal. They can wait while you see to your other needs."

This was the first word I ever heard in the Throne Room of the King's own needs rather than the affairs of the Kingdom, the strength of the army, and the requests of the common people. Had anyone but Izevel made the suggestion, Ahav certainly would have refused. Now he hesitated.

I recalled how Izevel stretched her arms out to him at the wedding, and he bowed before the Baal. Ahba still pressed her face to the floor, the red cloth clung tight to her back. The King rose unsteadily to his feet, just as he had at the wedding. He descended the three steps from his throne and turned toward the oaken door on the wall behind the scribes. Ahba stood in a smooth motion and followed him, eyes downturned. The guard stepped to unbar the door, and Izevel called out to his back.

"My Lord, a thousand apologies." He stopped with a half-turn. "The messenger awaits, let us hear his words and set him free."

The black-suited messenger bowed low. "I am your servant, my King. I will await your return."

"Nonsense," the Queen said. "A great King like my husband would never let an urgent matter wait. Speak your report. Is it of the fighting in Beit El?"

The messenger twisted his head from facing the King to look toward the Queen, above him on her throne. "Yes, my Queen."

Izevel shook her head, and her black hair fell over her shoulders. "A tragedy. One of my soldiers informed me this morning."

The King turned back to his wife. "Fighting?"

"A prophet and his disciples fought my men in Beit El. One of my father's soldiers fell, along with the prophet. In the end, order was restored." She turned to face the messenger. "Is that not so?"

The messenger's right hand closed around the scroll as he shrank beneath her gaze. Ahba took a step, drawing the King toward the door. The King stepped with her, though his eyes remained on the messenger, awaiting his response.

The messenger's eyes flickered back and forth between Izevel and the King. "Yes, my Queen, that is so."

Izevel gave her warmest smile and relaxed back into her throne. Her right hand returned to her belly, and the other reached out toward the young man. "You are to be praised. It is no simple thing to be the bearer of bad tidings. You may deliver the scroll into my hands."

The messenger bowed his head and placed the message in her outstretched hand. Guards pulled the Throne Room doors wide for Ahav and Ahba to pass. Izevel called after her husband, "We all await your return, my love."

Once he returned, the King moved quickly through the business of the day. Izevel paid little heed to the petitioners; even the nobility barely drew her attention. Her eyes remained on her husband, and her hand on her womb. Gossip would flow tonight in the kitchen, but there was no time for that. The King's absence made Court run late, and Raphael was waiting.

I dropped my kinnor and uniform at the musicians' quarters and went directly to Ovadia's house. "There's a prophet waiting for me at the gates," I said to Tamar. "I need bread."

Tamar stopped kneading. "A prophet? Who?"

"His name is Raphael ben Esek. He is a disciple of Master Yosef, or was. His master is now dead. I'll explain when I can, but now I must go."

Tamar looked me over. "Have you eaten today?"

"No, and surely neither has Raphael."

"Sit," she said. "There is no time to reach the cave and return before the closing of the gates, but there is still time to get out of the city. Tell me everything that happened."

Batya, who was silently listening in, brought me the Kohen's portion from the hearth, and I tore into the hot bread. Between bites, I described discovering Raphael among the beggars, then about Elifaz and Ahba in the Throne Room. "The attack in Beit El was clearly the moment Izevel was preparing for."

"Was it?" Tamar said. "I am not certain. Izevel may have delayed introducing Ahba until she had need, but I doubt the Queen acquired her for this alone. If Elifaz is to be trusted in his words, they must have planned Ahba's arrival for a month at least. I do not believe Izevel would bring another woman into the palace merely to rid herself of a single prophet."

"She said 'all great kings have great passions,' or something like that. She claimed this passion, unsatisfied, interferes with the King's justice."

Tamar's laughter held little mirth. "Ahav accepted this claim without protest? You see, Lev, even a King is subject to the weakness of men." Tamar turned a hard look on me. "This is why you must strengthen your will, for the weak of heart are easily manipulated. Izevel says indulging his desires is the path to justice, and the King runs out of the room with Ahba in pursuit of what? Justice? I think not."

Tamar's eyes bore into mine as if I had been the one to leave the Throne Room with Ahba. "Desire does not shrink when indulged—it grows. King Ahav will find no more justice with his concubines than King David found when he took Batsheva, killing her husband to have her himself. Such is the justice of those whose desire overpowers their will.

"Marry wisely, Lev. A wife should help a man strengthen his heart, bolstering him against base desires. I expect our King was left quite defenseless when his Queen led him to temptation rather than away from it." Tamar went back to her kneading, releasing me from her gaze. "Now, tell me more about Izevel."

"When she brought in Ahba?"

"No, I trust her guile enough to present the King exactly what she wanted him to see. From your description, that moment sounds well rehearsed. Tell me how Izevel looked once King Ahav left. Did she attempt to hold Court?"

"No. As soon as the doors shut behind the King, she signaled Dov, and we played music louder and faster than anything usually permitted in the Throne Room. After that, no one spoke other than the pages who brought her treats."

"Where did her eyes go? Did she look at her subjects?"

"No, her eyes were over our heads the whole time."

"When the King returned, did she come off her throne to greet him?"

I thought for a moment. "No, he climbed up to her."

"Was she disgusted with him?"

"Disgusted? Not at all." I could picture her face perfectly. "I've never seen her look upon him with more warmth. She held his hand through the rest of the day."

"Let me guess, her other hand rarely left her womb?"

"Yes, but her eyes remained fixed on Ahav. She looked…proud."

"Proud like a wife, or proud like a mother?"

"More like a mother."

"One hand on each of her children." She sighed and sat on a stool opposite me. "Perhaps when the birth comes she'll turn her attention to her child, though that seems unlikely, especially now that she has another tool with which to ply her evils."

"You think Ahba is dangerous?"

Tamar dismissed my question with a shake of her head. "Ahba is a toy, not a tool. I speak of the King's desires. Whatever Izevel said about being distraught to find the King without concubines when she arrived, she would have been far more troubled to find the King with a favorite son, even a bastard one. Now that she carries his seed, Izevel no longer fears other women. They can be her minions to weaken her husband's will. At least if she were disgusted with the King afterward, there would have been some hope of restraint."

Tamar stood with a sigh. "It is growing late. Go to Raphael now while the gates are still crowded."

"Who is there?" Peleh called out from the cave entrance.

"The footsteps are Lev's," Sadya said, "but he brings another."

"I bring the prophet Raphael ben Esek, a disciple of Master Yosef," I said.

Sadya put a hand on Raphael's shoulder as we entered the passageway. "Is all well with Master Yosef?"

Raphael walked with bent head. "The Holy One is a righteous judge."

Word spread quickly of Raphael's arrival. Whenever a new prophet reached the cave, his brothers gathered in the main entranceway. It was a greeting, but the prophets also hungered for news from the outside world. They sat in two circles, the prophets within and disciples around them.

Uriel said, "It brings us great joy to know you are alive, Raphael."

Raphael faced the floor, and in the weak lamplight, I could not see his expression. "Thank you, Master Uriel."

"Tell us now of our brother, Master Yosef."

"Master Yosef has been gathered to his fathers."

Uriel's head dropped, and a murmur passed through the prophets. Raphael continued, "Only a week ago, he said to me, 'this is my home. The Holy One brought me here, and here I will remain.' I believe he saw what lay ahead."

"Did any others escape?"

"What others? All others left long ago, though some have fared no better. Only Master Yosef and I remained."

"How did you escape when the soldiers came?" Uriel asked.

"I didn't." Raphael's shoulders shook, and the prophets waited in silence as his tears pocked the dust of the cave floor. "They bound my hands and legs and shoved me into a sack. As they carried me out, they told me that if I moved or screamed, they would cut my throat."

"What did you do?"

"I kept as still as I could, and bit at the ropes binding my hands."

"They bound you in front?" Pinchas asked. "I suppose they had no choice. They wished you to appear dead. Had your hands been bound behind you, a careful eye would notice."

"It took me most of the night, but I finally bit through my bonds."

"They carried you this whole time?" Uriel asked.

"Yes."

"How did they get out of the gates of Beit El?"

Raphael shrugged. He would have seen nothing from within his sack.

Pinchas answered, "The guards must have opened for the Queen's soldiers."

Several prophets shifted at his words. Until now, soldiers of Israel had not supported Izevel's troops in battle. The King was unaware of the attack. Did this mean Izevel issued an order to the King's soldiers to open the gates at night?

Raphael continued, "When the soldiers laid me on the ground, the sun had risen. Clearly, they planned to rest during the day and carry me off at night. They did not remove the sack, not even to offer bread or drink. It was fortunate, for they also did not notice that I had broken through the ropes. I waited until I heard their snores, then loosened the ropes on my feet.

"When I escaped my captivity, I saw we were not far from the King's Road. I slipped in among a group of men walking north. The men turned off at Shiloh, and one invited me to join his family for Shabbat. I was afraid to face the soldier at the gates to the city, so I walked alone until I found a spring not far from the road. I rested there through Shabbat, then walked through the night to Shomron."

"How did you know to seek Shomron?" Uriel asked. "Did Master Yosef have word of our hiding place?"

"I cannot say why I came here, only that I was drawn."

Hold fast to instruction, do not let it go. Keep it, for it is your life.

Proverbs 4:13

12

The Price of Redemption

My fingers ached from kneading. The incompetence which excused me from baking did not extend to matzah. The dry, unleavened dough required more strength of hand than skill of touch, so even my untrained hands were put to work.

"It's called both the bread of affliction and the bread of freedom." Tamar rolled out a thick disc.

"Affliction I understand." I shook out my tired arms.

"It's the bread we baked when we were freed from Egyptian slavery. Don't confuse the freedom of our world with life in the Garden of Eden, Lev. The prophets suffer because they are free. Now, keep working that dough."

I pushed against the hard mixture of flour and water, which slowly softened beneath my hands. "The prophets are not free. They're prisoners in a cave."

"The prophets can leave the cave any time they wish. Not only would they be safe in the land, the King and Queen would honor them. All they must do is bow before the Baal, and the gates would open. They imprison their bodies so that their souls are free to attach to the Holy One."

Hiding in a cave hardly seemed like freedom to me, yet I knew it was pointless to argue with Tamar. Could Uriel consider himself free? I received my answer two nights later. On the first night of Passover, we gathered in the entranceway of the cave as the sun faded, and told the story of our exodus from Egypt.

"Once our fathers were slaves in Egypt," Uriel began, "but today we are free." Silence filled the cave. Would no one, not even Pinchas, raise a voice of objection? "Our fathers descended to Egypt, and there they became a nation, mighty and awesome."

"Too mighty," Peleh said. "The Egyptians feared us, and so enslaved us."

"When slavery only increased our strength and numbers," Uriel resumed, "the Egyptians killed the newborn boys, letting the girls live."

"Why kill the boys?" Yissachar asked. I was surprised to hear such a question coming from an elder among the masters. "Surely if they desired slaves to build their cities, better to have men than women. If they wished to break apart the people, it is still better to eliminate the girls. Let the boys mingle with the daughters of other slave nations and so be drawn after their gods."

"The Egyptians feared the men of Israel would join with their enemies and defeat them in battle," Ariel said.

"If they wished to be rid of us so badly, why not set us free to return to our land?" Yissachar asked.

"They became too dependent," Pinchas said. "They could not imagine thriving without us there to serve them."

"Thus the master became the slave, trapped by his own weakness," Yissachar said. "True freedom is found in mastering oneself."

Back and forth the prophets went through the night, with Uriel breaking in periodically to move the story forward. "The Holy One struck Egypt with ten plagues."

"Why ten?" Yissachar asked. "Surely the Holy One could have destroyed Egypt in one stroke."

"The Holy One wished for the freedom of the Israelites, not for the destruction of Egypt," Uriel replied. "The plagues gave the Egyptians a chance to recognize their folly and rectify their deeds. Pharaoh hardened his heart against them, bringing destruction upon his nation. At last, his heart was broken by the death of the firstborn, including his own son and heir."

The discourse went on, the prophets never pausing until the dawn. I attempted to follow their talk, but at some point in the night, exhaustion overtook me. In the morning, for the first time since Sukkot, the prophets did not offer supplications to the Holy One for rain. Just as Sukkot marked the beginning of the rainy season, Passover marked its end. Late rains could still fall, as they had the year before when they destroyed so much of the barley crop, but such occurrences were rare. Six more moons would pass before the people would again look to the skies in expectation. Now even those who knew nothing about Eliyahu or his battle with the Baal knew for certain that we were in the midst of a devastating drought.

As the dawn of my thirteenth year approached two weeks after Passover, I knew there would be no feast in my honor, but I chose to spend the final Shabbat of my boyhood in the prophets' cave. As the day waned, I climbed out above the cave to watch the sun descend toward the sea. When darkness fell, I would finally be deemed a man, though for most of the past year I had been living the life of one.

The sun sank over the horizon, and I climbed down to the cave while light remained to pick my way through the rocks. By the time I reached the entrance, the first stars were visible in the sky. The prophets were assembled, waiting for me.

To mark my coming of age, they had gathered together all the discarded lamps in the cave, neglected since we ran out of oil a month earlier. Sadya had squeezed out the linen wicks and scraped their clay bottoms to recover whatever oil remained. The result was the first flicker of firelight to enter the cave since mid-winter. The cracks in the ceiling provided enough light during the day to see vague forms in the main cavern, but nothing compared to lamplight.

I studied the men around me: their gaunt faces, deep-set eyes, and hollow cheeks. I saw no sadness on their faces, only pride. One after another, they stepped forward to lay their hands on my head and blessed me upon coming of age.

"Lev, may you grow in wisdom and body."

"May you restore the holiness of the Kohanim to the Kingdom of Israel."

"Lev, may you wed the one predestined for you, the one who will complete your soul, and build a home and family in Israel."

Uriel was the last to come forward, led by Raphael, who rarely left my master's side. The old prophet's hands trembled on my forehead. "Lev, may you fulfill your destiny amongst our nation, relieve the suffering of the people, and return the Kingship to the House of David."

Return the Kingship to the House of David? Could Uriel be confusing me with my father, who dreamed of a reunification of the Kingdoms? I studied his milky eyes, searching for any signs that might shed light upon this strange blessing, but the flame went out, and we were plunged back into darkness.

I saw Ovadia almost every day in the Throne Room when he came in to discuss various matters with the King and Queen. He rarely lingered there, and of course, we never spoke. I also went to his house each morning to work with Tamar, but took pains to avoid meeting him there. So, I was surprised when Batya greeted me at the door of the house one morning and told me Ovadia wanted to meet me outside the city.

I finished playing for the day, headed out of the gate, turned down the path Batya had described, and waited beneath a stone overhang that shielded the spot from view. The days had grown longer now as summer approached, and I had more time between finishing in the palace and sunset. The sun moved toward the hills on the western horizon, and I shifted back and forth on my feet. The gates would close soon. Did Ovadia intend for me to spend the night outside of the city? Was he detained by some urgent errand of the King? Or was he being watched?

The shadows grew long around me, and I had all but decided to return to the city when I noticed Ovadia approaching. He was not alone; a grey-haired man and a young boy of not more than five followed behind him. From where I stood in the shade of the overhang, I could see them easily, but remained invisible to them. That must have been Ovadia's intention, for once he was certain no one was watching, he pulled out two blindfolds. The man first blindfolded the boy, then himself. Once he was satisfied that neither of them could see, Ovadia led them to me.

"Are you truly a Kohen?" the man asked when he stood in front of me.

I turned to Ovadia, shocked he would reveal my secret, but at his nod, I answered. "I am."

"You sound young. You are of age?"

"I am," I said again.

"I bring my son before you, to be redeemed."

"Redeemed?" I asked.

Confusion spread across the man's face. "The firstborn son must be redeemed by a Kohen. Do you not know?"

"Of course I know," I said. Uncle Menachem had made me recite verses from the Torah of Moses every night. Though I could recite the verses by heart, I'd never heard of anyone actually being redeemed, and I had no idea how to do it.

The man pushed forward his young son. "I was supposed to redeem him at 30 days of age according to the custom, but there was no Kohen in the land. I have waited until now. You will redeem him for me, will you not?"

I could not refuse, but I had no idea how to proceed. I turned to Ovadia with a pleading look.

"Wait," Ovadia said to the father, "do you need redemption? If you are a firstborn, and your father never redeemed you, you take precedence over your son."

A nostalgic smile came over the man's face. "I am indeed a firstborn. I was eight years old when my father brought me for redemption. There was no need for blindfolds then. We went to the Kohen Yochanan, who was then in the land."

"What did he do?" I asked, eager to hear of my father.

"The redemption itself was nothing. My father gave Yochanan five pieces of silver, as it says in the Torah of Moses, and I was redeemed." The man opened his hand to display five pieces of silver, dull with disuse. "After the redemption, Yochanan placed his hands on my forehead, and told me I was now part of a tradition stretching back over five hundred years, to the night of the Exodus itself." A tear leaked from beneath his blindfold. "I want my son to be part of that tradition as well."

"He shall be." I had to restrain myself from revealing that Yochanan was my father. These were dangerous times—better that the Kohen and the faithful not know one another. I would bring the boy into the tradition, and through him enter into my own, the tradition of the redeemers. It was my father, and his father, and his father before him, all the way back to Aaron the Kohen, who were the redeemers of Israel.

I took the tarnished metal from his hand, shocked at the amount of wealth passing to me, and dropped them in my pouch. I placed my hands on the boy's head and felt the dampness in his thin hair. He trembled at my touch. I leaned over and spoke softly in his ear. "More than five hundred years ago, our people were slaves in the land of Egypt. The Holy One took us out with a powerful hand and an outstretched arm, striking the Egyptians with ten plagues. The last blow was the worst, the death of the firstborn sons. The Egyptian sons were killed, but the sons of Israel were spared.

"It is no small thing to be granted life while others die around you. The firstborn sons of Israel were consecrated through the mercy of the Holy One and became obligated to serve. But the children of Aaron were chosen by the Holy One to inherit this service. They redeemed the obligation of the firstborn, taking it upon themselves. I am a descendant, father to son, of Aaron the Kohen. In receiving this silver from your father, I have redeemed your obligation. You are free to live your life, no more obligated than any other, but as part of a tradition that stretches back to the birth of our nation."

I kissed the boy's forehead and gave him the blessing of the Kohanim. "May the Holy One bless you and guard you. May the face of the Holy One shine upon you and be gracious to you. May the face of the Holy One turn toward you, and give you peace."

I turned back to his father. "Now go. It is unsafe to linger with me."

The father nodded, and Ovadia led the two away, removing their blindfolds as soon as I was again hidden from their view. I took the five pieces of silver from my pouch. As I stared at them, I recalled my conversation with Dahlia only a year before, about how long a shepherd would have to labor to buy a piece of rocky hillside. My prospects improved upon becoming a musician in the Court, but even that paled beside the horizon which now opened before me.

This man had waited five years to redeem his son. How many other boys were scattered throughout the Kingdom waiting to be redeemed? Even with multitudes turning toward the Baal, many devout remained. Their firstborn sons alone could number in the hundreds. For all of these boys, I might be the only one capable of redeeming them. If so, I could soon be a wealthy man.

I sighed and put the five pieces of silver back into my pouch. That was yesterday's dream. I told the boy he was now free to live a normal life, but such was not my fate. The Kohanim were the redeemers, not the redeemed. The power to redeem came with the obligation to serve. Great wealth might pass through my hands, but it wouldn't remain there. The silver would go to Ovadia in the morning. The price of grain had risen sharply when summer arrived, but five pieces of silver would still purchase several days of life for the prophets.

The one who sows injustice shall reap misfortune.

Proverbs 22:8

13

The Tattooed Soldier

Five soldiers with cedar tree emblems emblazoned on their tunics entered the Throne Room and bowed before Izevel, who sat alone on her throne. That morning, she had presented Ahav with yet another concubine, reminding him that for a King to be just, he must not allow his desires to go unquenched. The maidservants whispered in the kitchen that Ahba was already with child, and the King had been spending less time with her of late. A line of petitioners waited to be heard, as did the general of the King's army, who had arrived soon after the King departed. Izevel ignored all but the Tzidonians.

Earlier in her rule, Izevel interrupted her messengers, but now she listened to the entirety of a report before responding. Tamar said this showed she was maturing, for those who know how to listen learn far more than those eager to speak. Her restraint made my task more difficult, for when listening silently she gave fewer cues than when shouting down a messenger. Fortunately,

I'd also become more adept at watching. I could tell from the thin line of her mouth that she was displeased with today's report.

I felt someone's eyes on me, but when I glanced up from my music, I noticed nothing. When the feeling grew, I paused in my playing and lifted my kinnor in front of my face to tighten the strings. I scanned the room through the kinnor but still saw no one looking.

I watched the Queen closely, hoping to discover more about the report, when at last she did interrupt. She held up a hand to stop the officer who was speaking and turned her attention to one of the other four soldiers. An icy grip grasped my heart when I saw what angered Izevel. The soldier's attention had drifted, focusing neither on his officer's words or on his Queen. Instead, he'd been watching me.

He faced the Queen with bowed head, but once Izevel's attention returned to the report, a predatory smile crept over his face. My hands shook, but I didn't dare glance at him. Only when Izevel dismissed the officer, and he led his men out of the Throne Room did I venture one more peek. Black dots stretched down his neck, extending beneath his tunic. The tattooed soldier. The one who killed Shimon. He must have felt my stare, for he paused to turn before exiting the oak doors, and we locked eyes.

"Is everything alright, Lev?" Dov whispered. We did not often speak in the Throne Room.

"Just tired," I lied.

Dov nodded. "I've been working you hard lately. You can skip the banquet tonight. We have enough without you."

When King Ahav retook his throne, Izevel reached over, grasped his hand, and ran her thumb back and forth across his fingers. She never seemed more pleased with him than when he returned from the concubines.

The general stepped forward for his audience. He spoke before the King in low tones, and Dov urged us to play louder so the conversation could not be overheard.

Court ran late due to the King's absence. In the kitchen, I found the food laid out for the servants already gone. Once the rainy season ended without a break in the drought, the cooks began preparing less food for palace servants, and everyone rushed to receive their share. No longer could I arrive late and expect anything to be waiting. I ran out to the courtyard without taking the time to change. By the time I reached the courtyard, it was empty.

Darkness had already fallen, and the sound of drumming signaled a sacrifice to the Baal at the Temple. I raced through the palace gates to the main road. An old olive grove rose by the side of the road, the trees wide and knotted. They must have been planted hundreds of years before King Omri built the city around them.

Something moved between the trees and my heart pounded in my chest. I searched, but saw only darkness. My legs twitched with the desire to run, but I kept my pace steady, not wanting to draw attention. Perhaps I was too well trained. Sometimes a panicked run can save your life.

A twig snapped behind me, and I turned. Too late. A hand stifled my scream while a powerful grip hoisted me into the grove. A hard knot of olive wood drilled into my back as I was thrust against the trunk of one of the ancient trees. The hand under my arm released, returning to place a dagger against my throat.

"Don't move. Want answers before you die."

The tattooed soldier released his hand from my mouth, but kept his blade pressed under my chin. I kept silent—screaming would only end my life sooner.

"Simple boy help grandfather through roadblock. Then boy in Throne Room, watching Queen. Boy not so simple, I see." His breath was hot on my face, and evil seethed in his eyes.

My legs shook. Ovadia had warned me to never be caught without a story, but what could I possibly tell this murderer to convince him I was harmless?

"Old man with you is prophet, yes?"

Even if I denied it, he would not believe me. I just stared at his hand on the knife.

"Speak, or I cut out tongue. One with scars friend, yes?"

I forced myself to answer. "Yes."

"Also prophet?"

"No."

"You lie." The metal pressed against my throat, and I shrank back against the tree. "Not matter. He wore sword from Tzidon. He killed soldier of Tzidon?"

"They attacked us."

"I knew soldiers. They attack vile prophets. If friend kill them, friend was prophet." He leaned his face close. "I ask again, old man was prophet, yes?"

I trembled. The soldier pulled the knife away from my throat and held the blade before my eyes. "Many ways to kill. Fast ways, slow ways. Painful ways. You answer, I kill you fast. Not answer, I take time." He placed the dagger behind my ear, pulling it forward until I felt metal almost break skin. "Old man, he prophet, yes?"

What would Ovadia say in my place? The soldier already knew Uriel was a prophet. Shimon's stolen sword, along with my confession that we were together, confirmed that. I needed to gain the soldier's trust, make him think I was going to tell him the entire truth. "Yes, he was a prophet."

"Good. Where is prophet now?"

"Hiding in a cave."

"Good. Where is cave?"

I hesitated and felt a sharp pain from the blade. A drop of blood trickled down my neck. "In Emek HaAsefa."

"You lie. I go to Emek HaAsefa. No prophets there." He moved the dagger between my legs. "One more lie and I cut. Where is prophet now?"

A shadow detached itself from the darkness of the grove. The soldier spun at the sound, but too late. A sword slashed, catching the Tzidonian in the neck, cutting right through his tattoos. He fell in a heap, never to rise again.

My savior stepped forward into the moonlight, which illuminated the grey streaks in his square-cut beard. It was the general of the King's army. He sheathed his sword and stepped toward me. "You can't help me with the body, can you Lev?"

"You know—"

"That you're a Kohen? Now I do. Until this moment it was only a guess. No matter, I'll take care of this garbage myself." He slipped his arms under the corpse, lifted it over his shoulder, and stood with a practiced motion.

"You followed me?"

"I followed him. I read the malice on his face in the Throne room, and when I left the palace, I saw him lingering outside the gates. I know when a soldier has blood in his eyes. He was so focused on watching for you that he failed to notice me."

None of that explained how he knew my name or that I was a Kohen. "Why did you save me?"

He kicked at the parched dirt, covering the soldier's blood. "You expect me to let foreigners come into our land and kill our people?"

"Isn't that what—"

His eyes rose back to meet mine. "Enough questions. Run home, Lev. Tell no one what you saw here tonight, and I will tell no one what I heard."

He carried his burden through the grove. I ran the other way, to the main road, heedless of the noise from my footfalls. Hopefully, the general would keep his end of the bargain, but I had no such intention.

Ovadia told me never to go to his house at night except in an emergency. I broke off my run, calming my footsteps well before turning down his street. This felt like an emergency to me.

"You gave no hint of where Uriel was hidden?" Ovadia's face had remained calm throughout the whole story.

"No, I told the soldier he was in Emek HaAsefa. He didn't believe me, but he never got the truth out of me. Still, the general heard enough to know I'm connected to a prophet."

"He's not the one I'm concerned about," Ovadia said. "If he's willing to kill a Tzidonian soldier, he won't be quick to turn on the prophets. Did you believe his words that he followed the soldier because he didn't like foreigners killing his people?"

"I'm not sure."

Tamar had listened in silence until she heard my answer. "That's not good enough, Lev. I have been training you to see, whether you were paying attention or not. Where were his eyes when he said this?"

I summoned up an image of the general standing over the soldier's corpse. "Focused on the ground. He was covering the blood."

"Did he drop his gaze when he said it, or was he already looking at the ground when you asked?"

"When I asked."

"He's hiding something," Tamar said to Ovadia.

"Agreed." Ovadia tapped his fingers on the table. "The fact that he knew Lev was a Kohen confirms it. Nonetheless, I expect there was still truth to his words. The King has not allowed his soldiers to interfere with the Queen's hunt. They may follow orders, but that doesn't mean they like them."

"As the general showed," Tamar added, "if pushed hard enough, our soldiers may even act against their orders."

"What are you saying?" Batya asked.

"The general followed because he saw something suspicious," Tamar said, "but he did not have to act. He kept hidden and listened, only attacking to save Lev from harm. Why not strike earlier? My heart says he wanted to learn as much about the prophets as possible."

"You think the King's general is loyal to the prophets?" Batya asked.

"If so," Ovadia said, "he could be the ally I have been seeking."

"What are you thinking?" Batya asked.

"Until now, we've only had two options: the cave or the drought. Either we're waiting for the Holy One to save the prophets or we're waiting for the people to bow to Eliyahu's will. There is a third way."

"War?" I asked.

"We are already at war. If Yoav brought the army of Israel to our side, they could eliminate the Tzidonians from the land in a day."

"What about the Queen?" Batya asked.

"She's a bigger problem. King Ethbaal wouldn't invade Israel over the loss of soldiers, but he might for his daughter."

"What if the general's *not* loyal to the prophets?" I asked.

"Then he is a dangerous enemy." Ovadia stood and paced the room. "If he's loyal, the more he knows, the more he can help. If he has no special concern for the prophets, if he simply resents foreigners killing his people as he says, telling him anything is a risk."

"You said he's not the one you're concerned with." Batya turned to her husband. "Who is?"

"The other four Tzidonian soldiers. It will not take them long to realize their brother is missing."

I hadn't thought of the others. "Do you think he told them his suspicions about me?"

"Even if he did not, they might have noticed him watching you in the Throne Room, or even known that he was waiting outside the palace for you. When he fails to return, they could pick up his trail at you."

"The Queen could have noticed as well." My voice barely escaped my throat.

"True," Ovadia said. "The Queen rarely pays attention to her servants. But if a soldier focused on anyone but her, the insult alone might have drawn her notice."

I swallowed the lump in my throat. "What do I do?"

"You cannot change anything now," Ovadia said. "The risk is too great. If you fail to report to the Throne Room immediately after her soldier's disappearance, it might draw attention. We must prepare a convincing story in case they do trace his trail to you. To be caught without an excuse is certain death. No more coming here or to the prophets' cave until we are sure you are not being watched."

The next morning, Izevel's eyes jumped from the scroll in her hands to examine me. Not once, but three times. That had never happened before. My palms grew slick with sweat, and I struggled to play even our simplest melodies. Did she already know the tattooed soldier had disappeared? Was the scroll in her hands a message about his death? Did it mention me?

She would do nothing in the Throne Room. If she seized me in public, the King would want a full explanation. The Queen would take her revenge quietly. Who would wonder about the fate of a lowly musician? Even Dov would assume I got homesick and returned to Levonah.

Of course, I could only expect a quick death if she sought revenge alone. If Izevel suspected my connection with the prophets, she would force whatever information out of me she could.

I ran over the story Ovadia made me memorize the night before. I had been traveling with two prophets. One of them was killed at the roadblock. The other was old. I hid him in a small cave outside of Shomron, toward the sea. I brought him food each day, as much as I could manage. Between the lack of food and the winter cold, he died.

Ovadia had described a small cave he knew until I could see it before my eyes. If forced to show them where I hid the prophet, I could probably locate the cave. But what if they wanted to see his grave?

Izevel looked up from her scroll a fourth time, her eyes again going right to me. I could feel her studying me. Sweat beaded on my forehead.

Tuval slapped me on the shoulder. "Stop staring at the Queen. You're making her nervous."

I turned away, a sudden grin breaking through my sigh. Was I drawing her attention through my stares? She might know nothing about me, perhaps not even that her soldier was dead. Tamar told me the frightened man forgets to breathe. I took breath after breath, letting the tension in my shoulders flow out through the strings of my kinnor.

If I was not a suspect already, I couldn't let my behavior make me one.

I lingered in the palace kitchen for as long as I could, but when the sun set, I knew I had to move. Vulnerable as I was during the day, it would only be worse after dark. As I left the safety of the kitchen, I saw a group of servants crossing the courtyard toward the gate and dashed to catch up with them. If soldiers waited to grab me, they would do it while I was alone.

Once outside the gate, I heard the pounding of a familiar drum. I had not seen Zim since he moved into the Temple, almost two months prior. Could he protect me now? At worst, the Queen's soldiers had suspicions. Only a fool would think me capable of killing that tattooed brute on my own. If they saw me with Ovadia, I would endanger us both, as well as the prophets. If they saw me with Zim, would I be safer? He was also once connected to the prophets, but none would suspect him of remaining loyal.

I turned off the road toward the Temple of the Baal. Zim sat on a stone bench against the wall of the Temple, his drum between his knees. I quickened my step toward him, but a hand grabbed my shoulder before I reached him. I turned to face my attacker, and instead found a smiling face

"Lev, you're here too?"

There was something familiar about the young man before me, but I could not place him.

"I am Elad. I was a disciple of Master Yosef. Do you remember?"

"Elad, yes." During my brief visit to Master Yosef's, the disciples had studied me with their eyes closed. It was Elad who noticed my discomfort with being observed. "What are you doing here?"

"Continuing my studies," he said.

I swallowed my surprise as Tamar had taught me, showing only curiosity in my face. We stood before the Temple of the Baal, and his master was dead. What studies could he mean?

"What about you?" he asked.

"I'm a musician in the King's Court." I patted the strap of my kinnor which hung over my shoulder.

"You play before the King and Queen?" Elad gave a low whistle. "You have come a long way from playing for the prophets."

It was best to agree with him. "Indeed."

He looked me head to toe, taking in my linen garments slung over my arm. "It was a relief to find Zim already at the Temple when I arrived." He lowered his voice and leaned toward me with a knowing look. "Not many faces around from the old days."

"No," I shook my head in agreement. "Maybe just the three of us."

"There are more," Elad said, "though they have not yet arrived in Shomron. I was not the only disciple to feel the change in the winds."

A voice called out from behind us. "Elad!"

Elad turned toward the call, and I followed. I was safer in his presence than even in Zim's. Elad could swear that my contact with the prophets was temporary and insignificant.

He headed to a low doorway at the back of the Temple. Inside sat a man in dark violet robes hunched over two scrolls open on the heavy wooden table. "You called, Master?" Elad said, eyes lowered.

I recognized the wizened, hairless face of Yambalya's teacher, but he had eyes only for his disciple. "What is the meaning of this passage? If Balaam was permitted to journey, why was he punished for it?"

"I will show you, Master." Elad nodded to me with a smile of dismissal and entered.

I stepped away, but not before stealing a glance around the small room. It was a bare cell, except for the table and scrolls of varying heights and thicknesses stacked on a shelf in the corner. I had seen those ancient scrolls once before, a year earlier at Master Yosef's.

One's heart devises their way, but the Holy One directs their steps.

Proverbs 16:9

14

The Long Journey

The next day found me still alive, as did the day after that. Within a week, I felt invisible again in the Throne Room. The very idea that a boy like me could present a threat to a trained killer like the tattooed soldier even seemed funny.

The sun of summer rose to its peak, turning the fields a dusty brown and drying the hillsides to bone. People spoke of rain with a longing I had never heard. The crowd attending the Baal's nightly sacrifices grew as more and more looked to the storm god for relief.

Hunger was not yet widespread, though the beggars by the gate increased every week. Grain was not as scarce as I feared, for the past winter's early rains allowed many to save their barley by hand-watering, and those with spring-fed fields even saved much of their wheat. By the end of summer though, the ground was dry and cracked; no plow would break the soil until the rains fell.

I joined the prophets as they gathered at the end of the Sukkot festival for the annual prayer for rain. A year ago, Uriel stood in a downpour and begged the Holy One to bring the winter rains. At the time, his words seemed futile as the ground was already saturated, but now I understood that today's blessings were no guarantee for tomorrow. As he had done the year before, Uriel sealed his prayer with the traditional ending, "Master of the world, you and only you cause the wind to blow and the rain to fall."

None of the prophets objected, and I would not argue with my master in front of them, but his words felt like a lie. I waited until we were alone in the darkness of his cavern to confront him. "Master, you are praying to the wrong source."

"Am I, Lev?"

"Yes, Master. The Key of Rain is in Eliyahu's hands—*his* will holds back the rains. If we wish to plead for the drought to end, we must plead with *him*."

Uriel paused as he took in my words. "Very well. You may go to him. I will not stay your hand."

"Me?" I had not intended to volunteer. "This should be a message from the prophets."

"No, Lev, it must come from you."

"Master, I could easily direct one of the prophets or disciples how to find him."

"I am not sending you because you know his location, Lev. It is clear to me from the *ratzon* in your voice that you must make this journey yourself. It is your will."

"Master, do we not all share the desire for the rains to return?"

"Of course, but no one else objected to my prayer."

"My apologies for speaking out of place, Master."

"The prophets know that though Eliyahu holds the Key of Rain now, this is only because it is given by the Holy One, who rules over all things." My Master sounded uneasy.

"I bow to the wisdom of the prophets."

"You misunderstand me, Lev. I am not defending the prophets who accepted my prayer in silence. Sometimes innocence discerns where wisdom has gone astray. You walk in the sunlit world while we hide here in the darkness." The old prophet sighed in frustration. "Perhaps we have become overly passive. When our people were trapped between the sea and the army of Egypt, Moses too prayed for salvation. Do you recall what happened?"

Every child knew the story. "The Holy One split the sea in response to his prayer."

"Wrong." Uriel's joy was unmistakable. "The Holy One responded, 'Why do you cry out to me? Tell the people to move forward!' Prayer is not always a substitute for action."

"If this is a time for action, why not send a prophet or disciple?"

"Because only you were roused to object. Only you felt we must take action. That is the essence of *ratzon*. Everything in this world emanates from the will of the Holy One. Thus, the will to act can itself be a sign, for it can mean the Divine will seeks outlet through you. You tracked the ravens because they were a sign which only you saw. So too your *ratzon* to confront Eliyahu means you must be the one to seek him out."

My master's words made no sense. I had never felt a stronger will than to follow the priestess of Ashera into the orchard. Was that a sign as well? I wanted to ask, but I was ashamed to admit I played before the enemy's idols. "Does this mean King Ahav was right to depart the Throne Room with Ahba, because he desired her?"

Uriel threw the question right back at me. "What do you think?"

"It can't be," I said with a confidence I did not feel.

"One of the great tasks the Holy One has given us in this life is to distinguish between our base desires and our true will. But," he said, "this is far from simple."

"How can I know the difference, Master?"

"Only your heart can guide you, Lev. But I can teach you this: When a base desire is fulfilled, it brings in its wake only weakness and more desire; when it's overcome, it brings strength. Achieving your *ratzon* may demand fundamental sacrifice, but you will only grow stronger from it. And woe to the man who fails to express his true will, for it will drain his life away."

Was journeying to Eliyahu my *ratzon*, as my Master believed?

As if hearing the question in my head, Uriel said, "Listen to the voice of your heart—it is your true essence."

This time I had no need to follow the ravens. Nonetheless, as the sun dipped toward the sea on the afternoon of my first day's journey, I climbed a hillside in the hope of catching sight of the birds. So long as they fed Eliyahu, I knew the eyes of the Holy One remained on the land.

I chewed my evening bread as I watched the skies. My fingertips tingled, drawing my attention toward Shomron. Soon, two tiny black dots appeared against the white of the walls, growing moment by moment. The ravens still bore their burdens, and I kept my eyes on them until they disappeared into the haze in the east.

The next morning, I discovered I didn't need to search the skies to find them. When I awoke, a dull pounding pulsed in my ears and my fingertips tingled. My eyes were drawn to the sky, and I immediately spotted their path. Even after the birds passed from sight, the pulsing continued. Then all at once, it ceased.

What was this strange connection and why had it suddenly sprung up? I felt nothing like it on my journey the year before. A smile came to my lips as I realized my master already answered this question. Uriel said my desire to plead with Eliyahu was an expression of the Divine will. That made me a messenger of the Holy One, just like the ravens. Perhaps I sensed their passage because one will moved us to the same destination. I felt a surge of hope. With such a clear sign that I had aligned my will with the Holy One's, could my journey fail to succeed? I pushed down the trail with a new lightness in my step.

Just before sundown that night, the crag loomed above me. I was halfway up when I felt a tension in the air. My ears rang and my hands throbbed. The ravens were on their way. I touched one hand to my chest—the pounding was in rhythm with my heartbeat.

I rushed to reach the top before they arrived, even though I could now track them with my eyes closed. At the top, I put myself directly into their path, and the birds veered around me, eyes focused straight ahead. They were close enough to reach out and touch, yet I knew they would evade my hands as easily as they had the knives of the cooks.

Only one thing had changed. The ravens now carried gigantic portions. It was hard to believe one bird could even fly holding four pieces of bread in its claws, or the other with such a large chunk of meat. Of course, these birds were messengers of the Holy One—they would carry as much as they were commanded. But why should Eliyahu merit such generous portions while the prophets starved?

The next morning, I reached the final hilltop above Eliyahu's hiding place just before the time of the ravens' morning delivery. I decided to wait for them, to meet Eliyahu when he came out to retrieve his bread and meat. I sat with my back to the eastern sky as the world grew light, gazing over the ridges I had just traveled. I felt and saw nothing. Something was wrong.

I went to Eliyahu's encampment and called out, "Master Eliyahu?" No response.

I descended into the cleft of Nahal Karit. The once vibrant reeds were yellow and dry, and no sound of water met my ears. I slipped between the grey rocks and crashed through the undergrowth, trying in vain to move quietly. Water still stained the face of the cliff, but it was barely enough to wet the cracked mud at the bottom of the pool below. Eliyahu must have held out for as long as possible, but Nahal Karit could sustain him no longer.

The birds brought Eliyahu bread and meat, but only the nahal gave him water. A man could survive a long time without food, but only a few days without water. Could Eliyahu have died? If he did, would the Key of Rain return to the Holy One? Or would it be lost forever?

I climbed back up from the riverbed. As a Kohen, I was forbidden from entering a cave with a dead body, but I had to know the truth. I couldn't return to my master with a report that Eliyahu *may* have died. I stepped through the dark entrance and peered around in the dim light. Nothing. Not a crumb, not a garment, and no Eliyahu.

Perhaps the gigantic portions the birds carried were meant to sustain him on a journey? The ravens could have continued to deliver him food while he traveled. Why stop because he left the nahal? Whatever the reason, I hadn't felt their presence that morning, and my heart told me they would come no more.

The sun broke over the ridgeline above me, and I realized I had a more immediate problem than wondering about the birds. Expecting to refill when I reached the nahal, I had been less than careful with my water. One skin was empty, as was a quarter of my second. Even if I turned back now, it would be a hard journey back to Shomron, and I couldn't leave without first seeking answers.

The ravens came the night before, so Eliyahu couldn't have been gone for long. The pool in the nahal would gather water during the night, then lose it during the heat of the day. Eliyahu must have begun his journey at dawn after drinking whatever water had collected during the night.

If it were me, I would follow the nahal downstream toward the Jordan River, hoping to find water there. But would a man fed by ravens choose the obvious path? I couldn't risk starting off in the wrong direction.

I had felt the ravens on their way to Eliyahu, but lost the connection once they fulfilled their mission. I had guessed that I felt them because we were all Divine messengers, but didn't Uriel believe I had also received a sign the year before? So why had I not felt them then? What had changed in the past year? Only that Tamar taught me to watch, to listen, to feel. If I focused my heart, could I feel Eliyahu as well?

I pictured Eliyahu when we first met, with close-cropped hair and nobleman's clothes. Then I pictured him as I found him in the nahal, with hair and beard matted, his clothes in tatters. No matter how I imagined him, one feature remained unchanged: his eyes. I pictured those eyes now, staring into their fire as I could never do in person.

I felt nothing, just the heat of the sun on my back. Sweat trickled down my neck, and I felt the first touch of fear. If I lost any more time, I might not make it back to Shomron at all. I pushed the fear aside and squeezed my eyes shut. If the Holy One had mercy on the prophets, I would find Eliyahu.

I felt a tug at my heart. There was no pounding in my ears as I'd felt with the ravens, but as I focused on this pull, the hair on the back of my neck stood on end. I gazed downstream toward the Jordan but felt nothing. I turned to face the mountains and felt the tug drawing me on, upstream.

The sun reached its midpoint in the sky as I climbed. I knew neither how far I would have to pursue Eliyahu, nor if I would find water along the way. The wise decision would be to seek shelter and rest through the heat of the day, conserving my water. But if I stopped, I might lose Eliyahu. I had lost all connection with the ravens after they reached their destination—would the same hold true with the prophet? Perhaps not. The ravens became normal birds once they fulfilled their mission, but Eliyahu would never be an ordinary man.

I reached the head of the streambed and turned north. A hard-packed trail dipped in and out of the folds between the hills, and the sun pounded mercilessly on my head. Up and down I tramped, until at the crest of yet another ridge I tipped back my skin to take my last swallow of water. As I brought my eyes to the valley before me, a swath of green stood out from the yellow-grey hills around it.

Racing downhill, I forced my way through thick brush. I smelled the water before I saw it, and soon I was kneeling next to a cool trickle emerging from the rocks. I drank my fill directly from the spring, splashed my face and neck, and refilled both water skins. Only then did I notice a sandal print in the mud on the far side of the spring.

The sun was already dropping toward the west when I descended into the broad Jezreel Valley. Ovadia owned land somewhere near here, not far from where the King and Queen were building a second palace. This project had been the source of much discussion in the Throne Room. The Queen didn't like being isolated in the mountains, barely accessible to foreign merchants and dignitaries. She wanted a palace easily reached by chariot. But there were good reasons the kings of Israel built their capitals in the mountains; the very accessibility of the valley made it vulnerable to attack.

The valley was broad enough to fit Shomron ten times over, and it wasn't just an army that would be exposed here. A man walked alone across the valley ahead of me. I took a deep draught of water and set off at a run. It was the perfect place to encounter the prophet—he had nowhere to hide.

Eliyahu didn't increase his pace or even turn at my approach. "Welcome, Lev ben Yochanan," he said without surprise.

"Master Eliyahu, I come bearing greetings from the prophets."

"Greetings, are they?" Eliyahu's full face contrasted with the gaunt cheekbones of the prophets in the cave.

"Greetings and a question."

He looked over at the setting sun, then back at me. "I wondered if I would see you today."

"Why today, Master Eliyahu?"

"Do you not know what day it is?"

I had thought it merely luck that I reached Eliyahu's cave on the very day he left, but his tone made me wonder. "No, Master, what day is it?"

"One year to the day since we met in Jericho."

I nodded with sudden understanding. My friend Seguv died during Sukkot the prior year, and it was a few days after the festival that I left Emek HaAsefa to visit his family in their mourning. It was there that Eliyahu declared his curse. "Master Eliyahu, it has been one year since you brought the drought. The prophets want to know if it will now come to an end."

He did not look at me as he replied. "Have the people turned away from their idols?"

"No, Master. The people turn more to the Baal and Ashera every day. Queen Izevel tells them the rains have not come because the Holy One has abandoned Israel. The drought itself strengthens her gods."

Eliyahu's eyes narrowed. "Nonetheless, this is the justice of the Holy One, as stated by Moses, father of the prophets."

"What of the Holy One's mercy?" I asked. "Did it not hold back the drought despite the idolatry?"

"Indeed, for the Holy One is patient. Yet, I was granted the Key of Rain."

"The people suffer more every day," I said. "Has justice not been done?"

"Can there be justice while sin continues?"

This was going nowhere. Was Uriel mistaken about my coming to Eliyahu? "Then why do you journey?"

"Nahal Karit has run dry."

"The entire land has run dry," I said. "Soon no one will have water."

"The Holy One brings water to the righteous. I journey because I am sent to one who will sustain me through the drought."

So, that was where we were going, probably to some wealthy man who had remained loyal to the Holy One, one who could easily provide for a single prophet. Eliyahu would continue to eat while the rest of the nation suffered under his drought. I saw it was useless to speak to him and almost turned back to Shomron. At least there I could do my part to ease the burden of the prophets, but I knew I couldn't return to my master until I learned his destination.

We approached a cluster of houses surrounded by unplanted farmland, and I felt eyes on us from within. "The King seeks you day and night. Do you not fear being spotted crossing the valley?"

"The Holy One sends me. Who shall I fear?"

Eliyahu stared straight ahead as we walked, much like the ravens that brought his food. I watched the windows as we passed the farm, catching the eyes of the farmers sitting idle within. This was the time to turn their fields to ready them for the winter planting. Yet, their seeds would die if planted in this dry soil, and the harder they worked, the hungrier they would grow.

How would they react if they knew the one responsible for their suffering passed in their midst? Of course, even if they had heard Eliyahu's name, the ragged man crossing their field looked more like a beggar than a prophet. Only if they got close enough to see the burning eyes beneath his unkempt hair would they feel the presence of one who would never beg from men.

I felt Eliyahu's indifference as I walked beside him. I was connected to the prophets, so he didn't consider me an enemy, but I was hardly an ally. I couldn't shake the feeling that it didn't matter to him at all whether I succeeded or failed in keeping the prophets alive.

Not another word was spoken between us during the next three days. Our journey continued through the mountains of the Galil and then descended westward to the Tzidonian coast. Eliyahu woke before me each morning, but never departed until I arose.

At the end of the second day, Eliyahu finished the last of his bread and meat. The next morning, he watched me chew a piece of stale bread. I would have shared with him, but knew he would never ask, and respecting the silence between us, I didn't offer. Besides, I ate the Kohen's portion, which was forbidden to him.

Signs of the drought followed us into Tzidon, but grew less severe. We passed many springs but found them all guarded, so we were unable to refill our skins on the last leg of our journey.

Near sunset on the fourth day, we reached the village of Tzarfat on the Tzidonian coast. As the first houses came into view, we spotted a woman hunched over at the edge of a field, gathering sticks. Though we were now deep into Tzidon, she wore her hair covered in the manner of women of Israel. Eliyahu had barely spoken our entire journey, but now his restraint broke. He had not had a sip of water since that morning. He drew near to the woman and called out to her through parched lips. "Bring me please a cup of water that I may drink."

The woman stood with a startled look, then set off to bring water. She had only gone a few paces when Eliyahu called to her again. "And bring me please a small piece of bread in your hand."

The woman dropped her gaze to the ground. When she looked back up at the prophet, her eyes were filled with sadness. "As the Holy One, your Lord lives..." she began. I started at her words—she knew exactly who he was. Could she be connected to the one appointed to sustain Eliyahu?

"As the Holy One, your Lord lives, I have not a thing baked," the woman said. "All I have is a handful of flour in a jar and a bit of oil in a cruse. I came out to gather two sticks so that I could prepare a small cake for myself and my son. We will eat it and die."

Was there no wealthy man to feed Eliyahu during the drought? Could this poor widow, who did not even have enough to provide for herself and her son, be the one appointed to sustain him? Why would the Holy One send Eliyahu on such a long journey just to arrive here?

Eliyahu hesitated, but only for a moment. "Fear not. Go do as you have said, but first, make a small cake from your flour and bring it to me."

Would Eliyahu take the last morsel of food from the mouth of her child?

The fire kindled in Eliyahu's eyes, and his voice rang out across the field. "Afterwards you will make for yourself and your son. For so says the Holy One of Israel, your jar of flour will not be spent nor your cruse of oil fail until the day the Holy One sends rain upon the earth." His throat might be dry, but his voice carried the same power as when he issued his curse in Jericho. The widow ran off to fulfill his command.

Eliyahu looked around as if seeing his surroundings for the first time. His expression echoed that of the ravens after they completing their mission. The prophet had arrived at his destination. He called down a miracle from the Holy One, not merely to provide for this woman and her son, but for himself as well.

A jar of flour and a cruse of oil would sustain the three souls for the duration of the drought. It was a far cry from the meat and bread that Eliyahu had eaten from the King's table, but he would survive, even as others died of starvation.

The woman returned, followed by a boy not much younger than me. She carried a small piece of bread and two cups of water. She set the bread and one cup on the ground before Eliyahu and held out the second cup to me. Unlike the dregs that remained at the bottom of my skin, the water was cool and clear.

While the woman took Eliyahu to her mud home and showed him a place in the back where he could sleep, her son Yonah took me to the well. Like all wells we had seen in Tzidon, this one was guarded, but Yonah entered unhindered. "Will you be staying with us as well?" he asked me.

"It is time for me to go home." Even as I spoke the words, I wondered exactly where home was. I would do my duty and return to the musicians' quarters. That was my place now, more so than the prophets' cave or even Levonah.

One thing was certain: I did not belong here in Tzarfat. I had delivered the prophets' message and tracked Eliyahu to his new location. The time had come to return. Though the sun was setting, I shouldered my water skins and trekked south to Shomron.

Death and life are in the power of the tongue.

Proverbs 18:21

15

The Bitter Drops

I returned to Shomron via the coastal road where many of the springs and seeps near the sea still flowed. I finished my last piece of hard bread on the morning I turned east toward Shomron, and I walked the last day into the hills without a bite to eat. My duty was to report to my master, but I was too hungry to walk past Shomron. Dusty from more than a week's journey, I drew no notice from the crowd of beggars before the gates.

I went directly to Ovadia's, hoping the Kohen's portion might still be hot from the day's baking. Batya opened at my knock, and as I slipped in, I saw the donkey was already loaded and waiting in the courtyard.

"Where's Tamar?" I asked as soon as the gate swung shut behind us.

"I don't know." Batya's shoulders tightened. "She left this morning, not saying to where. I've had to do the baking myself."

My legs were weary, but the prophets needed to eat. I paused long enough to have a single piece of bread, then led the donkey out of the courtyard.

"Can that be Lev?" Peleh exclaimed. "We thought you lost in Egypt."

"Egypt?" I asked.

"You went to seek one of our brothers. It is an old story that ends with being sold into slavery." I could see Peleh's expectant smile in the dim light of the entrance.

Sold into slavery was the key. Joseph went to seek his brothers and did not return because they sold him into slavery in Egypt. Peleh was asking why I was so late in returning from Eliyahu. "If you want to hear my words, gather the prophets. I have both bread and a tale."

I recounted my journey as they ate in silence. No questions were asked, even when I told how I had tracked Eliyahu from Nahal Karit. I described the widow in Tzarfat, and I was struck by a strange expression on Uriel's face. "Why do you smile, Master?"

"The Holy One speaks to us in many ways, not only through prophecy. Messages come constantly to those who learn to listen."

"Listen to what, Master?"

"All that we encounter speaks to us in a single voice. The wise learn from all. Ask of everything you experience what it has come to teach you, and you will never fail for lack of wisdom. Do you hear what the widow says to Eliyahu?"

"She said he could stay."

Uriel almost laughed. "Not the words she said to him, Lev, but the fact she is appointed to sustain him. Every detail of your journey is a lesson to the knowing ear. First was Nahal Karit. The Holy One could have hidden Eliyahu by abundant waters; we ourselves are blessed with a spring whose flow did not diminish in the heat of the summer. Eliyahu was forced to watch as his source dried, eventually digging for water to survive."

"So he could not close his eyes to the drought?" I asked.

Uriel nodded. "Without question. For the past year, he has done little but sit alone and watch as all life around him withered and died. He could not help but know how much the people were suffering as well."

I pictured Eliyahu striding across the Jezreel Valley. "Forgive me, but Eliyahu cares little for the pain of others. He said any suffering was justice by the hand of the Holy One as revealed in the teachings of our Master Moses."

"It is not the only truth found in the Torah of Moses. It also says one should not oppress the widow or the orphan. This is the next part of the story."

"Which communicates what, Master?"

"The need for mercy. You are wrong that Eliyahu cares not for the pain of others, Lev. I imagine the pain he feels is beyond what you could imagine, for he feels, like a knife in his flesh, the Holy One's pain at the betrayal of Israel. This is what allows him to bear the suffering of Israel without mercy. Now each day, each hour, he will face the very people he is commanded to protect as they descend into cruel death through his curse."

"Isn't he the one keeping them alive, Master?"

"He is prolonging their suffering through his miracle, but even if they live, he must know thousands like them are not so blessed. We can only hope this will stir him to be merciful toward the people."

"What of being merciful to the cruel?" Pinchas asked. "Do we learn nothing from King Shaul?"

"What does Eliyahu have to do with King Shaul?" I turned toward Pinchas.

"I refer to the destruction of Nov," he replied. "Surely you know the stories of your tribe."

My face flushed and in my exhausted state I could not hold down my anger. "I had no father to teach me, and my duties to the prophets have left me little time to learn."

"True." There was no apology in his voice. "Well then, learn this. The Holy One commanded Shaul, our first King, to destroy the memory of Amalek. He killed their men in battle and poured out their blood like water. But when Shaul came upon their King, he had mercy." Pinchas' voice rose as he warmed to the story. "Yes, mercy. Shaul kept the King alive and saved the best of their flock for sacrifices."

"What does this have to do with Eliyahu?" I asked.

"Patience. Not long after, the price of his failure came due. In a fit of rage, our King commanded the death of an entire city of Kohanim."

I gasped, though I could not see the connection. "Why would the King kill Kohanim?"

"Because they aided our master David when he fled from Shaul."

I had always loved the stories of King David, but Uncle Menachem never told me this one. "The Kohanim preferred David as King?"

"We will never know, but Shaul believed they did. David was still the chief of Shaul's army when he fled. The Kohanim could not know Shaul was consumed by jealousy and sought David's head, so they gave David bread and a sword for his journey. When Do'eg the Edomite, master of Shaul's flocks, cursed be his name, told the King, Shaul assumed the Kohanim were in league against him. In his fury, he demanded their blood. Only Do'eg was low enough a creature to fulfill such a command, and he did."

Whatever lesson Pinchas was trying to convey, I didn't understand it. "What does a city of dead Kohanim have to do with Amalek? And what do either of them have to do with Eliyahu?"

"We learn from Shaul that those who begin by having mercy on the cruel will end by being cruel to the merciful. You can decide for yourself what this says about Eliyahu."

I turned from Pinchas to Uriel. "Is this true, Master?"

"Master Pinchas speaks truth about King Shaul, though there are many other stories he could tell. An act of true mercy is a creative force, whose full consequences cannot always be known. After all, were it not for the mercy of another, you would not live."

"How is that, Master?"

"When he struck down your parents, Yoav desired your death as well, but could not bring himself to kill a child."

I clenched my fists at the mention of my parents' murderer. "He left me to die."

"Indeed. His was only a small act of mercy, but sparing you from the sword was mercy nonetheless. We never know what plants may sprout from the seeds we sow, Lev. You are alive from Yoav's small act of mercy, and now you sustain the prophets."

"Even if Pinchas is correct," Master Yissachar said, "the Holy One did not send Eliyahu to the cruel, but to a widow and orphan of generous heart. I agree with Uriel; the message is one of mercy."

Pinchas was not deterred by the opposition of his elders. "We may debate whether the Holy One calls Eliyahu to mercy," he said, "but Lev's words bear a different message for us."

"Which is what, Pinchas?" Uriel asked.

"Even a prophet may ignore the hints which the Holy One sends through the world. Lev said Eliyahu hesitated when he saw the widow. Rather than relent, he called down a miracle to keep the three of them alive. Can there be any greater sign that he remains on the path of strict justice? No mercy bends his will. We must prepare for another winter of drought, and if we are faced with starvation or battle, I will take the sword."

When I returned to Shomron the next morning, Tamar hadn't yet reappeared. She had never before left Ovadia's house except to deliver bread. Batya was close to panic, fearing she might have been caught or worse, but I couldn't stay to wonder about her.

"You look like one who comes from a long journey, not a long rest." The squint in Dov's eye told me his words were more than jest. During Sukkot, he had us working harder than ever to cover all of the festival banquets. To get away, I begged time to return to my family and rest. He had granted me a week, and now I was almost a full week late in returning, and even more drained than before.

Fortunately, the walk back from Tzidon had given me plenty of time to think of excuses. "It was good to see my family, but rest was not to be. The spring near my Uncle's farm is nearly dried, and they would not hear of my returning to Shomron until we'd finished digging a cistern should the rains fail again."

"May the rains fall for your uncle and all of Israel," Dov responded as he bent to tighten the strings of his nevel. "Nevertheless, you were missed."

"Surely three was enough for the Throne Room."

"In normal times, perhaps, but the Queen began feeling the pains of labor two days ago," Dov said.

"Two days ago? Has she not given birth?"

"Not yet, but the Throne Room has been chaotic since it began."

"She has not retreated to her quarters?" I asked.

Peretz shook his head in disbelief. "You watch, she'll sit on that throne until the moment the baby comes."

Dov raised a hand in caution, looking around before he added in a quiet voice. "The King refuses her nothing now. Indeed, no one dares to deny her. We have been playing without break. That is why we missed your kinnor."

The guard at the door banged his staff before I could respond, and we took our positions. The King and Queen entered, hand in hand. Izevel's free hand rested upon her swollen belly, which was far larger than any woman's I had ever seen. There had been whispers of twins in the palace kitchen for months, though one of the maidservants maintained that Tzidonian women just got that way when with child.

The royal couple sat, and I looked toward Dov for the signal to shift into the softer Court music, but it never came. Now I understood what he meant about missing my kinnor. Petitioners would never shout in the Throne Room, but that morning they raised their voices to be heard over the music and a few times the King leaned in to capture their words. Servants flowed in from the kitchen bearing delicacies for the Queen, and Dov led us through every fast-paced song we knew. The Throne Room had become a banquet hall.

The business of Court crawled along, interrupted by the Queen's every desire, but the King never raised a word of objection. Shadows were already showing through the western windows, and eight petitioners still stood in a group by the rear wall, when a royal messenger rushed in with a report. Dov signaled us to play softly, though we did not break our melody.

"My King," the young man bowed, "I bring report from the border country of the north. Yesterday morning, four of the Queen's men discovered a group of prophets sheltered in a valley near..."

I would never learn whether the prophets were caught or killed, because at that moment the Queen let out a gasping groan and screamed out, "Summon the midwives!"

Izevel clearly wanted to distract the King from the report. Dov waved for us to play louder, and I watched her face contort in pain. Her hands pressed up against the underside of her belly as she breathed in short, heavy grunts. This was no act.

Before the pages could even run to do Izevel's will, a woman appeared from nowhere, rushed up to Izevel, and slid an arm behind her back. With surprising strength, she hoisted the young Queen off the throne and led her toward the main door of the Throne room. The midwife's scarf hung low over her forehead, shading her face from view. As she passed back down the aisle, she shot a glance toward the musicians and caught my eye. Tamar.

Ahav stood for a moment, the desire to follow plain on his face, then he collapsed back into his throne. The birthing room was no place for a man. The messenger looked at him expectantly, but Ahav waved him off.

We had broken off playing at the Queen's shout, but at a gesture from the King, Dov resumed.

We had barely regained our rhythm when the doors of the Throne Room flew open. In strode Mot, his frayed robes flapping in his haste. Two women dressed in plain linen clothing, their hair uncovered in the Tzidonian style, followed behind him. "Word reached me that the hour has come. I bring the Queen her midwives," he said. "Where may I find her, my King?"

"She is surely already on the birthing stool," the King replied.

"She has her own birthing stool, sent by her father, King Ethbaal, along with these two midwives. They awaited her call in the Queen's quarters as instructed. Why were they not sent for directly?"

Otniel exchanged a shocked look with the other scribe. One did not demand answers from the King in his Throne Room, but Ahav did not appear to notice. "One of our midwives came when she called."

"And took her where?"

"To her quarters, I presume," Ahav said.

"Nay, we came from there." Mot looked around the Throne Room. "Is there another birthing room in the palace?"

The King leapt to his feet at Mot's question, but only stood confused before his throne.

One of the pages stepped forward from behind the scribe's table. "There is another birthing room, my lord, where the maidservants go to birth. Perhaps the Queen was brought there."

"Take me there," Mot commanded, and without another word hurried him from the room. The midwives followed behind.

The King watched them go with a lost look. No one dared approach him as we waited.

Dov led us through one song and the beginning of another. We broke off at the sound of a woman's shriek coming from outside the Throne Room doors.

"What is that scream?" The King asked. "That is not Izevel. Whoever it is, bring her to me."

The door guards left the Throne Room, returning soon after leading Mot and Tamar. The old priest held Tamar's arm above the elbow.

"Let me go, foul priest!" Tamar pulled back, but Mot's grip was of iron.

"What is this?" the King said.

One of the guards answered. "The priest was attempting to drag this midwife out of the palace, my King."

Ahav turned to Mot. "What is the meaning of this?"

"I caught her trying to kill the Queen," Mot replied.

"I tried no such thing," Tamar cried out, yanking her arm free at last. "I brought the Queen to the birthing stool, you saw me yourself, my Lord. If any harm comes to my lady, it will be the fault of this fool. Her hour had arrived when he burst in and dragged me out."

"Ha!" Mot sneered at Tamar. "I harm the Queen? I have been her servant since before she was born."

The King turned from one to the other, mouth agape. His eyes came to rest on Mot. "What makes you think she was trying to kill the Queen?"

"The Queen's midwives awaited her in her chambers. If this woman meant no harm, why did she not bring the Queen to them?"

"What say you?" the King asked Tamar.

"My King," Tamar bowed her head to him, "I came to the servants' quarters to aid one of your maidservants who took ill. I was on my way out of the palace when I heard the Queen's scream for a midwife. I have delivered many babies in the palace and brought her to the birthing stool. I knew nothing of the Queen's own birthing stool or midwives." She threw Mot a venomous look.

The King turned back to Mot. "I hear truth in her words. Why do you not believe her?"

"My lord," Mot bowed his head as well. "My duty is to protect the Queen. A woman is never closer to death than as she brings life into the world." He half-turned to face Tamar. "It is the perfect time for her enemies to strike."

"I am no enemy of my Queen," Tamar said.

"Perhaps," Mot replied. "That was what I intended to find out."

Tamar turned a pleading look on Ahav. "My King, this man violated the birthing room and endangered the Queen's life by pulling me out. It is he who acts as the enemy." She lowered her eyes. "To say nothing of his desire to take me I know not where had your guards not saved me."

"Where were you taking her?" the King asked.

"To learn the truth," Mot replied.

"My Throne Room is the seat of truth in this land." Anger reddened Ahav's face. "If you suspected her of evil, why did you not bring her to me?"

The Throne Room fell silent, but Mot did not reply. No doubt he had more effective ways of learning the truth than anything the King would employ. Though would even his most brutal tools succeed in driving a confession from Tamar?

Finally, Mot broke the silence. "It is as you say, my King: This is the home of truth in Israel. Therefore, I humbly suggest a test." He looked into Tamar's eyes. "You claim to have no ill intent toward your Queen. If so, I am sure you would not object to beseeching her gods for mercy in her moment of trial." His eyes blazed as he rose to his full height and held out a threatening finger. "Take your choice, bow to Baal or Ashera, and I will admit my mistake."

The King asked Tamar, "Will you bow?"

Tamar dropped her eyes to the floor. "Is it the King's will, my Lord, that all of Israel must forsake the Holy One to live in our land?"

Ahav sat back on his throne with a start. "Certainly not."

"If my King does not require it," Tamar said, "I will not bow to foreign gods."

Mot's laugh dripped with mockery. "How many in the Kingdom, my King, would refuse to bow to save their lives? Very few. Very few indeed. Only the ones who are also willing to kill for their god."

Tamar ignored Mot and spoke to Ahav. "Does believing in the One who brought our people up from Egyptian slavery and elevated your father's house to be Kings over Israel, make me a murderer?"

Ahav turned back to Mot. "I will shed no blood on your fancy. The Queen called for help, and this woman ran to her aid. She deserves reward, not death. If you suspect her, you must bring me proof."

"You want proof?" Mot gave his widest grin. "You will find it under her cloak."

"Meaning what?" the King asked.

Mot did not bother answering. He knew he held the attention of the entire Throne Room and Tamar could not escape. "Do you know why I ran to your palace when I heard the Queen's time had come, my King?"

"I do not."

"I have studied the ways of the prophets. They harbor a deep hatred of the gods and our Queen. They do not hesitate to kill to drive Baal from the land. But what can they do?" Mot held up his hands with a shrug. "The King in his wisdom has taken my Lady as his wife. Killing her would not remove Baal nor return the prophets to power. You, my King, would have your revenge, as would my Lord King Ethbaal." He paused and looked the King in the eye. "He would not take the murder of his daughter lightly.

"If these murderous prophets wished to kill our Queen, they are wise enough to make it appear an accident. Any woman, even a queen, can die in childbirth, my King." Mot let his words hang for a moment before he continued. "No one would suspect a midwife of murder. She is the perfect killer—the Queen dies birthing your heir, and none would be the wiser.

"It was I who insisted King Ethbaal send Queen Izevel her own midwives from Tzidon." Mot tapped his chest. "It was I who set watch on her to see if any tried to interfere. It is a good thing for you I did, or else we would now be mourning the death of your wife and child.

"You want proof this woman intended to kill your Queen? I say again, you will find it under her cloak. Search her, and you will find her weapon of murder. If a knife, it will be so small and sharp that none would ever see the cut. If poison, you will find it in a vial."

Mot lifted his accusing finger against Tamar a second time. "Search her now or risk allowing your wife's murderer to go free."

If Tamar was afraid, she did not show it. She threw back her shoulders with a laugh as she addressed the King. "These priests of the Baal care nothing for truth, my King. They trade only in blood and fear. The lives of the innocent matter not at all, so long as those who remain turn toward their abomination."

"My King," Mot said, "I have presented two proofs. These prophets would sooner die than bow to the god of another, that is why I will be satisfied if she humbles herself before my god. If the law of the land does not allow for such a trial, let her be searched. Surely you cannot object to the search of a woman who would spill the blood of your Queen?"

The King turned back and forth between them, but before he could reply, Tamar spoke. "This man speaks of murder?" She gestured to Mot's robes in disgust. "For months, his priests and their henchmen have spilled the blood of the prophets like water along the whole length of the land, and he dares use that word?" Tamar paced, stepping behind Mot toward the King's side of the aisle. "Now that there are no true prophets left, he wishes you to fear shadows." She spun on the last word, pointing back at Mot.

"Another proof, my lord," Mot called out. "I ask you, oh wise King, are these the words of a midwife?"

Tamar ignored Mot's interruption, striding behind him once again, directly toward me. "I have done nothing. Nothing but run to the aid of my lady, your Queen, yet this priest," she spat out the word as if it had a bitter taste, "will gladly give my life to bring you under his sway. Do you think my death will satisfy him? No, my King, the priests of the Baal know well that they rule only through fear. Without it, they have no power."

I expected Tamar to turn again, to pace back toward the King, but she kept coming toward me. "If you condemn me, who will be next? It could be any of us." She spoke now to the commoners, huddled together against the wall. "Anyone who refuses to bow before them could die. My King, the servants of the Baal care not whose blood they spill so long as it feeds your fear. The prophets, a soldier in your army, the scribes of your Court, or even this boy."

Tamar threw out her hand with the last word, leveling her finger directly at me. She was close enough to touch, and as her arm extended, I saw something hidden in the fold at the bottom of her sleeve. It was the tiny vial she brought out to Ovadia months earlier when suggesting Ahba's death. In a flash, I realized she meant to pass the poison to me, but how to get it? If I reached out to her, all my secrecy would vanish. She placed her hands on my shoulders. "I ask you, does this fair youth deserve to die so that their fear may rule us?" Her hand drifted toward the collar of my tunic.

"Stop her!" Mot screamed out and ran toward the musicians. Tamar's body blocked his view, but all of Tamar's power over the hearts of men held no influence over him. Mot didn't need to see, his intuitions were right, and he knew it.

Tamar's hand dropped away from my shoulder, and the vial disappeared up her sleeve. "Stop me from what?"

"From passing your knife. You claim to protect the innocent? You would hand a boy a murder weapon and let him die in your place?"

"You are the only murderer in this room." Tamar's eyes held the same fire as Eliyahu's as she stared down Mot, then the fire extinguished as she turned back to Ahav. "My King, this man cares nothing for our laws. He wished to drag me from before your justice and kill me away from your watchful eyes.

If not for your faithful guards, my blood might already stain his altar. Another offering to his angry god."

She lifted her hands again. "You, my King, were appointed by the Holy One to uphold justice in Israel. This idolater offers no witnesses, brings no evidence, only declares his thirst for my blood, and seeks for me to bow to his god in exchange for my life. Do not make this day of rejoicing, the day your first child enters the world, into the day when the nation is given over to the justice of the Baal."

Ahav looked around the Throne Room. Scribes, commoners, guards, and pages all stared at him. I had heard case after case come before the King over the past year and had learned the law of the land from his lips. The law was clear in matters of life and death—two witnesses were required to prove guilt.

Tamar had spoken well. Too well. Mot spoke the truth when he said her words were not those of a midwife, and Ahav knew it. Tamar had abandoned her power to bend men's eyes as she rose to meet Mot's challenge. Now she stood before the King as she truly was, a woman of strength, a prophetess unmasked.

"Search her," the King said, and two guards jumped to obey. "If she is innocent, she has nothing to hide."

"I have nothing to hide, my King." She wrapped her arms across her chest, holding her robe tight. "But I do have something to protect—the dignity of a woman of Israel. Is there no woman who can search me?"

"The midwives from Tzidon may search her, my Lord," Mot said.

"Nay," Tamar said, "they would shed no more tears over my blood than you, priest, and perhaps you have already given them a weapon you intend them to find?"

"No matter." Mot smiled as he scented his prey. "Let the King's guards search them first—they will not hide behind their modesty."

"You see, my King, how little he cares for any but himself? He would take the very midwives away from the Queen only to find the innocent guilty."

"No assistance will be taken from the Queen," the King said. "Fetch two maidservants."

A page ran out and soon returned leading two maidservants, who blushed before the stares of the Throne Room. They bowed to the King as they approached his throne. "Take this woman and search her thoroughly," the King said. "Whatever you find, bring to me. Guard, go with them and watch the door against her escape."

Had Mot or his servants searched Tamar, they would surely find the poison, but I had little doubt Tamar could hide her secrets from two ordinary maidservants. Before long they returned, and one of the maidservants held the tiny vial aloft. "We found only this, my King."

Ahav looked at Tamar. "What is in this vial?"

"A tincture that eases the pain of birth, my Lord." Tamar bowed her head as she replied.

"May I?" Mot took the vial from the maidservant's hand. He released the stop and took a cautious sniff. "Oh yes, one who takes this potion will feel no more pain. Ever."

"You claim it is poison?" the King asked.

"Poison, my King, without question. Particularly deadly. If you still doubt my wisdom, there is a simple test." Mot pointed at Tamar. "Let her drink it now. If it is as she claims, no harm will come. If not, then let the death she intended for the Queen fall upon her own head." Mot's face broke into a grin—he had won his game.

Tamar opened her mouth to protest, but the King spoke first. "Drink."

She took the vial and raised it to her lips, but Mot stopped her. "I want to see it pour out," he said. "Every drop."

She held the clay vessel above her mouth and tipped it back. One, two, three slow drops fell. Tamar closed her mouth before the third drop hit her tongue, and it landed upon her lips. She wiped her mouth with her sleeve before any could stop her and her face contorted. "The taste is foul, it is true, but there is no greater remedy for pain."

"You spilled it out!" Mot screamed. "She must have emptied it with the maidservants, my King. We can still find it. It will be on the stones or even on her clothing. I know the smell; I will find it." He sniffed at Tamar like a dog on a scent.

"Look on the ground if you must," the King said, "but leave her unmolested." He motioned to one of the guards. "See that she remains until we know what effect the drops have."

All eyes were on Tamar, who stood calmly, arms at her side. Only the training she had given me allowed me to see her suppressed pain. Mot searched the ground, scrambling around Tamar's feet, then worked his way up the aisle of the Throne Room, sniffing for signs of the poison. He had almost reached the great oak doors when they flew wide.

"Twins!" Ovadia declared as he strode into the room. "My King, you have been blessed with a son and a daughter. Two nations came forth from your loins on the same day. The midwives say the Queen and your children are well. You may visit them now, my King."

The King stood from his throne as the room filled with music and cheering. It was only after the guards closed the doors behind him that I remembered Tamar. I searched the room, but she was gone. Mot stood alone before the King's empty throne, his face black with rage.

Covenants

Mot struck three blows upon the solid oak door.

"Who knocks?" Gershon, the High Priest of Israel, called out.

"A humble servant of the Queen."

There was a sound of shuffling within, and the door opened a crack. "I do not often receive priests of the Baal." Gershon failed to keep the tremble from his voice. "The Queen sent you?"

Mot sneered. "The Queen sends me nowhere. May I come in?"

Gershon took a half-step back, and Mot slipped through the doorway. "Cold evening," he said. "Cold and dry."

Gershon closed the door, but he stepped no further into the room. "I already told the Queen I will not fake the ceremony."

"Yes, I know." Mot drew back his hood, showing the delight in his eye. "A brave decision, though perhaps a foolish one. I would not wish to be the one to draw the blood of Izevel's firstborn son. But let the Queen devise her own revenge. I come not to obstruct, only to understand. May I sit?" Mot gave his widest, gap-toothed grin until Gershon gestured to a chair.

"What do you wish to understand? The circumcision?"

Mot sniffed and shook his head. "That seems simple enough. We too offer blood to Baal."

Gershon laughed, though his voice remained strained. "This is no blood offering. It is the sealing of a covenant."

Mot sat up at his words. "A covenant? Nonsense. A covenant has two sides. You may bind the child to your god by spilling his blood, but the gods do not bind themselves to us."

Gershon shook his head. "You do not understand at all."

Mot leaned forward and placed his hands flat on the table. "Precisely. I have spent weeks pouring over your ancient scrolls, trying to grasp the covenant of your patriarch Abraham, but it makes no sense to me. How can man bind the gods? Why would they consent?" He locked eyes with the priest of Israel. "That is why I am here. Teach me."

Confusion clouded Gershon's face. "I? Teach you? To what end?"

Mot sat back and placed his hands upon his chest. "If we are to be neighbors in this land, should we not seek to understand one another?"

"Neighbors? Is that how you see us?"

"For now, yes. Let the gods battle for dominion. I seek only understanding."

"Understanding of what?"

Mot's voice dropped. "I wish to understand the power of your god in this land."

Gershon frowned. "So that you can break the people's connection to the Holy One?"

A hungry light filled Mot's eyes. "I seek knowledge, nothing more."

"For my part, I understand your god all too well," Gershon said. "You give blood in exchange for fear." Gershon raised an accusing finger. "You do not share your secrets, why should I help you?"

"Fear?" Mot spread his hands wide. "Surely you do not fear an old man?" He gave a predatory smile. "As for secrets, it is true I have amassed much knowledge I have never shared, but only because so few come to ask." Mot bowed his head, his hands still outstretched. "I lay my secrets at your feet. Ask what you will. I am in no hurry. I will satisfy your questions, then seek answers to my own."

Gershon stood silent, disarmed by Mot's approach. Finally, he shrugged. "I have no questions for you other than why you seek me out."

"If you will be so kind as to hear my questions, perhaps your answer will become clear."

Gershon tipped his head, and Mot leaned in toward the High Priest. "Why does your covenant depend on cutting the foreskin?"

"It is the one part of the body whose purpose is to be removed."

"So it is a flaw?"

"Hardly." Gershon laughed. "Thus man was created, and no flawed work comes from the Holy One's hands."

Confusion knit Mot's brow. "If it is destined to be removed, it is unnecessary, which makes the work of your god imperfect."

"Only one who worships the works of their own hands would speak so." Gershon's face shone with a sudden likeness of his father. "The Holy One left the body incomplete so we could become partners in our creation."

"Partners?" Now it was Mot's turn to laugh. "We have nothing to give the gods but our devotion. They require nothing from us."

"Then why create the world?" Gershon asked.

"Why?" Mot hesitated. It was a question he had never asked. "The world has always been. The gods shaped it according to their will."

"Our Torah teaches that the Holy One brought forth creation out of nothing. For a purpose." Gershon leaned toward Mot. "In your eyes, whose creations are greater—those of your gods or those of man?"

"The gods of course."

"Oh? What do you consider greater, barley or bread?"

Mot sneered. "Don't think that because we can act upon their creations, that our actions matter to them."

"So you believe their creation is perfect?" Gershon asked.

"Indeed." Mot held out an open hand. "When the gods are appeased, their world provides us all we need. Should we be foolish enough to anger

them," he clenched his hand into a fist, "we will suffer and die. Do not tell me you believe your god created an imperfect world?"

"Not imperfect, incomplete. Such was the will of the Holy One."

"To what end?" Mot asked. "That the merit of your work ease your suffering in the underworld?"

Gershon's face glowed as he replied, "To make this world a place of growth, a place where we can perfect ourselves."

"You believe the world was created for your sake?"

"Indeed."

Mot shook his head. "Now the drought comes to punish you for angering your god?"

"It was Eliyahu, not the Holy One, who grew angry."

"A man alone cannot stop the rains," Mot said.

"No, not alone. This is the power of the covenant—we too bring the world into being through our actions."

"Even actions that bind your god?" Mot asked.

Gershon nodded. "Even to bind the Holy One."

Mot pushed himself to his feet. "I need to find myself a true prophet."

"A true prophet?" Gershon asked.

"Yes, a true prophet, like your father." Mot's eyes flashed as Gershon went pale. "Yes, I know who you are, Gershon ben Uriel. Be glad the Queen does not." Mot laughed. "Not that it still matters. Your father long ago gave his life for his god." His words landed like blows. "You spout the same rubbish I have heard from Elad and the others who left the prophets for Baal. I can't accept a word of it."

"These are our beliefs," Gershon stuttered as he struggled to regain his calm.

"No, it is clear they are not," Mot rose and turned toward the door.

"Why do you say this?" Gershon asked.

"Elad would lick the dust from my sandals if I said Baal willed it, and twenty more who once worshipped your Holy One would come behind

him to take their turn. Yet, mighty Baal cares little for their devotion. Could a man leave a true covenant for this?"

Gershon nodded. "It is sad, but many have been drawn after the illusion of power—"

"Do not speak to me of illusions." Mot slammed his fist on the wooden table. "You are no different, you who bows before the Golden Calf."

Gershon's face went white again.

"I seek a true prophet, one who knows of the Holy One's full power. Instead, I find only cowards like yourself and Elad. I believe nothing you say."

Gershon set his jaw. "A coward, am I?"

"You disagree? There is an easy proof. I see that dagger hidden beneath your cloak. Am I not an enemy of your god? Do your scriptures not say to strike me down? Do it." Mot raised his arms, exposing his body to Gershon.

The High Priest did not move.

"Come," he goaded. "I am an old man and unarmed. You can dispose of me easily."

Gershon's hands trembled.

Mot dropped his arms and spat on the stone floor. "Bah, you see? A coward, as I said. Surely not your father's son. He, I promise you, would have no such qualms." Mot rose to his full height, and a threatening light filled his eyes. "Nor do I."

Gershon gave a bitter smile at the tiny old man. "You mean to strike me down then?" He pulled out the dagger and placed it on the table between them. "Go ahead, take it. Am I not an enemy of your god?"

Mot stared at him in scorn. "You? An enemy?" Mot laughed as he stepped toward the door. "You are too insignificant to be an enemy of mighty Baal. Indeed, I consider you an ally. By the time Yambalya arrived in Israel, you had already taught the people to compromise their covenant. My priest had only to finish the task."

Mot stepped out of the house, back into the cold night, not bothering to close the door behind him.

"You think it was murder?" Izevel lay in the center of her large wooden bed, swaddled in furs. Her linen robe and youthful beauty contrasted with the rasp in her voice as she pronounced the last word.

"I am certain of it, my Queen," Mot replied.

"You did not catch this woman?"

Mot's hands clenched. "I had her, but she slipped through my fingers."

"You believe she was a prophetess?" When Mot nodded, Izevel fell back on her pillows. "How did one of the prophets enter our palace?"

"Our watch has not been as tight as it must be. This is the price of your King allowing the lowly of the land entrance to his Throne Room. In your father's palace, there could never be such a breach without the help of a conspirator inside the gates."

"You do not believe there was a conspirator here?"

Mot paced. "I am not certain. It's possible she acted alone. But she needed to do more than gain access to the Throne Room, which any commoner can do. She needed to wait in the palace, perhaps for days, until your moment came. She needed to know the instant you were in need and reach you before your midwives could arrive. A conspirator would be invaluable for such a plot."

She sat up in bed, eyes blazing. "Who would dare?"

The old priest looked closely at the Queen. "Who indeed? Is there no one in your palace loyal enough to the Holy One to desire your death? Someone who knows all of the secrets of the palace, who could hide the prophetess, and alert her at the proper moment?"

"Ovadia?" There was a note of doubt in her voice.

"If you are certain, he dies tonight." Mot turned as if to go.

"Wait!" She held out her hand, and he paused. "You would dare strike the King's steward?"

"There is nothing I would not dare, my lady." His lip rose in a sneer. "What is a steward or his King before Baal?"

"We must be certain first."

"Why? If there is even a chance he plots against you, better to remove him from your midst."

Izevel motioned him closer and dropped her voice. "You do not understand his power."

"What is there to understand?" asked Mot. "If he is so powerful, then all the more reason to eliminate him now before he discovers we suspect him."

"You do not know his hold on Ahav. The King relies on him with total faith."

He looked at her huddled among the covers. "You boasted that you hold the King's will in your hands."

She flushed but did not shrink. "So I do, but not entirely. Not yet." She smoothed her black hair over her shoulders. "Ovadia's loyalty is an absolute truth to Ahav. We cannot move against him without cause, or we risk awakening the King's opposition."

"Your father did not send me here only to leave a snake among us."

"Leave him? I have no such intention." Her smile was warmer than his but no less cunning. "What we need is proof. Or something which looks like it. I will shake my husband's trust in Ovadia, then he can die like any other."

"So we must put our eyes on Ovadia. How do you hope to watch him?"

"I will find a way." Her eyes narrowed. "What of this prophetess?"

Mot smiled at the hint of fear in her voice. "I am certain she is still in the city, and I have placed a watch at the gate. If she still lives, we will find her, my Queen."

"Do so." She settled deeper into her furs. "Ovadia is the one arranging the brit milah. Perhaps I should stop it?"

"No," Mot shook his head. "From what I have learned, your son will never rule without entering their covenant. Besides, the ceremony will show us exactly who remains loyal to their Holy One."

"What if seeing us bow to this covenant, the people's hearts return to their god? This could undermine our progress."

Mot's smile grew darker than hers. "Have no fear, my Queen. I have a plan."

The refining pot is for silver, and the furnace for gold; but the Holy One tries the heart.
Proverbs 17:3

16

Mercy to the Cruel

Batya emerged from Tamar's quarters holding an empty cup of the tincture that had boiled over the hearth for a week. "She wishes to speak to you," she said to me. "Go now while she can speak."

I had never been in Tamar's room, and I ducked to avoid hitting my head on the low ceiling as I entered. Tamar lay on the floor, covered in skins, but trembling with fever.

She opened her eyes and looked into mine. "I am sorry, Lev."

"Sorry? For what?"

"It was foolish to try to pass you the poison. I ruined your disguise."

"No one realized," I said.

"Do not be so sure. Beware of Mot. His eyes are open."

"So it was true? You tried to kill Izevel?"

Tamar nodded. "I could have succeeded."

"But for Mot?"

She shook her head. "I could have given Izevel the poison right away, told her it was for the pain. She would have taken it."

"Why didn't you?"

"I couldn't bring myself to kill the b-babies," she stammered. "I thought to wait until they were born."

"You had mercy on them," I said.

Her eyes burned with a feverish light. "Mercy, yes. Those who show mercy to the cruel, bring cruelty upon the merciful. They are babies now, but they will grow, and under the tutelage of Izevel, there is no telling what evil they will bring upon the land."

"You cannot know that." I recalled Uriel's response to Pinchas.

"Had I killed Izevel, I may have brought this war to an end. I spared the mother to save the children, and now it will continue. More prophets will die because I stayed my hand."

Uriel would have known how to respond, but I didn't. "Is that why you called me in, to ask my forgiveness? I give it to you fully."

"No, Lev, that's not why I called you." She winced and struggled to sit. "There's something I must tell you while I still can."

"What is that?"

"Do not despair." Tamar's eyes locked on mine. "You are never alone. The Holy One watches over you. Help will come when you need it most."

That's when I knew Tamar was leaving me as my parents left me, as Shimon left me, as Uriel was sure to leave me soon.

She closed her eyes. "Go now. I must rest."

I closed the door to Tamar's quarters behind me just as Ovadia came storming into the house, his face a deep red.

Batya dropped her dough when she saw her husband's face. "What's happened?"

"Izevel's done it."

"Done what?" Batya asked.

"I've been growing suspicious for days," Ovadia said. "There have been no instructions from her other than to prepare for the *brit milah*. It was unlike her, but at first, I thought she was just recovering from the birth, or perhaps had grown cautious due to Tamar's attempt on her life. But I feared that she was planning something, and I was right."

"What's she planning?" I asked.

"The Queen just announced a celebration for her daughter's naming."

"Won't the daughter be named together with her son tomorrow at the *brit milah*?" Batya said.

"That's what we all assumed, but Izevel has other plans. I should have known." Ovadia shook his head. "Her daughter will have her own celebration, led by Zarisha."

"The King agreed to this?" Batya asked.

"What could he say to a wife who gave him twins, and who is accepting the *brit milah* against her will?"

"When will it be?" Batya asked.

"Tonight."

"Tonight?" I said, "but that will—"

"Undermine the *brit milah*. I know, the timing is perfect. The *brit* is called for dawn tomorrow, so all of Israel that comes to celebrate will arrive by this evening. Izevel and Zarisha will treat them to a night before Ashera, and then they will drag themselves to the *brit*."

Ovadia put a hand on my shoulder. "I mostly came to find you, Lev. Dov will be looking for you. It's best if he finds you in the musicians' quarters."

I shook my head. "He's given me the morning off. We are to meet at midday outside the gates for our last rehearsal."

"Not anymore. Izevel wants her festival to outshine the *brit*. She will expect all of you to play before Ashera tonight, and to play perfectly. Dov will be frantic to get the music right."

I arrived back at the musicians' quarters just before Dov burst in. "Rehearsal, now! You, too." He kicked Betzalel awake. "We need everyone tonight. Meet outside the gates as soon as you can."

We practiced until the sun hung above the western horizon, but the music was still a mess. Visiting musicians kept arriving during rehearsal, undermining our minimal progress. In a last desperate act, Dov told Zim to lead the musicians during the ceremony, knowing that he had played for her before.

I had never seen Shomron in such chaos. A company of soldiers guarded the gates, which would remain open through the night to receive the numbers of people pouring into the city. The requirement to hold the *brit milah* on the eighth day meant that many of those arriving had not made arrangements for where to sleep, but Izevel's all-night festival made such provisions unnecessary. The travelers simply brought their donkeys and packs with them to the festivities.

When I first played before Ashera, there were twenty priestesses, mainly from Tzidon. Now there were over a hundred crimson-clad women and girls filling the clearing, and I could hear from their chatter that most of the recruits were daughters of Israel. Day faded, and Zarisha signaled to Zim to strike up the first rhythm. Younger priestesses climbed onto the shoulders of the taller ones to drape the tree with swaths of crimson cloth. They wove the decorations between the bright green leaves which hung heavy and full. The Ashera was not cracked and dried like the other trees in Shomron.

Once again, the tree transformed before my eyes. Jewelry glistened off its branches, reflecting the firelight, fabrics hung like braids of woven hair, and carved wooden breasts were hoisted against the trunk. Clouds of incense filled the clearing as the priestesses bowed before the tree, obscuring my vision enough to make the apparition appear real. The tree became a woman, mighty and awesome.

A shofar blast stilled Zim's drum, and the crowd parted as soldiers pushed their way into the clearing. Led by two torchbearers, the King and Queen entered, with Izevel cradling a baby to her chest. Zarisha reached in, took the child from her bundle of blankets, and held her up naked, so all could glimpse the week-old princess. The crowd roared in approval, and the baby wailed.

Zarisha dipped her finger into a jar of date honey and smeared it onto one of the wooden nipples of the Ashera tree. She took more honey and placed her finger in the baby's mouth. The child stopped screaming, pacified by the sweet syrup. Zarisha brought her to the trunk, slipped her finger from the child's mouth, and, before she could cry again, inserted the honey coated wooden nipple instead. The priestesses let out ringing ululations as their new sister nursed from their goddess.

The baby's scream once more hushed the crowd as she was pulled away from the tree and wrapped in a tiny, crimson robe. Zarisha held her aloft and yelled out, "I give you all Atalya, Princess of Israel."

This time, the crowd's cheer drowned out even the child's cry. Atalya was passed back to her mother, and then quickly on to a wet nurse, who eased the baby back to sleep. Zarisha waved to the musicians, and we dove into a fast-paced melody. Dov took back control from Zim and led us in a song we already knew from the royal wedding. Later in the night, no one would notice if we stumbled over the new tunes we had practiced that afternoon.

Every *brit milah* was also a sacred feast, and Izevel had no intention of allowing her ceremony to be outdone. Servants spread through the crowd carrying trays of roasted meat, bread, and wine. The quantities of food flowing from the roasting pits surpassed anything I had seen since the wedding. The crowd grabbed at the food. Was this why so many had poured into Shomron for the celebration? Had the promise of meat drawn them at a time when the shadow of hunger grew at home?

As the festival progressed, revelers again disappeared with priestesses into the darkness beyond the firelight. I kept my eyes down and focused on my fellow musicians. Master Dov smiled at me, taking my focus as an expression of devotion to my task. Little did he know I could not allow myself to look at the crowd. We played our wedding songs twice and had just begun a new melody when movement at the corner of my eye caught my attention.

A young priestess bore a clay goblet of wine. For some reason, she ignored the other musicians, even Betzalel, who extended a hand toward the goblet as she passed. Usually, only Zim received such personal attention, but the priestess stopped in front of me, cup outstretched. "Drink," she said.

A blush rose to my face, and I shook my head as I lifted my kinnor, my fingers never slowing.

She nodded but did not lower the cup. "Even a musician must drink." She gave an innocent smile. "What is your name?"

"Lev."

"Lev." I felt a flush of heat as she said my name. "I am Dinah. Drink, Lev. When you finish, I'll bring you more."

"Thank you, Dinah," I said and nodded for her to put the goblet by my feet. Once she left, I could spill out a bit of the wine so she would think I had accepted her gift. But Dinah didn't leave, she only raised the cup to my lips.

The smell of wine filled my nostrils as I examined her over the top of the goblet. She must have only just come of age. Her cheeks were smooth, her eyes big and brown. She was trembling. "How long have you been a priestess?" I asked.

"Two weeks." She dropped her eyes. "This is my first festival."

I peeked below the goblet to take in the rest of her. She blushed but did not shrink from my gaze. Her crimson robes could not hide her narrow frame. Her arms were bone thin, and her sash was tied tightly around a slim waist. "The drought?" I asked.

Tears welled in her eyes as she nodded. "My parents had no other choice. They could not feed both me and my younger brother." She pushed the goblet against my lower lip. "Please drink."

Normally there was safety in my appearing so young and innocent. Most priestesses looked right past me because I was hardly a man at all. This was what drew Dinah toward me, for she was hardly a woman herself. The cup trembled against my lip as she held my eye. We came to a pause in the melody, and I bent my head to the goblet. She tipped the strong wine into my mouth, and I downed a quarter of the cup before pulling away. "Thank you, Dinah. That is all I want."

Dinah set the goblet by my feet and placed a soft hand on my arm. "I will return soon to see if you want more. Lev." She said my name as if it were a plea, then turned to walk away, avoiding the eyes of the men she passed.

Once the meat and wine had made their way through the crowd, the dancing began in earnest. Our music rose with the energy of the festival. After a few songs, Zim's drumming dropped away when a priestess pulled him into the dancing. Dov scoffed, but Zim took no notice. He was the first musician to leave his post, but he would not be the last. Dov had drawn every musician in Shomron together for the celebration. We had a full company playing, including two visiting musicians who arrived during the festival itself. None of us would be missed.

Dinah still circulated with a wineskin, one of the few priestesses not dancing. Soon she returned as promised, and, noticing my still full goblet, brought it to my lips and tipped it back until I drowned it to the dregs. She refilled the cup and again disappeared.

As the wine took hold, a looseness infused my music with energy and passion. I reached down and took another deep draught from the goblet at my feet, enjoying the strength of the wine. With Zim gone, my kinnor drove the music forward. I looked for him, but both he and the priestess had disappeared.

I drained the second goblet on my own, and Dinah, true to her word, appeared out of the trees at the edge of the clearing and refilled it. This time she lingered, swaying with the rhythms flowing off my kinnor. As I watched her dance, I wondered how many girls were like Dinah, pressed into serving Ashera by the drought itself? How many more would there be before the drought came to an end?

She gave me one last smile, then disappeared back into the trees. How much longer could she continue to hide? Hesitant as she was now, a year from now would she not be like the other priestesses, full-bodied from a steady flow of food, and resigned to her duties?

The remaining dancers circled wildly around the trunk. Would any of us even be alive a year from now? In all this desperate crowd, only I had seen the stubborn fire in Eliyahu's eyes. Looking out through the cloud of incense, I was stabbed by the realization that he would never relent. How much longer could the land sustain itself without rain? Even if the land could hold out, would Ovadia? The price of grain was rising steadily now that another winter had arrived with no sign of rain. More than eighty prophets crowded the Cave of Dotan. Where would he get the grain to feed them for another year?

Could Ovadia himself even hope to survive that long? Izevel hated him for refusing to bow before her gods. He said that only the King's favor kept him alive, but that had been a year ago when Izevel was still a bride. Now she had born the King a son. A son brought the promise of stability to the Kingdom, allowing the crown to pass from one King to the next without war. She had crushed the prophets and was strong enough to move against Ovadia. She wouldn't even need the King's consent; her soldiers could ambush him on one of his many journeys outside of Shomron. Or she could arrange for him to die in his bed like Yishai ben Avraham.

With Ovadia gone, there would be no hope for the prophets. What would become of me? Last time I played before Ashera, Tamar had shamed me afterward. Now Tamar would never shame me, nor anyone else, ever again. Who would know or care what I did?

I knew these thoughts were the wine speaking, but that didn't make them less true. Uncle Menachem often said, 'when wine goes in, secrets come out.' The wine helped me see what I had known for months but didn't want to face. We were fighting a losing battle. Tamar lay on her deathbed, and it wouldn't be long before Ovadia and the prophets followed. I was the safest of them all. I could remain a palace musician, eating from the King's bread until that too ran out and we all perished.

Powerful drum beats lifted the rhythm from behind me. Zim had returned, and his drum raised the intensity of the music. The air hung thick with incense and sweat as people danced. I drained my third goblet, and my head spun. In an instant, Dinah appeared at my elbow, but this time she held no wineskin.

She placed her hand on my arm again, feeling my muscles tighten as I plucked the strings of my kinnor. Her other hand found the back of my neck, rubbing away the tension. My heart burned with desire. The hand on my arm moved down until it found my fingers, pulling them away from the strings. My kinnor fell silent, and she spoke into my ear, "Come, Lev."

I staggered to my feet, and her arm found my waist, bringing me balance. I left my kinnor beside Zim, who sent me off with a wink. In the world of Ashera there was no shame, only pleasure.

We walked away from the dancing, to where we could be alone. Dinah kept her hand around my waist, but once we left the firelight, I was the one supporting her. She'd been forced into a role she did not want, but with my help, at least this first festival would be on her terms. We were sheltered among the trees now, and I heard a voice in the darkness say, *"Don't do this, Lev."*

It was not the first voice I had ever heard. Twice during my first year alone with the flock, when I felt the approach of danger, I heard my uncle's voice repeating instructions he had given me months earlier. And the year before, when my aunt sent me away from home, had I not seen my master's face calling to me?

The voice fought against the clouds covering my heart. It was as if my master, lying blind in a cave, saw the path I walked and reached out to rescue me. But the voice was not Uriel's, it was Yonaton's. I had not thought of Yonaton since I returned to Shomron, and the very image of him tugged at my heart. He was stronger than I, more pure. He would have resisted Dinah's advances. He would have pushed on with the prophets until the end, even if he knew it was a losing battle.

Dinah's arm slipped from my waist and turned to face me. I smelled the incense in her hair. Yonaton's voice echoed through my head, and again, I heard, *"Lev, don't do this."* The voice came stronger now, almost in my ear, but I pushed it away as I stepped into Dinah's embrace. Tamar was dying, Dahlia beyond my reach. Soon Ovadia and my master would perish as well. Even my position in the palace would not save me from the devastation to come. Nothing remained to protect.

Dinah's hair brushed my face as I closed my eyes. At that moment, a hand grasped my shoulder and spun me around. I gaped in confusion as Yonaton said one last time, "Lev, don't do this."

He looked older than I remembered, with a tuft of hair sprouting from the tip of his chin. But his eyes were the same, peering into mine with strength and understanding. My feet found their balance, and, standing straighter, I turned back to Dinah. She stepped back, her face a mix of anger and relief. "Will you at least wait with me a little while, Lev? So the priestesses think…"

"Of course," I said. Dinah looked so frail, standing in the darkness in a crimson dress too loose for her. Tonight, I would stay with her, but Dinah's innocence wouldn't last. She had not chosen the path of Ashera, but she would walk it in the end.

Despite this, I felt a surge of hope. Yonaton was back. Yonaton would never resign himself to accepting the Baal or Ashera. Just seeing him bolstered my strength. Tamar was right—when I needed help most, it appeared. Even if we were fighting a losing battle, at least now I would not fight alone.

"What are you doing here?" I asked once my shock passed.

"I told you I would return when I came of age," Yonaton replied.

"You came of age months ago."

"True, but there was too much work to do at home. We watered the crops by hand all last winter. Since then, we've been digging cisterns and storage for our grain."

I felt a stab of guilt. We had both known of the drought from the beginning, but while Yonaton prepared his family, I refused to even tell mine. "You saved the barley crop?"

"The winter wheat as well."

"Must have been a tremendous amount of work."

"It was. Both donkeys carried water non-stop," he said, and I caught the reference to Uriel's old donkey Balaam, which Yonaton brought back to his farm.

"What are you doing here now?"

"When I received the message from Dov calling for musicians to come for the *brit milah*, I knew it was time to return. There will be no more planting until the rains return, and as long as I remain at home, I am another mouth to feed. The journey to Shomron took longer than I expected, and I arrived just in time to see…" Yonaton didn't finish his sentence, just gestured with his head toward Dinah, who shrunk further into the shadows.

I burned with embarrassment, and Dinah took this as her cue to speak. "We can go back now," she said, her eyes on the ground.

I walked back to the clearing at her side. She waited long enough for us to be seen returning together, then disappeared into the dancing. Zim gave me a knowing grin as I picked up my kinnor. Then he noticed my companion.

"Yonaton!" he yelled and rose to wrap him in an embrace. Yonaton's face shone as he hugged Zim back.

As Ovadia feared, the crowd assembled before dawn outside the city gates was bleary-eyed from reveling before the Ashera. Zim and a few other musicians had slipped off at the end of the all-night festival, but one new musician joined our ranks for the *brit milah*.

"Daniel!" I cried, and ran up to embrace him.

He gave me a weak hug and smoothed his long beard with two hands as we faced each other. "I wondered if I'd see you and Yonaton here."

I knew Master Dov sent notices far and wide calling for musicians to gather in Shomron, but somehow I hadn't anticipated seeing either Daniel or Yonaton. "You weren't at the festival last night," I said.

"I came to play for the ceremony of the covenant. Copper is always a boon, especially in times of drought. But I won't play before Ashera, not for any amount of silver." He intended his words to sting, and I understood the coolness of his embrace. Daniel would be proud if he knew the truth, as my aunt had been, but this time I held my tongue. The fewer who knew our secret, the better.

Dov struck the opening notes of the melody we had practiced for the ceremony. I fell in with him, and the others followed right behind. We passed through an entire round of the song, and my eyelids drooped from the slow pace of the music. I fixed my eyes on Master Dov, not wanting to miss a cue in my exhaustion.

I didn't even notice the King and Queen as they came out of the gate with their son, but I saw Dov signal for a halt. I silenced my strings with an open hand and the deep voice of Gershon the High Priest rang out over the crowd. "In the beginning days of Israel, the Holy One made a covenant with our father Abraham, commanding him to remove the foreskin from himself and every male of his household." Tall like his father, Gershon stood a head above the King and Queen. "Since then, it has been the duty of every father in Israel to circumcise his son on the eighth day of his life, marking his flesh with the sign of the covenant and binding him to the people and the Holy One." Gershon turned to Ahav. "My King, will you perform the circumcision yourself, or do you appoint me in your stead?"

Silence fell over the crowd as Ahav hesitated. He looked at his son, sleeping in the Queen's arms, and then he scanned the faces of the crowd. Izevel inclined her head toward the High Priest, but Ahav ignored the gesture. His eyes flitted across the crowd until they came to rest on Ovadia, who gave the slightest of nods. Izevel's eyes burned at their wordless communication.

"I will enter my son into the covenant with my own hands." Ahav stepped forward.

Gershon's tense brow relaxed. "The Holy One said to Abraham, 'Walk before me and be perfect.' Wasn't all of the Holy One's creation already perfect? The answer is no. The Holy One created man incomplete, and gave the covenant to our fathers so Israel could live our destiny as co-creators in this world." Gershon handed Ahav a small, sharp knife. "The child before you today was not born perfect, but his father will complete his creation with the removal of the foreskin, bringing him into the covenant the Holy One sealed with Abraham."

Izevel did not bother to conceal her sneer at the idea of her son's imperfection. If he lacked anything in her eyes, it was only the training she and her priests would supply. But this covenant held the key to her son one day ruling over Israel, so she could do nothing to stop it.

Gershon took the boy and sat on a special chair prepared for the occasion, holding the baby tight. Ahav glanced toward Izevel, without quite meeting her eyes, then declared, "I now bring my son into the covenant of our father Abraham, as commanded by the Holy One of Israel." He bent forward over Gershon's lap and made a quick motion. The baby's cry pierced the morning.

The High Priest pressed a clean cloth to the cut. "May the One who blessed our fathers Abraham, Isaac, and Jacob bless this tender child. His name shall be called in Israel…?"

Ahav whispered in the priest's ear.

"Ahazya ben Ahav, Prince of Israel."

A cheer rose from the crowd, but not from Izevel. She took her son back in her arms and returned to the palace. She would not stay for the celebration, nor did she attempt to hide her rage.

The next day, the morning meal for the palace servants included roasted meat. This was not generosity on the King's part but a testament to the success of Queen Izevel's plan. Zarisha's ceremony reduced the crowd at the *brit milah,* and those that came failed to consume all the prepared foods, even during this time of drought. I arrived at the kitchen early to hear the morning gossip, but all I heard was that the Queen had not emerged from her quarters once since the *brit milah*.

I kept helping myself to more meat, even as the shifts of servants in the kitchen changed, for anything not consumed now would spoil. I was reaching for my fifth piece when three trumpet blasts sounded in the hall. "That can't be the call for Court already." Tuval jumped to his feet. "It's far too early."

Otniel, the only other person still in the kitchen, said, "It is not for us to determine what time Court begins. Our task is to be ready when the call comes." As he already wore his scribe's garments, he headed straight for his writing table. Tuval and I threw on our musicians' uniforms and ran out after him.

In the hallway, all was chaos. Tuval and I just managed to duck into the Throne Room before the doors shut behind us. Dov and Peretz were due to play with us, but neither took their morning meal in the kitchen and would not arrive at the palace for some time. The musicians were not the only ones left short by the sudden announcement. Otniel was the only scribe at his table, and there were no pages in position behind the thrones. Two heavy knocks sounded against the door, and Tuval and I struck up our music.

All stood as the doors opened, and the Queen marched in alone. Normally, she walked straight to her throne, not sparing a glance for her servants. Today, she scanned the room upon crossing the threshold and had not reached halfway to her throne before she stopped.

The music caught her attention first. It was a good thing Tuval and I were eating in the kitchen or else no one would have been playing, but even we were not enough. "Where is Dov?" she called out to us. "I expect more than two musicians to play at my entrance." I trembled at the smoothness of her voice. When the Queen yelled, her anger faded. The quiet evil in her words told me her rage would only be satisfied by vengeance.

Tuval couldn't answer without removing his halil from his mouth, so he shot a glance at me. I opened my mouth to reply, having no idea what to say, but was spared. Izevel had already turned her venom elsewhere. "Just one scribe? Are matters of royal decree of such little importance that I am afforded only one scribe?"

No doubt the other scribe waited outside the locked doors of the Throne Room, but no one was allowed entrance until the Queen took her throne. Otniel made to answer, but again Izevel moved on.

"Where are my pages?" She directed her attention to the empty spot where the pages normally stood.

"This Throne Room is a disgrace. In my father's Court, such incompetence would cost someone their head." Even the guards at the door shrank as she swung her gaze around the room. "Ovadia will answer for this. He is the King's steward—the servants are under his authority. Summon him to me!"

The Queen gave the order, but no one moved. All of the pages were trapped on the other side of the Throne Room doors. A wry smile came across her lips as her eyes fell back upon the empty pages' station. Her voice took on a melodic tone that sent shivers up my spine. "If Ovadia thinks his incompetence at organizing the pages will save him from being summoned before me, he is mistaken. Who here knows where to find him?"

Otniel spoke. "He was here earlier this morning, my Queen, but I saw him leaving the palace shortly before Court began."

"Do you know where he lives?" Izevel asked.

"I do not, my Queen."

It was a risk, but a moment such as this was why Ovadia placed me in the Throne Room. If anyone else went, they would not warn him of all he needed to know. Worse yet, they might see things in his house best kept secret. I called out, "I know where he lives, my Queen."

"Go, boy. Tell Ovadia I require his presence immediately. Run!"

I lay my kinnor next to Tuval and raced out. A guard opened the doors just wide enough to let me slip through. The hallway was crowded with the pages, the second scribe, and Master Dov all waiting to get in.

"What's going on?" Dov asked, but didn't press me when I shrugged. He didn't need me to tell him the Queen was on the warpath.

I ran out of the palace, still in my musicians' clothes, and dashed down the hill to Ovadia's house. I banged hard on the gate, and when Batya opened it, I ran past her into the house.

Ovadia sat in the kitchen having his morning meal with Yonaton, who had spent the previous night with me in the musicians' quarters. "Queen Izevel—," I began, but Ovadia put up his hand to stop me.

"Is looking for me?" He asked.

"More than looking," I said, surprised at his calm. "She ordered me to bring you back to the palace."

"You? Why you?" The skin between his eyes tightened. "Does she know of the connection between us?"

"No. She was looking for someone who knew where you lived. I thought it better that I bring the news than another."

"She may come to wonder how you know me." Ovadia raised an eyebrow.

My shoulders slumped. "I hadn't thought of that."

"It is of no matter," he said, waving it away. "Perhaps we can turn it to our advantage." He took another bite of his bread.

"She's furious," I said. "You'd better hurry."

"Why should I hurry to meet her anger?" he asked.

"Because she might—"

"Get even angrier? She already wants my head. What more can she do if I delay? Cut off my arms as well?"

Batya snorted.

"Why does she want your head?" Yonaton asked.

"For no better reason than because it still sits upon my shoulders," Ovadia said. "She's seething over the *brit milah.*"

"You said she wanted it," Batya said.

"Only because she wants the people to recognize her son as heir to the Throne, and she knows they won't tolerate an uncircumcised King."

"She ruined the *brit milah* with her festival the night before," I said.

"The *brit* brought her son into the covenant with the Holy One. Nothing Zarisha did can take that away."

"She blames you?" Batya asked.

"No, she blames her husband. Performing the *brit milah* himself shows he still honors the very devotions she wants to wipe from the land. But there is nothing she can do to King Ahav. She seeks to vent her rage, so she will take revenge by striking a blow against one who will not bend his knee to the Baal, who is beneath her, and who she believes she can treat as she pleases."

"On you?" Batya said.

"Precisely. I am sure the fact that I hold the keys of the palace, and that Tamar managed to get in and draw her away from her midwives, only heightens her suspicions of me."

I had thought little of Tamar these last few days. "Is she…?"

"Tamar still breathes, barely, but has not yet awakened."

Ovadia took another bite of his bread. What would I do now? The Queen awaited my return. "How long do you plan to avoid Izevel?" I asked.

"Not long," he said. A knock came against the outer gate. "If that's what I think it is, the time has come." Ovadia went to answer, opening the gate just wide enough to peek out. He stood there a moment, then locked the gate and returned to the house.

"Who was that?" Batya asked.

"A page. I told him to inform me the instant the King entered the Throne Room."

"You think she will drop her revenge because the King is there?" I asked.

"No. It is never safe to have an enemy as dangerous as the Queen harboring ill will against you. She will not like that I avoided facing her alone, and she has many tools of revenge at her disposal. Before she can craft a more devious plan, we must supply one of our own."

"What does that mean?" I asked.

"Yonaton and I have been working on our next steps."

I had assumed Yonaton came over to Ovadia's house on his own that morning, but now I wondered. Before I could ask, Ovadia said, "Come, we must move quickly, before the Queen chooses an alternate path of action. Lev, you go. Tell the Queen I am on my way. Make it clear that you ran back."

I turned to run out of the house, but Ovadia stopped me. "Wait. Two nights ago, you played before Ashera, did you not?"

"I had no choice, Dov—"

"You've also played before the Baal, correct?"

"Yes, but—"

Ovadia waved away my objections. "Let the Queen know this."

"How?"

"Go now. Remember, arrive out of breath."

I ran all the way back to the palace, and my lungs burned as I entered the Throne Room. Two petitioners stood before the King while the Queen stared away, her face livid.

Her eyes found me as soon as I entered. "You were gone a long time."

I bowed before her. "I had to bang on the gate of his courtyard many times before he came, my Queen."

"You delivered my message?"

"Yes, I told him it was important, and he must hurry. I ran back to report to you, my Queen."

"Very well," she replied. She cast a sideways glance at her husband.

It was not long before the doors swung open to admit Ovadia, trailed by Yonaton. When Ovadia was halfway to the Queen, Yonaton asked him, "Why not?"

Ovadia glared at him. "I tell you for the third time, no!" He muffled his voice, but could not hide his frustration.

"My Queen," Ovadia said, situating himself before Izevel.

Yonaton's eyes went wide as he noticed the Queen and quickly stepped back from Ovadia's side to where the petitioners stood. The Queen's eyes followed him, and a smile crept to her lips.

"Ovadia," she said in her sweetest voice, "what is this disturbance?"

"My apologies, my Queen." He bowed his head. "Your messenger said your summons was urgent, so I came before I could properly dismiss this urchin. His request is beneath the interest of your majesty." Ovadia waved his hand as if brushing away a fly. "Please, what do you require of me?"

"Oh no, Ovadia, there is nothing too small for my concern." Her eyes gleamed. "Have you not said the Throne Room of Israel is the place where any of my people, even the most meager, can have their grievances judged?"

Ovadia took a step back. "Your attention is most generous, my Queen, but I assure you I can handle this small matter on my own."

"Boy!" Izevel called to Yonaton. He took a half-step forward and glanced over his shoulder at the Throne Room doors, as if calculating his chances of escape.

"Come here," she commanded, signaling him with her long fingers. "There is no need to be afraid."

Yonaton stepped toward the throne, his eyes on the ground.

"What is your name, boy?"

"Yonaton, my Queen."

"Do you know what this room is, Yonaton?" Izevel asked.

Yonaton's voice was barely loud enough to be heard. "You said it is the Throne Room, my Queen."

"Precisely. This is where the people of Israel come to resolve their disputes. They come before their King and Queen to seek our wisdom and justice. Whatever we decide is the law of the land. Do you know what the penalty for disobeying the law is?"

"No, my Queen."

"Death." The word hung in the air. With a flick of her wrist, she said, "Oh, you need not look so grim. We rarely kill those who come before us. As the penalty for disobeying is so severe, no one dares disobey." She glanced at Ovadia as she said this. "Thus, justice and peace reign in the land. Do you understand?"

"Yes, my Queen."

"Now, tell me. What do you ask of the palace steward?"

"As Master Ovadia said, it is nothing, my Queen. I'm sorry for the disturbance."

"I assure you, it is no disturbance at all. As Queen, my only desire is to help and guide my people as best I can. No matter, once it has entered the threshold of the Throne Room," she shot another glance at Ovadia, "is beneath my attention."

"If it pleases the Queen," Yonaton said, "I withdraw my request of Master Ovadia. I should never have made it."

Ovadia had instructed Yonaton well. The more he withheld information from her, the more she wanted to know. Izevel turned to Ovadia. "As the boy does not wish to share, you will tell me what this is about."

Ovadia took a step toward the Queen's throne. He shot a glance toward the King, as if looking for help, but the King had given only one curious glimpse at the beginning of the conversation before returning to the two petitioners. Seeing that he was alone, Ovadia bowed his head before the Queen. "This boy was one of the musicians at the royal wedding. The city was so full then that I allowed him and that other boy, Lev," Ovadia pointed in my direction, "to stay in a spare room in my house. Now this one has returned to Shomron at Master Dov's request to play for this week's celebrations and wishes to remain. He asked to sleep in my house once again."

"Is the room available?" Izevel asked.

"Well yes, my Queen." He frowned, choosing his words carefully. "But my home is not an inn. I only took in the boys during the wedding as a service to my King." He raised his voice on the last word, but Ahav did not turn from his deliberations. "At that time, the musicians' quarters were overcrowded. There is now ample room, as I am sure Lev can tell you. That is where he has lived since returning to Shomron, and I see no reason Yonaton should not join him."

"Lev," the Queen called, "do come here." I put down my kinnor and approached with a bow. "This is how you knew to find Ovadia's house, because you stayed there in the past?"

"Yes, my Queen, during the wedding."

"You have chosen not to stay with him now?" the Queen asked.

I saw the direction of Ovadia's plan and answered, "Not by choice, my Queen. When I returned to Shomron, I also asked him if I could stay, but he directed me to the musicians' quarters." I gave her my most miserable look. "I cannot blame him for not wanting us, my Queen. I expect he wants his privacy, and when I play for Yambalya or Zarisha, I don't return until the middle of the night."

The Queen's eyebrows pricked up at the mention of her priests. "Are these musicians' quarters comfortable?"

"I have no complaints, my Queen."

"Of course you do not," she snapped. "You are a servant boy; it is not your place to complain." She added with a smile, "Are these quarters as comfortable as Ovadia's house?"

"Oh no, my Queen. At Master Ovadia's I had a bed of my own. With fresh straw!" I tried to look excited. "But the musicians' quarters are fine. There's a patch of floor in the corner where I lay out my mat."

"A patch of floor you say? How many musicians are in these quarters?"

"Four right now. Yonaton will make five."

"Five musicians in one room?" She turned back to Ovadia. "Is that how you treat our servants?"

Ovadia flushed. "The room held three times that number during the wedding."

"Only because they practically lay on top of another," Yonaton muttered, much to the Queen's delight.

"Nevertheless," Ovadia said, "there is certainly enough room for one more right now." He stood straight and met the Queen's eye. "My room is not available."

The Queen looked from Ovadia to Yonaton, but when she spoke, it was again to me. "Lev, you played the other night when Zarisha named Atalya, did you not?"

"Yes, my Queen."

"Do you enjoy playing before Ashera?"

"Very much. The priestess doesn't pay as well as some, but there are other benefits," I added with a smile. "Yonaton also played that night, despite arriving in Shomron after the festival began."

Izevel turned to Yonaton. "Did you enjoy playing before Ashera?"

"Oh yes, my Queen. Master Dov sent me notice asking me to return for the *brit milah*, but after playing for the priestess, I decided to stay in Shomron rather than returning home."

"I am delighted to hear it," Izevel said. "Musicians add to the glory of a capital, and we must do whatever the glory of the Kingdom requires. Isn't that right, Ovadia?"

He bowed his head in defeat. "Yes, my Queen."

"It is unfortunate, but we must remember we are a young city. There are not enough homes, and the builders are hard at work on our Temples. You have said the city must grow, have you not, Ovadia?"

"Yes, my Queen."

Izevel licked her lips. "I fail to see the problem. The room sits empty, and the boy has stayed there before. Was he an unpleasant guest?"

"No, my Queen."

"Then what is the difficulty?"

"It is my home. As Lev said, my wife and I enjoy our privacy."

"We all value our privacy, Ovadia, but an empty room is a small sacrifice for the glory of Shomron. Cramped quarters are no way to attract musicians to our growing capital." Her eyes shone as she announced her verdict. "You will take the boy in. In fact," she added, passing her tongue over her lower lip, "you will take them both in."

"Both? Lev is perfectly happy in the musicians' quarters."

"He is a servant of his King and Queen, so he does his duty and does not complain. A virtue I would recommend to some others." Their eyes met for an instant before Ovadia dropped his head.

"That is your wish, my Queen?"

Izevel leaned back in her throne. "It is my will. As you know, Ovadia, my will in this land is law." She reached out and placed a hand on the King's arm, and he turned to take her hand. Ovadia retreated from the Throne Room.

You can get horses ready for battle, but it is the Holy One who gives victory.

Proverbs 21:31

17

The Fighting Cave

"Fire!" Yonaton called out, pointing to a black column rising in the sky. "Hurry, we can help."

"Not until after we deliver the bread," I said. We had turned off the King's Road for the trail to the cave. It was Yonaton's first bread delivery, and hopefully, now that he was here to take my place, one of my last.

"You have to get a fire fast, before it spreads," he said.

"After the bread."

Yonaton half-turned back toward the head of the trail. "Someone could be trapped."

"Go if you must. I'll join you after I drop off the bread."

Yonaton shot me one last look, then ran off in the direction of the fire. I also ran, but toward the cave. When I arrived, Sadya said, "There is a fire."

"I know. You pass out the bread, I'll return for the donkey after." I ran toward the pillar of smoke. The smell of burning grass filled the air. By the time

I arrived, the fire had consumed three fields despite the twenty or so men and women fighting to bring it under control. More farmers ran in on barely visible trails, summoned by the smoke. Yonaton held a crude torch fashioned from dried grasses, which he used to set a small fire beyond the edge of the blaze.

"What are you doing?" I asked, gasping for breath.

"It's the only way to stop it—if there's no fuel to burn, it'll go out." His fire raced toward the main flames, and he motioned for me to join him stomping on its edge. "Let it burn back toward the center, only stop it if it threatens to spread the other way."

Helpers poured in from the surrounding area. After so many months without rain, it wouldn't take the fire long to reach their homes and fields if it wasn't stopped. Soon, more than fifty small fires like Yonaton's burned around the great blaze in the middle. A cheer went up when the entire perimeter was burnt, leaving nowhere for the main fire to spread. As it ran out of fuel, it smoldered and split into many smaller blazes that would eventually die on their own.

Yonaton and I walked back toward the cave. "It's a good thing there was no wind," he said, "otherwise we never would have contained it so easily."

"That was easy? It took over fifty men!"

"The bigger it gets, the more people you need working together. That's why I wanted to get there so quickly."

I heard the criticism in his words, but I held my tongue as farmers were still dispersing on the trails around us. We took a seat in the shade of an oak until we were alone on the trail, and only then did I lead Yonaton to the cave. After I was sure he could find the path by himself on the next trip, we retrieved the donkey and headed home.

We walked for a while on opposite sides of the donkey until I broke the silence. "We can't save them all, Yonaton."

"All who?"

"Israel. We cannot save them all. Some have already died, and many more will before the drought breaks." He looked away as I spoke, so I halted the donkey and waited until I had his attention. "We can't save them all."

Pain mixed with confusion on his face. "Shouldn't we try to save those we can?"

"We're committed to saving the prophets, and that's where our loyalties must lie."

"If we can save others as well—"

"Then we should. But only if it doesn't endanger the prophets. Each time I go to the cave, I pass starving beggars at the city gates. I pass them with a donkey load full of bread, yet I barely spare them a glance."

"Don't you care?"

"Of course I care, but I would be taking food from the mouths of starving prophets to feed them.

"Running to the fire wouldn't have taken bread from the prophets," Yonaton said. "Just delayed it a bit."

"What if someone opened our saddlebags? They might be looking for something to fight the fire with. What would they think of all this bread?"

"They'd wonder where we got it and where we were taking it."

"Exactly." I recalled Tamar's words the night I rescued her. "Never forget we are at war. If even a whisper of what we do reaches the ears of Izevel's soldiers or spies, everything is lost."

"Are you always this cautious?" he asked.

"Always."

Yonaton nodded, and I knew he would accept my words. But had he learned from Tamar, he would have paid more attention to my tone. In truth, I'd let my guard down too many times. I couldn't shake the feeling that sooner or later one of my mistakes would lead to disaster.

Yonaton's appearance didn't free me from bread deliveries after all. If his excuse for staying in Shomron was to be a musician, he had to live like one. As the drought deepened and the shadow of famine spread across the countryside, Izevel only increased the sacrifices to the Baal and Ashera. Spurred on by the desire for her favor, nobility hosted private sacrifices as well, and musicians were in high demand. Yonaton had no lack of work at night, and he gave what little energy remained to help Batya bake during the day. Her face grew thin from laboring day and night, and now she was also nursemaid to Tamar, who still hovered on the edge of life. While the rest of her withered, Batya's arms grew strong, their muscles showing hard under her skin from the constant grinding and kneading.

When I wasn't playing in the palace or delivering the bread, I too spent every spare moment baking, though my hands would never make up for the loss of Tamar's. Still, between Yonaton's return and moving back into Ovadia's, my life had taken a turn for the better. The same could not be said for the prophets. When I arrived at the cave and found Raphael sitting in the shadow of the olive tree which hid the entrance, I knew something was wrong. "What are you doing out of the cave?" I asked.

"Waiting for the bread," he said. "I will take it from you here. You may not enter."

"Why not?" I asked. After all this time, what secrets could the prophets possibly have from me?

Raphael's head sank. "The Holy One is a righteous judge."

I understood. There was no secret in the cave, only death, and as a Kohen, I was forbidden to enter. Raphael risked waiting outside to warn me. I thought of my master, so weak the last time I had seen him. "Master Uriel?"

Raphael shook his head. "Master Yissachar."

Yissachar had been wise and kind. He had not been strong even before entering the cave, and it was only from strength of will that he survived this long. "When can I come back?" I asked.

"We will return his body to the earth tonight, after the moon sets. Your master bids you return tomorrow night, and to bring Ovadia and Yonaton as well. A council has been called."

"Our fathers taught us to make war through wisdom and said victory comes through council." Uriel's words were no empty phrase, though we sat in total darkness. The entrance hall was full, with every prophet who could stand gathered together.

"Is it victory, then, that we seek – or survival?"

"Peace, Master Pinchas. The plans of the Holy One encompass the ancient hills as well as the dew that melts with the dawn. Survival and victory can often look the same. Every voice will be heard, but only once we know the truth of our situation." Uriel's words were met with a murmur of approval. "Ovadia, we will begin with you, as you hold the staff of life. How much grain remains?"

"Less than I hoped, but more than I feared," Ovadia said. "Already last winter I sent my household servants for secrecy to my land in the Jezreel Valley. They hand-watered the wheat and barley all winter. But it's a small farm, and even in a good year, the crop would not feed eighty. Now the dirt is dry as dust, and we have neither enough servants nor enough water to bring in another harvest."

"How long can you hope to sustain us?" Uriel asked.

Ovadia sighed. "The Holy One will provide."

"You need not tell us what the Holy One will or will not do," Pinchas said. "All of the grain stores in the cave have already been depleted. How much do you have?"

"Six sacks. Enough to sustain us for two weeks."

The prophets received this verdict in silence, as if hearing a death sentence.

Ovadia spoke again. "This is not the first time our stores have been so low. I found a way before, and I will find one again."

"No one doubts your abilities or your efforts, Ovadia," Uriel said. "We are grateful for every morsel we have."

"May I now speak?" Pinchas' voice conveyed demand rather than question. "It is not the way of the prophets to sit idle while the enemy takes over our land. Perhaps if Ovadia brought hope, my words would be different. But he does not. Is it not better to die by the sword in the light of day than to starve here in darkness?"

"Do you suggest reducing the mouths to feed by offering the enemy your throat?" Ovadia asked.

"The drought dried the entire land," Pinchas continued. "Lev tells us it struck Tzidon as well. Where does the Queen find grain to feed her soldiers?"

"Her father, King Ethbaal, imports grain by ship from Tarshish," Ovadia answered. "It comes in caravans from Tyre."

"There is our source of grain!" Pinchas said. "The Holy One ceased sending down manna for the people when Joshua led us into the land. Our ancestors ate by seizing the grain of their enemies, strengthening themselves and weakening their foes at the same time. Let us do the same."

"This grain feeds more than our enemies," Ovadia said. "Many who would starve now sell their labor to the King and Queen for bread. If famine comes to Shomron, Izevel's soldiers will be the last to go without."

"What is it Izevel pays our people to do?" Pinchas asked.

"Building mostly. They are improving the roads, constructing a new palace in Jezreel, and," Ovadia hesitated, "constructing temples to her gods."

"Then they have passed judgment on themselves already." In the darkness, Pinchas could have been Eliyahu. "Better the prophets eat than those who give honor to Izevel's abominations."

"The people care not for honor, but for keeping their families alive," Ovadia said.

"What is life without honor worth?"

"By fighting, you may lose more than you gain, Master Pinchas," Uriel said. "If you sneak off to attack the enemy, you risk our secrecy and all of our lives."

"True, yet I still say it is better to die by the sword than starve."

"Starvation is not yet at our door," Uriel said. "We have grain for now."

"Do you believe Eliyahu is close to relenting?" Pinchas asked. "Have the people turned away from desecrating the name of the Holy One?" No one could dispute his words. All I could think of was the fire in Eliyahu's eyes. A shift in Pinchas' voice made it clear he was speaking to the entire assembly when he announced, "I will not continue eating the bread of shame."

"There is no shame in the bread I provide," Ovadia said.

"No shame?" Pinchas said. "No shame in lying hidden while another feeds me by the sweat of his brow? No shame in knowing others may starve because of the bread I took from their hand? The fewer mouths you have to feed, Ovadia, the longer you may sustain those who remain."

"It is clear, Master Pinchas," Uriel said, "that your heart is set on the sword. I will hinder you no longer, but I have not the strength for battle. I suggest a division."

"A division indeed," Pinchas said. "We are already too many between these walls. I will leave and welcome any who will join me. If we fail, our blood will be on our heads. If we succeed, we may feed you all. Agreed?"

"Agreed." Uriel sighed. "Take those who will fight beside you and prepare for battle. I implore you to hold the lives of your brothers as dear as your own. Do not invite death unnecessarily upon yourselves while grain remains to sustain us. Agreed?"

"Agreed. I will need at least twenty men. I know not the caves in this part of the Kingdom. Is there another that might shelter us?"

"I know of one," Uriel said. "It overlooks the sea, on the far side of Shomron."

"Near the sea is good, for the caravans from Tyre must pass on the coastal road," Pinchas said. "Is there clean water nearby?"

"There was," Uriel said, "but we cannot be sure the spring still flows, nor that the cave is still secure. We must send someone to investigate."

I knew what was coming next. Of all the assembled, only two of us could walk the Kingdom freely without attracting attention.

Yonaton and I woke before the first light so we could hunt for the second cave before I needed to be in the Throne Room. He was strangely quiet as he slipped into his clothes. "Lev, I want you to do me a favor."

"Of course, what is it?"

He hesitated for a moment. "I want you to buy me."

"Buy you what?" I asked.

"Not to buy me anything," he said. "I want you to buy me. I want to become your slave."

I would have laughed, but the expression on his face told me he was not kidding. "Why would you want to be my slave?"

"So I can eat *challah*."

The *challah* was my bread of shame. The commandment to separate a portion for the Kohen meant I always had bread in abundance, but could not share it with anyone else. Only a Kohen and his dependents could eat consecrated bread.

"You have more bread than you need," Yonaton said, "while everything I eat comes from the mouths of the prophets."

"You're not taking from them, you're feeding them," I said. "I know you already give Ovadia the copper you make from your music. That more than pays for what you eat."

"Still," Yonaton said, "I eat twice as much as any prophet."

"You're working hard each day, while they're trapped in the dark, moving as little as possible to preserve their energy."

"If I could eat *challah*, two more prophets could eat off my earnings."

I grinned at him. "The only way for you to eat *challah* is to become my slave, and then all of your earnings would belong to me anyway."

"You'll do what with my earnings? Build yourself a palace?"

I sighed. If he was my slave, a bit more bread could be spared for the prophets, but I still didn't like the idea. "We'll ask Master Uriel later. If he agrees, I'll do it."

Yonaton nodded.

"In the meantime, you can bring water and wash my feet," I said.

Yonaton's sandal came flying across the room and hit me in the leg. "I'm not your slave yet!"

"If that leaves a bruise," I said, "you'll rub it with ointment until it heals."

The other sandal came flying, but this time I was ready and dodged it. "I won't abuse this," I told him, suddenly serious.

"I know."

The King's Road descended west of the gates of Shomron, winding between slopes of white stone as it dropped toward the sea. We were far below the level of the city, but still high enough to see out across the plain to the ocean, when we turned north onto a faint trail marked by nothing but a bend in the road. As we walked in the half-light, I counted out five hundred and fifty paces, as my master had instructed. When our path passed beneath a cliff overlooking the ocean below, I stopped and looked at the layered stone. Tiny holes in the cliff face appeared to be bird nests or flaws in the rock, but I knew they were windows into a cave beyond. We inspected the holes, but none were big enough for even a child to enter. We continued past the cliff and climbed up the hillside until we stood above it.

The top of the cliff was nothing but a flat hilltop. In richer seasons, it would have made good pasture, and I imagined sitting with my flock as they grazed, watching the sea roll back and forth in the distance. Now only a few yellowed thorn bushes maintained their grip on the dusty soil. A small boulder sat alone, almost at the center of the rise, and because I knew to look, I saw the gap beneath its eastern edge. It took both of us to roll the rock back and expose a dark hole beneath.

"You want to go first?" Yonaton asked.

There was no telling the depth of the pit or what awaited us at the bottom. Snakes, scorpions, even jackals could have slipped through the gap. "Slave," I said, "I command you to go first."

Yonaton grinned at my fear. "You could have asked me. At least lend me a hand, will you, oh brave Master?"

Yonaton sat on the edge of the hole. I held his hands as he slipped in, but his feet hit the ground when he was only chest deep. "It's got to be deeper than that," I said.

"It slopes downward," he replied.

"Go feet first, just in case." In case of what, I didn't know, but if anything was down there, better to encounter it with his feet than his head.

Yonaton ducked into the darkness. His slow, scraping progress became a slide. "Whoa!" was all he had time to say before he hit the cave floor with a thump. "It's OK, come down."

I lowered myself into the hole and scooted in after him. Light from the entrance above revealed a worn passage. It grew steeper, and I scrambled to find a handhold, but the walls were too smooth. The tunnel widened out as it became almost vertical, and, as I dropped, I glimpsed Yonaton, lit by the cracks in the cliff wall behind him. Two men held him tight, one with a hand over his mouth. As I hit the ground, someone grabbed me. I struggled, but he wrenched my arms behind my back, and a fourth man placed a sword across my chest.

"Who are you?" the man with the sword asked.

It was like my first encounter with Pinchas, except then I knew I was going to meet prophets. Now I had two stories I could give—in one I was a royal musician, loyal to the King and Queen. In the other, I served the prophets. The wrong story could cost me more than my life.

"We are two friends out exploring," I said. "You have nothing to fear from us." There was no need to fake my terror.

"Two friends out exploring?" I heard the doubt in his voice.

"Yes!" My skin burned as he gripped me tighter. "We saw the rock and guessed there might be a cave. We hoped to find hidden treasures, not hidden men. Please, we are at your mercy."

My eyes were adjusting to the dim light, and I took a closer look at our captors. They wore linen clothing, once fine, but now tattered and worn.

"Indeed you are at our mercy." The man who held the sword flat against my chest was beyond my eyesight, but I didn't dare to turn and face him. "Now I must decide whether you are deserving of it. I kill no man without cause, but mercy has little place in war." He pressed the flat of the sword against my chest. "How did you find this cave?"

It was less his words than how he said them, like a prophet, but I had to be sure. "My master sent me to this cave," I said.

"Your master? What master? You're his master. I heard him say so above."

"I'm not his master," I said, "not really."

"Then why did he call you that?" His curiosity gave me an idea.

"He wants me to buy him. For his own sake."

"For his own sake?" His confusion was plain, but the blade at my chest did not waver. "Why? For grain?"

I took a deep breath and made my choice. "He wants me to buy him so he can eat *challah* to survive the drought."

The men looked at one another. The one holding his hand over Yonaton's mouth relaxed his grip. "What's your name?" the leader asked.

"Lev ben Yochanan HaKohen."

"Yochanan's son lives?" The sword dropped away from my chest, but the grip on my arms remained firm.

"The faithful are all but driven from the land, son of Yochanan. Who still separates *challah* now that there is no one to receive it?"

"If you knew my father, you know I have not shared this information lightly. I have revealed myself, now tell me with whom I speak and who you serve."

"Very well, Yochanan's son." At a nod from my captor, the man behind me released his hold. "I am Kenaz ben Ulam, and I serve only the Holy One of Israel. My disciples and I took refuge in this cave after the cursed Tzidonians discovered our camp and slaughtered our brothers and sisters."

"You are a prophet?"

He rose to his full height. "I am."

"Then release my friend. We found this cave on the direction of Master Uriel."

"Uriel lives as well?" Kenaz sheathed his sword and leaned close to see my face. "The son of the priest appears from nowhere, bearing news from the father of the prophets. There is more to your story, Lev ben Yochanan. Why did he send you here?"

"He and many of your brethren have taken shelter in the Cave of Dotan, but their numbers have grown beyond what the place can hold." I saw no need to share the decisions of the council with him yet.

"So your master thought to send more to our little cave?" Kenaz said.

"He did not know we would find it occupied," I replied.

"We are already twelve. How many more must come?"

"I do not yet know. I expect at least twenty. Perhaps as many as forty."

"It will be difficult to receive so many," Kenaz said. "How will they eat?"

"We will supply them with bread, as we do now."

The surprise was plain on his face. "Your story deepens at every turn. Though we will not eat *challah*, son of Yochanan, not even as your slaves. That is merely the false hope of an ignorant boy."

Yonaton started at the insult. "My father taught me that the slave may always eat from the table of his master."

Kenaz shook his head. "A man of Israel belongs to the Holy One, never to another man. You cannot sell your body, only your labor. According to our laws, only a foreign slave owned by a Kohen can eat *challah*." Only a prophet would teach even in the midst of battle.

Yonaton's chest fell.

"This is of no matter," I said. "The *challah* I eat is separated from the bread baked to feed the prophets."

One of the disciples spoke up for the first time. "I have been in the Cave of Dotan. For it to become crowded many of our brothers must have sought refuge there. Who can supply that much grain?"

Even though I was speaking to a prophet and had already mentioned the Cave of Dotan, I hesitated about saying Ovadia's name out loud. "We eat by the grace of the Holy One."

Kenaz laughed. "Boy, after what we have seen in the last year, there is no need to teach me we all eat from the Holy One's hand. I will not ask where the grain comes from, just tell me how long it can hold out?"

"I do not know," I said.

"And when that is exhausted?" Kenaz asked. "Is this hiding place to become our grave?"

"The Queen transports her grain along the coastal road. If need be, those who come to this cave will seize grain from the Queen herself."

"Under whose leadership?" Kenaz asked. "Yours?"

"Master Pinchas ben Asaya."

A murmur passed among the disciples. "As I said, there is more to this story. I have no doubt we will hear it full when the time is right. It is a worthy plan, son of Yochanan, but not all of us are fighters."

"My master will welcome at Dotan those who do not wish to fight."

Kenaz returned his sword to his sheath. "If you can feed our hungry, we can shelter your homeless. Come, I will show you."

He led us into a second cavern, and from there into a third further under the hill. It was less than half the size of Dotan, but the absence of passageways left plenty of sleeping space. It was better lit than Dotan, with light seeping in from the cave wall overlooking the sea, though the innermost chamber was entirely dark. "Will it suffice?" Kenaz asked.

"Very well. We could sleep forty and be no more cramped than in Dotan."

I noticed Kenaz ignored Yonaton but spoke to me like I was an equal. I added, "The best part for our purposes is its defensibility. Even if discovered, only one soldier can enter at a time."

Kenaz laughed. "You've proven yourself to be more than you appear, son of Yochanan, but you have no knowledge of warfare. This cave is a deathtrap. True, only one soldier can enter at a time, but why try to enter? Two soldiers could hold the exit against us all. If they built a fire outside the cliff face, the smoke would suffocate everyone inside."

I blushed at the rebuke and changed the subject. "What about water?"

"There is a well which flows not far from the sea."

"How do you get there without being seen?"

"We slip out in the middle of the night. We catch fish the same way."

We left Kenaz and his disciples and rolled the boulder back into place over the entrance. It felt different than leaving Dotan, where I walked out upright. Crawling up through a hole in the ground and plugging it behind me felt like sealing them in a crypt.

A second council was held in Dotan that night. Well after darkness fell, Yonaton arrived leading Kenaz and his disciples. We sat in the main cavern in a three-rowed circle so we could all fit. Ovadia spoke first. "With our new arrivals, we now have precisely one hundred prophets and disciples. Our father Jacob divided his camp before meeting his brother Esau, reasoning that should Esau attack one camp, the other could survive. The actions of our fathers are lessons for their children. We will divide as well. One group will remain hidden here, the other will go to a second cave and prepare themselves should we need to fight."

"Jacob did more than divide his camps in preparation for battle," Uriel said, "he also appeased his brother with gifts and turned to the Holy One in supplication. I no longer have the strength to fight, nor do I have any gifts to offer. I will remain here and continue to pray for salvation."

"I will depart to the cave by the sea," Pinchas said, "and lead those seeking battle with our enemies. Know now, those of you who will accompany me, you must hold the lives of your fellows more precious than your own, for if caught, you must give your own life rather than reveal the location of either cave. If you cannot make such a commitment, better you should remain here."

"I have now spent nearly a year in the cave by the sea," Kenaz said. "I know where to find water. I know passageways to the coast and coves hidden from the road where we can fish. I will join the fighters and share my knowledge."

One by one the prophets spoke as the disciples sat silent. Of the twenty-three prophets, only eight chose to join the fighters, most of the others being too old or weak to fight. Raphael was the last prophet to speak, not only because he was the youngest among them, but because his path was unclear even to himself. "My master Yosef taught me to always fight for justice. When the soldiers came for us, he killed the first to step through the door. But I was little help fighting by his side. I believe in Pinchas' mission, and I would like to join, but I do not feel fit for battle."

"If you would hear my counsel," Uriel said, "remain here, Raphael. Yours are the hands of a healer, they were not formed to spill blood."

"If I can heal, then should I not join my brothers, so I can tend to the wounded?"

"Uriel is right," Pinchas said. "If we need your healing, we will send for you. We have room only for those ready to fight."

I agreed with Pinchas' decision, if not with his actual words. In truth, a healer would be quite valuable amongst the fighters. However, Raphael was clumsy and a bit too trusting, traits ill fit for a warrior. Was that the actual reason Pinchas rejected him? My suspicions were bolstered when a disciple named Elon spoke. "I will fight if called upon, but I have striven for years under my master to pursue the paths of peace. I believe I am more suited to remain here."

"Elon," Pinchas said, "you walk through the passageways of this cave as quiet as a cat. Twice you sought me out in my cavern, and neither time did I hear you approach. You say you will fight if called upon? I call upon you now."

Elon was an exception, as more disciples wished to fight than could fit in the new cave. Pinchas told several of the less able to remain in Dotan.

"What of Sadya and myself?" Peleh asked. "We guard the entrance here. Does that not make us fighters in the non-fighting cave?"

"Does it take two to guard one hidden entranceway?" Pinchas said. "Let one of you remain here as guard, and the other can join me."

Peleh and Sadya exchanged a glance. Peleh spoke first. "For a year I have held a sword, each day knowing I would be useless if ever called to use it."

"So you wish to remain?" Sadya asked.

"No, I wish to go, if Master Pinchas will have me. It is time to train my hands to fight."

Once the groups were divided, Ovadia stood in the middle of the circle. "The moon will set in one hour's time, and those going to the cave by the sea will depart with it. Whoever has weapons shall bring them here. One sword only will remain in Dotan to protect the entranceway. The rest go with the fighters."

Yonaton and I left ahead of the fighters to spy out any travelers on the road. Fortunately, the journey was a quiet one. When we were all assembled in the cave by the sea, and the boulder rolled safely back into place, Pinchas broke the silence. "Sleep now while you may. Our training begins with the sun."

"What about bread?" one of Kenaz's disciples asked. It had been many months since they tasted bread, and the trip to Dotan and back could not have been easy for them.

"Ovadia will provide bread in the morning," Pinchas said.

"How will it get to us?"

"I will bring it," Yonaton said.

"And water?" one of the new arrivals asked. In Dotan, they at least had a steady source of water within the cave, though the spring had slowed to a trickle.

"We will bring you to water before dawn," Kenaz said. "For now, finish what is in the skins at the back of the cave."

Yonaton and I found a spot in the back of the innermost cavern where we were least likely to get stepped on. Not a ray of starlight penetrated its blackness, but I had long ago lost my fear of the dark. I snapped my fingers lightly, a trick I had learned in the Cave of Dotan, hearing the echoes off the walls, sensing their distance with my ears.

"It's a shame you weren't able to buy me," Yonaton said as he lay on the bare stone with his arm under his head. "A master is required to provide his slave a pillow."

A mass of people huddled along the western wall of Shomron as we approached the gates in the early light. "Who are they?" Yonaton asked. "Beggars?"

"Beggars wait by the gates." There were more than ten of them, men and women mingled together, some sitting with their backs against the wall. A moaning reached us. "It's the diseased." I turned my eyes away with a shudder.

Yonaton stared, fascinated. In his village, such a large crowd would only be seen at a wedding. Or a fire. "They just sit there?"

"They have no choice. They're forbidden to come within ten *amot* of the gates, much less enter."

"How do they live?" Yonaton asked.

"They don't live long."

I kept my gaze straight ahead as we passed through the gates and rushed up the road to Ovadia's. I had just enough time to grab my linen tunic and make it to the palace kitchen while the servants were still eating. But when Batya opened the gate, all thoughts of hurrying vanished. "You look like someone died," I said.

"Not yet, but perhaps soon."

"Tamar?" A shudder passed through me.

Batya shook her head. "Your uncle."

The heart alone knows its bitterness, no outsider can share in its joy.

Proverbs 14:10

18

Evils of Drought

I paused only long enough to pack bread and water, then got back on the road, grateful to walk alone in the quiet of the morning. The heat rose as the day progressed, and travelers were few. In the mid-afternoon, I climbed up from the King's road toward Levonah and circled around to my Uncle's farm. I met total silence. No children played outside the house, no one worked in the orchards. The flock was gone from the pen, and when I touched the oven in the courtyard—it was cold. How long had it been since my family had baked bread?

When I entered the house, there was no one downstairs, but a head appeared over the edge of the loft at the sound of my footsteps. "Lev!" Shimi cried out. He came down the ladder, jumping from the third wrung right into my arms. He hugged me hard around the neck, and his tears wet my cheek.

"Lev?" The croaking whisper was a shadow of my Uncle's voice.

I put Shimi down and climbed the ladder. All of the family except Eliav surrounded my uncle's bed. Uncle Menachem was too weak to sit up to greet me, but I saw no shame in his eyes. We examined each other before a wave of coughing took him. He turned toward the wall as spasms wracked his body.

Aunt Leah reached over to take my hand, but her eyes didn't leave her husband as he shook. When the coughing ceased, Uncle Menachem turned back toward us and said, "Leah, take the children. I'd like to speak to Lev."

Aunt Leah kissed his forehead, then led everyone down the ladder and out of the house without a word. Uncle Menachem waited until he heard the door close. "You remember Asher ben Yaakov, the merchant?" I nodded, confused by the question. "He often travels to Shomron. On his last trip, I asked him to look in on you." Menachem's gaze held me; it, at least, had not grown any weaker. "When he inquired at the palace, they told him you went to visit your family."

My uncle's eyes grew stern, but only for a moment. Then he smiled, like one in on a joke. "When he told me, I guessed you were on a mission for the prophets. Was I right?"

I had hidden my loyalty to the prophets for so long, but he knew anyway. "Yes, Uncle."

"You know this is not the path I wanted for you, right Lev?"

"Yes, Uncle." Tears filled my eyes, and I bent over his body, which lay so frail and helpless on the bed. It would have been so easy for me to save him. "Forgive me," I gasped.

"Forgive you? What is there to forgive? This is the way of all flesh, Lev, in good times and in bad."

"This is all my fault. I knew about the drought. I could have warned you."

Uncle Menachem placed his hand behind my head. "There was nothing you could have done, Lev. Your warning reached my ears. Dahlia told me about the drought as soon as you left."

I stared up in alarm, my eyes going dry. "What?"

"Have no fear, boy, your uncle is not as slow as you think. Dahlia also told me why you swore her to secrecy. I stored both grain and water before it was too late. By then, others already spoke their fears in the gates. Prices had risen, but not so high yet that I couldn't secure sufficient grain to last us a couple of years. A cistern also seemed a wise idea, given that the spring was sure to dry up before the end of summer. No one suspects you played a role, not even Eliav."

Relief washed over me with my uncle's words. Did Dahlia share my doubts about Eliav, or had he worked that out on his own? "Where is Eliav, Uncle?"

"With the flock, of course." Uncle Menachem smiled at my look of surprise. "Yes, the flock lives, though I had to sell off more than half of it to pay for the grain. Eliav has quite a march each day to find water and grass. He has grown since I took to my bed. Soon he will be the man of the family."

"Uncle!"

"My path has reached its end, Lev." As if to punctuate his point, another coughing fit came over him. When it passed, he met my eyes. "In drought, even water and grain may not be enough. Disease grows as the land withers, and it does not spare the hungry or the fed."

"While there is life, there is hope."

"Hope itself can be a burden, Lev. It is better this way. I have settled all of my debts and said goodbye to those I love. Only you remained, and now you are here." His eyes held the peace of acceptance. "Did I ever tell you how much I admired your father, Lev?"

"No, Uncle."

"Your father was fearless." Uncle Menachem stopped. "No, not fearless. He felt fear, but he did not let it rule him. Yochanan did what he believed was right, no matter the risks."

"That got him killed," I said.

"True, that is why he died, and your mother as well." Uncle Menachem sighed. "The cost of living for what you believe can be high. I wanted you on a different path. On my path. The path of safety. But look at me now, Lev. The way of flesh awaits us all. If I could live it again, I expect I'd still choose the path of safety. But I wanted you to know, despite the differences in our choices, I always admired him."

Uncle Menachem leaned back and closed his eyes. "I must rest. Please leave me for now, Lev."

I bent over, like Aunt Leah had done, and kissed Uncle Menachem on the forehead. As I turned to go, he took my hand in his, giving it a feeble squeeze before releasing me and turning away.

Dahlia fired the oven for the evening baking. She watched me approach, then dropped her eyes when I was close enough to meet her gaze.

I put my hand on the warm oven. "It was cold when I came."

Dahlia nodded. "We're only baking once a day now. There's less of everything."

"You told your father about the drought."

Dahlia pushed a curl from in front of her eyes. "I'm sorry, Lev, but I couldn't let—"

"Thank you," I said.

She cocked her head. "You're not angry?"

"When I first heard he was sick, I thought I was responsible."

"No, Lev. You've done all that you could."

I sighed. "It wasn't enough."

"Enough for what?"

I gestured toward the house.

"Enough to save my father?" Dahlia asked. "Enough to save the prophets?"

I shrugged.

"Enough to defeat the Queen, perhaps?"

I dropped my eyes back to the oven.

"You're barely of age, Lev. I doubt you'll be able to overthrow the Queen until you're at least sixteen." She threw me a mischievous glance. "It means a lot to my father that you've come. I haven't seen him this excited in a week."

"And you?"

She looked down at the dough in her hands. "Shelah approached my father for my hand a month after I came of age."

The oven grew hot beneath my fingertips. "What did your father say?"

"He said, 'drought is not a time for planting.'"

"And Shelah?"

"He was surprised. Remember, only we knew the rains would not return." Dahlia's eyes sparkled. There were other benefits of her breaking my trust. "Shelah understood that he wasn't rejected, but…" Dahlia held my eyes, and I pulled my hand from the oven, which grew too hot to touch, "he wasn't accepted either."

I heard bleating in the distance, and looked out to see Eliav walking at the back of the flock, which was now less than twenty sheep. Eliav waved his staff hand in the air in greeting. He had grown taller and carried himself like a man. I went to meet him, and he threw his arms around me in a rough hug. "You came back to see my father?"

I nodded. "He sent me a message."

"Thank you for making the trip. I'm sure it means a lot to him." Even his tone was different.

"Can I help settle the flock?" I asked.

"There isn't much to do," he said. "As you can see, it's much smaller than when you were here last."

I opened the gate of the pen, and Eliav drove the sheep in. There was a confidence in the way he worked, an ownership I'd never seen in him before. He set to work cleaning the lambs and milking the mothers, humming to himself as he picked burrs from their wool.

I circled behind the house and toward the rocky hillside. Our spring was dry; only brown stains showed were the water used to flow. At the foot of the chalky cliff were signs of digging and a heavy wooden cover on the ground: the cistern. I stooped to lift it and then thought better of it. Who knew how long its water had to last? Why waste even a drop to satisfy my curiosity?

Aunt Leah called us to eat, bringing the food outside so we would not disturb my uncle's sleep. The meal was a quiet one, though I felt the eyes of my younger cousins on me as we ate. Naama whispered to Ruth, and they both laughed. "What's so funny?" I asked.

"You're getting a beard," Naama said.

I touched the soft hairs sprouting from my cheeks, hardly the makings of a beard. I stroked my chin, letting my fingers pass through long, imaginary hairs. They both giggled. Aunt Leah didn't look up from her food, barely noticing the rest of us were there.

Uncle Menachem didn't wake once during the evening, nor in the morning, nor any morning after that. My Aunt must have known the moment was coming, for she didn't allow me to sleep in the house that night. Eliav eyed me as I brought my sleeping mat outside, but said nothing.

In the morning, the men of Levonah gathered. Aunt Leah called me to join her behind the house. She wrapped a length of cloth around my neck and right arm and tied it behind my neck.

"What are you doing, Aunt?"

"You hurt your arm," she said.

"I did? How?"

"I shut the door on you when you were coming in last night."

"You didn't even allow me into the house last night."

"Of course, I did," she said, "that's when you hurt your arm. Or, if you don't like that story, come up with another."

"Why?"

She frowned at my slowness. "So no one will expect you to carry Menachem."

I should have thought of that. It was a great honor to bear the dead. My uncle would go to his grave carried by his family and the men of greatest stature in the community. Uriel called it true kindness, for unlike acts of kindness to the living, it could never be repaid. It was an honor which a Kohen was forbidden to give except to his most immediate family, and though he had raised me, Menachem was my uncle, not my father. Without an excuse, all would wonder why I failed to perform this kindness.

Most men of the city came to escort my uncle to the burial cave. Eliav took hold of the funeral bier along my uncle's right shoulder, Yoel ben Beerah took the left. Shelah supported one of his hips, and even Shimi was allowed to hold one of his feet. I stood at a distance, drawing occasional glances, but few paid much attention to Menachem's orphaned nephew with his arm in a sling.

The custom was to allow the dead to rest in the burial cave for a year before their bones were gathered to their fathers, but the drought had taken so many in Levonah during the past few months that there was no room in the cave to lay my uncle. In the end, they removed the bones of a man who had died only nine months earlier to make space.

They were going to need more caves.

One of the men at the funeral traveled regularly to Shomron, and I sent word through him to Master Dov that I would remain in Levonah through the seven days of mourning. My family sat upon the ground in their home, barefoot and weeping. Women brought food and sat with Aunt Leah. Men came and sat with Eliav. Few paid me any attention.

According to the customs of the land, I was not a mourner, so I could do things forbidden to my aunt and cousins during the week of honoring the dead. I took out the flock each morning, leading them to a distant spring that Eliav told me still trickled.

It was considered a disgrace to the community for mourners to have to eat their own bread. For a man like Menachem, well known through the whole city, it was not unusual for a house of mourning to have so much excess bread that some went to waste. Despite the visitors who crowded in to pay their respects, there was barely enough in the house to feed the children for the week. On the third day after the burial, I considered baking bread for the family, but no one in Levonah had ever seen a man bake. I couldn't afford to arouse questions.

All week long, stories of Uncle Menachem's life were told and retold. I had never before heard the story of how he and Aunt Leah came to marry, but by the end of the week, I'd heard it so many times that I could have told it over myself. My grandfather, Aunt Leah's father, first refused the match as Uncle Menachem, who had not yet inherited his family's farm, was too young and poor. Uncle Menachem defied my grandfather by approaching Aunt Leah next to the stream where she did her family's wash. For over a year, he visited her by there, and at the same time built up his flock. When he approached my grandfather again a year later, he was hardly a rich man, yet he showed he was moving in the right direction. Even more importantly, he now held my aunt's heart, and though Aunt Leah described her father as a strong man, his strength did not hold up long against his daughter's desires.

Had the same thing happened with my mother? If my grandfather was anything like my uncle, he would not have approved of his daughter marrying a landless Kohen. Had my grandfather's will been broken by my mother's devotion to my father?

The week of mourning came to a close, and with it went all discussions of the past. No one in the house said it, but all feared a future without Menachem. Making matters worse, there were now two heads of the family. Eliav was the eldest son, and the land went to him. With it came the responsibility to provide for his mother, and for Naama, Ruth, and Dahlia until they were married, and for Shimi until he came of age and inherited a portion of the farm. Eliav was eleven, not even of age himself. It was no small responsibility to care for an entire family, particularly during a drought.

Then there was Aunt Leah. Until Eliav came of age, she ruled the family, but she couldn't afford to assert too much will. She needed a strong son to provide for the family—she could ill afford to make him feel like a child.

As soon as he rose from mourning, Eliav took me aside. "Thank you for coming, Lev. You brought honor to the living and dead." There was a formality to his voice—he spoke not as Eliav, but as the head of the household.

"Of course," I said. "Your father was as a father to me too."

Eliav nodded. "It was a blessing having you take out the flock all week." He frowned and looked at a spot over my shoulder. "It would have been hard without you."

His words held more than simple gratitude. We both knew the reason I could take the flock was that Uncle Menachem was not my true father.

"Now you'll be returning to Shomron?" He shifted on his feet, his composure eroding.

"Yes, I am needed at my post."

Eliav's shoulders relaxed. As the elder, my presence challenged his role as the man of the house, but I could see in his eyes that more than pride and authority were at stake. "How much grain do you have?" I asked.

"Nine months. A year if we stretch it. Maybe more, if…"

His voice petered off, but one thing was clear from his words, the longer I stayed, the quicker his grain would dwindle. I looked up at the clear sky. It was already early afternoon, too late to make it back to Shomron before the gates closed. "I plan to leave at first light," I told him.

He nodded, and we stood in silence for a few moments. Eliav would never ask me to leave, but he was grateful I would not remain. When he spoke, it was no longer about grain. "You didn't hurt your arm last week," he said quietly.

"No, I didn't." I looked him in the eye. "It was your mother's idea."

"Was it also her idea that you sleep outside the night my father died?"

"It was."

"Why?"

Such a simple question. An image of Eliav sprawled in the dirt before the Baal rose in my heart. Of all the family, he was the one I least wanted to learn the truth. I hesitated. He already knew enough to work out the answer on his own. He might not be as sharp as Dahlia, but he wasn't stupid.

"I'm a Kohen," I said.

"A Kohen?" His eyebrows rose in understanding. "That is why you have no land?"

"Yes." A year ago, his words would have stung. "Your father never wanted to tell me, but I learned the truth not long ago."

Eliav's forehead contorted in thought.

"Both your father and mother felt it best to remain a secret. I'm not sure why," I lied. "Since they didn't want anyone to know, it's best if you share this with no one."

Eliav gave me a questioning look before nodding once. "I won't." He patted me on the shoulder, much like his father used to do. "I'd best see to the flock. They've yet to be out today."

Eliav did go out with the flock, but not alone. Aunt Leah went out with him. It was not unheard of for women to shepherd. It even made some sense, as learning to lead the flock would allow Eliav to take over Uncle Menachem's tasks around the farm. Yet, there was so little work to be done around the farm during the drought that I rejected the idea. If Aunt Leah accompanied Eliav, it was because they had something to discuss.

Aunt Leah returned an hour later, alone. I had Naama riding on my shoulders and was running circles around the house to the sound of her giggles.

Aunt Leah watched us for a moment, then said, "Naama, could I have Lev to myself for a bit?"

I put my little cousin down and followed Aunt Leah along the same path she walked earlier with Eliav. We started in silence, until Aunt Leah said, "Eliav wants to marry Dahlia to Shelah."

A lump rose in my throat. "Didn't Uncle Menachem refuse him?"

"Menachem never said no, just that it was not the right time."

"Didn't he say drought is not a time for planting?"

She walked on without looking at me. "Indeed, those were his words."

"So why not hold by his wishes?" I asked.

"Menachem is no longer here, Lev, and Eliav is only eleven. Even without Dahlia, he has to provide for his mother and three siblings."

Eliav told me he could stretch his grain to a year, perhaps longer if something happened. Was this the something? Giving Dahlia in marriage could stretch his grain for another two months.

"Why to Shelah?" I asked.

"Shelah's a good man."

"He's already twenty-five, at least," I said.

"The gap in age was even greater between your mother and father," Aunt Leah said as she stopped and turned toward me, "and rarely has love burned as theirs did. Shelah has his own farm—he can provide. Dahlia would never be far away."

Everything Aunt Leah said made perfect sense. I always knew Shelah was the more likely suitor. Still, the story I had heard all week of Uncle Menachem pursuing Aunt Leah came to mind. He was rejected by my grandfather but won out because he held my aunt's heart.

"What about me, Aunt Leah?" My chin trembled, and my voice stuck in my throat, but I pushed out the words I needed to say. "Would you give her to me?"

Aunt Leah stopped walking. "Lev, I have long known of your feelings for Dahlia, and of hers for you. I discussed marrying her to you, both with Menachem and now with Eliav. You know Menachem's wishes—he wanted his daughter provided for. Shelah has land. When Menachem heard you were playing before the King, he came close to changing his mind." She turned away, but not before I caught the flash of tears in her eyes. "You walk a dangerous path, Lev, even more than your father before you. Does Dahlia love you more than Shelah? Of course. But love grows with time. Menachem felt Shelah was the right choice."

"What do *you* say?"

"I deferred to my husband."

"And now?"

"Now Eliav fears that if the drought lasts much longer, he won't be able to feed us all. I never shared with him what Dahlia told me about the drought, but that makes Eliav's concerns all the more real. I would prefer to give Dahlia a few more years before making a choice, but the drought does not allow that luxury. She's another mouth to feed at a time when every bite is precious. For some reason, you told Eliav you're a Kohen, so now he knows you will never own land. He's his father's son. He believes stability comes from an inheritance."

"Not during a drought," I said.

Aunt Leah's eyes shot back up to mine. "What do you mean?"

I took a deep breath. "Land doesn't bring stability without rain. Dahlia warned Uncle Menachem of the drought, but Shelah had no such knowledge."

"The drought will not last forever, Lev."

"Perhaps not, but it will get worse. How much grain does Shelah have stored away?"

Aunt Leah hesitated. "I don't know."

"You had better find out before you marry off Dahlia. If he was caught unprepared, you might gain mouths to feed rather than losing one."

Aunt Leah grew silent as she started walking again. "You may be right," she said at last, "but what am I to do?"

"You won't consider giving her to me?" I tried again.

"Lev, I have nightmares about you. When Asher came back and told your uncle that you'd taken leave to visit your family yet never arrived, I feared you dead." Aunt Leah rubbed the tears from her eyes. "I will not lose Dahlia as I lost my sister."

"And if I could promise that Dahlia would not be at risk? That I could keep her safe?"

"That's a promise you cannot make." Aunt Leah took a deep breath, and let her tears flow. "She no longer has a father to look after her. She needs a husband who can provide for her and protect her. You've chosen a dangerous path. I won't tell you to choose any differently, but if you marry Dahlia, her fate is bound up with yours. Do you expect Eliav to care for her if anything happens to you? Do you know how hard it is to marry off a widow?"

The last word stung coming from her. "What if we didn't marry?" I asked.

Aunt Leah turned to me, fire in her eyes. "What are you saying, you would treat my daughter like some concubine?"

"No, never." I shrank from her anger. "Aunt Leah, look at my hands."

Her eyes calmed as she studied my fingers. "I've never noticed how calloused they were."

"That's what's left from the burns I've received from baking bread. I'm better at it now. I rarely burn myself any longer. I spend most of my evenings baking bread to feed hidden prophets."

"Oh Lev, not just Uriel?"

"No, Aunt, there are a hundred. This past week, while we sat in mourning, was the first time I had a full night's sleep in a month."

"What are you saying?"

"You said yourself you would rather wait to marry off Dahlia, that you would only do so now to have one less mouth to feed. There's another choice. I can take her back to Shomron, without committing her to marrying me or anyone else. She can live in Ovadia's house, where I live now, earning her bread by baking for the prophets."

Aunt Leah again walked on in silence. "You are certain Ovadia would take her?"

"We need the help, Aunt. There are so few people we can trust. I trust Dahlia, and if I vouch for her, Ovadia will trust her as well."

Aunt Leah sighed. "Serving another man's family is hardly the path Menachem would have chosen for his daughter."

"Nor is marrying her off during a drought. At Ovadia's, she will have sufficient food, which is more than either Eliav or Shelah can promise her." This last point was a stretch. I knew neither how long Ovadia's grain supply could last, nor how much Shelah had saved away. But at the moment, truth was not my main concern.

"Dahlia was prepared to marry whenever, and to whoever, Menachem deemed most fit," Aunt Leah said. "She was not prepared to serve another outside of marriage. I will put your option to her. If she chooses it, she will have my blessing."

Aunt Leah turned around and led me back to the farm. Everything now rested in Dahlia's hands.

Aunt Leah and I agreed Dahlia's joining me in Shomron was not a pledge of marriage. Yet, anyone seeing Dahlia's face that evening would have sworn she became a bride. She and I had spoken little since her father died, and she almost never made direct eye contact—knowing her father's death might necessitate her marriage to Shelah. Now that her mother was sending her to Shomron, her eyes almost never left me as she knelt before the oven, baking bread for her family one last time.

Dahlia packed her belongings—three times. Then there were the goodbyes—long, tear-filled goodbyes between Dahlia, her mother, and her siblings. Eliav and I were the only ones tearless, though it was hard to say which of us was happier with the arrangement.

As much as Eliav wanted to marry off Dahlia to Shelah to preserve his supply of grain, that plan would still require him to feed Dahlia until the marriage, then provide for the wedding feast, which despite the drought would require him to give a ram from the flock and a portion of his remaining grain. Then there was the chance, as Aunt Leah no doubt warned him, that Shelah's own grain supplies were lacking.

Yet, Eliav's joy flowed from more than preserving his grain. He cared for us both and was genuinely happy to see us set off together. Of course, he didn't know Dahlia would be feeding hidden prophets. Eliav thought she would be serving in the house of the King's steward, earning her bread in a respectable manner which still allowed for marriage to Shelah after the drought's end.

When we finally set out, the sun had already risen above the eastern hilltops. I carried Dahlia's bundle as she walked along at my elbow. "When my father died, I thought for sure they would give me to Shelah. Last night, when my mother told me I could choose, I never dreamed the other choice would be serving the prophets." She blushed and looked away. "I expected it to be you."

We turned north on the King's Road, with no other travelers in sight. For the first time, we were alone. "I asked for your hand," I said. "Your mother refused."

"Really?" Dahlia giggled. Dahlia never giggled. It made her look so young. "You asked?"

"She feared I would be killed and you left a widow." It was a harsh truth, but she needed to understand where we were headed.

"Perhaps when the drought is over, and the fighting has ended—"

Though she voiced my own hopes, I felt the blood rising to my cheeks. "Do not plan for after the drought, Dahlia. We are not at the drought's end, perhaps not even at its middle. There is no knowing if either of us will live to see the next rains."

She did not shrink from my words. "Very well, Lev. I will not speak of the future. I will bake bread for the prophets as you wish."

As I wished. Her mother gave her the choice between Shelah and the prophets, and she chose me. Of course, I had done the same. I wasn't bringing her to Shomron to help the prophets, but to stop her marriage to Shelah. "I'm bringing you into the middle of a war, and I didn't even ask you."

"I was already in the middle of a war," she said. "I lost my father to it."

I'd planted this idea in her head the year before. "Ovadia will accept help only from those devoted to the prophets, from one who would never betray them no matter what the cost. He may question you when we reach his house."

"I've never met a prophet, but I'll never betray you."

"And if I should be killed?"

"Then I'll marry Shelah or whoever else my mother sees fit. But I'll take our secrets with me to the grave."

This was the Dahlia I knew. I'd frightened her the previous year when I sprang the truth on her. Now that she had absorbed it, her will was more powerful than her fear.

"Still want to see the Queen?" I asked.

"Once I wanted to look upon her beauty. Now I only wish to understand who it is we're fighting." She hesitated, then asked, "Lev, is it true what they say about the priestesses of Ashera?"

I turned my eyes away. "I don't know what you've heard."

"Yes, you do."

I sighed. "Yes, it's true."

"Have you…" She broke off, hugging her arms across her chest. "No, don't answer. I'd rather not know."

I felt a rush of gratitude toward Yonaton for saving me. "Dahlia, it's impossible to serve the prophets and Ashera at the same time. I made my choice."

Though physical contact was forbidden between us now that we'd both come of age, Dahlia reached over and took my hand. "And I've made mine."

Dahlia's eyes grew wide as we approached Shomron. The capital was many times larger than our small town, with the palace towering over the city walls and soldiers guarding the gates. Though Dahlia stared at the guards, particularly the strange uniform of the Tzidonian one, they took no notice of us as we passed through the city gates. Dahlia was as invisible as I.

I banged on the gate of Ovadia's house, and Batya opened it a crack to peek through. She saw me first, then her eyes found Dahlia. It was a risk to allow a stranger into the house, but even more dangerous to question me in the street. After a moment of indecision, she opened the door wide enough for us to slip into the courtyard. As soon as the gate was shut and locked behind us, she turned on me. "Who is this?"

The door of the house opened. The woman who stepped out looked more like a corpse than person, her skin was deathly pale, and her eyes looked huge in sunken sockets. Yet, Tamar stood upright, her hands covered in flour, with no signs of fever upon her brow. "This must be Dahlia," she said.

Dahlia pushed her curls out of her eyes and said, "I have come to help."

There are many designs in one's heart, but the Holy One's plan is accomplished.
Proverbs 19:21

19

The Lost Prophecy

In the coming months, I could not shake the feeling Tamar came back to life solely to mentor Dahlia. The idea was absurd, for Tamar had been standing already when we returned. Nevertheless, from that day forward, I rarely saw the two of them apart. Dahlia did the kneading, which Tamar was still too weak to handle, while Tamar baked on the indoor oven. The kitchen never fell silent while they worked, though rarely did they speak loudly enough for me to overhear anything. At first, Dahlia's voice dominated, while Tamar listened and responded. After a few weeks, Tamar did most of the speaking, with Dahlia only interrupting when she had a question. That's when I knew Tamar had found herself a disciple.

When we first arrived, Dahlia snuck glances at me from the kitchen, and I felt the promise that coming to Shomron meant more than just aiding the prophets. Once she began listening to Tamar, she kept her eyes upon her work when I was in the house, though I could tell from the color in her cheeks that this cost her some effort.

Even at night, there was no hiding from Tamar's watchful eyes as Dahlia slept in her quarters. While Dahlia had been in Levonah, I went weeks without thinking of her. Now that she was in Shomron, I thought of her constantly, but even speaking to each other became a rarity in Ovadia's house.

The nights lengthened toward midwinter without any sign of rain. As the soil turned to dust, Izevel finally took an interest in the suffering of the petitioners who crowded the Throne Room.

"The spring lies within my inheritance," said the younger of two farmers, who came in with an increasingly common dispute. "He has no right to the water."

"I have taken water from that spring my entire life," the other responded, "as my father did before me, and his father before him."

"As long as it flowed strong, I was happy to let you take your needs," the first one said, "but now that it slows to a trickle, I must put my family first."

"The water seeps through the rocks on your land, but that does not make it yours," the older one said.

The King opened his mouth to respond, but Izevel placed a hand on his arm and leaned forward toward the petitioners. He looked at her in surprise but didn't interrupt. She licked her lips and said, "Your families have been neighbors for generations, and yet now you fight. You do know why, do you not?"

The younger one squirmed under Izevel's gaze. "It is the drought, my Queen."

"Indeed," Izevel said. "Do you know why we have the drought?"

Both men shook their heads. "No, my Queen."

"Eliyahu, a prophet, cursed the land in the name of his god."

The older of the two men, the one denied the water, clenched his hand into a fist. The Queen grinned at his frustration. "So long as his field is closer to the spring, he has first right to the water," she said, sitting straight. Ahav turned to his wife in shock. She was correct according to the strict custom of the land, yet the King always attempted to find a way to arouse compassion in such petitioners and encourage them to reach an agreement.

"What are we to do, my Queen?" the older one asked.

"Is there no priest of Baal near your home?" she inquired.

"There is, my Queen."

"Go to him," Izevel said. "I will give you a scroll to present to him, and he will give you enough water each day to keep your family alive."

The man stood tall, his pride aroused. "And if I do not wish to bow before his god?"

Izevel stared down at him. "Then you may lay the bodies of your children at Eliyahu's feet."

The farmer could not meet her gaze, and when his head fell, he mumbled, "Thank you, my Queen. I will take the scroll."

The two farmers had come to the Throne Room together, but each left alone. The younger one hurried out after the Queen pronounced her judgment while the elder one waited for Otniel to prepare his scroll. He exited with heavy steps.

I kept my face blank, masking my rising anger. The next petitioners attempted to step forward, but the magistrate held them back, waiving someone else forward from the back of the Throne Room. It was the white-haired general, the one who had rescued me from the tattooed soldier. Outwardly he looked calm, but his stiffened shoulders indicated that he too was swallowing rage at what just transpired.

I had not seen the general in many months, but the mystery of his actions had not diminished. Was he the ally we so desperately needed? I stared at him as he spoke directly to the king, but his back was to the musicians as he made his report. Even Tamar couldn't have learned anything from the way he stood. When he finished, the King nodded, and the general bowed as he stepped away from the throne.

As the general reached the oaken doors of the Throne Room, I felt a sudden clarity of will. I signaled to Dov that I needed a break. It was time to solve this mystery.

I left the Throne Room in such haste that it drew a few stares, but I did not want to lose my quarry. When I reached the palace gates, the general was already on the main road. I descended the hill, only to see him turn into the very grove where he had rescued me months before. I rushed to follow, but there was no sign of him as I entered the trees.

"I wondered if you would come." The voice was behind me, and I spun around as the general stepped from the cover of a thick olive tree. "You want answers. I suppose you are owed that much. Keep following, but this time don't look so obvious. When you enter my house, make sure no one sees."

He left the grove without looking back or waiting for my reply. I waited a few moments, then followed behind. I arrived at the corner in time to see which house was his. I lingered until the street was empty, then dashed forward to slip through the unlocked gate. A woman baked bread in the courtyard, but she didn't even lift her head as I walked past her into the house.

"Sit." The general pointed to a stool. He said nothing else, so I sat silently, waiting for him to begin. I had taken a great risk in following, but the clarity had not left my heart. I needed to know. I was mustering myself to ask a question when the woman from the courtyard came in, stoked up the fire in the hearth, hung a kettle of water over the coals, and left. Even once she exited the room, he said nothing, just looked me over. His eyes paused longest on my face, but he examined my arms, chest, and even legs as well. He grinned at the trembling in my hands, but overall he appeared disappointed with what he saw.

I broke the silence. "Why did you save me?"

"Should I let these foreigners come into our land and kill our people?"

"Isn't that what our King is doing?" It was a stupid thing to say to the King's general, but the words sprang from my mouth. Ovadia would have scolded me for my recklessness.

The general's hand clenched into a fist on the wooden table. "Yes, that is exactly what our beloved King is doing."

His reply encouraged me to push further. "So you protect the people when the King is not looking?"

The general snorted. "I am not that sort of fool. That soldier's blood was the first I've shed since these pigs came into our land."

"Then why did you save me?" I asked.

"I saw the way he watched you in the Throne Room," the general said. "He had death in his eyes. When you left the palace, I followed."

It was precisely what he said on the night of the rescue. If he was loyal to the prophets, why hold back now? If he wasn't, how did he come to know that I was a Kohen? I asked for a third time, "Why did you save me?"

It was the same question, but this time, his whole body tightened up. He brought his fist to his mouth, pressing the knuckles against his lips as if afraid to speak. Finally, he said in a low voice, "Call it a debt I owed."

"A debt to whom?"

"Your father."

His answer was so unexpected that for a moment I was struck dumb. "My father? You knew my father?"

The door creaked open, and the woman from the courtyard entered to stir the kettle over the hearth. The general motioned me to be silent, and only when she left did he nod for me to continue.

"Knowing my father is a secret you keep even from your wife?"

He eyed the shut door. "She is a concubine, not my wife. My wife is dead."

I had never heard of a man of the general's importance without at least one wife. If his wife died at the hand of the Tzidonians, or even from the drought, that might explain his willingness to kill their soldiers. Maybe this had nothing to do with the prophets. I had to be sure. "When did she die?" I asked.

"Over a decade ago," he said.

A decade? So her death had nothing to do with the Tzidonians or the drought. But if it had been so long, then why was he still alone? "You have not remarried in all this time?"

"No, Lev." He paused as if it hurt to say my name. "I will neither remarry nor have children. I took a barren woman as a concubine, and that is all I will ever do."

This made less and less sense. "You have no children either?"

"None. My wife died in childbirth." His eyes bore into mine as he said this, as if I were responsible for her death.

A decade ago, I was only a baby, losing my own parents. In a flash, it all fell into place. I jumped to my feet. "You're Yoav!"

"Keep your voice down, boy. Yes, I am Yoav ben Alon." He swallowed hard. "I made you an orphan."

I glared at my parents' murderer. A lifetime of anger struggled to spill out, and I clenched my hands as if to strike him. But the memory of the tattooed soldier was strong. Yoav had killed my parents and saved me from certain death. My heart raced, and I wanted to scream. I dreamt of this moment, of hurting the one who had taken my parents, and now I owed him my life.

Tamar taught me not to struggle with my rage, but to let it rise and pass through me. Tears welled in my eyes as I forced breaths in and out. As I gained control, both anger and gratitude gave way to confusion. "You should be dead!"

"Dead?" A sad smile flitted across his face. "Why do you say so?"

I remembered every detail of Shimon's story about my parents' death. At the recollection of his name, another wave of fury pulsed through me and I gritted my teeth. "You were to fall slaying Tivni."

"Ah…that bastard soldier was right. You have been with the prophets." His eyes gleamed as he spoke. "I wondered if you'd only lied to save your skin. You know about Uriel's curse. Did you not hear it all?"

I thought back to the story in the cave. Shimon told it a few days before he died at the hands of the tattooed soldier. I could still picture Uriel and Yoav's confrontation as my father lay dying, though the scene burned with a new clarity now that I knew Yoav's face.

"Your future is in your own hands," Uriel said. "You are a man of strength. Turn your strength inward, conquer your anger, and live."

"And if I don't?" Yoav asked.

"Then your greatest act of valor will be your last. King Tivni will die by your sword, but you will fall as well."

Shimon portrayed Yoav as a man of burning anger. It never occurred to me he might conquer himself. Yet, here he sat before me in the posture of one whose passions were firmly in his hand. His words made it clear he had accepted the reality of Uriel's curse, if not its justice. Though his jaw clenched as he spoke of the ruin of his family, his voice remained calm.

"How did you discover who I was?" I asked.

"I heard the head musician call you by name—that got my attention. You look like your father, and you're the right age. But I didn't know for sure until I asked if you could help me with the body."

"So you saved me as penitence for killing my parents? Do you expect me to forgive you now?"

"I make my penitence before the Holy One, boy." I saw the pain in his eyes. "I need no man's forgiveness, not even yours. I called what I did paying a debt, and so it was. But there is also the prophecy."

"Prophecy?" I asked. "What prophecy?"

Yoav squinted at me. "You don't know? You know the story of my curse, and that soldier said you were with some elderly prophet. I assumed it was Uriel."

"It was." My heart pounded again, but this time with neither fear nor anger.

His confusion grew. "Uriel told you why my wife died, but not why your parents died?"

I hesitated. Uriel had shared little; it was Shimon who spoke. Did he hold something back, or was there more to the story than he knew? "I thought you killed them for crossing into the Kingdom of Judah?"

Yoav shook his head. "That was the justification, not the reason."

"Was it because my father wanted to reunite the Kingdom?"

Yoav laughed. "Your father was hardly the only one who wanted that. Then or now." He let his words hang before continuing. "Many thought the solution to the civil war was for both Omri and Tivni to step aside and allow the King of Judah to once again rule over the entire land."

"Why did you kill him then?"

"Because of a prophecy," Yoav said. "One I wished to destroy, and indeed thought I did. Until I saw you."

"What was the prophecy?"

"Uriel never told you?" Yoav passed a hand over his face in disbelief. "But he's been training you nonetheless," he said with sudden energy. "It's no coincidence he's taken you under his wing all these years later. Or that you are here in the palace at such a time. The prophecy is still alive for him, as it is for me."

Uriel told me he took me under his wing because of my father. Was that only part of the truth? "What prophecy?"

Yoav took a deep breath. "That through your father, the House of David would be restored to the throne."

I dropped back in my seat as my whole life came into focus. Now I knew why King Omri wanted my father dead. I understood Uriel's secrecy. The dangerous power of prophecies often led the prophets to keep them hidden.

Which raised another question. "The prophets are careful with their words. How is it you knew about the prophecy?"

"That was your father's undoing. He spoke of it often, perhaps to build support for reunion."

I hung my head as my heart absorbed his words. "So you killed him to stop the prophecy from coming true?"

"Yes, and until a few months ago, I believed I succeeded. Now I'm less certain. Prophets die more easily than their words."

"Less certain? My father is dead, and Omri's son sits on the throne. The prophecy failed."

"Did it?" Yoav asked. "A prophecy is the word of the Holy One. Can an ordinary man like me stamp it out?"

I felt a growing discomfort in my chest. "What do you mean?"

"I wonder now if we all misunderstood the prophecy from the beginning, and it has yet to come to pass."

"You killed my father," I said.

"I did, and I intended to kill you as well, but I couldn't bring myself to do it. Instead, I left you to die. You would not have lasted more than a day by yourself. But you didn't die. Uriel found you. After all these years, you are here, in the Throne Room of the King."

The general had a hungry look in his eye. He wanted something from me. I didn't know what it was, but I drew back. "What are you saying?"

"Perhaps the prophecy wasn't speaking of your father at all. It said, 'through him, the Kingship would return to the House of David.' 'Through him' could also apply to his son. As long as Yochanan's seed lives, the prophecy can still come true." His face lit with hope. "It can be fulfilled through you!"

"Me?" I pulled back and my heart raced. "You think I'm the one destined to restore the Throne to the House of David?"

"Why not you? You're Yochanan's son! All we lack to throw the foreign yoke off our necks is someone to rally the people. There are enough still alive who remember your father, who remember the prophecy." He stood and held out his finger at me. "They would rally around you."

Was this the true reason Uriel made me his disciple? Was this why mentioning my father's name had such an impact on Pinchas and Kenaz? Did they see me as a savior? Uriel warned me it was dangerous to let people know I was a Kohen, for any Kohanim in the land were a challenge to the legitimacy of the current priests of Israel. Yet, the Kohanim were mostly forgotten in the Kingdom, and the few who remained blended in amongst the people. Had Uriel lied to me? Was the source of danger *my father* and not *my tribe*?

"This is the real reason you followed me that night?" I asked.

Yoav nodded. "If the prophecy is going to come true, you need to live. When I saw the way that soldier looked at you, I knew I needed to act."

Something still didn't make sense. "Why do you want the prophecy to come true?"

Yoav looked like he was slapped. "Sorry?"

"You killed my father to end the prophecy. You helped the House of Omri win the Throne, and now you serve King Ahav. You want him to fall from power?"

Yoav kept his voice calm, but only with effort. "He already has."

"What?"

"Open your eyes, Lev. The King may sit on the Throne, but he bows to the gods of Tzidon. Tzidonian soldiers hunt our prophets, and King Ahav does nothing to oppose them. You ask if I want this prophecy to come true? Absolutely. Better that Israel bow to the House of David than the House of Ethbaal."

My eyes narrowed. "You would overthrow King Ahav?"

Yoav took a breath, then shook his head. "I would not spill the blood of a King of Israel."

"And the soldiers of Tzidon?"

"Should King Ahav give the order, I would rid the land of every last one of the vermin."

"And their Temples?" I asked.

"I'd burn them to the ground."

"And Queen Izevel?"

"I'd hang her from the walls of Shomron if I could, but exile would be the wiser course."

For the first time in months, I felt hope. "Do many feel as you do?"

"Among the army, certainly. We do not like foreigners coming into our land, killing our people at will."

Yoav knew I was connected to Uriel, but did he suspect we had so many hidden prophets? Would he rise to their defense? I decided to test him with one more question. "What of the Golden Calf?"

Yoav blinked. "The Calf? What does the Calf have to do with this? Once the Kingdom is reunited, the Calf can give way to the Temple. Until then, it is our connection to the Holy One."

One cannot serve two masters. I had learned that lesson already. Those dedicated to the prophets did not bow to the Calf. Despite how powerful an ally Yoav could be, I would not tell him about the Cave of Dotan. As my father's murder showed, the secrets of the prophets should not be revealed lightly.

My heart was still pounding as I rose to leave. I saw disappointment in Yoav's eyes. No doubt he wanted me to stay, to plan how I could rally the people around me, yet he did nothing to prevent me from going. I knew I ought to thank him for saving my life, but I couldn't. I hadn't mastered my heart that deeply.

One thing still bothered me. How could my master have lied to me all this time? Why did Uriel not tell me the truth about my father? I stopped on the threshold of his door. "You are certain Uriel knew of this prophecy?"

"Absolutely," Yoav said. "He was the prophet."

Do not boast of tomorrow, for you do not know what the day will bring.

Proverbs 27:1

20

Grain and Blood

I left Yoav determined to confront my master, but it was not to be. Death stalked the prophets at Dotan, and twice I was turned away from even entering the cave. When I finally did succeed, I found the old prophet too feeble to even sit in the darkness. Rather than confront him, I gave him what comfort I could—holding a cup to his lips and distracting him with stories from the Throne Room.

Winter passed and spring came, but I kept the prophecy to myself. Neither Dahlia nor Yonaton would understand. I could have opened my heart to Tamar, but I feared what she might say. I didn't know what would be worse: if she told me the prophecy had failed, or that it was still bound to come true. The ground grew hard as iron and a yellow haze hung in the sky. Disputes over food and water became common, and the King kept extending Court later and later to accommodate all the petitioners. No matter how Ahav ruled, Izevel made sure that all who came left knowing Eliyahu was the true source of their suffering.

I continued to take my meals in the palace kitchen, though now I ate very little. As long as Ovadia fed the prophets, there would be no lack of *challah*, and in the kitchen, the cooks prepared less and less for the servants, so eating there felt like taking food from the mouths of others.

One evening, only one cook stood at the hearth. One of the pages eating in the kitchen called out, "It's the silence of the dead in here."

It was Eder. As a page, he stood quietly most of the day and liked to relax by running his mouth after Court. When no one responded, he added, "I miss the ravens."

His comment drew a weak laugh from a couple of maidservants, but the cook's shoulders tightened. "They must have grown wise and gone elsewhere for their food," he said. "A page could do worse than learn from a bird."

"The cooks must have improved their aim, otherwise wisdom says the King's kitchen is the easiest place for a bird to find a meal," he paused and looked around at the listening servants. "At least they were in no danger here." This drew a real laugh and some admiring looks from the maidservants. Few dared to mock the cooks in their kitchen.

"Curse them! Those were no ordinary ravens." The cook swore under his breath and turned back to the hearth. "Anyway, I expect they've gone on to raid fuller pantries."

"Fuller pantries?" Eder asked. "Whose pantry is fuller than the King's?"

"Anyone with decent grain storage and not so many big mouths to feed." The cook said.

The servants laughed at Eder's blush, but their smiles faded quickly when the cook turned back toward them. His face was serious. "The King must have stores of grain," one of the maidservants said.

"The King *had* tremendous stores." The cook leaned in. "But if you haven't noticed, not much wheat was gathered last year, and this year there will be no harvest at all."

"A failed harvest is no threat to the kings of Israel." This came from Amram, one of the scribes. "In the days of King Omri, five years' worth of grain were stored. When King Ahav rose to power, he heeded Ovadia's words and raised it to ten." He flicked a bit of dust from the sleeve of his linen tunic. "I myself wrote the order."

"Scribes always know, eh?" The cook's grin was not unfriendly. "Do you also know that ten times as many people eat from the King's table as did two years ago?"

Silence fell. "That can't be," Eder said.

"No?" the cook asked. "The servants of the Court alone have doubled. The Queen insists on musicians in the Throne Room now." He pointed to Tuval and myself.

"I don't eat that much," Tuval said.

"You eat your share and then some." The cook turned back to the scribe. "But that's just the beginning. Two hundred and fifty priestesses of Ashera and two hundred priests of the Baal eat from the Queen's table each day." He held up another finger to make each point. "Then there are the poor and diseased who have descended on Shomron from around the Kingdom seeking the King's mercy. You won't see them, as Queen Izevel won't allow them near the gates, but we send them bread each day by Ovadia's orders."

"Are you saying the King's stores are going to run out?" Amram asked.

"When Queen Izevel arrived in Shomron for her wedding, there were four grain shafts, all full," the cook said. "Now three are empty, and each time I go into the fourth, I have to descend further to get to the grain. I don't know how many more steps until I hit bottom, but it can't be too many."

"How long until we run out?" Eder asked.

"We would've run out already if not for the wagonloads of grain King Ethbaal sends down from Tzidon. That's most of what we've been eating the past month. Haven't any of you noticed the difference in the bread?"

From the faces of the servants, it was clear no one had.

"Is there no drought in Tzidon?" Eder asked.

"I suppose not, if their King has grain to spare."

Only I knew he was mistaken. The grain didn't come from Tzidon, where the rain had also ceased to fall. It was brought by Tzidon's merchant fleet all the way from Tarshish. But I wasn't going to risk my secrecy to prove the cook wrong.

"How much of the Tzidonian grain is left?" Amram asked.

"That's the last of it there," the cook waved his knife toward a pile of sacks in the corner. "I'm told there is another load coming tomorrow, but the caravans have been late before. If it doesn't come, I'll be going back into our grain stores in two days' time, and we'll keep digging toward the floor."

I still had half a piece of bread before me, and I finished it in two bites. I was in a sudden hurry to leave, but after what the cook had said, I could hardly leave it uneaten. If he was right that there was another caravan of grain arriving the following day, I needed to get word to Pinchas tonight.

"What happened?" Yonaton asked as he opened the gate and saw my face.

"Inside."

He followed me in, and all three women paused in their chatter, though not in their kneading, to listen. "How much grain do we have left?" I asked.

"That," Yonaton said, pointing to a half-empty sack in the corner, "plus two more in the courtyard."

Batya sighed, "Is that all?"

"Do you know how Ovadia plans to get more?" I asked her.

Batya shook her head. "I don't even know where he got the silver for this last batch. I fear he's been selling land. Or worse, borrowing on interest. Why?"

"A caravan of grain is supposed to arrive tomorrow from Tzidon," I said. "I thought to alert Pinchas."

"Have you spoken to Ovadia about it?" Batya asked.

"No, I was hoping to find him here. Do you know when he will return?"

"No."

A ram's horn blast echoed in the distance. "Is that the first horn for the gates closing or the second?" I asked.

"It's the first I've heard," Yonaton said. "We can make it if we run."

It should have been Ovadia's decision whether to tell Pinchas of the caravan or not, but there was no time to wait for him. We needed to go now or miss our chance. I still held my musicians' clothing in my hand. "I'll put away my tunic, and we'll go."

"I'll do that for you," Dahlia said, taking the tunic from my hands. "Be careful."

I barely had time to meet her eyes before Yonaton grabbed my arm, and the two of us ran out toward the gate. We were not the only ones racing down the main road of the city—this was the one time of day we could run through the gates without attracting attention. We squeezed through just before the guard blew the final blast on the ram's horn and pulled the gates closed behind us.

Only once out did I stop to think how ill-prepared we were. In our rush, we had brought neither bread nor water, and I would not reduce the prophets' portions by taking from them. The sun was already beneath the horizon, and the moon wouldn't rise for several hours, leaving us to walk most of the way in darkness.

When we finally arrived at the cave, I whispered, "It's Lev and Yonaton," into the cracks of the cliff as we approached, knowing they would hear our footsteps. When we reached the top of the hill, the boulder had already been rolled back, and Ariel stood beside it, waving us in.

"You come with news?" Pinchas asked as soon as my feet hit the cavern floor.

"Yes, Master Pinchas. A cook in the kitchen said he expects a caravan of grain to arrive tomorrow from Tzidon."

"It will come along the coastal road?"

"I expect so."

"You expect? What does Ovadia say?"

"I could not find Ovadia, and there was no time to wait if I wished to bring you word before the closing of the gates."

"Do you know what time tomorrow they expect the caravan to reach Shomron? It might still be some distance away."

"No, Master Pinchas. The cook wasn't even sure it would arrive tomorrow at all."

"What would you have us do? Lay in ambush in case it comes?"

"That is for you to decide, Master Pinchas."

"I would like to know precisely when it will arrive two days in advance so we can pick the right spot to attack. I would like to know how many wagons are coming, and more importantly, how many soldiers are escorting it. I'd like to track them during the day, mark the spot where they make camp for the night, and attack before they wake."

Pinchas paced across the cave. "It is less than I want, but perhaps more than I have a right to expect. Before I make my decision, does anyone wish to speak?"

"I can go look over the road," Elon said. "It's a cold night. If there's still even a remnant of a fire, it will be visible at a great distance."

"Go."

"We could prepare ourselves at the barrier rocks where the road rises from the coast," Ariel said as Elon headed up the tunnel entrance. "From there, we can watch their approach and only attack if we have greater numbers."

"How many could we hide in the rocks?" Pinchas asked.

"If we are certain of attacking, twenty-five can hide long enough to take them by surprise. But if we chose not to attack, they would see us as they passed. More than ten cannot hope to remain secret."

"Ten is too few."

Elon returned to the cave. "There are three fires close together along the road to the north."

"How far away?"

"I would guess an hour's walk."

"Only a large company requires three fires," Pinchas said. "How long until the moon rises?"

"There is already a glow in the eastern sky."

"I will lead a small group," Pinchas said. "Eight men, no more. We will investigate, then decide our next step."

"Will eight men be enough?" Ariel asked.

"To investigate, yes. To attack, most likely not. Ariel, you remain here in command. Be ready to lead the others. We will send word whether you are to join us at their campsite or the barriers. Elon, you come with me." Pinchas chose several more fighters, all on the smaller side, focusing more on stealth than strength. "Lev, you come as well."

"Me?" I was no fighter.

"I need someone who doesn't look like a fugitive."

Yonaton was stronger and more agile. I was about to suggest Pinchas should take him when I recalled Kenaz calling the cave a deathtrap. Sitting in the darkness, waiting for word if the mission was successful, or if the group would return with soldiers in pursuit, felt worse than anything which lay ahead. I followed Pinchas out with the other disciples.

Two hours later, I entered the enemy camp alone. As we approached, Pinchas gave me a tattered sleeping mat, and I strapped it to an empty pack taken from one of the disciples. My disguise was completed with a worn skin, empty save for a sip or two of thick water. I hummed a familiar tune as I continued up the road from where Pinchas halted the group, around a bend from the firelight.

One soldier sat alone by a fire built in a broad hollow a stone's throw from the road. As I stepped down the embankment, I saw the open space was filled with wagons, circled around tents and a larger fire pit. The moon lit a row of donkeys tied to a massive tree trunk at the far side of the camp. I called 'hail!' as I left the road, like any honest traveler, and the soldier waved me toward the fire. The cedar tree emblem of Tzidon was clear on his tunic as I approached.

"Do you have any water?" I called out, holding up my skin.

"Shhh!" he lifted a hand to quiet me.

Some instinct told me to ignore him, and I shook the empty water skin in front of him. "Water, I need water. Even a mouthful!"

"Quiet, fool!" He half rose from his seat. "You wake whole camp." I nodded silently, and he motioned me to take a seat by the fire. "I have water," he said. "You have copper?"

"Copper!" My voice rang loud in the quiet of the night. Had things grown so bad that a traveler must pay for water? Or was that the Tzidonian way? "I am a poor shepherd returning from my master's flock. The copper I earned is to buy grain for my family."

"No shout," he hissed, and motioned for me to lower my voice. "Many sleeping." Then his eyes lit up. "You buy grain?"

This was the caravan. "You have grain to sell?"

"More grain than you can eat here." Then he shook a finger at me. "Not to sell."

I laughed at his boast. "So you say, but I'm a shepherd, not a fool. Where would a common soldier get such wealth in these days of drought?"

I could tell from his frown that the Tzidonian did not like my laughter, nor being called common. "King's grain," he said. "I guard it."

"It can't be so much grain if you sit alone to guard it."

Now he smiled. "Shepherd know sheep, not war. Big camp mean small guard." He gestured toward the darkness behind him. "Twenty men sleep here."

I leaned forward over the fire. "Twenty men must escort much grain," I lowered my voice to a whisper. "Sell me a sack full."

The soldier's face blanched in the firelight. The Tzidonians were famous for their punishments. "I guard, not merchant."

"Come," I pressed, "with so much grain, who would notice if one sack goes missing?"

He nodded with a frightened laugh. "The master notice."

We sat without speaking for a few moments, then I finished the last swallow in my skin, grimacing as the warm liquid slid down my throat.

"You buy water now?" He asked again. When I shook my head, his face turned harsh. "Then you go, shepherd." He spit out the last word, but it was an insult that had long ago ceased to bother me.

I shrugged. "It will be a thirsty walk home." I rose from the fire and headed back into the dark. When I reached the road, I paused for a moment to look back at the camp behind me. Shadows moved in the darkness between the wagons.

The plan had been for the others to investigate the caravan while I distracted the guard, but I saw Pinchas and the others moving along the edge of the camp in the dark, each with a heavy burden on his shoulder.

Standing there risked alerting the guard. I needed to head along the road, and in my haste, I made a mistake. An honest traveler would have continued up the road in the direction he had been going, but I turned back the way I had come. It was enough to arouse the guard's curiosity.

He called after me, "Boy, stop."

I hesitated. I could tell him I'd passed a proper place to sleep earlier but had pushed on in hopes of finding water. Or I could ignore him and hurry on my way—he wouldn't leave the camp unguarded to chase a shepherd. Danger mounted with every step the guard took from his fire—soon he would notice the thieves.

A shadow rose behind the approaching soldier, and a rock flashed white in the moonlight. A single cry escaped the soldier as he fell, ringing loud in the silence of the night. It must have been one of the disciples who struck him. Pinchas would have used his sword, knowing that a sharp blade is a silent killer.

We didn't wait to see what his cry awoke. The disciples ran back up the road, each carrying a massive sack of grain on his shoulder. We halted at a rocky outcropping which overhung the road after a bend. It was a strong defensive position in case we were pursued. Pinchas had us wait in silence, but no attack came. The guard's groan must not have woken the other soldiers, and given how hard Elon had struck him, it would be quite some time before he roused himself. If he ever got up at all.

At a silent signal from Pinchas, we took to the road again but soon left it to trace a route among the winding goat paths in the hills above the eastern side of the road. When we reached the cave, he whispered "We're back," as we passed the cracks of the cliff face, and by the time we got to the top, the boulder was rolled back from the entrance. Ariel was waiting. "How many did you kill?" he asked Pinchas when he saw the sacks of grain.

"Maybe one, perhaps none."

"There is no pursuit?"

"Not yet, but there will be," Pinchas said. "Our hiding place should be secure, but set a two-man guard just in case."

"I will stand guard myself through the night," Ariel said. "The other disciples may set a rotation for joining me."

I slipped into the cave once all the grain was brought in, seeking out a quiet corner. Ovadia would want my eyes on Izevel in the morning, and I didn't want to have to fight to keep them open as I played my kinnor. I lay down on the rocky floor and dropped off to sleep, exhausted from hours of travel and flight.

When Yonaton shook me awake, I saw grey light coming through the cracks and realized it was almost dawn. "It's time we got back," he said.

I nodded silently and followed Yonaton toward the cave entrance. Together we were strong enough to roll back the boulder when we were outside the cave, but from inside the tunnel, there was not enough room for us both to push it off.

I woke Peleh and asked him to help us. He gave a tired smile and said, "Of course I will release you. We are commanded to redeem captives."

Peleh wormed up into the entrance tunnel, and I followed close behind him. As the boulder shifted under his force, light flooded in through the open space and I smelled the sea. He pushed again, and the boulder tipped, dropping a single, pearly-white barley kernel into the tunnel at his feet. My stomach clenched. Was there was a hole in one of the sacks?

"Peleh, stop!" I called.

"Why?" he said, turning back with a confused face.

The question saved his life, as the sword which struck through the opening pierced his shoulder rather than his head. A quick retreat from the entrance was not possible with me behind Peleh and Yonatan below me.

"Yonaton, pull!" I screamed and grabbed Peleh's feet. Yonaton grabbed my legs, and the three of us slid back into the cave, falling into a heap on the floor.

Tzidonian soldiers must have followed a trail of barley right to the cave. My warning hadn't so much saved Peleh's life as delayed his death. We were trapped.

Pinchas ran over and hoisted Peleh to his feet. "They've gained the entrance? Where's Ariel?"

"He must be dead," Peleh gasped, clutching his bleeding shoulder.

"Master!" cried Elon. Three soldiers appeared through the gaps in the cliff wall. Two held armfuls of dried grasses and wood. The third carried a torch.

The disciples thrust their swords through the larger holes in the cliff wall, but it was no use. The blades were too short to do anything other than surprise the soldiers.

The Tzidonians laid their burdens at the base of the cliff, and more soldiers came behind them. As the pile grew, I realized that they had prepared their attack for hours. The torchbearer lit the grasses, and the sun-dried fuel burst into flame. As the fire kindled, the soldiers continued to throw grass on top, and smoke poured through the cliff wall. A few disciples spat mouths full of water through the crack, but it only added steam to the smoke.

The boulder blocking the cave entrance was rolled back into place, and the cave filled with a choking haze. Avner suggested that we roll it back off, but Pinchas stopped him short, saying it would only make the tunnel a chimney and draw more smoke through the cliff.

My eyes burned, and I lay on the dirt floor with several disciples, sucking at the last of the air. All around me, disciples hacked and coughed from the smoke. Master Pinchas stood with grim determination in the center of the cave, a wet cloth wrapped across his mouth. "Bring me the Ashera." Though his voice was muffled, the disciples leapt to do his will.

Ashera? Why would the prophets have an idol in the cave?

Ten disciples hauled a massive burden out of the deepest reaches of the cave. They reemerged into the smoky main cavern dragging a tree trunk, freshly felled.

"Positions!" Pinchas called. "Elon, take Ariel's place. Kenaz, behind me!"

Elon unsheathed his sword and stepped to the front of a column of fighters which formed on the left side of the tree trunk, Pinchas moved to the front of a second column which lined up across from them. The remaining disciples lifted the Ashera.

"Strike!" Pinchas cried. The disciples surged forward at the cliff wall. A dull thud shook the cave, and more smoke poured through the wall. "Again!" he called. Our best chance was to break through before the Tzidonians realized what was happening. Their main force was on top of the hill. No one would expect an escape through the cliff face.

Pinchas crouched with Kenaz by the wall at the head of his fighters, waiting for the next blow. Even if they broke through, any gap their ram opened would be tiny. Even if one man could crawl through, he would have to face whatever onslaught awaited alone—one nearly starved man against multiple trained killers. It was suicide to lead, but one look at Pinchas left me no question as to who would be the first one out. The prophets expected no one else to die for them.

The trunk swung again and with a loud 'crack!' the entire wall collapsed. The men holding the trunk fell forward to the ground, many of them with their arms pinned beneath the Ashera. The two columns poured through the opening, Pinchas and Elon at their heads. After a stunned moment, the remaining disciples followed, gasping at the fresh air.

"Look," Yonaton said to me as we stepped through the shattered cliff, "they chiseled it out." The stone to our side had been cut away, leaving just enough for the wall to hold together. Pinchas had planned this escape.

By the time the cave was empty, the battle outside was over. Seven Tzidonian soldiers lay dead. Only one remained alive, and he knelt in the center of a circle of disciples. Unlike his companions, he wore a simple woolen tunic, with no cedar tree emblem.

As the circle of swords closed in on this last enemy, his right hand flew up, not to defend himself but to cover his eyes. "She'ma Israel!" he cried out, speaking a phrase declaring the unity of the Holy One, the last words a man of Israel utters before meeting death.

These words saved his life. Kenaz raised a hand, and the circle halted. He stepped forward and leaned over the man. "Who are you?" he asked.

The man shook, too frightened to answer.

"Speak man, if you would save your life!"

"A waggoneer, my lord."

"You were hired to haul grain from Tzidon?" Kenaz asked.

"Yes, my lord." He kept his head down.

"Where are you from?"

"From Dan, my lord." The waggoneer's voice trembled.

"You are a man of Israel, and you fight with the Tzidonians?" Kenaz asked.

"Mercy, my lord." He lifted his eyes to the prophet, sensing death might not be certain. "They gave me no choice. A man must defend his caravan."

"Indeed he must, waggoneer." Kenaz grabbed his arm and hoisted him to his feet. "Go now and return to your caravan."

The waggoneer blinked at Kenaz. His eyes dropped to his weapon on the ground. "May I take my sword?"

"Does the sword belong to you or the Tzidonians?" Kenaz asked.

"It is mine, my lord."

"Very well, then take your sword," Kenaz said. "Just remember who are your brothers and who are your enemies."

The disciples stood by in silence—no one contested Kenaz. The waggoneer snatched up his sword and with a frightened look bowed to the prophet. "Bless you for your mercy, my lord!" He fled toward the road. I looked around for Pinchas. Surely he would never agree to let one who fought with the Tzidonians, who knew the location of the cave, leave alive and with his sword?

Then I noticed our dead. The first fighters out of the cave had followed Pinchas without hesitation, and their bodies lay beside his at the base of the cliff.

"Neither my wife nor my daughter is receiving enough to eat," the petitioner said. It was unusual for a slave to stand before the King, but Ahav gave the man the same attention any petitioner received. Izevel focused on the musicians, showing no sign that she noticed the lowly stature of the petitioner, except perhaps for a deepening of the sneer which she always wore when a commoner spoke before the Throne. The absolute boredom on her face told me she knew nothing of the grain stolen that morning. Or of the soldiers killed.

"It is the drought, my King" the slave's owner replied. "Even my own family goes without."

"You look well enough fed yourself," the King said.

The man blushed. "Fed, yes, my King, but not well fed. I eat what I must to labor while I may."

"The laws of Israel are clear," the King said. "Your duty to your slave and his family come before even your duty to yourself. You have a choice: feed them or free them."

The owner bowed his head in acceptance of the King's word. The next petitioner made to step forward, but the magistrate put up a hand to stop him and waved forward three men from the back of the Throne Room. Two wore the cedar tree on their tunic.

One of the men had his right eye swollen shut, the entire side of his face purple and bruised. It was the guard who tried to sell me water the night before. Beside him walked the waggoneer, flanked by another soldier of Tzidon. The Queen snapped her fingers at Dov to play louder. Dov launched into a new melody—the very one I had hummed as I entered the enemy's camp.

The wounded guard looked up with a start of recognition. I raised my kinnor before my face, limited shield though it was. Surely he would not think to look for a shepherd boy in the Throne Room of the King.

The Queen's hands clenched the arms of her throne as she listened to their whispered report, and even the King's face grew dark. The waggoneer's presence told her that prophets lived, and where they were to be found. Kenaz was wise enough to have all of the men and the grain hidden by now, but when the Queen's men reached an empty cave, her wrath would only grow. Then where would her vengeance fall?

The attack the night before had been made without Ovadia's knowledge or consent. Nothing connected him to the attack, but that didn't matter. As Ovadia had warned me, she sought any justification to attack him—that's why he wanted me on the watch. Her power had grown, and she no longer needed excuses to strike. Would she lash out against him to vent her wrath? Even without the deaths of Pinchas and the others, Ovadia's life would be too big a price to pay for seven sacks of grain.

It was at the end of the day when Mot surprised me. He was waiting in the narrow passage which led off from the courtyard between the main palace and the servants' buildings. I had passed it every day on my way to the kitchen, only I never noticed it was the perfect place for an ambush.

When he grabbed me, I was too shocked to struggle and before I knew what was happening the old priest was dragging me into the darkness. He stopped beneath a torch burning in a bracket and pushed me against the stone wall with surprising force.

"You are the spy!" he hissed.

A wave of panic washed over me. How did he know? Fortunately, my fear prevented me from doing anything more than stuttering, "W-what?"

"The spy," Mot leaned close. "You are the one the Queen placed in Ovadia's house."

I shook my head. "I'm no spy."

"Fool! Wasn't it clear why she put you in Ovadia's house? I must know what he is plotting."

"Plotting?" I asked, hoping to gain time. Once again I was caught without a proper story.

"Yes." Mot released me and stepped back. "What have you seen? Who comes to his house? Is he often away at night?"

"I only return to his home to sleep."

Mot frowned. "The Queen assured me that you knew your business and would not fail." He held a leathery finger up to my face, "You do know the price for failing your Queen, do you not?"

I nodded. There was no need to ask.

"Tell me this," his voice dropped to a whisper, "what does he do with all the grain he buys?"

In that moment, Tamar's training saved me. Inside my heart raced, but I managed to answer him with a questioning look.

"Grain?"

"Yes, grain! He has been buying large quantities quietly for some time. But not quietly enough." The torchlight danced in Mot's eyes as they went wide. "What I do not know is why?"

I had to distract him, put him on the wrong path, but it was all I could do to hold down my fear. Mot continued to mutter to himself. I turned the question on him. "Why would he buy so much grain? For profit?"

"In drought, one who controls the grain controls the hearts of men."

As Mot answered my first question, I tried another. "To what purpose?"

"It could be a plot. Some treasonous plan to stir rebellion in the city." He looked straight into my eyes. "Have any noblemen been visiting him?"

Silence would not satisfy his hunger, so I said the first name that came to me. "Micha. Micha ben Yehudah. Once when I returned from a festival, they were speaking together in the courtyard."

"Yes," said Mot to himself, "it could be, then. It could be Ovadia plots against his King, hoping grain gives him power as the drought grows."

Despite my fear, I felt a pang of regret. I knew nothing about Micha ben Yehudah, other than he had conspired with Izevel and Elifaz at the Queen's birthday feast. "It cannot be," I ventured in a small voice.

"What?" Mot's eyes came back into focus on mine. "Why not?"

"I've learned that Ovadia is foreign born. He owes everything to his King."

"Bah!" Mot scowled. "Loyalty fades before the lust for power."

I forced myself to breathe and shook my head. "The people of Shomron would never follow a foreigner against their own King."

"What do you know of such things, boy? The people of Israel are sheep. They will follow whoever leads them." Mot hesitated. "Why does Ovadia hoard grain?" He asked again, and I heard doubt enter his voice. "I want you to keep an extra close eye on him."

"As you say, Master."

Mot paused at my choice of words. He placed his hand on my shoulder. "Boy, if it is a master you seek, you could do no better than I. Uncover for me the secret of Ovadia's grain, and I will make you my servant." He gave a smile so warm that I trembled at its force. "It is good to have a powerful master in uncertain times."

That night, Yonaton brought word that the remaining prophets were safe in the Cave of Dotan, along with the stolen grain. When he returned home, Ovadia himself said nothing about the attack. Unlike the Queen, he was a master at hiding his emotions.

The next morning, before the sun had risen, I heard the door to the house open and slam shut. I sped down the ladder to find Ovadia by the entranceway.

The women were already baking their second batch of dough.

"What's wrong?" Batya asked.

"Eight of the sick who shelter beneath the city walls disappeared last night."

Batya took a step toward him. "Why do you say disappeared? Surely they left?"

He shook his head. "I should have said 'were taken.' Those who remain tell a terrible story of hooded demons who appeared out of the night and dragged them off for their blood."

Batya was shocked into silence.

"Mark my words, Izevel's hand is behind this," he added.

"Why would the Queen take the sick?" I asked.

"Revenge."

"Against those feeble souls?" Batya asked. "What could they have possibly done?"

"They may be the victims of her wrath," Ovadia said, "but her target was the prophets." His eyes blazed as they met mine.

"How is that revenge on the prophets?" Dahlia knew the least of our struggles, but she was never one to let a question go unasked. Or to allow anyone's wrath to fall on me.

"Why does the King feed the weak from his limited grain stores?" Ovadia asked back.

"I thought you were the one who ordered the bread for the infirm?" I asked.

"It is not my grain to distribute as I see fit." Ovadia turned back to Dahlia. "Do you know why the King consents?"

Dahlia had rarely spoken to Ovadia since binding herself to Tamar, and now she blushed before his anger. "Because it is the right thing to do."

"Is it?" Ovadia asked. "The Queen does not think so. She believes the right thing to do in time of need is to provide first for the strong, thus keeping the nation powerful."

"That's not what my father taught me," Dahlia said.

"Nor is it what the King's father taught him, which is why he consents. But who taught this to your father and his?"

"The prophets." Understanding dawned on Dahlia's face.

"Precisely. The Queen's message is clear. If the prophets attack her grain, neither she nor her soldiers will suffer. They are only taking food from the mouths of the neediest, those she has no desire to feed at all."

"Why take them away?" I asked. "Why not just cut off their bread?"

"The grain comes from the King. Izevel holds Ahav in her hand, but she does not yet own him entirely. She still pretends mercy is a value they share. She cannot starve the sick without exposing herself to him. But she can spill blood without the King's consent."

"Why only eight?" Tamar asked, and Dahlia slid back into her shadow.

Ovadia hesitated at her question. "What do you mean?"

Tamar continued kneading as she spoke. "Izevel's rage knows no boundary. If she has unleashed it upon the defenseless, why not kill them all at once and leave no witnesses to tell the tale?"

"Perhaps by leaving the rest alive, she is spreading fear and threatening that further thefts will result in further murders."

"I think not," said Tamar. "If that were the case, then why risk capturing more than one or two? If Izevel has moved to murder so many, there is more to this story than we can see. Are you certain she is behind the disappearance?"

"Who else would do such a thing?"

"Blood is power. There are many types of evil which might seek it out. We must know for sure whether this is the Queen's doing." Tamar looked toward me. "Lev will root out her secret. It is what I have trained him for."

Ovadia nodded. "Tamar is right. Go now, Lev, and bring back word from the palace."

I ate my morning meal with only Tuval for company, hearing no whispers about the disappearances from either him or the cooks. As I tuned my kinnor, I wondered how I was supposed to uncover the Queen's role in the disappearance. Her henchmen would not report to her in the Throne Room, and even if they did, the musicians would hear nothing. A large group of commoners gathered by the rear wall, but no messengers even waited to be heard. The King and Queen finally entered. Ahav's face was set and regal as they walked up the aisle, and Izevel's lips curled back in a satisfied smile.

Then I understood Tamar's words. Izevel's anger would boil until she had her revenge. One look at her face as she walked toward her throne told me all I needed to know. The Queen was pleased with herself. It wasn't the type of evidence which would persuade the King of the evil dwelling in his midst, but in one glance I knew what the Queen had done.

The Initiation

The priests of the Baal held their initiation on the night of keseh, the concealment of the moon, when the stars burned brightest in the sky. A steady rhythm accompanied the almost three hundred priests as they ate and drank. At midnight, the drumming shifted. The boom, boom, boom echoed off the stone walls of the Temple like a heartbeat. The priests rose silently and made their way into the Temple. The pounding of the drum only faded when the oak double doors shut behind them.

A golden Baal stood on an altar in the center of the celebration, its war helmet reaching more than halfway to the ceiling. He held a lightning spear pointed down at Yambalya, who danced alone beneath it. Around him danced an inner circle of twenty priests, all Tzidonian. The next ring of priests was a mixture of Tzidonian and Israelite, all but eight in violet robes. Two more rings of Israelites surrounded them. The priests chanted as they danced around their god, the energy of their voices rising with each pass around the golden statue.

Yambalya raised his scarred arms, and, with a flourishing drumroll, silence fell. The giant priest fell to the ground before the Baal. Once his forehead touched the ground, the rest of the men bowed as well.

Yambalya rose, and all rose with him. "All praise to mighty Baal!"

"All praise!" The voices of the three hundred priests shook the wood of the rafters.

"All praise to the master of the storm wind!"

"All praise!"

"My brothers, tonight eight men seek to join our ranks." Yambalya's eyes passed over the crowd. "Come forward, you who desire to bind yourselves to Baal."

Eight men separated from the crowd and stood shoulder to shoulder facing Yambalya, directly beneath the spear of the Baal. Five wore the woolen garments of commoners and three the linen tunics of nobility—both equally alien in the Temple. Two priests stripped the initiates of their tunics, leaving the men in nothing but their undergarments. Their skin appeared smooth in the torchlight, so different from the scarred chests of the priests surrounding them.

Yambalya handed each of them an iron knife. "Cut yourselves over the heart, and offer your lifeblood to Baal."

Usually, the priests cut themselves in a frenzied state, dancing to the rhythms of their god. Except for their first time. Now they had to cut themselves in pure silence, with three hundred priests looking on.

One of the noblemen raised his knife and drew it across his chest, but barely a trickle of blood rose to his skin.

Yambalya pulled out his own knife, resting the tip above the nobleman's heart. "You cut, or I cut!"

His face paled, but he pushed the blade deeper into his flesh. The blood came pouring out.

Yambalya drew his knife back. "Now, give your blood to Baal!"

The man slapped the cut with the flat edge of his knife, and blood spattered on the base of the golden idol.

"Bow!"

The man pressed his face to the ground before Baal.

"Rise!"

He rose to his feet, leaving a bloody stain on the stones. A priest stepped forward and caught his blood in a golden bowl while another threw a violet robe around his shoulders.

One by one the others stepped forward to complete the initiation until the floor was slick with their blood. Only one candidate remained. Yambalya approached Elad, the former disciple of the prophets, knife outstretched. No doubt the priest's cut would be worse than his own. Elad drew his knife across the skin over his heart, cutting deeper than any who went before him, and blood gushed out. He slapped his chest with the flat of the blade, speckling the statue, then bowed with his forehead to the ground.

Once Elad's blood was collected, Yambalya added wine to the blood bowl, swirled it around, and poured it out into eight goblets. "You are bound together by the blood of brotherhood. Drink!"

All eight emptied their goblets. The drumming resumed as the priests hollered in approval and danced.

"Silence!" Yambalya threw up his arms, and the rhythm stopped as the priests stared at him in confusion. "You have sworn your allegiance to Baal," Yambalya looked at the initiates, holding each one's eyes in turn. "Now we will put that allegiance to the test."

The new priests exchanged glances.

"As servants of Baal, you are not only priests but soldiers. We are in the midst of a war, and in war a soldier must be prepared to fight, to kill, to die."

Yambalya grabbed Elad's arm and pulled him into the center of the circle, next to Baal. "This time, you go first."

The muffled sound of a struggle came from a corner of the Temple. The color drained from Elad's face.

"The enemy brought drought upon the land. Baal now battles their god for control. When Baal is victorious, the drought will end."

Yambalya walked a tight circle around the Baal, holding the eyes of the assembled priests. "Two years ago, I came to this land with twenty priests. Now we are three hundred. Two years ago, the enemy prophets roamed this land. Now they are dead or driven into hiding. Victory is at hand."

A roar rose from the priests. Elad remained silent, green in the torchlight.

"The enemy know they cannot win. They do not even try. They aim to bring complete destruction upon the land. If they must die, they want all to die with them.

"The great King Ethbaal sustains us with grain from Tzidon. The enemy steals whatever grain they can. They tell King Ahav he must take from the strong to feed the weak. Such mercy is how disease spreads through the land. Their mercy makes the strong weak. They want all to perish before mighty Baal rules this land."

The priests from Tzidon cheered his words, but many from Israel joined in only quietly, while a few, like Elad, stood in stunned silence.

"Until now, we have not fought back against the enemy's treachery. We had the means to fight, and the will to fight, but it was not yet the time to fight." Yambalya stopped beneath the golden spear and rose to his full height. "Now is the time! We will no longer be restrained. The enemy will weaken us no longer. We will spill the blood of the weak, and with it water the Kingdom of the strong."

Yambalya extended his arm toward the corner of the Temple under the loft. "Bring the first offering."

Two Tzidonians dragged a man through the crowd, his arms tied behind his back, his head covered in a sack. His coughs rang loud in the now silent Temple. The priests pushed the man onto his knees before Yambalya.

Yambalya pulled the sack from the man's head and flipped him onto his back so that he stared straight up at the Baal. The High Priest turned to Elad. "Now you will show your allegiance to your new master, Baal, mightiest of gods. When Baal's faithful spill the blood of those loyal to the enemy's god, we strengthen Baal's hand and extend his dominion over the land. Spill out this diseased blood before Baal. Show your allegiance. Bring Baal victory!"

Elad looked at the old man and then at the golden statue. Baal's war helmet extended up toward the heavens, and his jagged spear pointed down at Elad's chest.

He turned toward the door of the Temple, and Yambalya gave the slightest shake of his head. Leaving was not an option. Elad had offered his blood to Baal and drunk that of his brother priests. He had sworn allegiance to the Baal, and there was no going back. A hundred priests stood between him and the door—he could not run if he wanted to.

Yambalya unsheathed his knife, his eyes fixed upon Elad. The message was clear. Either Elad would spill the old man's blood, or Yambalya would spill the blood of them both.

A hacking cough racked the old man's body. Even left to himself, he did not have long to live. Elad swallowed, took one more look at the massive priest and his knife, and bent over the old man. But Elad's surrender was not complete. He positioned himself so his head was almost against the old man's ear and breathed out the word, "She'ma."

Even in the Temple of the Baal, the victim was ready to declare the power and unity of the Holy One. "She'ma Israel!" His voice rang as loud as his sick chest could bear. Before Yambalya could do anything to stop him, the old man reached the final word of the declaration, "echad!" Elad's knife fell, silencing him forever.

One who stops their ears at the cry of the wretched,
they too will call and not be answered.

Proverbs 21:13

21

Resurrection

Ovadia received the King's permission to station soldiers outside the walls at night. Even so, the kidnappings continued, and reports came in of similar disappearances around the Kingdom, where he was powerless to respond. Hardly a week now passed without one or more prophets dying in the Cave of Dotan.

Autumn arrived, and with it the festival of Sukkot. On the final day, the prophets gathered to pray for rain. Uriel was now too weak to lead us and passed the task on to Raphael, who had thrived in the cave. Though far thinner than when he entered, he appeared healthier than ever. He spent his days caring for ailing prophets and drawing from the great wisdom around him.

"The first time the rains ever fell, there was only one righteous man in existence, yet you watered the entire world for his sake," Raphael began.

"Master of the World! Look at the men around me. They have given their entire lives to serving you, and here they lie, on the brink of death. Is there not among them even one man worthy of life? If so, I beg you, bring the rain for his sake."

The tears streamed down Raphael's face as he called out, "May the rains come as a blessing and not as a curse!"

The prophets, with as much energy as they could muster, called back, "Amen."

Raphael raised his eyes to the roof of the cave. "May they come for life and not for death!"

"Amen."

"May they come for abundance and not for scarcity!"

"Amen."

"Master of the World, you and only you cause the wind to blow and the rain to fall."

The final words fell flat, for Eliyahu still held the Key of Rain. Silence filled the cave, disturbed only by the sound of weeping. Uriel's voice spoke out in the dim light. "It will soon be the second anniversary of the drought. If the first anniversary brought a change, the second may as well. Lev, it is time for you to return to Eliyahu."

My legs were longer and stronger than they'd been the year before, and as I covered ground on my road north, I realized how much I'd grown. It had been a year and a half since I came of age, and I finally felt like a man. Twice before I had journeyed to Eliyahu. The first time seemed a fool's errand, tracking ravens through the sky. The second time had proved to be one, fueled by a foolish hope that I knew the Holy One's will. This year, I was done playing the fool. I had no mere hope. I had a plan.

It was near nightfall five days into my journey when I reached the outskirts of Tzarfat, and almost full dark when I reached the widow's small dwelling. The next morning marked the second anniversary of Eliyahu's curse and one year since he fled Nahal Karit. Part of me wanted to wait until the morning to confront him, but my waterskin was empty, and I dared not go to the well alone. Strangers were attacked in Tzidon for taking water without permission.

The widow spied me as I approached, and stepped into the doorway to block my entrance. "What do you want?"

I leaned in close. "I am seeking Eliyahu."

Her eyes widened, then she regained her composure. "There is no one by that name here."

The words were hardly out of my mouth when a hand rested on my shoulder. "This one is known to me," Eliyahu said. "To you as well, if you'll recall. He followed me here a year ago. Welcome, Lev ben Yochanan."

"Ah, it is that one." The widow backed away, allowing me to step into the small house.

By the dim light of the hearth, I saw Yonah, alone in the corner. Like me, he had grown in the past year, but his growth made him look stretched, not stronger. His eyes appeared huge inside sockets that were nothing more than skin drawn across bone. Of the three in the house, he was the only one who seemed pleased by my arrival. "Lev," he said, "you've returned."

"I do hope it's not in search of food," the widow said, "for we have none to share."

"Food, no. Water would be welcome."

"Water we have." She took a skin from its peg on the wall and filled me a cup.

Eliyahu followed me into the low, single room of the hut. "I do not receive many visitors, yet you keep coming back."

I finished my water in one gulp. "Tomorrow will be two years."

"You came to see if I relented?"

"There is no need to walk all this way for that. One look at the sky tells me you have not, to say nothing of the wasteland I walked through to get here. The past two years have brought tremendous suffering, and few in the land will live through another. I fear none of the hidden prophets will be among them. I have come on their behalf to beg that you allow the rains to return."

"What will tomorrow bring that I should do so?"

The question told me one thing that had not changed was Eliyahu and his stubbornness. Was he determined to destroy the world rather than relent? "Perhaps nothing, but has not justice already been done? Is now not the time for mercy?"

"Have the people turned away from their idols?"

Eliyahu was a two-day journey from the northernmost part of the Kingdom, and I doubted he ever left his hiding place on top of the widow's house. Did he even know what was happening with the nation? Even if not, I knew better than to lie outright to a prophet. I swallowed. "Many have."

The widow turned back and forth between us. She owed her life to Eliyahu's miracles, but it was the drought which endangered her to begin with. Now she watched a struggle in which her life and many like hers hung in the balance. Did she admire Eliyahu's stance, or share my desire? Either way, I doubted her opinion would have any more impact on Eliyahu than mine.

"And the King?" Eliyahu asked.

I knew this question was coming. "The King has not repented."

"If the sin persists, then mercy is unjust."

I had not expected him to hear my pleas. "There is another way," I said.

"Oh?" A bemused smile came over Eliyahu's face.

My heart thumped as I looked the prophet in the eye. "Do you know of Uriel's prophecy concerning my father?"

Eliyahu's smile disappeared as he nodded. "I know of it."

"Yoav, the general of the King's army, knows of it as well. We have spoken. He but awaits an opportunity to take action."

"What action?"

I had his attention. Now I must shift his will. "To rid Israel of the Tzidonians. Their soldiers, their idols, their priests, their temples. Even the Queen herself."

"You believe the army would act at Yoav's word against their King?"

"The army does not like having foreigners in our land, killing our prophets. All they are waiting for is leaders to take up the fight."

"Who are these leaders you propose?"

"Yoav already leads the army, and he believes in the prophecy. He will follow me as his soldiers follow him. The people know of your power and would rally behind you if you promised to return the rains. With the three of us at their head, we can lead the nation to victory and wipe idolatry from the land."

"Three may lead in war, but the people accept only one head. Who do you believe will rule when the battle ends?"

"None of us, Master Eliyahu. Let the King of Judah rule." My voice rose as I let the vision take hold. "The twelve tribes will be reunited, the prophecy fulfilled, and the Golden Calf can again give way to the Temple."

"You believe the general of Israel would step aside and let another King rule?"

"Yes, Master Eliyahu. He wants to see the prophecy fulfilled." It was the moment for my strongest proof. "Yoav saved my life and risked his own in order that the prophecy not fail."

Eliyahu's face was a mask. "You will discover that it is far easier to seize power than relinquish it, Lev."

"Yoav will never have full power, he will never be more than one of the three."

"Yes of course, for he will be sharing power with the reclusive prophet and the boy Kohen."

"The plan will work, Master Eliyahu." I put my whole heart into the words.

"Work to accomplish what, Lev?"

"To wipe the Tzidonians and their foreign gods from our land."

"You believe this is about the Tzidonians?"

"They first brought trouble to our land. Izevel brought her soldiers, priests, and gods as her dowry. If we eliminate them and get rid of her, why would the people not turn back to the Holy One?"

"Why indeed?" He fixed his eyes on mine, and the terrible feeling he was laughing at me burned my insides. "The trouble, as you call it, neither began with Izevel nor will it end by her removal. You and your general may burn the Temple of the Baal to the ground, but can you uproot the fear of the Baal from the people's hearts?"

"But the prophecy…"

"Is indeed the will of the Holy One, but do not let your limited understanding lead you into foolhardy adventures. You will only understand the prophecy when it is fulfilled."

"We can fulfill it now!" Desperation rose as I felt him slipping away. "My plan will work, Master Eliyahu."

"Work to do what? To bring the bodies of the people back to Jerusalem, even as they curse the Holy One in their hearts?" He snorted in disgust. "Your vision of victory scarcely resembles mine, Kohen. I will not buy the people's loyalty with the rain, nor uproot the Baal with a sword. Let Israel turn their hearts back to the Holy One and the rain will come. Otherwise…" Eliyahu did not finish his sentence, only turned and walked out of the house.

"You may sleep here tonight," the widow said to me. "At first light, begin your journey home. There is nothing for you here."

I spread out my sleeping mat on a narrow section of bare floor, my heart bleeding but not yet broken. I would leave the next day, but not at first light. First I was determined to see if the second anniversary of the drought would bring any change.

I awoke to pre-dawn light pouring in through gaps in the curtain covering the entrance of the mud hut. I rose as quietly as I could and stepped outside to breathe the sea air. I had become fascinated by the sea. The land had ceased to produce its fruit during the drought, but the ocean remained a source of life. Many who could no longer farm turned to fishing, and even the King's grain came from distant lands across the sea.

A shriek roused me from my thoughts. I ran back to the house to find the widow crouching over her son. Yonah's face was blue, and his wide eyes darted back and forth, seeing neither his mother nor myself. A rasping sound rose from his throat as he tried to draw breath. His eyes went white, and his face darkened.

I ran out of the house and up the ladder to Eliyahu's attic. I jerked aside the curtain only to find the room empty.

Below the widow cried, "Yonah! Yonah!"

Back in the house, Yonah's head lay slack against the ground. His mother slapped his cheeks, but the boy didn't move. She let out a final scream of pain and collapsed over his body, wailing.

Eliyahu appeared in the doorway.

The widow rose from her son's corpse and pointed an accusing finger at the prophet. "You! You did this!"

Eliyahu's face paled.

She dropped to her knees again and hugged Yonah's lifeless body against her bosom, rocking him back and forth. "Why? Why did you come and bring this destruction upon me?"

Eliyahu stood motionless.

"What is between me and you, man of the Holy One, that you came here to recall my sin and put my son to death?"

He opened his mouth to reply, but no words came.

Her voice rose to a wail. "Get out! Leave my house. Leave me to my misery and bring your destruction elsewhere."

The second anniversary had arrived. Once again, Eliyahu's sanctuary was ripped away. My shock over Yonah's death was pushed aside by a wave of hope.

He crossed the room in two steps. "Give me your son." The widow looked at him in confusion but didn't resist as Eliyahu's strong arms lifted Yonah. He carried the dead boy out of the house, and up the ladder to his attic.

I ought not to have followed. As a Kohen, I was prohibited from entering a house with a dead body. But it was too late anyway. My carefully guarded purity was lost the moment Yonah died. I climbed the ladder to find his body stretched out on the prophet's bed.

The prophet turned his eyes upwards and called out, "Master of the World! My Lord, have you also done evil to the widow who shelters me, to bring death to her son?" He gazed upon Yonah's limp form, as if his accusation against the Holy One would resurrect the boy. Yonah just lay there, lifeless.

Pain creased the prophet's face. His hands rose and fell, like one fighting an enemy. Or facing an impossible decision. Eliyahu's fists clenched, and he closed his eyes. A groan escaped his mouth that shook his entire body. With a last shudder, his face grew resolute. When his eyes opened, they no longer burned.

Eliyahu leaned forward and stretched his body over Yonah's. He put his hands on Yonah's hands, his belly upon Yonah's belly, and his forehead against Yonah's. Eliyahu sat up, gazed upon the dead boy, and bent over him a second time. Then a third.

Rising from Yonah's body, Eliyahu's voice filled the tiny room. It held a softness I had never before heard from him. "Holy One, my Lord, please restore the soul of this boy within him."

He collapsed in a heap on the floor, trembling in the spirit of prophecy. On the bed, the dead boy coughed.

Yonah drew one raspy breath, then another. Soon his breathing grew smoother, and the color returned to his face.

Eliyahu emerged from his prophecy and lifted himself to his feet. He picked up Yonah, whose breath still rasped in his throat, and carried him down the ladder. His mother waited at the bottom.

"See," he held out the boy. "Your son lives."

She grabbed Yonah from Eliyahu and hugged him to her chest. She beamed at the prophet, saying through her tears, "Now I know you are a true man of the Holy One, and the Merciful One's word in your mouth is true."

My remaining hope died as I saw joy light the widow's face. When Yonah died, and she commanded Eliyahu to leave her house, I thought this was the change I came to witness. Perhaps then Eliyahu would have given ear to my plan. But that moment was already forgotten. Now that Eliyahu had resurrected her son, there was no way the widow would evict him from her home.

Had one boy's life been purchased at the cost of a third year of drought? Even as I watched, the fire rekindled in Eliyahu's eyes.

The second year of the drought had ended without any change, and as I headed south, I struggled to accept that most of Israel would not survive the third. The hidden prophets would all die, as would most others in the land. The animals and vegetation would wither, the ground itself turn to dust. All but the most powerful would have to flee the land or die.

I walked the deserted coastal road, seeing devastation everywhere. Most on the King's road averted their eyes from fellow travelers from fear that they might ask for food or water. But hungry faces of the living were not as bad as the unburied dead. Twice I passed travelers who would never reach their destination. Signs of fire were everywhere, and the forests of the Galil, which I had passed through only the year before, were all scorched now, their bare and blackened branches offering no shade from the ever-present sun. Even if the rains returned, it would take many years for these forests to be restored to their glory.

No more caravans passed here to supply Izevel with grain. The little still being sent to Israel arrived by ship and was escorted to Shomron under heavy guard. Even those shipments must eventually come to an end. To conserve water, I walked mainly at night. As I traveled along, I passed fishermen on the seashore, casting their nets into the tidal pools and sand flats, hoping to catch the one source of food still abundant in the land: fish.

I approached Shomron in the middle of the night and, knowing the gates were shut, circled around the city to walk directly to the Cave of Dotan. When I reached the end of my trail, I hesitated beneath the olive tree before entering. How many more had died since I left? Was there a dead body in there now, prohibiting me from entering?

"Lev?" Sadya called out at the sound of my footsteps. "Is that you?"

"It's me. Can I enter?"

"Oh yes, we've been awaiting your return."

The moon was only a sliver, and the light which shone in through the entrance did not allow me to see anything more than darker patches among the shadows. Still, I sensed the presence of most of the prophets gathered in the main cavern at a time when I expected them to be asleep. I felt their expectant silence as they stared at me in the darkness, but I said nothing. How could I tell them they would all surely starve?

"Come," Sadya said, "you must speak immediately to your master. He has been anticipating your arrival."

My heart sank, knowing what my news meant for the old prophet. I walked down the narrow passage, one hand against the stone for guidance, hearing my footfalls as they echoed off the walls ahead. The prophets rose behind me. From the sound of the footsteps, every man who sat in the great chamber followed me to Uriel's cavern.

"Lev," Uriel's voice was weak, and I didn't hear him until I reached his chamber, "I have been waiting."

"It was a long journey, Master. I came as quickly as I could."

I entered and sat next to him where he lay, with my back against the wall. Prophet after prophet squeezed into the cramped space, and the rest filled the passageway. I dreaded telling my story. They were desperate for good news.

"What did you see?" Uriel asked.

"Nothing has changed, Master. Eliyahu will not relent."

To my surprise, a ripple of dry laughter moved through the prophets.

"What Eliyahu will or will not do is beyond your ability to report," Uriel said. "I asked you what you saw." My master's voice was weak, but there was an unmistakable spark of hope under his words.

I told Uriel of the burnt trees, the empty fields. Dust. Death everywhere and no man a friend on the road. The images were so fresh I could see them. "When I reached Tzarfat, the widow and her son still sheltered Master Eliyahu. I delivered the message that the hidden prophets wished him to allow the rains to return."

"And?"

"He asked if the people had repented, and said that rain would be unjust so long as sin persists."

"Then what happened?"

Then I had told Eliyahu about my foolish plan to overthrow the King and return the Kingdom to the King of Judah, but I would not repeat my words here. "The next morning, Yonah, the widow's son, couldn't breathe."

"What did Eliyahu do?"

"Nothing. He was not there. The boy died."

"You are certain he was dead?"

"Yes, Master." Yonah's eyes floated before me, huge in the darkness.

"And then?"

"Eliyahu came, and the widow blamed him for Yonah's death."

"Because he died from the drought?"

"No." I had pondered the widow's words many times on my journey home. "At least, not directly. When I arrived, Yonah looked much like the starved I had seen dead along the road, but that's not what the widow said. She said Eliyahu caused the Holy One to recall her sin."

"What sin?"

"She didn't say."

"I do not know that it matters," Uriel said. "If she knows of Eliyahu's righteousness, any sin could make her feel unworthy in his presence. What did Eliyahu do?"

"He took Yonah from his mother, brought him to his attic, and laid his body on the bed. Then he called out to the Holy One."

"What did he say?"

"Master of the World! My Lord, have you also done evil to the widow who shelters me, to bring death to her son?" I tried to put some of the anger I had heard into Eliyahu's words.

"Did the boy come back to life?" Uriel asked.

"No. Nothing happened."

"I thought not. What happened then?"

Uriel seemed to know much of what I was telling him, but there was no way he could know all. I hated to quench whatever hope the prophets had found, but I must tell him all I saw. "Eliyahu appeared to debate something within. Once he decided, he lay over Yonah three times."

"How did he look?"

"Resolute. His anger had passed. He called out, 'Holy One, my Lord, please restore the soul of this boy within him,' and then…"

"Then the boy came back to life?"

"Yes, Master."

"Praise be the One who gives life!" Uriel's words were quiet but spoken with some of his former strength.

"What praise, Master?" I could not keep the bitterness from my voice. "When Yonah died, the widow told Eliyahu to leave the house. Even he may have had to relent or die. Once he brought back her son, all returned to the way it was. Now we will all die."

"Life never returns to the way it was, Lev. Each step brings change. No matter how we cast our eyes backward, we can only move forward through life."

"I saw his eyes, Master. They still burned with the same fire."

"Nonetheless, much has changed."

"What, Master?"

"Most importantly, Eliyahu no longer holds the Key of Rain."

"The Holy One took it back?" I asked.

"No, once given, it was Eliyahu's to return."

"He gave it back?"

"As when he first took the key, I was granted a vision. My first since coming to the cave."

"What did you see, Master?"

"Eliyahu pleading for Yonah's life. Such visions are a narrow window. You showed me the rest of the picture."

"What do you mean, Master?"

"You told me Eliyahu accused the Holy One, calling it evil to strike down Yonah. He found it unjust that she who sustained him should lose her son. But justice could not allow the boy to live. The widow herself saw the root of Yonah's death in her own sin, whatever that was."

"So Eliyahu called for mercy?"

"Indeed. For two years, he has been out of balance, held by a vision of absolute justice. But justice failed him. Seeing the dead boy's face, Eliyahu asked for mercy."

"Because he asked for mercy, the Holy One brought Yonah back to life?"

"As we judge, so are we judged, Lev. He could not demand strict justice for all of Israel and receive mercy for Yonah at the same time. To receive mercy, he first had to awaken mercy within himself."

"But he did not bring the rains," I said.

"No, he did not. Had Eliyahu allowed the mercy he felt for Yonah to extend to all of Israel, he could have restored the rain. Then perhaps his plea for mercy would have revived the boy on its own. But the heart opens slowly, and Eliyahu could not give up on the justice of his cause. Instead, he sought a second key."

"A second key, Master?"

"Recall the three keys that are never given into the hand of man: the Key of Rain, the Key of Life, and the Key of Resurrection."

"Eliyahu sought the Key which resurrects the dead?"

"This was my vision. I saw him ascend to the Throne of Glory and demand it."

"The Holy One agreed?"

"The angels raged in protest. Should flesh and blood hold two of the three, and the Holy One only one? The angels insisted that Eliyahu first relinquish the Key of Rain."

"But there is still no rain."

"No, but there will be." Uriel's voice was brighter than at any time since entering the cave.

"When, Master?"

"I do not know. Perhaps the fate of the rain is still tied to Eliyahu. Perhaps since he ended it, the Holy One will allow him to restore it. But I do not believe we will suffer through another year of drought."

A wave of excited whispers passed through the gathered prophets and disciples, but I couldn't share their hope. The prophets were dying quickly. For them to have any chance to emerge from this cave, they needed rain now. "Shall I return to Eliyahu, Master?"

"No, Lev. My heart tells me our task now is to wait. But the shifting winds make our wait easier."

One who is bent on evil, upon oneself it shall come.

Proverbs 11:27

22

Trial by Fire

A week passed. Then a second. Each day, I studied the sky for signs of rain, but saw only the yellow haze of dust.

Hope sustained the prophets in their hiding, but the people lacked even that. Despair turned to terror as winter advanced without rain, and death stalked the land. Even the abundance of King Ethbaal wavered. When the latest grain shipment passed through the gates of Shomron, it was guarded by thirty soldiers all the way from the port, but for the first time, the wagons held disappointment. The people of the palace would eat, but there was no fodder for the King's horses. I didn't need to look at Izevel to feel her rage. The entire Throne Room slinked around her, hoping to avoid becoming a target for her wrath. King Ahav did not seem to share his wife's anger but sat lower in his throne.

The next morning, I stood alone in Ovadia's courtyard at first light, loading the morning bread, when someone rapped at the outer gate. I threw a blanket over the donkey's back and a second one over the few remaining sacks of grain.

Ovadia raced into the courtyard as the banging rang out a second time. "Who knocks with the dawn at my gate?" he called out.

"It is I," came the whispered reply. There was something familiar about the voice.

Ovadia's eyes grew wide, and he moved to pull open the gate. After one step, he paused, as if seeing me for the first time, and pushed me to the ground next to the grain. I pulled the grain's cover over me, leaving enough of a gap to see through.

Ovadia opened the gate, and in slipped a man tightly cloaked and hooded. Even when Ovadia locked the gate behind him, the guest looked around every corner of the courtyard before lowering his hood. As he exposed his face, I beheld King Ahav. I had not seen him outside the palace since Ahazya's *brit milah,* and I had never before seen him alone.

"Such an honor, my lord. Please, come into the house. Let me tell my wife we have a guest so she may cover her hair." Batya always covered her hair; Ovadia's request was an excuse to make sure all signs of baking were well hidden.

"There is no need," Ahav said. "We depart at the opening of the gates."

Ovadia did not blink at his words. "Very good. Where do we go, my King?"

Ahav's eyes tipped up to the sky, turning light above the houses. "Let us inspect the springs and nahals around Shomron. Perhaps we will find grass to keep the horses and mules alive so we will not lose all of the beasts."

"An excellent idea, my King." Ovadia opened the door of the house a crack to retrieve his cloak, then the two men stepped out of the gate with their hoods pulled over their heads.

I threw off my covering, packed the remaining bread into the donkey's saddlebag, and rushed after them. By the time I drew the donkey into the main square, the gates were open, and I could not pick out the two men among the farmers and travelers leaving the city. Unable to track the King, I continued toward the Cave of Dotan to deliver the bread. Halfway up the trail, I found Ovadia sitting on a boulder, alone.

"Aren't you supposed to be checking the springs and nahals for grasses?" I asked.

Ovadia laughed. "Is there anyone in Israel who does not know what they will find in the springs and nahals?"

"Apparently, the King," I said.

"True." Ovadia sighed. "He did nothing when the prophets were being slaughtered, but now that his precious horses are endangered he will even search for grass himself."

"You told him it was an excellent idea."

"So it is. The world looks different when viewed from the Throne. Let him look upon the devastation his idolatry has brought upon the land."

"Where is he now?"

"We split up to cover more ground. He went east, and I told him I would look north. I thought I might as well accompany you to the cave."

Ovadia turned up the trail, but I could not follow him right away. Given a moment to himself, the donkey searched for grasses among the rocks by the side of the trail. The poor animal had no more success than the King Ahav would—whatever once grew here had long ago been consumed by beast or fire. I grabbed the donkey's lead rope and pulled it back onto the trail.

Ovadia gasped and fell on his face across the trail. So, the King was not as oblivious as we thought. He was not searching for grasses but testing the loyalty of his steward. I prayed he had not overheard our conversation or he'd recognize Ovadia for what he was.

Ovadia called out, "Is it truly you, Master Eliyahu?"

Eliyahu? I hurried forward until I saw the man Ovadia bowed before. I took in Eliyahu's tattered garments, his wild hair, and his burning eyes.

"It is I," he called out in his deep voice. "Go. Tell your master Eliyahu is here."

"What is my sin that you would hand your servant over to Ahav for him to kill me?" Ovadia asked.

"Why would he kill you?" Eliyahu asked.

"There is no nation nor Kingdom where King Ahav has not sought you. When they replied that you were not there, he made them swear they could not find you. Now you wish me to tell King Ahav that Eliyahu is here?"

"Yes. Why do you not go?"

"As soon as I leave, a wind from the Holy One will blow you beyond our reach. When the King fails to find you, his anger will burn against me. Since our battle began, it has been his hand alone which kept me safe. Should he not find you, I will lose his favor and my head with it."

Eliyahu frowned at Ovadia but said nothing.

"Have you not heard all I have done to save the prophets from Izevel's wrath? I have hidden a hundred prophets, sustaining them in two caves with bread and water. Now you tell me to say, 'Eliyahu is here?' The King will kill me when he doesn't find you."

"As the Holy One lives, before whom I stand, I will show myself to Ahav today."

Ovadia had enough experience of Eliyahu's oaths to need no further reassurance. He stood and smoothed his cloak. "Stay here with Master Eliyahu," he said to me. "I will return with the King."

"Lev ben Yochanan," Eliyahu said to me once Ovadia sped up the trail, "how is it the Holy One guides your steps to so many critical junctures?"

I had asked myself the same question many times. Now I shrugged in response.

"You think it chance?"

"I do not know, Master Eliyahu."

"There is no chance." He looked closely at me, perhaps for the first time. "You have a role to play in the unfolding of the Holy One's plan. Of that I am certain."

Eliyahu continued to study me. "Something disturbs you. Speak, one who has seen the dead rise must have courage."

"When will the rains come, Master Eliyahu? When I returned from Tzarfat, Master Uriel told me you returned the Key of Rain. Yet, the sky is still sealed."

"You would have the rain fall immediately?"

"The people suffer. The prophets are dying. The land has turned to dust. We need rain."

"The land may need rain, but the people need to know rain comes from the Holy One." Eliyahu's eyes showed no light of mercy. "The people will have their rain, but first the Holy One has commanded me to appear before the King."

"Then why are you here?"

"What?" My question seemed to surprise him.

"Why reveal yourself to Ovadia rather than directly to the king?"

The prophet's smile was almost as frightening as his anger. "Who is the greater King, Ahav or the Holy One? Let the lesser King appear before the servant of the greater."

A voice rang out in the distance. "Where is he?"

"Just ahead, my King."

"You're certain he's still there?"

"I would not leave him alone, your Majesty. I came upon one of the King's loyal servants, the musician Lev who plays in the Court. I ordered him to guard Eliyahu and follow him if necessary, so we would not lose him again." Ovadia spoke his words to protect me, lest the King become suspicious when finding me with Eliyahu.

King Ahav breathed heavily, as if he had just halted a run. When he saw Eliyahu, he tipped his head in confusion. With his long hair and frayed clothing, the prophet little resembled the man who declared a curse before the King in Jericho two years prior. "Is it you, troubler of Israel?"

Eliyahu rose to his full height and pointed one finger at the King. "It is not I who have brought trouble on Israel, but you and your father's house in forsaking the commandments of the Holy One and turning after the Baal."

"I have been out to look upon the land," Ahav said. "It is all dried up, and the people are dying. We must bring back the rain."

"The rains shall come. First, you must know there is only one true power over Israel."

Ahav's eyes narrowed, but he held his tongue.

"Gather all of Israel to join me on Mount Carmel," Eliyahu said. "Bring the four hundred and fifty priests of the Baal and the four hundred priestesses of Ashera who eat at Izevel's table."

"If I do this, you will return the rains?"

"I will."

"When shall they gather?" Ahav asked.

"One week from today."

"As you say, so it shall be." Ahav's eyes fell upon me, and his eyebrows pricked up. "From now until we meet at Mount Carmel you have my protection. None will seek your blood. And I give you my servant Lev, one of the men of my Court, to wait upon you."

I was surprised to hear King Ahav even knew my name, then recalled

Ovadia had wisely used it a moment before.

"Lev, come here." The command returned to Ahav's voice as he addressed me.

"It is my will that you to attend to Eliyahu. You will leave his side for no cause, is that understood?"

"Yes, my King."

"Ovadia, you will provide Eliyahu with anything he needs from my treasury." The King's eyes were still on me. "Speak with him now to know if he requires anything."

Ovadia knew his master's will. He drew Eliyahu aside so the King could talk to me.

"Boy," Ahav put a hand on my shoulder and leaned close to my face. "You will stay with Eliyahu no matter what happens, whether he desires your service or not."

"Yes, my King."

"If he tries to flee, you are to follow him and send word of his location as soon as possible."

"I understand, my lord."

His eyes grew hard. "I have sought this prophet for two years in every land from east to west. If he fails to appear at Mount Carmel in a week's time, I shall have one of your heads. If you lead me to him, you will be greatly rewarded. If you lose him, I will take yours instead."

I forced myself to look frightened. Of the three men before me, it was only Ahav's words which I doubted. Eliyahu said he would come to Mount Carmel, so he would. But would the King bring the priests of the Baal and Ashera as he promised?

Ovadia returned. "I have received all of his instructions, my King."

"You may take your leave, Eliyahu," the King said as if addressing a servant. "We will meet in one week's time at Mount Carmel, with all of Israel assembled."

To my surprise, Eliyahu bowed his head. King Ahav and Ovadia turned back toward the city.

Once they were gone, I said, "I am at your service, Master Eliyahu. Where shall we go?"

Eliyahu smiled, an expression that appeared out of place on his grim face. "Am I not a prophet? Take me to the prophets' cave."

"It is Lev, though he arrives late!" Peleh called out as I entered. "No doubt your delay was from searching the skies for rain. Did you find that which you sought?"

"I did."

"Truly?" Peleh's joke was thrown off by the serious tone of my answer. "Have you seen then a wisp of cloud in the vast sky of blue?"

"Not yet. Still, I promise you the rains will return in one week's time."

"You bring promises with your provisions?" Peleh took the lead rope of the donkey from my hand. "Have you been gifted with a vision? If so, perhaps you should hide here, and I will go out to haul bread."

"Better than a vision." I couldn't help but grin.

"What could be better than the word of the Holy One?" Peleh's smile fell as he turned back toward the entrance. "Whose footsteps are these behind you?"

"I bring Master Eliyahu."

Sadya gasped. "Master Eliyahu, is it truly you?"

"It is I."

"Have you come to take refuge with us?"

"I have come to join your company for several days. After that, I hope none of us will need to hide again."

Peleh laughed. Sadya said, "Is there anything we can provide you, Master Eliyahu?"

"A place to rest. I have had a long journey."

"Come with me," Sadya said. "I will take you to a cavern where you can sleep."

I left the bread with Peleh and slipped down the passage to my master's cavern. "How beautiful are the footsteps of the messenger!" Uriel said. "Lev, I can hear your excitement. Tell me all that has happened." Uriel sat silently as I related the story of Eliyahu's appearance and the coming assembly. Once I finished, he asked, "King Ahav called Eliyahu the 'troubler of Israel?'"

"Yes, Master." Why of all my news was that detail of most interest to the prophet?

"Did you see any remorse in the King for his part in bringing about the drought?"

I pictured Ahav as I had seen him on his throne for nearly two years. I could see his genuine care for the suffering of the people, but there was no remorse. His posture before Eliyahu had been defiant rather than repentant. "No, Master, I did not."

"Did this anger Eliyahu?"

"Yes, Master." I had flinched when Eliyahu threw the title of troubler back at King Ahav.

"Why do you suppose it angered him, Lev?"

It was a strange question, for the answer seemed obvious. My heart told me Master Uriel wanted something more from me, but after a long pause, I could think of no alternative. "The King insulted him by saying the suffering of Israel was all Eliyahu's fault."

"You believe Eliyahu holds his honor so dear?"

I did believe Eliyahu cared for his honor, but I held my tongue for my master clearly thought otherwise. "Why else would the King's words anger him, Master?"

"Because Ahav's defiance showed his drought was a failure."

"Why do you call it a failure, Master?"

"In Eliyahu's eyes, the drought was a just punishment, and as such should have brought the King and the people back to the Holy One. In that moment, Eliyahu saw he had failed even to make the King take responsibility for his behavior, much less change it." Uriel paused. "His encounter with Ovadia must also have been upsetting."

"How is that, Master?"

"Is there any more righteous man in all the land than Ovadia? He has labored mightily and risked everything to keep the prophets alive when he could have been safe from the drought himself. If anyone in the entire land should see the justice of Eliyahu's curse, should it not be him? How did Ovadia react when seeing Eliyahu?"

"He was terrified." I paused to picture Ovadia's face. "I have never seen Ovadia so scared, but before Eliyahu, he trembled for his life."

"Indeed. Ovadia, wholly devoted to the prophets, feared Eliyahu would allow all his efforts to come to naught. King Ahav, whose idolatry brought on the drought, failed to show any remorse. What greater sign could there be that the drought failed to achieve its goal with the righteous or the wicked?"

"So what will happen now, Master?"

"Eliyahu must have a new plan. We shall see if this time he succeeds."

Eliyahu slept through much of the day, but the other prophets didn't. There was too much excitement at the revelation that their period of hiding might soon come to an end. The day's surprises were not yet over. Late in the afternoon, Ovadia and Yonaton arrived leading three donkeys laden with food and drink.

"What is this abundance, Ovadia?" Peleh asked when they entered the cave.

"The King opened his treasury to provide for Eliyahu. It did not seem right that he eat alone, so tonight we feast together from the King's table."

Laughter and cheering greeted this statement. There were only small portions of meat, though the prophets could hardly handle more after two years without, but there was no lack of bread, fish, and wine.

Ovadia brought olive oil as well, and for the first time since I came of age, we lit lamps in the great chamber. Some of the prophets hadn't left the cave in more than a year, and even this tiny fire stung their eyes. The light also allowed many of us to see each other for what seemed like the first time. The faces of the prophets were much like Yonah's before his death. I felt a pang of guilt as they looked at me, fat with my meals in the palace and the Kohen's share of their bread.

Ovadia took one of the lamps and unfurled a scroll. "The King sent out this decree today to all corners of the Kingdom." He read, "*Drought and division plague the people of Israel. King Ahav commands every man of age to gather to Mount Carmel on the fourth day of the third week of the eighth month, and promises the rains will follow.*"

"King Ahav promises?" Peleh called out.

"He must trust the prophets," Ovadia said, "for he has made Eliyahu's promise his own."

"He does not trust us that much," Peleh said, "for he said nothing about uniting the people before the Holy One. He still doubts who will prevail."

"Perhaps," Ovadia said, "but there is more news. King Ahav has decreed, and the Queen consented, that nothing will be done to hinder Eliyahu or any other 'enemies' of the Kingdom from peacefully reaching Mount Carmel."

"That is significant," Kenaz said, "for they know where Eliyahu is going and when he is going to arrive. There would be no easier time for an ambush."

"Indeed," Ovadia said, "but Eliyahu has shown the ability to evade them before, and a failed attempt at his life could further prolong the drought. They want the rains to come."

This brought the loudest cheer yet. Several of the prophets raised their goblets of wine in celebration. However, one man did not cheer. He slipped in unnoticed until he stood right beside Ovadia in the lamplight.

"Is this a time for feasting?" Eliyahu's eyes burned as he gazed on the assembled prophets. "The people bow to the Baal while the prophets drink wine?"

A stunned silence filled the cave. Eliyahu continued, "You celebrate the return of food to your bellies and the promise of again walking beneath the sunlight. Do none of you hold the Holy One's honor above your own?

"Lev, take enough bread to last the two of us the week. I do not belong here. I stand alone amongst the prophets of Israel."

With these words, Eliyahu stepped out of the cave, never to return.

Two days before the gathering on Mount Carmel, Eliyahu and I walked north in the full light of day, on roads crowded with all Israel making their way to the mountain. Eliyahu's unkempt hair and tattered clothes drew stares, but all turned away when they met his gaze.

Despite the signs of poverty and disease, a mood of excitement pervaded the travelers. Friends called out to each other on the road and strangers chatted loudly with one another, discussing the coming gathering. Eliyahu had not spoken since we left Dotan, and no traveler's greeting would make him break his silence.

On the second day of our journey, trumpets sounded behind us. The crowd parted to make way for a dozen horsemen, who rode through flying the royal ox of the House of Omri. The King's chariot followed, and the people cheered him like a savior. Ahav caught sight of Eliyahu and ordered his charioteer to halt. The prophet and the King locked eyes. Ahav nodded, pleased to see Eliyahu on his way to the mountain, then rode off without a word.

Ovadia halted beside us. "Is all well?" he asked me.

"All is well."

Eliyahu asked, "What of the bulls, the wood, and the jugs?"

"All has been arranged according to your instructions."

I turned to Eliyahu with a questioning look, but he took no notice. Whatever his plans, he felt no need to share them with me.

"What of the priests?" Eliyahu asked.

"Yambalya was quite pleased by your proposal. He awaits you on Mount Carmel together with all of his priests.

"And the servants of Ashera?"

"The Queen has refused to send her priestesses."

I sucked in my breath. Eliyahu's words to Ahav were clear. If Ashera did not arrive, would that be the end of Eliyahu's promise to restore the rains?

Eliyahu replied, "It is no matter. Baal and Ashera are one in the eyes of the people, and all are equally powerless before the Holy One."

I exhaled, relieved to hear Eliyahu's plan would continue. I could not bear the death of this hope. But why did he let this slight pass? Did he have no choice now that he no longer held the Key of Rain?

"What of the Queen?" Eliyahu asked.

"Do not expect her to appear on the mountain. She has journeyed to her new palace in Jezreel so she can receive report of what happens as quickly as possible."

Eliyahu turned back to the road, his face showing neither surprise nor disappointment, and Ovadia rode off after the King. Whispers now swirled around us. The name of Eliyahu circulated along the road, and the travelers gave us a wide berth as we passed, much as they had for the King. But none cheered Eliyahu.

That night, we slept at the foot of the mountain. Hundreds of campfires lit the slopes around us, but I didn't attempt to approach any of them. I was sure to be swarmed with questions if I left Eliyahu's side, and I knew nothing of what would happen tomorrow.

The priests of the Baal lit a massive bonfire as night fell, and the familiar pounding of Zim's drum echoed across the mountaintop. As darkness settled in, chanting joined the drumbeats, growing in volume as thousands of voices joined together. I lay awake listening to the Baal's song as Eliyahu slept soundly beside me.

Few understood why they had gathered at Mount Carmel. They knew the King called the people together to restore the rains, they knew Eliyahu and the priests of the Baal had arrived, but they knew nothing else. When they woke in the morning, all eyes turned toward the King's camp for direction, but when Ahav finally emerged from his tent, his eyes sought out Eliyahu. The people followed their King and fell in behind the prophet as he ascended the mountain.

Mount Carmel rose gradually from the sea, lacking the steep sides of the mountains near Jericho. When Eliyahu reached the highest point, the entire nation surrounded him, leaving a wide circle of space out of respect or fear. Only I stood by the prophet's side, and, as I looked around, it struck me that I was the one person out of place. My mission was complete. I no longer belonged with Eliyahu, but with the people. Without a glance back, I stepped away from Eliyahu and into the crowd, taking my position beside Ovadia. The King smiled in my direction.

Eliyahu turned a slow circle, looking at the men around him. A hush fell over the crowd. "How long will you waver between two hearts? If the Holy One is the true power, then devote yourselves. But if the Baal is the true power, serve him. You cannot be loyal to both."

Complete silence overtook those gathered, only birdsong from the trees around us could be heard. No one answered Eliyahu's challenge.

"I alone remain a prophet of the Holy One. The priests of the Baal number four hundred and fifty men."

Yambalya stood at the edge of the crowd, surrounded by a sea of violet-robed priests, fingering the handle of his knife. Excitement lit his eyes. He only needed to kill this last prophet to be victorious.

"Let two bulls be brought," Eliyahu said. "The priests of the Baal shall choose one for themselves, slaughter it, cut it into pieces, and place it upon wood. They shall light no fire. I shall prepare the other bull. The priests of the Baal will call out in the name of their abomination, and I shall call out in the name of the Holy One. Whichever answers by bringing down fire to accept the offering, you will know to be the true power."

A murmur passed through the crowd. I heard calls of "so shall it be," and "it is good."

Yambalya released the handle of his knife and nodded. As the challenge was issued before the entire nation, he had no choice but to accept.

At a signal from Ovadia, two men pushed through the crowd leading identical brown bulls, their black horns sharp as spears.

Eliyahu and Yambalya locked eyes. Eliyahu said, "Choose one for yourselves and prepare it first, for you are many and I am but one." Yambalya chose, and Eliyahu himself took the lead rope and drew it to the priest.

More men entered the clearing with wood, and the priests of the Baal set to work building their altar to the beat of Zim's drum. The dirt and stone altar rose swiftly with four hundred and fifty men at work, but one priest stood off to the side among the people and lent no hand to their labor. He had discarded his dark violet robes for a woolen tunic with the hood drawn forward over his head. Still, I recognized the narrow eyes of Mot.

A bellow pulled my gaze back to the altar. Yambalya had slashed the bull's throat before the golden Baal. The animal crumpled, kicking on its side as its lifeblood spilled onto the ground. Priests descended upon the carcass, the first to receive a bowl of blood and the rest to chop it into pieces. They poured out the blood at the feet of their god and arranged the animal's flesh on the dry wood. The crowd roared in protest as a priest brought forward a flaming torch, but Yambalya used it only to light incense before the golden statue. He poured out wine which mingled with the blood on the feet of Baal, flowing out into the dirt. When Yambalya fell to his knees and pressed his face to the ground before his god, all the priests followed, as did many of the assembled crowd.

Yambalya rose, and the priests danced around their altar, whirling and leaping to the sound of Zim's drum. Hundreds broke from the crowd and moved toward the altar, joining in the ecstatic dance. I felt the call of Zim's music; my fingers itched, and my legs longed to move, but I held them back. At the royal wedding, I told myself there was no harm in just dancing, but I knew better now. The prophets of Israel had been slaughtered in the Baal's name, and I would do nothing to add to its glory.

The priests of the Baal worshipped at night, but today they danced with fury as the sun rose in the sky. When it reached its high point directly overhead, Yambalya called out in his booming voice, "Baal, answer us! Send down your fire and make all Israel fear you!"

Neither spark nor smoke issued from the altar.

"Call out louder, for he is a god!" Eliyahu mocked. "Perhaps he is in a conversation and did not hear." Laughter rippled through the crowd. "Perhaps he is relieving himself." Yambalya's eyes burned with hatred. "Perhaps he is on a journey, or maybe he sleeps and must be wakened."

With the King and the entire nation watching on, Yambalya could do nothing to violate the challenge, but the High Priest of the Baal had not yet exhausted his power. He tightened the belt around his waist and slipped his arms out of his robes, letting the top of his garment fall toward the ground.

A gasp rose from the crowd as they eyed Yambalya's scarred back and chest. His priests bared their torsos as well. Some were as scarred as Yambalya, while others, like Elad, displayed the smooth skin of a new recruit. Zim's drumming took on new life, his frenzied rhythms preparing the crowd for the offering of blood.

Yambalya unsheathed his knife, still speckled red from slaughtering the bull. He held it high for all to see, then drew it across his chest. A fountain of blood erupted, pouring over his stomach and staining the robes around his waist. Yambalya slapped the cut with the flat of his blade, spattering the statue with blood. "Baal, answer us!"

The dry ground around the statue grew muddy with the blood of four hundred and fifty priests cutting themselves and screaming out, "Baal, answer us!"

All of Israel watched Yambalya, the priests, and the altar, but my eyes kept returning to Mot on the edge of the crowd. He spoke in hushed tones to a nobleman with thick black eyebrows which contrasted with the grey of his beard.

"I think Mot is planning something," I said to Ovadia.

"You do not recognize that man with whom he speaks?"

"Should I?"

"You have seen him before, though not for a couple of years, and the last time he would have looked quite different, sitting on the ground in ripped clothing."

That was why I had been struck by his eyebrows, they were identical to Seguv's, my friend who died during the rebuilding of Jericho. "That is Hiel of Beit El?"

"Indeed. Between losing his sons to Joshua's curse and witnessing Eliyahu's oath, he has turned from the Holy One and become quite the devotee of the Baal. If you think they're conspiring, best to tell Master Eliyahu."

By the time I reached Eliyahu, Mot had slipped back into the crowd. "I think the priests of the Baal are plotting something with Hiel of Beit El," I whispered.

"I am certain of it."

"You knew this?"

"I know their god cannot answer them and that they will not accept defeat. The hour for Yambalya's offering is almost over. He is desperate to show the power of his god."

"Even if his actions are a lie?"

"Why not? His god is a lie."

"Won't you do anything to stop him?"

"There is no need. The Holy One's power is real."

A group of priests massed between Hiel and the altar. Yambalya stood on the far side, before the golden Baal. "People of Israel," he called out. As all eyes turned to him, Hiel ducked between the priests and crawled toward the altar. "Observe and see the true power of Baal, most powerful of gods." Hiel pulled a flint and a flask from beneath his tunic.

Yambalya stepped further away, keeping the people's attention far from the altar. A small plume of smoke rose from the wood, but it did not yet look like the act of a god. "Mighty Baal!" Yambalya called, "send down your fire to consume this bull, and forever disprove the false god of Israel."

I expected Eliyahu's eyes to burn in anger, but the prophet laughed. How could he be so calm?

A pounding rang in my ears, the same sensation I felt when the ravens carried bread and meat to Eliyahu. I searched for the birds, but the skies held nothing. I closed my eyes to focus and felt that the force did not come from above this time but from below. Something moved on the ground through the crowd. The pounding grew in intensity as its source drew closer. I sensed it directly behind me, and I opened my eyes in time to see a brown viper slither between my sandals.

I jumped back, but the venomous creature paid me no heed. My uncle taught me such beasts attacked for two reasons, food and defense. They were deadly dangerous, but shy—no viper would willingly enter a crowd of people. The pounding in my ears told me this snake feared no man, just as the ravens feared no predator.

"People of Israel." Yambalya stretched out his arms. "The moment has come. For the past two years, your adherence to the falsehoods of your fathers has angered Baal, and he has withheld the rain. Cast aside your false beliefs and embrace Baal, and the storm god will reward you with rain."

The plume of smoke grew darker, and the crowd closest to the altar shouted and pointed. The viper wound its way unnoticed between the priests who ringed the altar, blocking Hiel from view.

"See with your own eyes the power of the great Baal!"

The words were hardly out of Yambalya's mouth when Hiel's scream pierced the air. The plume of smoke sent out one more dark cloud, then died. Zim's drumming faltered.

Angry accusations came from the crowd, and they pressed close around the altar. Yambalya and his priests pulled out their knives, but Eliyahu stepped into the gap between them and the people. "You have failed," he said to Yambalya. "Now let the truth be seen."

The crowd parted before Eliyahu. He crossed the mountainside, leaving the altar of the Baal far behind. Nothing would stop the priests now from lighting the fire on their own, but their time had passed; no one would believe them.

The prophet stopped before a pile of moss-covered boulders, a ruined altar from many generations ago. He scraped away the dried mud and grasses, exposing twelve large stones which he used to rebuild the altar. Eliyahu called for a ditch to be dug all around. After two years without rain, the ground was like stone, and no one had arrived on the mountain with farming tools. Nevertheless, the men gathered around and struck at the dirt with their staves and scraped with sharp stones. The task would have been impossible had there not been so many willing hands. We dug a trench shin deep around the base of the altar while Eliyahu arranged the wood on top. When all was complete, he called for the bull.

I felt the bulge of my knife against my thigh. When I first arrived among the prophets, Shimon rebuked me for using it to cut a melon. "This is not a tool for cutting fruit," he said. "It has one purpose, and should be used for nothing else." As I watched two men lead the bull toward Eliyahu, I knew this was its purpose. I unstrapped the knife from beneath my tunic and shouldered my way through the crowd to hand it to Eliyahu. He turned it over, examining it. He met my eyes and said, "Thank you, Lev."

The bull stood perfectly still as Eliyahu drew one quick slash across its throat, and made no sound as its blood splashed to the ground. When its death throes ceased, Eliyahu cut up the animal and arranged it on the altar.

"Fill four jugs with water and bring them to me," Eliyahu commanded.

The people stirred. No spring flowed on the mountaintop. The prophet meant for the people to sacrifice their water. After more than two years of drought, he might as well ask for their lifeblood—water was the most precious thing they had. One could no longer count on finding water sources on a journey, so those making the trip had brought enough water to arrive at Mount Carmel and return home. The King had promised them a renewal of the rains, but he had not said when it would arrive.

At a signal from Ovadia, four men came forward carrying large clay jars. Palpable relief spread on the faces in the crowd as they saw the King had supplied water. Yet, the men barely exerted themselves as they placed the jars beside the altar. They were empty.

I still carried half a skin full of water, all that remained of the water I brought for Eliyahu and myself. Running out of water was risking death, but if the drought continued, death was a certainty. I unplugged my skin and emptied it into the first jar. As I stepped back into the crowd, another man moved forward with his water skin. He pulled out the stopper and took a long swig, drinking as much as he could hold. Then he poured the rest into one of the jars.

One by one, more men stepped forward to empty out the remains of their skins. It took over a hundred men to fill the jars to capacity. When they were full, Eliyahu said, "Now pour it over the bull and the wood."

I wrapped my arms around the nearest jar, but could not even budge it. Two others grabbed hold, and the three of us carried the jar to the altar. The water sloshed inside. It hurt to watch something so precious fall onto dry ground. Two more men helped us hoist the jar high enough to pour over the sacrifice. There was a gasp from the assembled men as we emptied its contents. Many hands lifted the next three vessels, and water splashed over the bull and the wood, soaking the dirt around the altar. No deception of flint and oil would make this wood ignite, but it was still not enough for Eliyahu. "Do it a second time," he called out.

The empty jars were again positioned before the people. Those who hesitated the first time, holding back their water for the journey home, now stepped forward and added their share. A man who had only put in a few mouthfuls the first time now emptied the rest of his skin into the jar. Others approached from further back in the crowd. Little by little, the jars were filled again

So many men rushed forward to carry the second round of jars that I didn't get a chance to help. Now the bull and wood were fully soaked. Only a miracle would start a fire beneath the altar.

"A third time," Eliyahu said.

Those who wished to give their water had already done so, and few stepped forward now to fill the jars. The sun hung low over the sea, and when it dropped past the horizon the time for the afternoon offering would draw to a close. King Ahav himself stepped forward and added two full skins to the nearly empty jar. He turned to the people, "Let all who wish the rains to come add their water now."

Their King had spoken. The people stepped forward in droves, with men pushing up from the back of the crowd to add the contents of their skins to the jars. When the last round was poured over the offering, even the ditch around the altar filled with water.

Eliyahu turned his eyes skyward. "Holy One, the Lord of Abraham, Isaac, and Jacob, let it be known today that you are the only true Power in Israel, and that I am your servant, and that I have done all of these things according to your word. Answer me, oh Holy One, answer me! Let this nation know that you are the Holy One and turn their hearts back to you!"

Every eye turned to the altar, waiting for the wood to ignite. Nothing happened. My heart pounded in my chest. Would Eliyahu also be humbled before the people?

A scream rang out behind me. Someone pointed skyward. "Look!"

A single cloud hung in the sky, lit orange by the rays of the setting sun. Except that as I watched, the cloud descended toward the altar, revealing itself as a tongue of flame descending from above.

The crowd fell back as the pillar of fire approached. The instant the flame touched the bull, it splintered in all directions. My arm flew up to shield my eyes from the burning light. Searing heat poured over me, and I fell to the ground, seeking sanctuary in the cool earth.

The wave of heat passed, and I lifted my head to see the pillar of fire ascending in the sky. Where the altar had stood, nothing remained. The offering was completely consumed, the water gone, and even the stones and dirt incinerated. All the people had fallen to the ground to take shelter from the heat. They pressed their faces to the earth and screamed out, "The Holy One is the Lord! The Holy One is the Lord!"

Only Eliyahu remained standing. When the fire came down, he neither hid nor shielded himself from the fire of the Holy One. "Seize the priests of the Baal." His voice cut across the people's cry. "Let not one escape."

The priests were four hundred and fifty strong, but they could not stand before the host of Israel. Elad tried to pull off his priestly robes before the crowd reached him. Even if he could have done so, there was no hiding the fresh cuts across his chest. Two men pinned him to the ground.

Those not taken in the initial onslaught gathered together in a knot, back to back with knives drawn. Few men of Israel carried swords, and their knives were shorter than those wielded by the priests, but most carried staffs. They rained blows upon the priests, blocking their slashing cuts as the crowd closed in. There were simply too many attackers for the priests to face. Whenever one man of Israel sustained a cut, three more appeared to take his place. Soon all were subdued but one.

Yambalya stood alone, a towering menace. One man stepped in and attempted to hit him in the back, but Yambalya spun and snatched the staff out of his hand, delivering a slashing blow to his face. Armed now with staff and knife, he held the people at bay. A circle developed around him, with none drawing within reach. Yambalya's staff swung with enough force to crack a man's skull, and he showed no signs of tiring.

The crowd parted as a champion stepped forward to face the High Priest. The Holy One had prevailed over the Baal. Now was the time for the Holy One's prophet to defeat the Baal's priest. But when the champion broke through the edge of the crowd, it was Yoav.

The aging general unsheathed his sword and advanced on his enemy. Yambalya stood a full head taller than Yoav, and his staff gave him even greater reach. Yoav's expression was grim, but he showed no fear. Nevertheless, I couldn't see how he hoped to prevail against such a powerful adversary. The two men circled one another, and Yambalya smiled. To defeat the general of Israel would redeem him in the eyes of the people. But all Yoav wanted was the priest's attention.

Yoav aimed a sword thrust at the priest's belly. Yambalya laughed as he parried the sword with his staff. Yoav stepped back to defend the counter-attack and gave a quick nod over Yambalya's shoulder. As the priest stepped in to deliver a deadly blow, one of the men behind him swung with his staff, hitting him square in the temple. Yambalya staggered, and another staff struck him in the chest. A third man stepped forward and jabbed the priest in the eye. Yambalya raised his knife to retaliate, and Yoav's sword came down on his wrist. The knife fell as hand separated from arm, and the High Priest of Baal collapsed under a rain of blows.

"Stop!" Yoav called. "Eliyahu asked for him seized, not dead."

All four hundred and fifty priests of the Baal were now subdued. Zim was unarmed and didn't attempt to fight, yet he too was seized. I looked around for Mot. He was nowhere to be seen.

"Take them to Nahal Kishon," Eliyahu commanded, "and kill them there."

The people dragged the priests of the Baal down the mountainside toward the dry riverbed. Zim struggled against two men. "Let me go! I'm not a priest, I'm a musician." He was almost crying, like a little child being punished for no reason. Zim was hardly a child, not even the boy I met playing with the prophets. He had grown into a man under Yambalya's watchful eye, feeding the Baal's evil with his music.

"Let me go! Please, don't kill me!" His captors pulled Zim backward as he kicked and fought. He shot a last, wild look around him, and his eyes met mine. "Lev!" his face twisted in a desperate plea. "Save me!"

Baal or no, I could not abandon my friend. Zim stood up for me in Shiloh and had looked out for me in Shomron. I fought my way through the river of people heading over the edge of the mountainside. "Don't touch him!" I yelled in my deepest voice, but the sound was lost in the tumult. The killing began as soon as the crowd reached the base of the mountain. They used the priests' own knives to cut their throats.

Zim had no knife, but one of his captors did. He slashed at Zim's throat, but Zim threw himself forward and caught the blade on his cheek. His face burst open in a spout of crimson as another man struck him with his staff. There was a loud crack as his nose broke.

"No!" I cried as I reached him and managed to catch his attacker's knife arm before the second blow could fall.

All of Israel had seen me beside Eliyahu that day. Zim's captors fell back, and their eyes widened in recognition. They released his arms, and I caught Zim as he fell forward. Blood soaked my tunic as I lifted him to his feet, and he threw an arm around my shoulder. Together we limped back up the mountainside.

Death raged on below us, and Nahal Kishon, dry for two years, flowed red.

When Eliyahu pronounced his sentence upon the priests of Baal, the King and his guard did nothing to hinder it, just as they had stood by while the Tzidonians slaughtered the prophets. Ahav had retreated to his camp on a shoulder of the mountain, out of sight from the river bottom. As I approached supporting Zim, two soldiers held out their swords, but at a sign from Ovadia, they lifted their weapons. A page came running bearing bandages, and I left Zim in his care for a moment as Ovadia drew me aside. "Are you mad! Why did you save him?"

I was still shaking from what I had seen below. "The prophets say one who saves a life in Israel saves an entire world."

"They also say those who show mercy to the cruel bring cruelty upon the merciful," he replied with a hard look.

I met his eyes without flinching. I knew it was a brash thing I did, but my heart said it was the right one. "We cannot know how the seeds of mercy will sprout. They are why I am here today."

Ovadia swallowed his response as his eyes shot to the edge of the camp. Eliyahu had returned from the slaughter and approached the King's tent. There was no need for Ovadia to signal the guards as the prophet drew near; no one would oppose Eliyahu today. Ahav stepped out to meet him.

"Eat and drink," Eliyahu said to Ahav, "for there is the sound of gathering rain."

The late afternoon sky was still bright above and empty of clouds. There wasn't even a whisper of wind moving through the trees which ringed the summit of the Carmel. Nevertheless, the King didn't argue. Ovadia brought food, and he sat to eat.

Without another word, Eliyahu turned and headed for the top of the mountain. One look from Ovadia sent me following at his heels.

At the summit, Eliyahu lowered himself to the bare grey stone, bent forward, and brought his head between his knees. He rocked gently back and forth until the familiar trembling began. I stood alone on the mountainside, as prophecy shook Eliyahu and the faint cries of killing rose from the valley below. The sky in the east was turning deep blue when Eliyahu's vision came to an end, and he lay back exhausted on the ground. After a moment, he caught my eye. "Lev, go look toward the sea."

I ran across the rocky outcrop to the western edge of the mountain. The setting sun hovered above the sea. I scanned the sky, but it was empty. I ran back to the prophet. "There is nothing."

"Go look again," he said.

This time I watched the sun sink into the water. The sky glowed red at the horizon, but above it was still clear. When I reported back to Eliyahu, he merely repeated, "Go again."

Seven times I ran back and forth between the prophet and the lookout. By the final time, I struggled to discern the line between the sea and the sky. Then I saw it. I ran back to Eliyahu. "There's a tiny cloud coming up from the sea," I said, breathless, "hardly bigger than a man's hand."

That was all the prophet needed to hear. "Go tell Ahav: hitch your horse and your chariots and descend, lest the rain stop you."

Wind whistled in my ears as I ran back to the King's camp. The King still sat at his meal, with Ovadia standing next to him. I bowed low before he gave me leave to speak. "My lord, Eliyahu bids you to mount your chariot and go lest the rains come and stop you."

A crack of thunder wiped the incredulous look from his face. Ahav dropped the bread in his hand. "Hitch the horses," he ordered Ovadia. "We must go." Ovadia raced toward the king's tent to arrange his departure, and Eliyahu himself appeared in the King's camp.

As Ahav's chariot was made ready, the prophet pulled the skirts of his robes between his legs and tied them off around his waist so he could run unimpeded. When the King was ready to travel, Eliyahu himself led the way, running before his chariot like the wind.

Another clap of thunder shook the mountaintop, and the skies opened.

The people cried out and turned their faces upward to catch the precious drops in their mouths. Rain fell in soaking torrents, but no one sought shelter.

I stood dumbfounded in the middle of the King's camp as servants hurried to pack. A mounted rider stopped beside me. "Come, Lev. We too must go." Ovadia extended a hand and pulled me up behind him on the horse. I grasped him around the waist and we picked our way down the muddy mountainside.

When we reached the road leading out from Nahal Kishon, Ovadia let the horse run. A chariot is no match for a rider, and we soon caught up to Ahav. Eliyahu still ran out in front, but we had not come to escort the King. Ovadia pulled the horse off the road and kicked its flanks. Mud splashed from the animal's hooves as we retook the road alone, and the royal chariot soon disappeared behind us.

Between the darkness and the rain, I could barely see the road. Ovadia rode on hard, pushing his mount forward. I pressed myself into his back, using him as a shield against the rain and wind. I knew neither where we were going, nor why we were in such a hurry to get there. I clenched my eyes shut and put my faith in Ovadia. Wherever our destination, hopefully we would arrive safely and in time.

Like dogs returning to their vomit, so do fools repeat their folly.

Proverbs 26:11

23

The Mother of Baal

The unrelenting rain made the night darker than any I could remember, but Ovadia somehow rode on. The horse slowed to a walking pace as it felt, more than saw, the way ahead. It was after midnight when we finally reached the newly constructed palace at Jezreel. "Open the gates," Ovadia called out. "The King approaches."

The King must still be far behind us, but the guards did not know that. They threw open the gates at the sound of Ovadia's voice. "The King will be here before long," Ovadia told the officer in charge. "Stand guard and leave the gates open."

We rode into the courtyard and Ovadia leapt from his mount to bang on the stable master's door, rousing him from sleep. "Come, take my steed and wake your boys. The King approaches."

I was drenched and shivering as I followed Ovadia into the palace. Word of our arrival spread quickly, and servants already raced through the halls.

Ovadia stopped two pages. "Build a fire in the King's quarters and prepare a change of clothing. The King will be cold and wet when he arrives. Let us make the palace welcome." Next, he went to the kitchens, woke the sleeping chefs, and told them to prepare a hot meal.

As we headed away from the warmth of the hearth, Ovadia drew me down a side corridor and into a small room. It held nothing but a chest and a neatly made bed of fine quality, but servants had already placed a small brazier of glowing coals in the corner. "What is this room?" I asked, holding my hands out to the heat.

"These are my quarters, for when the King requires me in Jezreel."

"Why am I here?"

"The Queen has surely heard of my arrival and now eagerly awaits the King. She will want a report the moment he arrives, and I am certain she won't want me present." Ovadia drew my musicians' clothes and kinnor from a niche in the wall. "I had these brought in case such a circumstance should arise."

Again, I was valuable because I was invisible, but after the day's events, this was less true than before. Fortunately, Izevel had not come to Carmel. She had not seen me with Eliyahu, and to her, a musician was little more than another tapestry decorating the walls of the Throne Room.

I pulled off my woolen tunic, soaked with rain and blood, but I paused for a moment before donning the linen garments. What if Izevel had already received a report of the day's events? I could be walking into a trap. I turned to Ovadia to voice my doubts and saw his face was resolute. He was no fool—he knew the danger of sending me before the Queen. He nodded once, and I slipped the musician's tunic over my head. It was a risk which must be taken—their conversation could determine the fate of the prophets.

The linen tunic was far thinner than my woolen one, but at least it was dry. I didn't realize how much my teeth had been chattering until I pulled on the soft clothes and my body calmed. These garments, which had been so baggy when I first got them, fit perfectly now.

Ovadia retrieved a tray of hot delicacies and a goblet of wine from the kitchen, then led the way into the Throne Room. Izevel sat on her Throne with Zarisha at her side. They broke off their conversation when we entered. "My Queen, King Ahav will arrive within the hour. He bade me ride ahead and make preparations for his arrival. He himself will report the day's events to you. In the meantime, I brought you a small something to sustain you until his arrival."

Ovadia nodded me toward a nook on the Queen's far right. I played softly so as not to draw undue attention. Izevel eyed Ovadia hard. He was hardly her favorite source of news, but she was desperate to know who brought the rains. She accepted the tray and the wine that went with it and dismissed him with a wave of her hand.

Even with a fire burning, the Throne Room remained cold and drafty. The storm still poured down outside, and water dripped through cracks in a roof that had not yet been tested by rain. No doubt Izevel would be more comfortable waiting for the King's return in her quarters, but that was not her way. The Throne Room was the seat of power. She would receive the news here and nowhere else.

The Queen spoke little to Zarisha, just sat with her eyes fixed upon the Throne Room door. An hour passed, then another. Finally, in the third watch of the night, a page entered. "King Ahav has returned, my Queen."

"Excellent. Tell him I wish to see him at once."

"Of course, my Queen."

The page left, but still the King did not come. The longer he delayed, the more restless she grew. No one waited to report good news.

When the door to the Throne Room opened, it was not the King but the general who entered. "My Queen, I bear tidings!" Yoav's voice was loud as he strode toward the thrones.

"You are not my husband," Izevel snapped.

Yoav stopped short and looked around the empty hall before bowing. "I begged leave of his majesty to bring first word to his Throne Room of the victory wrought in Israel today." Yoav did not lift his head as he addressed Izevel, but I could see the corners of a smile on his face.

Izevel went white, but only for a moment. Her hands gripped the arms of her throne, and she drew back, as if she were ready to strike the general. "Your tunic is stained with blood," she said with perfect calm. "Do tell me what happened on the mountain."

Yoav straightened. "Yambalya and his priests died by the sword after their god was proven false by Eliyahu."

Izevel's eyes blazed so fierce that he took a half-step back, and his hand dropped to the hilt of his sword. "It was a just trial, to which your priests agreed."

I was sure that she would have him seized—two Tzidonian guards stood outside the Throne Room doors. But Yoav rode at the head of the King's guard. She could not threaten him as she could Ovadia. "Where," she hissed, "is your lord, my husband?"

"I also bear a message from my King." The last word rang loud in the stone room. "The rains which Eliyahu brought have fallen in such abundance that even the short journey from the Carmel has made him unpresentable to my lady. He begs your understanding as he changes his mud-soaked attire and takes a hot meal before appearing."

"Leave me," she said.

"My lady." He bowed his head again and turned to go. As his glance crossed mine, he held my eye for a fraction of a moment.

Izevel sat brooding on her throne. My music was the only sound which disturbed the tension.

Zarisha broke the silence. "It is a setback, nothing more." Her voice held all the comforting strength of a mother. She spoke Tzidonian, but after two years of listening, I understood.

Izevel turned on her. "They killed Yambalya!"

"They did. You must now appoint a new High Priest in his stead."

"He was more than just a priest. The people cowered before him!"

"Tell me," Zarisha asked in a calm voice, "what would happen if Ahazya, your son, would die?"

The question was so unexpected that Izevel sat straight. "Who would dare threaten my son?"

"No one, love, no one." The tension drained from the Queen's body at the soothing tones of Zarisha's voice. "It is simply a question. The answer is that you would have another son."

Izevel swallowed before answering. "I suppose."

"Little would change as long as you, the Queen mother, remain."

"I see." An evil light glowed in Izevel's eyes.

"Ashera is the mother of Baal. The tree does not fail every time one plucks a fruit. Yambalya is dead, but as long as the mother remains, there can always be another priest."

The Queen basked in the priestess' smile, and it took all of Tamar's training for me to stay calm behind my instrument. I passed through half of a melody before Izevel spoke. "You do not fear the people will kill you and your priestesses next?"

Zarisha gave a smile which dripped with scorn. "All men are ruled by desire."

Izevel's hands closed over the arms of her Throne. She sat straight in her seat and scanned the room. Seeing no one else, she snapped her fingers at me. "Boy, go tell my husband I wish to see him at once."

I silenced my kinnor with a bow and ran. I had never been to the King's quarters in either palace, but I knew where to go. The two soldiers at the foot of the stone stairs saw me burst out of the Throne Room and didn't hinder me as I raced up the stairs to a heavy oaken door which stood ajar at the end of the hallway. It opened at my gentle knock, and I entered with a bow. Ahav sat alone before the fireplace, a steaming bowl on the table at his side. "My King, the Queen ordered me to summon you at once."

I kept my head bowed as I backed out of the room. "Stay," Ahav called. I froze on the threshold.

"My lord, the Queen bid me deliver her message and return immediately," I said. It was a lie, but I was eager to return to the Throne Room.

"You need not fear the Queen's anger," he said with a laugh. "I assure you, she will be perfectly angry no matter when you return."

"Still my King," I said with another bow, "I do not wish to keep her waiting."

"Come in, Lev." My eyes shot up at the use of my name. "Close the door behind you."

I stepped into his chamber, and a cold draft followed me as I pulled the door shut. The King examined me in silence, and I dropped my eyes from his gaze.

"How long have you been playing in the Throne Room, Lev?"

"Just over two years, my King."

"Two years?" He gave a strange smile. "So you appeared just as the drought began." He paused as if considering something. "But that was not my question. I meant tonight. How long have you been in the Throne Room tonight?"

"Only a short time, my King." I wanted to say that I had just arrived, but I sensed the danger of being caught in a lie. "No more than two hours," I said.

"Two hours? I only arrived half an hour ago, and you were still at Mount Carmel when I left. How is it you arrived before me?"

"The royal chariot is not very fast, my King."

"Faster than your legs can carry you, boy. I know you walked to Mount Carmel with Eliyahu. If you speak the truth, you can only have come by horse. Who brought you?"

I could think of no answer but the truth. "Ovadia, my King." I scrambled to think of a reason Ovadia would do such a thing. "He wanted me ready to follow Eliyahu, should the King desire. I have earned the prophet's trust."

"Should I desire. Indeed." Ahav rose from the table and paced before the hearth, his eyes on the fire. "It has not escaped my attention, Lev, that you keep appearing at pivotal moments."

His words left me numb. I had been so focused on deceiving Izevel, that I had paid little mind to the King.

"You were there in Jericho, visiting poor Hiel when Eliyahu called down the drought."

It was not a question, but still I answered. "Yes, my King."

"Not long after, you appeared in my Throne Room, and have been there since."

"True, my King."

"Last week, you were with Eliyahu when I found him. Ovadia claimed he left you to watch Eliyahu. I thought this wise, and I commanded you to do the same. Now I see I was a fool."

I swallowed. "My King?"

"You weren't watching Eliyahu. He goes where he will, and no man will hinder him." He turned to look at me. "Certainly not some boy. Ovadia was protecting you."

I said nothing.

"You were there serving Eliyahu, and perhaps you were serving him in my Throne Room as well. Ovadia knew this and lied to me." Ahav smacked a fist into his open hand. "That is how he found him when all my efforts failed! Ovadia is not loyal to me, he is loyal to Eliyahu!" Ahav stuck a finger into my chest. "And you are his spy!"

A King's fury is like a lion's roar, but his goodwill is like dew upon the grass.
Proverbs 19:12

24

The Queen's Message

The King was close to the truth. Dangerously close. But the parts he misunderstood could be more fatal than the truth itself. "You are wrong, my King."

Ahav started at my response, and I wondered if a servant had ever contradicted him.

"Ovadia is loyal to you," I said. "He never wanted drought or war, and until last week, he had seen Eliyahu no more than you." I took a deep breath and added, "my lord."

The King recovered quickly from the shock. "How can you be so sure of Ovadia's loyalties? Or what he has seen or not seen?"

Caught again. Ovadia would know how to answer, but I knew neither he nor anyone else would come through the oak door to my rescue.

The King did not wait for my reply. "Of all my servants, the one whose loyalty I never questioned was Ovadia's. Do you know why?"

"No, my King."

"His discretion." The King paused to let his words sink in. "Ovadia holds his tongue truer than any man in the Court, no matter what secret he may know. But you speak with confidence about where Ovadia puts his loyalty, what he wants, who he has seen." Ahav stepped closer to me, and I dropped my eyes to the floor. "Of course you may be a liar or a fool." He moved next to me. "Are you a fool, Lev?"

I swallowed. "If you believe so, my King."

"I do not take you for a fool, Lev. Life has taught me that when a person is always in the right place at the right time, it is either wisdom or providence. You would have to be great indeed for providence to grace you with all you have seen."

I trembled at the word providence. The King did not know who my father was and might not know about the prophecy, but if he did, would he conclude I was a threat to his Kingdom?

"I hear the wisdom of truth in what you say about Ovadia. I believe you that he does not serve Eliyahu. But I can't help but wonder, how do you know all of this? Why would a man of discretion put so much trust in anyone, let alone a servant boy? Only one answer comes to mind. He needed you. He placed your kinnor in my Throne Room so you could be his eyes."

"Ovadia never told me to spy on you, my King."

"You do not deny being a spy, merely that you were not spying upon me." Ahav was like a fox who had trapped his prey. "Ovadia placed you there to spy on the Queen, did he?"

My eyes darted to the door, but no help would come.

"He put you there two years ago, at the beginning of the drought, immediately after my dear wife began hunting the prophets. Ovadia is serving the prophets."

Silence seemed like the safest response to the truth. The King sighed and returned to his seat by the fire. "Do you like riddles, Lev?"

"Sorry, my King?"

"Riddles. Do you like trying to figure them out?"

I loved riddles, every shepherd did. There was no better way to pass the time alone in the hills without going mad from watching the sheep. Nonetheless, I did not like the direction this conversation was taking. "Not really, my King."

"Neither do I. The one asking the riddle invariably delights in your confusion, and it is never good for others to grasp the answer before the King. The people must believe in the wisdom of the head which wears the crown." He paused. "But I do love it when all of the pieces come together. There is something satisfying about that."

"Indeed, my King."

"Much has happened these past two years that I did not understand. But now all the pieces are in place. Mot was correct." He jumped from his chair and paced. "That woman in the Throne Room was a prophetess, and she did try to kill the Queen. She knew and trusted you, so when she was caught, she tried to pass you the murder weapon. All of this happened because Ovadia conspired against me. I could not see the truth because my belief in his loyalty blinded me."

"Ovadia never abandoned his loyalty to you, my King."

"Again you do not deny my other claims." The King stopped pacing and fixed his eyes on mine. "If Ovadia is a servant of the prophets spying upon my wife, how can you deny that he broke his loyalty to me?"

"I see no conflict in serving the King and the prophets of Israel."

"Even when a prophet devastated our land with drought?"

"I swear to you, my King, Ovadia did not serve Eliyahu. He only tried to save the lives of the prophets the Queen sought to kill."

"And attempted to kill the Queen herself."

"Ovadia had no hand in that, my King."

"But you know who did, do you not?" My breaking eye contact was as good as an admission. "You know too many things for a servant boy. There are prophets still alive in the land, and you know where they are."

I had watched for two years as the King listened to endless petitioners, but only now did I appreciate how closely he hearkened to their words. I had tried to answer him with cunning, but Ahav heard everything he wanted to know in what I said. And what I did not.

The King had learned enough already to have both my and Ovadia's heads. Even if I said no more, doubtless his next move would be to send soldiers to Ovadia's house. There they would discover Tamar, and immediately conclude that she and Ovadia had plotted together to kill the Queen. They would get no information about the prophets out of Tamar, but they were sure to beat the truth out of Batya, Yonaton, or Dahlia. It would not take them long to discover the location of the hidden prophets.

My heart told me there was only one path ahead. It might be a fool's hope, but I had to try. "Ovadia has hidden and fed one hundred prophets of the Holy One during the war, my King."

The King took a step back. He had not expected such forthrightness. "Where?"

"In a cave outside of Shomron. Only seventy now remain. The rest have died from starvation." I saw no need to mention the fighting cave.

"You can lead me to them?"

"I could, my King. But you do not want me to." It was not the place of a boy to advise the King, but I had already defied him beyond what any servant would dare.

If Ahav was offended, he didn't show it. "How can you presume to know what I want?"

"Because the drought has broken. The war is over. If you will it, peace can return to the land."

"If I will it?" He gave me a bitter smile. "You believe letting the prophets walk the land once again is the best path to peace?"

"Indeed, my King. It is the only path."

"Your confidence is matched only by your inexperience in war, boy. For over two years, war has raged between the prophets and the priests of Baal. The blood of the priests now soaks Nahal Kishon. Why should I not spill the blood of the prophets as well and rid the land of all these troublers in one stroke?"

"Killing the prophets will never bring peace."

"What can a boy know about the ways of war and peace?"

There was one more step I must take. "I am no ordinary boy, my King."

"No, you are a spy. Perhaps even now you play your game."

"Yes, I am a spy, and I learned much by watching your Queen. Still, I am more than that." I needed to win his confidence. I had gained the confidence of Pinchas and Kenaz by telling them my father's name, but with Ahav, that would only increase his suspicions that I was an enemy of his Kingdom. I tried a different approach. "I am also a disciple of the prophets, and I learned even more from them. Had you taken counsel with the prophets, as your fathers did before you, you could have avoided both drought and war. Do not ignore their wisdom now."

"You? A prophet?" Ahav threw back his head and laughed. "If I want to hear from a prophet, I will call Eliyahu to me now. He waits outside the palace walls. You saw the river run with the blood of his enemies, do you expect me to believe that following the prophets now will bring peace to the land?"

Eliyahu's way might eventually lead to peace, but many more would die before it did. First among them would be Zarisha, her priestesses, and perhaps the Queen herself. "Eliyahu does not speak for the prophets. I am not his disciple."

"Who is your master?"

"The prophet Uriel."

The King nodded. "Uriel is known to me." He scrutinized my face. "But I have thrice seen you with Eliyahu. Even if Uriel is your master, why should I trust that his way is any different from Eliyahu's?"

"You witnessed the proof yourself earlier today, my King."

"When?"

"When I saved the life of Zim, musician of the Baal."

"That was the man you carried into my camp?"

"Yes, my King. I rescued him from the hands of those killing the priests of the Baal."

"Why would a disciple of the prophets save a servant of Baal?"

"Because he is my friend. And because I do not want to live in a world of vengeance and murder. Master Uriel taught me that as we judge, so are we judged. That, my King, would be Master Uriel's message to you if he stood here now. You are the King of the land. If you fill your heart with mercy, mercy will fill the land. Spilling the blood of the prophets will only bring bloodshed and destruction in return."

The King shook his head. "You do not know of what you speak, Lev. I am a merciful King. I never sought anyone's life without cause, including the prophets. My mercy has brought only death and drought."

The King already had grounds to take my life. There was nothing to be gained by holding back now. Still, I took a deep breath before answering. "That is because your will is weak, my King."

"You go too far!"

"No, my King. I am simply the first to go far enough. When the prophets were driven into hiding, no one remained with the courage to speak the truth. The Queen rules in too many things. Your mercy means nothing as long as you nullify your will to her will."

The King stepped to the door and pulled it wide. "Summon the captain of my host," he called to a waiting page. He turned to me as he shut the door again. "You wish to see the power of my will? Very well."

Apologizing would not help—I had admitted to being a spy. He even knew I was connected to Tamar's attempt on the Queen. The only way out was forward. "Your pardon, my King, I lied to you earlier."

Ahav laughed. "You see the weakness of mercy? I call one soldier to my side, and you backtrack. I have been too merciful these past two years."

"No, my King, what I said about mercy was true. I lied when I told you the reason that Ovadia brought me back to the palace tonight."

"Yes, as soon as I learned you were a spy, I worked that out myself."

"Ovadia brought me here to listen to Izevel's reaction when she heard of Yambalya's defeat."

"Do not hope to buy your life with information. I need no spy to know my wife."

"Do you not?" I let the question hang. "Ovadia wished to know whether the war ended on Carmel, or if we needed to prepare for the next stage. Are you not curious?"

Ahav hesitated. "What did you hear in my Throne Room?"

"Zarisha will continue Yambalya's fight."

He waved my words away. "Lust is the handmaiden of fear. Without Yambalya, Zarisha's power will amount to little."

"No, my King. The Tzidonians say Ashera gave birth to Baal. Zarisha says as long as the tree remains strong, it can always produce more fruits."

"You are a capable spy, Lev, but repeating the words of others does not produce understanding. If Zarisha was willing to fight, she would have appeared on Mount Carmel."

"Her strength is not in battle. She manipulates the hearts of men so they will fight her battles for her."

The King paused at my words, and I pressed him further. "The Queen did not hope to win this war by fighting your will, but by capturing it. Did your concubines make you a more just King as she promised?" I summoned all the strength of my heart before I met his eye. "She bribed you with pleasures to buy your blindness. Queen Izevel usurped the Kingdom through your desires."

Ahav's hands balled into fists. Before he could speak, a knock sounded at the door, which swung open at the King's "Come!" Yoav took in the room with one glance, and only a flicker deep in his eye betrayed his surprise at seeing me there.

"This boy is a spy." The King's tone was cold, and the weight of all I said pressed on me.

Yoav looked me over, his eyes unreadable. "You are certain, my King?"

"He admits it. Do remind me, what is the penalty for spying upon the King and Queen?"

The King needed no reminding of the law of the land. He was merely stretching out the sentence as punishment for my affront.

"The penalty is death, my King." Would Yoav truly let me die? "Shall I kill him now?"

Yoav took a menacing step toward me, and my heart pounded. When we had last spoken, he had said 'far better that Israel be ruled by the House of David than by the House of Ethbaal.' Would he kill me now if he knew he was defending the Queen?

"Not yet. The boy also knows the location of seventy prophets hidden in a cave outside of Shomron."

"My King, you wish the army of Israel to spill the blood of the prophets?" Yoav's tone was soft, but the question itself was a challenge.

"Was this drought not caused by a prophet? Are they not at war with the priests of Baal?"

"The drought has broken, my King, and the priests of the Baal are dead."

The King studied Yoav's face. "Dead by the hand of a prophet."

"Dead at the hands of the people. Your people, my lord. We all saw the fire consume his offering. All the priests of Baal showed was trickery."

"How many stones did Eliyahu construct his altar with?"

Yoav frowned at the question. "I did not notice, my King."

"Twelve." The King turned to face me again. "Lev, does that number mean nothing to you?"

"Twelve is the number of the tribes, my King."

"Just as a disciple of the prophets should answer. Your master and his brothers have long dreamed of reuniting the tribes under the House of David. For that to happen, my Kingdom must fall, must it not?"

Silence filled the room. I faced the King, but his eyes were now on Yoav's. Ahav had not brought Yoav there to kill me. He needed to know where his soldiers' loyalties lay before he could decide his next steps. Would his army back the Throne or the prophets?

Yoav told me he would not raise a hand against a King of Israel. What if the choice were between Ahav and the prophets of Israel? With the priests of the Baal dead, one blow against the King could bring about the reunion of the Kingdom.

With Ahav gone, the road to Jerusalem could open again. The Golden Calf could give way to the Temple. If I spoke, would Yoav strike? With one blow, he could fulfill the very prophecy he tried to destroy when he struck down my father and tried to resurrect when he saved my life.

"This boy has shared his master's wisdom," the King continued. "He says that only allowing the path of mercy will bring peace to the land." The King's eyes bored into Yoav's. "Your sword has served the Kings of Israel for more than twenty years. What do you say? Will peace come from having *mercy* on the prophets?" Ahav stressed the word 'mercy.' Clearly, he knew about the curse which caused Yoav to lose his wife and son, and counted on the general's anger to sway his decision.

Yoav held his ground. "The boy speaks truth. All Israel saw the fire—who would dare fight Eliyahu now? Should the rains cease again, the land will be destroyed. As the captain of the host of Israel, I say this war must end."

The King went pale, and his eyes sank back into their sockets. Two wills warred across his face. Finally, he pointed at me. "Boy, go and inform the Queen I am on my way."

My escape from the room brought such relief that I considered running straight out of the palace, but now was not the time to fail in my duty. I felt Izevel's wrath before I reached the Throne Room. "What took you so long?" she barked as I entered.

"The King detained me, my Queen, but he is on his way."

Her face twisted in anger, and she opened her mouth to reply when the page by the door called out, "Our Lord, the King!" Her transformation was immediate.

"Ah, Ahav. I trust you have recovered from your journey?" It was her sweetest voice, and after two years in the Throne Room, I knew it to be her most dangerous. I slipped aside and lifted my kinnor, blending back into the background as King Ahav took his throne. "I have eagerly awaited you. Do tell me about your adventures on the mountain."

Ahav eased himself back as she leaned toward him. "Eliyahu brought the rains, as he promised."

"Yes, we noticed." She gestured to the drops falling on the Throne Room floor. "Your general tells me that Eliyahu murdered Yambalya and his priests." Her eyes grew hard. "You did nothing to stop him?"

"It was not Eliyahu, it was the people." The King braced himself on the arms of his throne. "Their hearts have returned to the Holy One."

"After all we have done these past years, the nation still prefers the service of your Holy One?"

"After what they saw on the Carmel, now more than ever."

Zarisha still stood behind the Queen's throne. "The heart of the people is easily moved by passion, my Queen. It can be won back."

"This is no fleeting passion." The color rose to Ahav's face. "You have shed too much blood in the name of your gods these past two years." He met Zarisha's eyes. "Yambalya failed to show the people Baal's superiority, and he paid with his life. The fighting must end. There will be no more hunting of prophets."

"Baal is not the only power," Zarisha said. "He sprang from the womb of Ashera."

"Eliyahu challenged Ashera to appear on Mount Carmel. You refused. Will you face Eliyahu now?"

Zarisha said nothing.

The King turned to Izevel. "This is my will. The hunting of the prophets ceases."

"And if it does not?" Izevel asked.

"Then I will do what I should have done two years ago. It will not take more than a day or two for the army of Israel to dispose of every Tzidonian soldier in the land."

"You dare!" The Queen rose in her throne. "You will answer to my father for every drop of Tzidonian blood you spill."

"I am King in Israel, not your father, and not you." She shrank at the harshness in his voice. "There will not be two armies in my Kingdom. His soldiers will leave this land immediately, and you will answer to me for every drop of Israelite blood they spill."

Izevel shot a glance at Zarisha, who nodded. The Queen's voice was soft when she responded. "If that is your will, my lord, it shall be so." She gave him her warmest smile. "Surely you will allow me to keep ten soldiers, as my personal guard?"

"That sounds more like a hunting pack than a personal guard."

"You have my word your prophets are safe. All except one."

The King laughed. "You would still hunt Eliyahu? Have you learned nothing?"

"He killed Yambalya."

"With the help of the entire people. Your beloved priest lost a fair contest."

"Eliyahu is a menace we cannot tolerate in the land."

"What do you fear? That he will come after your priestesses next?"

"He is a threat to your entire Kingdom."

"My Kingdom?" The King drew back. "You mean to your gods."

The Queen knew nothing of the twelve stones in Eliyahu's altar, but she could see she'd hit upon her husband's fears. "Not my gods, but yours. Will he bow to your beloved Calf?"

"To the Calf? Certainly not. In his eyes, the Calf is—"

"An idol," Izevel finished for him. "Mot taught me the prophets bow to their god only in their Temple." Izevel gave an evil smile. "They recognize Jerusalem as the eternal capital of your people, not Shomron. Is that not so?"

The King's resolve tottered. "What are you saying?"

"Today Eliyahu fights Baal, tomorrow it will be the Calf. What then?" She paused to let her question sink in. "Do you think he smiles upon the divided Kingdom?"

"No," the King shook his head without meeting her eyes. "None have since Ahiya the Shiloni, but the prophets cause little trouble."

"Until now." Her voice chilled my blood. "Eliyahu incited the people to kill Yambalya. Who will be next? You do not doubt he wishes to serve the House of David, and yet you think your head is safe." She reached out and placed her hand over his. "You will never rule in peace so long as he lives, my lord." She leaned close enough to the King that her hair brushed his arm and added in a whisper, "My love."

Izevel's eyes glowed with passion. King Ahav sagged back in his throne. "What would you have me do?"

"You need do nothing." She reached out and caressed his cheek, drawing his face close to hers. "You already have my promise that my soldiers will cease to hunt the prophets. Leave Eliyahu to me."

"You will not be able to harm Eliyahu."

"Then there is no reason for you to worry." Her hand moved up his arm.

"Ten soldiers cannot kill one that the Holy One and the people protect."

"I do not fear your Holy One, nor your people."

"You are mad. The people killed four hundred and fifty of your priests when Eliyahu called down fire from the heavens."

"Power is greater than signs and wonders, my love. What happened on Mount Carmel will soon be a memory, but our power remains real. By the time I find Eliyahu, the people will have forgotten why they protect him. But they will remember our power."

"Find him? There is no need. He is here."

"Here?" She bolted upright on her throne, and for a moment her spell was broken.

"He ran before my chariot all the way back from the Carmel."

"He must not remain in Jezreel." Her eyes darted to the door as if she expected Eliyahu to come striding through. "Every moment he lives, his presence undermines your rule."

"You will not kill him while he is a guest under our roof?"

"No." She shook her head and flipped her hair back over her shoulders. "His victory is still too fresh today, but by this time tomorrow, his miracle will fail to move the people. We must drive him away, but we cannot lose him again." She frowned in concentration.

The King gestured toward me. "This boy here was Eliyahu's servant for this past week, at my word." Izevel looked up as if seeing me for the first time. "I believe he earned Eliyahu's trust. Let him bear your message to Eliyahu now, and he will send us word of where he goes."

The Queen could not understand the King's intention, but I did. He lacked the strength to oppose her will, but he wanted the bloodshed to come to an end. He could not let me remain in the palace after revealing to Yoav that I was a spy, so he was arranging an excuse for Eliyahu and myself to flee together. That would save both of our lives and bring the war to an end.

Izevel motioned me forward with a finger. "Come here, boy. I wish you to give Eliyahu a message. Do you think you can remember it?"

"Yes, my Queen."

Izevel spoke her message and had me repeat it back to her until she was satisfied I knew it word for word. "Go now to deliver my message. Do not lose the prophet. Do this task, and I will see you well rewarded. If you fail, I will see your head on a pole."

"Your will is my will, my Queen." I bowed my way out of the Throne Room, clutching my kinnor to my chest.

Ovadia was asleep when I reached his quarters, and I shook him awake. When he heard the prophets could safely leave the cave, he called out, "Blessed be the Holy One. I could not have sustained them much longer. So, King Ahav is finally doing his duty to protect the people?"

"Not all of them. He bowed to Izevel's will regarding Eliyahu. They sent me to follow him once again."

"Eliyahu can look after himself."

"There's more. The King questioned me." I watched the creases on Ovadia's forehead deepen as I told him the story.

"It is all in the hands of the Holy One now. Be grateful we both still have our heads. You should sleep while you can. I will have the cooks prepare food for you and Eliyahu."

I had grown so used to snatching rest when I could that I dropped off as soon as I lay on Ovadia's bed. It seemed like only a few minutes later when he shook me awake. "It is time."

I dressed in my woolen tunic, which Ovadia had thankfully dried by the fire. First light had risen, the rain had stopped, and the sky was patched with clouds. I inhaled deeply—for the first time in two years the air smelled of life. I carried a bundle of food and a purse of silver from the Queen.

I found Eliyahu seated in the shadow of the palace walls. "You have returned," he said.

"I have been given orders to remain with you if you'll have me. I also bring a message from the Queen."

"Tell me the message."

"So may the gods do to me, and so may they do further, if tomorrow at this time I have not made your life like Yambalya's."

Eliyahu sighed. "So the fight goes on."

"For you. The Queen has promised to leave the other prophets in peace."

"That at least is something." He stood with a sigh, and I wondered if he had sat there all night. "But for now I must leave."

"You fear her threat?"

He shook his head with a sad smile. "I fear only the Holy One, but I have no more will to fight. Let us go. There is a long journey ahead."

"Where do we travel?"

"South, to the mountain of the Holy One."

A thrill sent my heart racing. "We are going to the Holy Temple?"

"No, I go to Sinai. I do not know where your journey ends, but we can begin together."

Eliyahu took up his staff from against the wall and started down the road from the gate. I shouldered my bundle of food and followed in the footsteps of the prophet.

Dear Reader,

Thank you for reading The Key of Rain. I first started working on The Age of Prophecy series over a decade ago, and one of the things that has kept me going during that time, especially during the last four years of working on The Key of Rain, has been the constant stream of reader feedback.

I love learning who my readers are, what they love and don't love about the books, and what they are most eager to see in the future. My personal email is Dave@TheAgeofProphecy.com, and I'd love to hear from you.

If you enjoyed the book, I'd love your help in spreading the word. Online reviews on sites like Amazon and Goodreads are a huge help in book promotion, as are social media posts. Please take a moment to leave a review on your favorite sites. And if you know of anyone you think would love The Age of Prophecy books, please pass on a recommendation.

Check out TheAgeofProphecy.com for a growing library of resources and bonus materials to help you get even more out of the books.

Thank you so much,

Dave Mason

Glossary

Ahav: Also known as Ahab.

Eliyahu: Also known as Elijah.

Emek HaAsefa: Literally, the valley of gathering. A fictional location.

Halil: A straight flute.

Izevel: Also known as Jezebel or Isabel.

Kohanim: Priests (plural).

Kohen: A Priest.

Kinnor: An instrument that most resembles an ancient lyre.

Nahal: A riverbed, typically one that flows only seasonally.

Navi: Prophet.

Navi'im: Prophets.

Navua: Prophecy.

Nefesh: The lowest level of the soul.

Neshama: A higher level of the soul.

Nevel: An instrument that most resembles an ancient harp.

Nigun: A melody, usually without words.

Niggunim: Plural of Nigun.

Ratzon: Will.

Shalom: Peace.

Shomron: Also known as Samaria.

Sukkah: The temporary huts built during the festival of Sukkot.

Sukkot: The festival when we build and live in temporary huts.

Tzedakah: Charity

About the Authors

Dave Mason

Mike Feuer

Dave and Mike have led bizarrely parallel lives. Born just four days apart, they both grew up in secular, Jewish, suburban communities, then found their way to Colorado College. Despite having friends, interests, and even one class in common, they remained complete strangers. Afterward graduation, Dave backpacked around the world while Mike lived in the woods for two years, immersed in wilderness therapy with at-risk youth.

Later, both turned their attention to the environment. Dave went to NYU Law and became a litigator for the Natural Resources Defense Council (NRDC). Mike studied desert agriculture and water resource management, but ultimately found his calling as a teacher.

Fifteen years after first becoming classmates, the two finally met as part of a core group formed to create Sulam Yaakov, a new Torah institution in Jerusalem. There, they became study partners, close friends, and ordained Rabbis. Dave was blown away by his studies about the inner workings of prophecy, and was surprised at how little exposure he had to this crucial part of his tradition. He began The Age of Prophecy series to bring more of this world to light.

Mike joined the project initially as a research assistant, contributing his expertise in the terrain, history, and stories of the Bible. Mike calls himself Dave's creative co-conspirator.

Professionally, Dave is a business strategist and sells cabinet hardware online through his website Knobs.co. He, his wife Chana, and their son Aryeh Lev live in the eclectic Nachlaot neighborhood of Jerusalem.

Mike lives with his family outside of Jerusalem, at the edge of the Judean wilderness.

Acknowledgements

Wow, another book done, another monumental effort by vast numbers of people. Mike and I feel such gratitude to all who came together to bring it to life. First of all, we'd like to thank our wives, Chana and Karen, both for your support as we've gone through this process and for the actual work you've put in to help get it out the door.

Interestingly, some of the most pivotal contributions to The Key of Rain came from those who we didn't turn to during the writing of The Key of Rain itself. That's the amazing thing about writing a series, so much of the work for the entire collection needs to be done before the launching of the first book, for all subsequent books are set in the world we created for the first one. So, we'd like to collectively re-thank all of those mentioned in the Acknowledgements of The Lamp of Darkness who helped this world come together in the first place.

We'd like to thank our editor, Yehudis Golshevsky, and all of our Beta readers who provided feedback on the book, including: Aryeh Lev Mason, Beth Shapiro, Moshe Newman, Amy Rothstein, Maayan Ziv-Krieger, David Grundland, Robin Moskow, and Daniella Levy.

We'd like to thank the Rabbis and teachers who helped us understand the Torah concepts that underlie this book, including Rabbi Daniel Kohn, Rabbi Yehoshua Gerzi, Rabbi Aaron Liebowitz, and two Rabbis who passed away this past year, Rabbi Yaakov Moshe Pupko and Rabbi Natan Segal, may their memories be a blessing.

We want to thank Juan Hernaz for creating another gorgeous cover, and to Zoran Maksimovic for doing the interior layout under tremendous time pressure. Mike wants to add a special thanks to JRR Tolkien and to his mom, who taught him how to write.

Finally, we want to thank two close friends who inspired characters in the book. At the launch party for The Lamp of Darkness, we held a story slam, with the grand prize being that the winner would get a cameo in book 2. We had not anticipated a tie, but in the end, Chaya Lester and Mottle Wolfe inspired two of our favorite characters in this book (we'll let you guess which ones).

Thank you all.